Miss Read, or in real life Dora Saint, was a teacher by profession who started writing after the Second World War, beginning with light essays written for *Punch* and other journals. She then wrote on educational and country matters and worked as a script-writer for the BBC. Miss Read was married to a schoolmaster for sixty-four years until his death in 2004, and they have one daughter.

In the 1998 New Year Honours list Miss Read was awarded an MBE for her services to literature. She is the author of many immensely popular books, including two autobiographical works, but it is her novels of English rural life for which she is best known. The first of these, *Village School*, was published in 1955, and Miss Read continued to write about the fictitious villages of Fairacre and Thrush Green until her retirement in 1996. She lives in Berkshire.

Books by Miss Read

NOVELS

Village School * Village Diary * Storm in the Village
Thrush Green * Fresh from the Country
Winter in Thrush Green * Miss Clare Remembers
Over the Gate * The Market Square * Village Christmas
The Howards of Caxley * Fairacre Festival
News from Thrush Green * Emily Davis * Tyler's Row
The Christmas Mouse * Farther Afield
Battles at Thrush Green * No Holly for Miss Quinn
Village Affairs * Return to Thrush Green * The White Robin
Village Centenary * Gossip from Thrush Green
Affairs at Thrush Green * Summer at Fairacre
At Home in Thrush Green * The School at Thrush Green
Mrs Pringle * Friends at Thrush Green * Changes at Fairacre
Celebrations at Thrush Green * Farewell to Fairacre
Tales from a Village School * The Year at Thrush Green
A Peaceful Retirement

ANTHOLOGY

Country Bunch * Miss Read's Christmas Book

OMNIBUSES

Chronicles of Fairacre * Life at Thrush Green
More Stories from Thrush Green
Further Chronicles of Fairacre * Christmas at Fairacre
Fairacre Roundabout * Tales from Thrush Green
Fairacre Affairs * Encounters at Thrush Green
The Caxley Chronicles * Farewell, Thrush Green
The Last Chronicle of Fairacre

NON-FICTION

Miss Read's Country Cooking * Tiggy
The World of Thrush Green * Early Days (comprising
A Fortunate Grandchild & Time Remembered)

News from
Thrush Green

Gossip from
Thrush Green

Illustrated by J.S. Goodall

News from Thrush Green
First published in Great Britain by Michael Joseph Ltd in 1970

Gossip from Thrush Green
First published in Great Britain by Michael Joseph in 1981

This omnibus edition published in 2008
by Orion Books Ltd
Orion House, 5 Upper St Martin's Lane
London WC2H 9EA

A CIP catalogue record for this book is available from the British Library.

ISBN 978-1-4072-1515-0

Printed in Great Britain by
Clays Ltd, St Ives plc

The Orion Publishing Group's policy is to use papers that are natural,
renewable and recyclable products and made from wood grown in sustainable
forests. The logging and manufacturing processes are expected to conform to
the environmental regulations of the country of origin.

www.orionbooks.co.uk

News from
Thrush Green

Miss Read

For Marjorie and Glen with love

'You are now collecting your People delightfully, getting them exactly into such a spot as is the delight of my life; 3 or 4 Families in a Country Village is the very thing to work on.'

JANE AUSTEN in a letter written to her niece Anna who was then writing novels

CONTENTS

* * *

1	For Sale – Tullivers	1
2	Who is She?	11
3	The Priors Meet Their Neighbours	16
4	A Shock for Dotty	25
5	A Problem for Winnie	34
6	A Dinner Party at Thrush Green	41
7	A Question of Divorce	51
8	Gossip and Gardening	58
9	Sam Curdle Tries His Tricks	67
10	Harold is in Trouble	76
11	Albert has Suspicions	87
12	Albert is Struck Down	95
13	Christmas Preparations	105
14	Sudden Death	114
15	Harold Takes Charge	123
16	Harold Thinks Things Out	132
17	Richard Contemplates Matrimony	139
18	Harold Entertains an Old Friend	150
19	Richard Tries His Luck	158
20	An Engagement	168

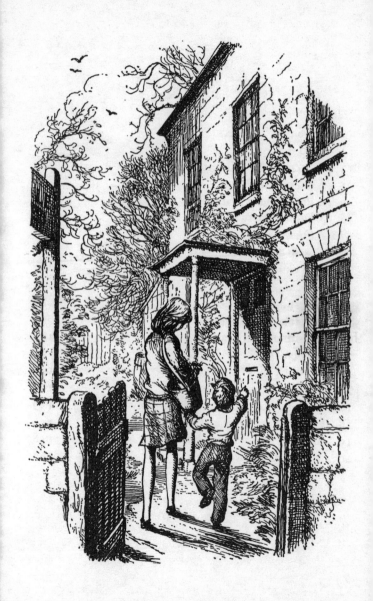

1. For Sale – Tullivers

If you live at Thrush Green you can expect your morning post between 7.30 and 8.15 a.m.

If it is Willie Bond's week to deliver the letters, then they will be early. But if Willie Marchant is the postman then it is no use fretting and fuming. The post will arrive well after eight o'clock, and you may as well resign yourself to the fact.

'It just shows you can't go by looks,' Thrush Green residents tell each other frequently. Willie Bond weighs fifteen stone, is short-legged and short-necked, and puffs in a truly alarming fashion as he pushes his bicycle up the steep hill from the post office at Lulling. His eyes are mere slits in the pink and white moon of his chubby face, and his nickname of Porky is still used by those who were his school fellows.

Willie Marchant, on the other hand, is a gaunt bean-pole of a fellow with a morose, lined face, and a cigarette stub in the corner of his mouth. He scorns to dismount at Thrush Green's sharp hill, but tacks purposefully back and forth across the road with a fine disregard for the motorists who suffer severe shock when coming upon him suddenly at his manoeuvres. He was once knocked off his bicycle as he made a sharp right-hand turn from one bank to the other, but escaped with a grazed knee and a torn trouser leg.

Doctor Bailey, whose house was nearby, had treated both postman and driver, and found that the motorist, though un-scarred, was by far the more severely shaken of the two. But despite this mishap, the violent remarks of later motorists and the advice given unstintingly by his clients on Thrush Green, Willie continues to proceed on his erratic course every other week.

The fact that both men have the same Christian name

might, at first sight, seem confusing, but there are distinct advantages.

As Ella Bembridge remarked once at a Thrush Green cocktail party, in a booming voice heard by all present: 'It's jolly useful when you're upstairs coping with your bust bodice or bloomers, and you hear whoever-it-is plonking down the letters on the hall table! I just shout down: "Thanks, Willie", and you know you'll be all right.'

There had been a sudden burst of animated conversation as Ella's fellow-guests, embarrassed or simply amused by Ella's unguarded remarks, sought to tell each other hastily of their own arrangements for receiving and disposing of their mail.

'I have had to install one of those wire cage things,' said Harold Shoosmith, the bachelor who lives in one of the handsomest houses on the green. 'Since the puppy came, nothing's safe on the floor. He ate a cheque for six pounds ten, and the rates' demand, all in one gulp last Thursday. I didn't mind the latter, naturally, but I hated to see the cheque going down.'

'We leave our letters sticking out of the flap,' said the rector, 'and Willie takes them!'

'Not if it's a north wind,' his wife Dimity reminded him. 'The rain blows in and drenches them. He has to open the door then, and take them from the window-sill.'

Winnie Bailey, the doctor's wife, said she usually put hers in the post-box on the corner of the green. It made her go for a walk, for one thing, and she sometimes wondered if Willie Bond read the postcards.

'Why not?' said Harold Shoosmith. 'I *always* read postcards, other people's as well as my own. Damn it all, if you don't want a thing to be read you put it in an envelope!'

Someone said, rather coldly, that was exactly why she *never* used postcards. One was at the mercy of unscrupulous busybodies. Her letters were left, neatly secured with a rubber band, on the hall table to be collected by whichever Willie was on duty.

Her companion said he left his in a box in the porch. Dotty Harmer, an elderly spinster as erratic as her name implied, vouchsafed the information that she hung hers on the gate in a string bag, and that they had blown away once or twice. Significant glances were exchanged behind the lady's back. What else would you expect of Dotty?

'My new next-door neighbour,' remarked Winnie Bailey 'leaves hers pinned under the knocker, I see. It must weigh seven or eight pounds. It's that great brass dolphin old Admiral Trigg fixed up years ago, you know. Nothing could get blown away from that thing!'

Suddenly, the subject of letters was dropped. Here was something of much greater importance. Who was Winnie Baileys' neighbour? Where did she come from? Would she be staying long?

The party turned expectantly towards Winnie, avid for the latest news from Thrush Green.

The house where the newcomer had recently arrived had been empty for two years. Tullivers, as it was called, had been the home of old Admiral Josiah Trigg and his sister Lucy for almost thirty years, and when he died, suddenly, one hot afternoon, after taking the sharp hill from the town at a spanking pace, his sister continued to muddle along in a vague, amiable daze, for another eighteen months, before succumbing to bronchitis.

'If it's not the dratted hill,' pronounced old Piggott the sexton gloomily, 'that carries off us Thrush Green folks, it's the dratted east wind. You gotter be tough to live 'ere.'

You certainly had to be tough to live at Tullivers after the Admiral had gone, for Lucy Trigg, in her eighties, could not be bothered to have any domestic help, nor could she be bothered to light fires, to cook meals for herself, nor to clean the house and tend the garden.

Winnie Bailey, the soul of tact, did what she could in an unobtrusive way, but knew she was fighting a losing battle. The curtains grew greyer, the window-panes misty with grime, the door-step and path were spattered with bird-droppings, and the docks and nettles rioted in the borders once tended by Lucy's brother and kept trim and shipshape with pinks, pansies and geums neatly confined within immaculate box hedges.

It wasn't as if Lucy Trigg were senile. Her mind, in some ways, was as clear as ever. She played a good game of bridge with her neighbours. She attacked, and overcame, the challenge of the *Daily Telegraph* crossword puzzle each morning, and played her dusty piano with fingers still nimble despite arthritis. It was simply that the squalor of her house did not affect her. Her world had shrunk to the few things which still had interest for her. The rest was ignored.

It was fortunate that Tullivers was a small house with a small garden. Doctor Bailey, as a young man, had been offered the major part of the next-door garden by the Admiral's predecessor. He had bought it for thirty pounds, enclosed it with a honey-coloured Cotswold stone wall, and planted a small but fine orchard, now at the height of its production. Thus the Baileys' garden was L-shaped, and the remaining portion of Tullivers' land, a mere quarter of an acre, allowed room for only a lawn, a few mature lilac and may trees and the flower border which had been the Admiral's particular pride.

An Albertine rose grew splendidly over one end of the house, and winter jasmine starred the front porch in the cold of the year. Inside were two fairly small square rooms, one each side of the front door, with a roomy kitchen built on at the back.

Above stairs were two modest bedrooms and a bathroom with Victorian fittings and a geyser which made threatening rumbles, wheezes and minor explosions when in use.

Tullivers, in its heyday, was always known as 'a snug house' by Thrush Green people. It stood at right angles to the road, and rather nearer it than most of the larger houses which stood back in their well-kept gardens.

It faced south, across the Baileys' front garden, towards the roofs of Lulling in the valley below, a mile distant. It crouched there, as snug as a contented cat, catching the sunshine full on its face.

To see Tullivers so neglected had grieved Thrush Green. Its decay over the past two years had been a constant topic of conversation. It had been left to a nephew of Lucy Trigg's, also a naval man, who put it in the hands of a London estate agent to sell for him whilst he was abroad.

'Pity he didn't let the local chaps have it,' was the general opinion. 'Keep a sharper eye on it. Should have gone within the month.'

There had been one or two prospective buyers, pushing their

way through the tall weeds, with papers describing the property's charms in their hands, but the general neglect seemed to dishearten them. Heavy snow in January and February kept other possible buyers away, and by the time the crocuses and daffodils were decking the rest of the Thrush Green gardens, Tullivers was looking at its worst.

Birds nested in the porch and in the guttering, and a bold jackdaw started to build in the cold unused chimney. Mice had found shelter in the kitchen, and spiders spun their webs unmolested.

The children at the village school eyed the blank windows speculatively, and the bigger boys fingered the catapults hidden in their pockets, longing to pick up pebbles and let fly at this beautiful sitting target. What could be more exhilarating than the crack of a glass pane, the dramatic starring, the satisfying hole? Two of the most daring had been observed in the garden by Miss Watson, the headmistress, who lived across the green at the school-house, and she had delivered dire warnings during assembly the next morning. The two malefactors had been displayed to the assembled school as 'Trespassers Loitering With Criminal Intent', and were suitably abashed. Thrush Green parents, fortunately, were still unspoilt by modern educational theories and heartily approved of Miss Watson's strong line. Miss Fogerty, who was in charge of the infants' class, added her own warnings when she regained the classroom, and the infants approached their morning's labours in a suitably sober mood. It says much for the two ladies, and the parents of Thrush Green, that the little house remained safe from children's assaults, despite temptation.

One bright April day, a red Mini stopped outside Tullivers and a tall woman, paper fluttering from a gloved hand, made her way into the house.

Miss Fogerty was on playground duty that morning. Standing on the sheltered side of the school, teacup in hand, she watched with mounting excitement. Around her squealed and shouted the sixty or so pupils of Thrush Green Church of England Primary School. During those delirious fifteen minutes of morning play-time, they were variously space-men, horses, footballers, boxers, cowboys or – among the youthful minority – simply mothers and fathers. The noise was ear-splitting. The bracing Cotswold air produces fine healthy lungs and the rumpus made at play-time could be clearly heard by fond parents who were safely half a mile away.

Agnes Fogerty, quiet and still as a mouse, and not unlike that timid animal in her much-pressed grey flannel skirt and twin-set to match, stood oblivious of the chaos around her. Somehow, she sensed that the stranger would take on Tullivers one day. There was something purposeful about that stride towards the front door, and the deft slipping of the key into the lock – almost as though the house were hers already, thought little Miss Fogerty.

And quite alone! Perhaps she was a single woman? Or perhaps her husband was working and she had decided to look at the place herself before they came down together? Or, of course, she might be a widow? The war had left so many attractive women without husbands. Miss Fogerty gave a small sigh for all that might have been, and then remembered, sharply, that the stranger was much younger than she was herself, and could not have been much more than a baby during the last war.

Not that widowhood could be dismissed quite so neatly, Miss Fogerty comforted herself. After all, the number of young men who succumbed to coronary thrombosis alone, not to mention the annual toll of influenza and road casualties, was quite formidable. On the whole, Miss Fogerty liked the idea of a sensible widow occupying Tullivers. Who knows? She might even become friendly with another well-read woman living nearby, and companionable little tea-parties and visits to each other's houses might blossom. Miss Fogerty, it will be observed, was lonely at times.

Meanwhile, time was getting on. Miss Fogerty consulted her watch, which she hauled up on a chain from beneath her grey jumper, and then clapped her hands for attention. It says much for her discipline that within one minute the playground was quiet enough for her small precise voice to be heard.

'Lead in, children,' she said, 'and *no pushing*!'

She followed the last child towards the arch of the Gothic doorway, pausing there for a last look across the green to

Tullivers. The stranger had vanished from view inside the house. The dashing red Mini-car waited by the kerb.

Here was something to tell dear Miss Watson! Warm with excitement, Agnes Fogerty entered her accustomed realm, the infants' room. As soon as school dinner was finished, and she and her headmistress were enjoying their cup of instant coffee, she would impart this latest snippet of news to her colleague.

Needless to say, many other people observed the stranger's entry to Tullivers. Thrush Green, to the uninitiated, might have seemed remarkably quiet that morning. The school children apart, not more than two or three people were to be seen. There were, of course, almost a dozen unseen – hidden behind curtains, screened by garden shrubs, or cocking a curious eye from such vantage points as porches and wood sheds.

Albert Piggott, languidly grubbing up the dead winter grass at the foot of the churchyard railings, kept the stranger comfortably in view. He approved of the red Mini. Must have a bit of money to drive a car, and that great leather handbag had cost something, he shouldn't wonder. He knew a decent bit of leather when he saw it. Plastic never deceived Albert Piggott yet. A handsome gal too, with a nice pair of long legs.

Not like his old woman, he thought sourly. He straightened up slowly, eyes still fixed upon the unsuspecting stranger. What on earth had made him marry that great lump Nelly Tilling? He should have known it would never work. Women were all the same. Wheedled their way into your life, cunning as cats, and once they'd hooked you, the trouble started.

'You ain't washed, Albert! Time you took a bath, Albert! Give over sniffing, Albert! You've got plenty of hankies what want using. I wants more money than this for housekeeping. And you can keep out of the pub, Albert! That's where the money goes!'

His wife's shrill voice echoed in his head. He hadn't had a day's peace since they were wed, and that was God's truth, said the sexton piously to himself.

Marriage never did anyone any good. He'd take a bet that that young woman at Tullivers' front door was single. She could afford to buy a house, to run a car, to keep herself looking nice.

Probably one of these career women who'd had the sense to keep out of matrimony.

Albert leant moodily on the railings, a fistful of dead grass against his shirt front, and pondered on the inequality of the bounty supplied by Providence. By now, the stranger had unlocked the door and entered the house.

For the first time that morning Albert became conscious of the warmth of the sun and the song of a bold robin perched upon the tombstone of Lavinia, Wife of Robert Entwistle, Gent., who had left sunshine and birdsong behind her for ever on 3 February 1792.

Nelly might be no beauty. She was certainly a nagger. But he had just remembered that she was preparing a steak and kidney pie when he had left her an hour ago, and Nelly's hand with pastry was unsurpassed.

Cheered by this thought, and by the hopeful signs of spring about him, Albert bent again to his task. Another warming idea occurred to him. Single women often needed a hand with wood-chopping, hedge-trimming and the like. It would be a good thing to have a little extra money coming in. With any luck, he could keep it from Nelly, and spend it as he used to, in his carefree pre-marital days, at The Two Pheasants!

Albert Piggott broke into a rare and rusty whistling.

But it was Ella Bembridge who had the closest look at the newcomer that morning.

She was about to cross from her cottage to the rectory on the green opposite to consult her friend Dimity Henstock about the advisability of having the boiler chimney swept.

Such mundane affairs had always been left to Dimity when the two women shared the cottage where Ella now lived alone. The rector's wife, as well as running her own ungainly house, found herself continuing to keep an eye on her old establishment, for Ella was the most impractical creature alive.

It was Dimity who defrosted Ella's refrigerator before the icy stalactites grew too near the top shelf. It was Dimity who surreptitiously threw away the fortnight-old stew which had grown a fine crop of pale blue fur upon its surface, or some shapeless mess which had started out as a fruit mousse and had collapsed into something reminiscent of frogs' spawn. She did not chide her old friend about her slap-dash ways. She loved her too well to hurt her, and recognized that Ella's warm heart and her artistic leanings more than made up for her complete lack of housewifery.

The little red car had just drawn up as Ella was slamming her gate. Ella had no scruples about staring, and she stood now, a sturdy figure, watching unashamedly as the stranger emerged.

The younger woman gave Ella no greeting, as country people are wont to do. In fact, she appeared not to notice the watching figure. She locked the car door (a precaution which most Thrush Green folk forgot to take) and consulted the paper in her hand before walking swiftly towards Tullivers.

Ella waited until the front door closed behind her with a groaning of rusty hinges, and then crossed the road to the rectory where she found Dimity in the kitchen beating up eggs whilst her husband made the mid-morning coffee.

Over their steaming cups Ella gave her account of the newcomer.

'About thirty, I reckon. Looks bright enough – might be useful in the WI. Nice dog-tooth-check suit in brown and white, and stockings with no seams. Come to think of it – they were probably tights. I didn't see any tops when she clambered out of the Mini.'

'Ella dear,' protested Charles Henstock mildly. 'Spare my feelings.'

'Nice pair of square-toed shoes, Russell and Bromley probably, and an Italian handbag.'

'How on earth do you know?' expostulated Dimity.

'I can smell Italian leather a mile off,' said Ella, fishing a battered tin from her pocket and beginning to roll a cigarette from the crumpled papers and loose tobacco therein.

'And I'd take a bet her earrings were Italian too,' she added, blowing out an acrid cloud of smoke. Dimity quietly moved the egg-custard out of range.

'Ears pierced?' asked the rector, with rare sarcasm.

'Couldn't see,' replied Ella in a matter-of-fact tone. 'But wears good gloves.'

Something sizzled in the oven and Dimity crossed the kitchen to attend to it.

'Not that I really noticed her,' continued Ella. 'Just got a passing glimpse, you know.'

The rector forbore to comment.

'But she's welcome to Tullivers,' went on Ella. 'There's a jackdaw's nest the size of a squirrel's drey in the kitchen chimney. Which reminds me – shall I get the boiler chimney done, Dim?'

Dimity sat back on her heels by the open oven door and looked thoughtful.

'September, October, November, December, January, February, March, April – yes, Ella. Get it swept now.'

'Good,' replied her old friend, rising briskly and dropping her cigarette stub into the sink basket where it smouldered, unpleasantly close to the shredded cabbage soaking in a bowl.

'I got my old hand loom out again last night,' said Ella conversationally. 'Thought I'd run up a few ties ready for the next Bring and Buy Sale and Christmas time.'

She looked speculatively at Charles, who was doing his best to repress a shudder. He already had four ties of Ella's making, each much too short, the colour of over-cooked porridge, and far too thick to knot properly. Fortunately, he wore his clerical collar more often than not, and could safely leave the monstrosities in the drawer without hurting Ella's feelings.

'Lovely, dear,' said Dimity automatically, putting the egg-custard into the oven carefully.

'I'll see you out,' said the rector, following Ella along the cold dark passage to the front door.

Outside, Thrush Green sparkled in the bright April sunshine. It was like emerging from a dark cave in the cliffs on to a sunlit beach, thought Ella. She was thankful that she did not have to live in the rectory. Could anything ever make that north-racing pile of Victorian architecture comfortable?

She looked towards Tullivers, and the rector's gaze followed hers. The shabby little house basked in the sunshine like some small, battered, stray cat grateful for warmth.

There was no sign of the stranger, and the red car had gone.

'Oh,' cried the rector, genuinely disappointed. 'I'd hoped to catch sight of her, I must admit.'

'You will,' prophesied Ella, setting off purposefully for her own cottage. 'Mark my words, Charles Henstock, you will!'

2. WHO IS SHE?

Two or three weeks later the red car reappeared. This time the young woman had a companion, as sharp eyes on Thrush Green were quick to observe.

A small boy, of about six years of age, clambered out of the car and jumped excitedly up and down on the pavement. He was a well-built child, flaxen-haired and fair-skinned, and seemed delighted with his first glimpse of Thrush Green. He pointed to Tullivers, obviously asking questions. He pointed to the fine statue of Nathaniel Patten, erected a year or two earlier by Thrush Green residents to honour one of their famous men, and he was clearly impressed by the church and the village school across the green.

The woman looked up and down the road, as though waiting for somebody. Her answers to the child appeared perfunctory. After a few minutes, she led the way to the front door, followed by the boy. Just as it closed behind them, the local builder's battered van screeched to a halt behind the red car, and out tumbled Joe Bush.

'Late as usual!' was the general comment of the hidden onlookers of Thrush Green as they watched him scurry up the path.

By standing on tip-toe, little Miss Fogerty could just see what was going on across the green. The Gothic window was uncomfortably high, installed by its Victorian builders for just that purpose – to make sure that children could not look out easily and so be distracted from their pot-hooks and hangers by the giddy world outside.

The sand-tray was also rather awkwardly placed beneath the window. Miss Fogerty made up her mind to shift it at play-time.

This week the sand-tray carried a tiny replica of Thrush Green with plasticine houses, duly labelled with their owners' names, the church, the school, and even a passable representation of Nathaniel Patten's statue. Some of the infants had proudly brought contributions to the scene. Toy lorries, cars, and even an Army tank, had found a place on the roads across the green, and though grossly over-sized for their surroundings they made an imposing addition to the sand-tray. It was unfortunate that the fine avenue of chestnut trees which flanked the north side of the green, had also been constructed of plasticine. The heat from the hot-water pipe nearby had caused them to bow to the ground with flaccid exhaustion. Loving fingers restored them to the upright position a dozen times a day, but Miss Fogerty decided that twigs set in a plasticine base must replace the present avenue without delay.

Miss Fogerty shifted a Virol jar full of paint brushes further along the window-sill, the better to follow the stranger's activities. The little boy aroused her keenest interest. He looked just the right age for her class, and very likely he could read already. What a blessing! And could probably manage his own buttons and shoe-laces too which was more than half her class could accomplish. It was truly disgraceful that Gloria Curdle, at the great age of six, was still unable to tie a bow!

'Which reminds me,' said Miss Fogerty to herself. 'Tears or no tears, that child's tin camel *must* be removed from the Thrush Green model. Looming over the church spire is bad enough, in all conscience, but having an Asiatic creature like that among the Cotswolds scenery just Will Not Do!'

Firmly she plucked the offending beast from its alien pastures and put it safely into her sagging cardigan pocket.

Across the green the little boy was jumping rhythmically. Good co-ordination, noted Miss Fogerty approvingly, and plenty of spring.

'I wonder if there are any more children?' speculated Miss Fogerty. A tugging at her skirt nearly precipitated her into the sand-tray.

'Child,' cried Miss Fogerty, with unusual sharpness. 'Don't pull people about in that rude fashion.'

'I can't wait,' said the child, with simple candour.

'Be quick then,' responded Miss Fogerty automatically, returning reluctantly to her duties, with a last glance at Joe Bush's retreating back.

'She's back again,' announced Betty Bell to her employer Harold Shoosmith.

Harold Shoosmith was a comparative newcomer himself to Thrush Green, having come to live there on his retirement from business in Africa two or three years earlier. Tall, spare and handsome . . . and, best of all, a bachelor . . . he was welcomed warmly by the community. It had been his idea to honour one of Thrush Green's famous sons, the missionary Nathaniel Patten, and the splendid statue of their nineteenth-century hero now graced the green.

The fact that Harold was happy to take part in village affairs, and had the leisure to do so, meant that he was on a dozen or more local committees. At this moment he was immersed in the Thrush Green Entertainments Club's accounts. He looked up from his desk. He had long since given up remonstrating with his slap-dash help about bursting into occupied rooms. If Betty Bell held a duster in her hand, she looked upon it as a passport to free passage anywhere in the house, the bathroom included. Early in their acquaintance she had bounced in to encounter her employer stark naked, except for an inadequate face flannel, but had not been a whit abashed. It was Harold Shoosmith who suffered from shock. After that, he prudently locked the door when at his ablutions.

'Who's back?' he asked apprehensively. Ella Bembridge, whom he found most trying, had just left him after delivering the parish magazine, and he feared her return.

'That new party,' responded Betty, flicking an African carving, knocking it from its shelf and catching it adroitly, all in a second. Harold, wincing, could not help admiring her deftness. Practice, he supposed, resignedly.

'Her that's coming to Tullivers,' continued Betty, attacking a small enamelled clock mercilessly. 'Got a young man with her this time,' she added archly.

'Husband, I expect,' said Harold, returning to his accounts.

'What! That age?' cried Betty, giggling at the success of her subtlety. 'He ain't no more'n six, I'll lay.'

She fell energetically upon a window-sill. A dozing fly burst into a frenzy of buzzing as it tried to escape from her onslaught.

'If you was to go out the front and down to the gate you'd get a good look at her,' advised Betty. 'She's hanging about for someone. Joe Bush, I expect. That place'll need a proper going-over before it's fit to live in.'

'I shouldn't dream of staring at the lady,' said Harold sternly. 'And, in any case, I think you are taking a lot for granted. No one knows if she proposes to buy Tullivers. If she does, then we shall call in the usual way.'

Betty Bell was not affected by the touch of frost in Harold's manner. Hoity-toity was her only silent comment, as she gave a final drubbing to the window-sill.

'Wantcher desk done?' she asked cheerfully.

'No thanks,' replied Harold shortly. 'I want to work on it.'

'Okay, okay!' replied his daily help. 'I'll go and put the curry on. Suit you?'

'Very well, Betty, thank you,' said Harold, his good humour restored at the thought of her temporary absence.

The door crashed behind her, and soon the sound of clashing saucepans proclaimed that his lunch was being prepared. Distracting though the noise was, Harold Shoosmith thanked heaven that it was at a distance.

He turned again to his accounts.

Across the green, young Doctor Lovell was having trouble too. The last patient at his morning surgery was Dotty Harmer.

He had to admit, in all fairness, that she did not worry him unduly with her ailments. She preferred to deal with them herself with a variety of herbal remedies ranging from harmlessly wholesome to downright dangerous, in the doctor's opinion.

His senior partner, Doctor Bailey, who was now too frail to take much part in the practice, had warned him about Dotty.

'Eccentric always – plain crazy sometimes,' he summed up succinctly. 'Father was a proper martinet, and taught at the local grammar school. His wife died young, and Dotty kept house for the old tartar until he died. As you'll see, the place is filthy, full of animals, and the garden is a jungle of herbs from which Dotty brews the most diabolical concoctions. I beg of you, young man, never to eat or drink anything which Dotty has prepared. We have a special complaint at Thrush Green known as Dotty's Collywobbles. Be warned!'

Since then, the young partner had frequently met those suffering from this disorder. Doctor Bailey, he realized early in their friendship, knew his patients pretty thoroughly.

This morning he examined a long angry gash in Dotty's forearm, caused by the horn of a young goat who was the latest addition to Dotty's motley family.

'Such a sweet disposition really,' said Dotty earnestly. 'It wasn't *meant*, you know. Just playfulness.'

'When was it done?' asked the doctor.

'One day last week, I think,' said Dotty vaguely. 'Or the week before, perhaps. The weeks pass so quickly, don't they? Monday morning it's Saturday afternoon, if you know what I mean. I treated it at once, of course.'

'What with?'

'Now let me see. I think it was one of dear Gerard's. From his *Herball*, you know. Yes, I remember now, it was All-Heale.'

'All-Heale?' asked Doctor Lovell, whose knowledge of sixteenth-century remedies was shaky.

'As a practising physician,' said Dotty sharply, 'you surely know Clownes Wound-Wort! You simply pound the leaves with a little pure lard and apply the ointment to any open wound. Gerard gives several examples of his success with the cure. I should have thought that all medical men would be conversant with the "poore man of Kent who in mowing of Peason did cut his leg with a sithe". He had the sense to apply All-Heale, and was cured within days.'

'I'll give you a shot of antibiotics,' said Doctor Lovell firmly. He scribbled a prescription, turning a deaf ear to his patient's protestations.

'The lotion should be used twice a day,' he continued, handing her the form, 'and keep the wound covered. Take the tablets night and morning. You'll be fine in a day or two, but come back if it gives any further trouble.'

Dotty took it in her claw-like grasp and surveyed the hiero-glyphics with distaste and doubt.

Doctor Lovell relented, and patted her bony shoulder. 'Most of these things are based on the tried herbal recipes, you know,' he said mendaciously.

Dotty looked relieved. 'I hope you're right, young man,' she said, opening the surgery door. Her eye lit upon the red car and Joe Bush's van.

'Have you met your new neighbour?' inquired Dotty.

'First I've heard of one,' said Doctor Lovell.

'You're the only person on Thrush Green who hasn't,' replied Dotty tartly.

Setting off for her cottage half a mile away, Dotty shook her untidy grey head over modern physicians. They seemed to know nothing about their really great forebears, and very little of the immediate world about them. It didn't give a patient much confidence, to be sure.

She fingered the prescription in her coat pocket. For two pins, she'd tear it up and forget it. But just suppose that her arm refused to heal and she was obliged to return to that silly fellow?

It might be prudent to give his nostrums a brief trial. Medical men were so touchy if one ignored their advice.

Nevertheless, as soon as she had traversed the alley by Albert Piggott's house which led to the path to Lulling Woods, and knew that she was out of sight of Thrush Green, Dotty stopped to extract a string bag from her pocket, and advanced purposefully upon a fine collection of weeds growing in the ditch.

'Best to be on the safe side,' said Dotty to herself, thrusting the pungent leaves into the bag.

Swinging it jauntily, she skipped homeward, well satisfied.

3. The Priors Meet Their Neighbours

In the months that followed, Joe Bush's van spent most of its time standing outside Tullivers. Not that the house was a hive of activity – Joe Bush's methods, and those of his two assistants, were both leisurely and erratic. There were frequent trips down the steep hill to Lulling High Street, where lay the builder's yard, for forgotten items. There were a prodigious number of 'brew-ups' during the day, so that work proceeded slowly.

Luckily, perhaps, only the basic repairs seemed to be tackled. Loose roof tiles were replaced, the jackdaw's nest removed from the kitchen chimney, and two faulty windows were rehung. Inside, a few rotting floor-boards were made good and a particularly hideous fireplace removed. Otherwise, it seemed, the house would be put into shape by its owner.

'Cor!' exclaimed Joe Bush, to the landlord of The Two Pheasants. 'She've got plenty to do there, I'll tell you. I shan't get fat on what she's spending, and that's the truth.'

'Maybe she ain't got it to spend,' replied the landlord reasonably. 'She being a widow, I take it.'

'And what makes you think that?' asked Joe, heavily sarcastic. 'She's got a husband all right.'

'Don't show up much,' commented the landlord.

'He's overseas,' replied Joe, putting down his empty glass and making for the door. 'I shouldn't wonder,' he added vaguely.

'Either he is or he isn't,' pointed out the landlord, understandably nettled.

'Well, that's what she told the kid last week when they was down. But you knows women. Crafty as a wagon-load of monkeys. Maybe he's doin' time and she don't want the kid to know.'

'Don't talk out the back of your neck,' begged the landlord. He flapped at the counter with a teacloth in a dismissive fashion. Joe took the hint and vanished.

The absence of a man in the stranger's life certainly intrigued Thrush Green. It was established that the handsome lady was a Mrs Prior, that her son was called Jeremy, and that they lived, at the present time, in a flat in Chelsea.

These interesting facts had been gleaned from the child, rather than from his mother, by Joe Bush's junior assistant, known as Sawny Sam locally, for obvious reasons, although his baptismal name was Samuel Ellerman John Plumb. It was Sawny Sam who held ladders, carried hods, mixed cement, wheeled barrows, fetched forgotten items from the yard, and brewed the tea six times a day.

He had a gentle, kindly disposition, and at seventeen years of age his intelligence was on a par with young Jeremy's. They got on famously, sharing a love of football, animals and stamp collecting.

On several occasions during the summer, Mrs Prior and Jeremy came down at weekends to decorate the interior of Tullivers. While his mother slapped vigorously at the walls with white emulsion paint, the child occupied himself happily in the garden. On Saturday mornings, the builders were at work, and it was then that the friendship grew between Jeremy and Sawny Sam.

'I'm going to that school,' said Jeremy, nodding across to the other side of the green.

'It's ever so nice,' said Sam heavily. 'My cousin Dave went there. He was a monitor.'

'Why didn't you go?'

'I lives up the street. I 'ad to go to St Margaret's School. We 'ad a beast of a 'ead.'

'What did he do?'

''It yer!'

'What for?'

'Anythink. Nothink.'

'He sounds cruel.'

''E were.'

'Is he still?'

'No. He's stopped now.'

'Why?'

'Dead,' said Sam perfunctorily.

He filled the kettle, and Jeremy set out the enamel mugs for the second tea-break of the day. He looked thoughtful.

'Are they cruel over there?'

'Nah!' drawled Sam derisively. 'There's only two old ducks – Miss Watson and Miss Fogerty. Like aunties, they are. Gives you sweets and that. Friday afternoons you can take any gear you likes to play with.'

'Like stamp albums?' asked Jeremy eagerly.

'Dinky cars, if you want to. Anythink – absolutely *anythink*,

Dave said. Except guns and catapults and that. Them two don't 'old with guns. Nothink dangerous.'

They sat companionably, side by side, on a low pile of bricks, and looked across at Jeremy's new school, while the kettle hummed.

'I shall like it,' announced Jeremy, with decision. 'Shall I learn things?'

Sawny Sam's mouth and eyes became three O's in astonishment.

'Learn? 'Course you'll *learn*. Them two'll learn you all right. Poitry, tables –'

'*Tables?*' exclaimed Jeremy. 'What tables? You can't *learn* tables. You eat off 'em.'

'You must go to a pretty soppy school if you ain't 'eard of tables. Multiplication tables! Twice two are four, three twos are six, four twos are eight, five twos are ten. I knows 'em all – well, nearly. Never quite mastered seven times and twelve times,' admitted Sam frankly.

'We work things out like that with milk bottles at my school,' said Jeremy.

'Must take a lotter time,' said Sam.

'And a lot of milk bottles,' responded Jeremy. They relapsed into silence, brooding vaguely upon elementary arithmetic. The kettle lid began to rattle cheerfully and Sam rose to attend to it.

'Tell you one thing,' he said. 'You'll do all right with Miss Fogerty. She learns kids a treat. Been at it a hundred years, I shouldn't wonder. My dad said so.'

It was a comforting thought.

It was that night that Winnie Bailey, next door to Tullivers, woke at two o'clock. In the other bed her husband tossed restlessly.

'Are you all right, Donald?' she asked softly.

'Sorry, my dear, to have woken you,' wheezed the old man. 'Just can't sleep, that's all.'

'I'll go and warm some milk. It will do us both good,' said Winnie, groping for her slippers. She shrugged herself into her comfortable ancient red dressing gown, and made her way downstairs. In the kitchen, as the milk warmed on the stove, she looked out upon the dark garden. In the distance, an owl screeched from Lulling Woods. A frond of jasmine tapped at the window, and turning to the noise, Winnie Bailey had a severe shock. A light was showing in Tullivers.

Could it be that someone had broken in? Could that attractive young woman have left the light switched on? Should she go and investigate? Or ring the police?

An ominous hissing from the milk saucepan interrupted her agitated thoughts. She filled two mugs, put them on a small tray, and then went to look cautiously from the front door across to her new neighbours.

To her surprise, she saw the little red car parked in the short drive to Tullivers. The light, she now perceived, was a very low one. She realized suddenly that it was a night-light, and recalled with a pang, her own children's early years, when a night-light burned comfortingly in a saucer of water to keep away those bogeys which come at night to scare the young.

But what an extraordinary thing, thought Winnie, mounting the stairs carefully. What could those two be sleeping on? And how cheerless it must be in that cold, empty house!

She had spoken once or twice to the young woman who had

introduced herself as Phil Prior, but Winnie had felt that the stranger did not welcome overtures too warmly, and so she had decided to 'make haste slowly', as Donald often said. No doubt, the girl had plenty to do in the short time at her disposal on each visit, and any interruptions were frustrating.

But really, thought Winnie, she must see that those two were all right in the morning. Why on earth didn't they put up at The Fleece overnight?

By the time she regained the bedroom, her husband had fallen asleep. She knew better than to disturb him. Sleep was of more value to the frail man than hot milk.

She sipped her own milk thoughtfully, turning over in her mind the conditions of the pair next door. There was something rather sad about them, she felt. Perhaps 'sad' was too strong a word to use about two young and obviously healthy people. On second thoughts, 'forlorn' fitted them better. As though they were faintly neglected – as though they had lost something desperately necessary.

Could it be, thought Winnie, a husband and a father?

She must certainly risk a snub, and speak to Mrs Prior in the morning. Putting her mug gently upon the bedside table, she slipped, within minutes, into troubled slumber.

Winnie Bailey was one of the very few residents of Thrush Green who attended the communion service at eight o'clock at St Andrew's.

No one was stirring at Tullivers as she returned to prepare breakfast, and it was almost ten o'clock before she heard the child's voice from the garden next door. The August sun was already hot, and Thrush Green was going to have a day of shimmering heat. Doctor Bailey was lying in the old wicker chaise-longue, a rug across his legs, and a battered panama hat tilted over his eyes.

He wished, for the thousandth time, that he was not such a useless crock. Doctor Lovell and Winnie had to work far too hard for his liking. There was no doubt about it, the time was fast arriving when young Lovell would need another partner, and a pretty active one too.

A new estate was growing rapidly along the lane leading to

Nod and Nidden. Two or three dozen families had moved in already, mainly young couples with one or two babies, and obviously more would come. The practice had almost doubled in size since he arrived there with Winnie in their young days.

How happy they had been, he thought! His mind dwelt on early patients, many now dead, and the welcome they had given him. He remembered, with affection, the matriarchal figure of Mrs Curdle, the gypsy woman who ran the annual one-day fair on Thrush Green every first of May. He hoped that young Ben, her grandson, who was now in charge, would call again next May.

His eye fell upon his pale wasted hands, and he wondered, without self-pity, if he could live long enough to see the fair again. He doubted it. As a medical man, he could gauge his future fairly accurately. Already, he told himself, he was living on borrowed time. And how good it was! Despite weakness and pain, life was still precious, and the companionship of Winnie the mainspring of his days.

He saw her now crossing the garden to the hedge, and heard the little boy from Tullivers answering her questions. Very soon a third voice was added to the conversation, but he could not distinguish the words.

Not long afterwards, Winnie came up to him and tucked the rug neatly round his legs.

'I've asked our new neighbours to come and have coffee,' she told him. 'It won't tire you?'

'Attractive women never tire me,' said her husband gallantly.

An hour later they arrived.

'Please forgive my piebald appearance,' said the young woman, gazing down at her black jeans and sleeveless black blouse. Both were liberally speckled and streaked with white paint. 'It seems to run down my arm and trickle off my elbow.'

'Try a roller,' advised the doctor.

'I simply can't manage one,' confessed the girl, and the comparative merits of brushes and rollers occupied them happily whilst Mrs Bailey went to fetch the tray, accompanied by a chattering Jeremy.

'And when do you hope to move in?'

'In two or three weeks, with luck. The men should have finished by then, they say.'

'Yes – well,' said the doctor, rubbing his bony nose doubtfully. 'That may be so, but if I were you I should move in even if they haven't departed. Joe Bush takes his time.'

'It hadn't escaped me,' replied the young woman, smiling.

Mrs Bailey returned with the tray.

'We've got *two* sorts of biscuits,' announced Jeremy excitedly.

'It's not very polite to comment on other people's food,' his mother told him gently.

'It sounded favourable comment to me,' said Winnie. 'We like that here.'

'We had rather a scratch breakfast,' said Mrs Prior. 'We stayed overnight for the first time.'

Winnie was glad that she had mentioned the burning subject first.

'Were you both comfortable?' she asked.

'Hardly. Our camp beds are the sort that Victorian explorers humped about!'

'Or probably their native bearers humped about,' suggested Doctor Bailey.

'Are they hard?' asked Winnie anxiously. 'We have two spare feather-beds. Or better still, come and sleep here. You would be quite free to come and go when you pleased.'

'You're very kind,' said the girl. She flushed in a way that made her look suddenly young and defenceless.

'Or The Fleece is very comfortable, I know,' went on Winnie, intent upon her visitors' well-being.

'Too expensive,' said the girl.

'Hotel prices are ruinous these days,' agreed the doctor. 'Sugar, Mrs Prior?'

'No, thank you. And as we're to be neighbours, do you think you could call me Phil?'

'That would be very nice. Short for Phyllis, I take it? One of my favourite names,' said Doctor Bailey.

'I wish it were.'

'Philippa?' asked Winnie.

'Worse still. My proper name is Phyllida. My parents were hopelessly romantic.'

'Henry Austin Dobson,' said the doctor. 'Born 1840, died 1921.'

'How on earth did you know?'

'My mind is full of completely useless bits and pieces, such as that,' he replied. 'But the things I want to remember – where I left my pipe, or if I gave my partner a certain urgent message, for instance – completely escape me.'

'Well, you're dead right about Austin Dobson. My parents were great readers of poetry and had a weakness for the light fantastic.'

'A pleasant change from the heavy dismal we suffer from everywhere today,' commented Winnie. 'No one seems to laugh any more.'

'I do,' said Jeremy. 'I laugh a lot.'

'Keep it up,' advised the doctor. 'Keep it up.'

'My daddy makes me laugh.' He turned to his mother. 'Doesn't he make me laugh?' he persisted.

'He certainly does,' agreed his mother.

'When's he coming to see the new house?' asked the boy, through a mouthful of ginger biscuit.

'Sometime,' said his mother evasively. She produced a crumpled handkerchief from her jeans' pocket and gave a deft dab at her son's mouth. 'My husband has to be abroad a great deal,' she explained. 'He's in a textile firm. I'm afraid Jeremy hasn't seen much of him this last week or two.'

'More like a month,' began Jeremy.

'It always seems longer than it is,' his mother said swiftly. She looked at a massive wrist-watch. 'Time we went back to our paint pots, young man,' she told him, rising. 'Thank you so much for the coffee. We shall work twice as fast after that.'

Winnie accompanied her to the gate.

'Now, don't forget. If you want to stay overnight, do let us help. We look forward to having you as neighbours.'

'We look forward to coming,' replied the girl. 'A London flat is no place to bring up a growing boy. I was country-bred myself. I know what Jeremy's missing.'

'You'll be happy at Thrush Green,' Winnie assured her.

The girl's mouth quivered. 'I'm sure we shall,' she said. 'We'll be here in good time for Jeremy to start school in the village in September.'

The two women looked across the green. The dew was drying rapidly, and from St Andrew's came the sound of country voices raised in praise. A pigeon clattered out from the avenue of chestnut trees, and landed nearby, strutting aimlessly this way and that, thrusting out its bright coral feet.

The girl sighed.

'It's all very comforting,' she said softly, as though speaking to herself. 'And now we must go home. Thank you again.'

They parted with smiles, and Winnie watched the pair run to Tullivers. It was good to see the little house in use again.

She returned to her own garden thoughtfully. Why did the girl use the word 'comforting' about Thrush Green? From what pain did she seek relief? From what torment was she flying? Who could tell?

4. A SHOCK FOR DOTTY

Half a mile away, Dotty Harmer was in trouble. She had gone down the garden to feed her hens, when she saw something move behind the garden shed.

An open-ended extension had been built on to house Dotty's winter store of logs. An energetic nephew, staying for a week of his vacation, had obligingly set some flag-stones at the entrance, so that his aunt could step from the path to the logs without getting her feet wet.

'Very nice, dear,' she had commented. 'And I can chop up the logs there. And marrow bones. So useful to have what my dear father used to call "an area of hard standing". It will be most useful, dear boy.'

Its use at the moment, when Dotty stood transfixed, hen food in hand, was unorthodox. For, lying in the sun, was a mother cat suckling five well-grown babies.

Charming though the sight was, Dotty's jaw dropped. How on earth could she cope with six cats – nay, six *more* cats! Already she owned two, a mother and daughter which she had

prudently had spayed. What would they have to say about this brazen intruder and her progeny?

Dotty peered through her steel-rimmed spectacles at the family. They were a motley crew, to be sure, but how engagingly pretty! The mother was black with white paws, and one of the kittens had the same colouring. There was a fine little tabby, and three tortoiseshell kittens.

Dotty's heart sank again. Ten to one the tortoiseshells would be female. How long before their first litters arrived? Something must be done before the place was over-run with wild cats.

She took a resolute step forward, and the kittens shot into the stack of logs and vanished. One young quivering triangular tail showed for an instant in a gap, and then was gone. The mother cat crouched defensively, facing Dotty, strategically placed between this enemy and her babies. She was pathetically thin and dusty, and Dotty's tender heart went out to this gallant battered small fighter.

'Good puss! Nice little puss!' said Dotty, advancing gently.

The cat retreated slightly, and spat defiance.

Dotty put down the hen food and returned to the house for a dish of milk. Through the kitchen window she witnessed a remarkable sight. The mother cat gave a curious chirruping sound, and the five babies tumbled from the logs, towards the steaming hen food. Within seconds six heads were in the pot, as the cats ate ravenously.

Dotty stood aghast. That cats, so fastidious as a rule, should fling themselves upon cooked peelings, meat scraps and bacon rinds, all bound together with bran, showed to what excess of hunger the poor things were driven.

She watched them lick the pot clean, their eyes half-closed with bliss, and then sit down to wash themselves.

'Well, that's the last of the chickens' mash,' said Dotty aloud, and philosophically reached for the bag of corn instead. Bearing this and the brimming dish of milk she went once more down the garden path. As before, the kittens vanished, but the mother cat stood her ground. Dotty fed the hens, put down the milk, and retreated to the house, there to work out the best way to cope with an embarrassment of cats.

It was a problem which was to puzzle her, and the rest of Thrush Green, for weeks to come.

One still, hot morning, in the week following Dotty's discovery, Albert Piggott was digging a grave. For this melancholy task Albert's glum expression seemed particularly suited, but although the occasion was a sad one, it was not the circumstances of his labours that troubled Albert that morning, but the worsening conditions of his own matrimonial affairs.

He was the first to admit that he was cunningly hooked at the outset. There were a few aspects of married life which, in all fairness, he would agree were an improvement on the single state, for a man in his position. His house was warm and clean. His clothes were washed and mended. And his meals – ah, his meals! – were superb.

But once you'd said that, Albert told himself, squinting along the side of the grave for any unsightly irregularities, you'd said the lot. Nagging, whining and money-grubbing, that's what Nell was, and lately he had detected a new unpleasant note in her diatribes. There was far too much about that oilman who came with his clanking van every other Thursday, for Albert's liking. A smarmy fellow, if ever there was one, a proper sissy, a regular droopy-drawers! And Nell was taken in by his soft soap, the great fool, and talked about it being 'so nice to see a gentleman for a change, and what a pity it was she had married beneath her'.

Albert set his spade to one side, pushed back his greasy cap and mopped his sweating brow. It was about time Sam Curdle arrived to give him a hand. He could do with it. Cotswold clay makes heavy digging in any weather. On a blazing August morning it was doubly intractable.

Sam Curdle, grandson of Mrs Curdle who once ruled over the fair, had been released from gaol early in the New Year. Most of Thrush Green thought, and said openly, that Sam Curdle had a nerve to return to the place where he had so misbehaved.

'How he can face that poor Miss Watson he stole from, and battered into the bargain, I really don't know,' they told each other indignantly. 'It's a pity he doesn't take himself off, with that blowsy Bella of his, and find a living elsewhere.'

But that is just what Sam was incapable of doing. Here, in Thrush Green, as well he knew, were a few soft-hearted souls who would give him a little work for the sake of the children – and a *little* work was all that Sam Curdle wanted. Bella had found a daily job at a farm at Nidden while he was doing time, and had developed into a passably good worker under the brisk direction of the farmer's wife. They still lived in the battered caravan, converted years ago from a bus, in a sheltered corner of the stackyard. Here the Curdles reckoned themselves well off, with water from an outside tap, free milk, and a dozen or so cracked eggs weekly.

'You can stay there as long as you go straight,' the farmer had told Sam. 'But you try any of your gyppo tricks here, nicking eggs, knocking off the odd hen, and that sort of lark, and you get the boot, pronto!'

And Sam had toed the line.

The rector had found him odd jobs to do, both in his own garden and in the churchyard. Albert Piggott was glad to have an assistant when it came to such tasks as grave-digging and coke-sweeping. The fact that Sam Curdle was a wrongdoer and had been in prison troubled the sexton not at all.

It was Albert himself, in fact, who had helped to bring him to justice. If anything, Albert felt now a certain proprietorial warmth towards the local malefactor. Just bad luck he'd been caught. He'd simply met a master mind, was Albert's opinion. Plenty of people were quite as bad as Sam, but got away with it.

A shadow fell athwart the grave and Albert looked up to see Sam's face peering down at him.

'And about time too,' grunted Albert. He indicated the second shovel with a jerk of his black thumb.

Sam jumped down and began scraping some crumbs of earth together in a languid manner.

'Don't strain yourself,' said Albert tartly.

Sam stirred himself to attack the other end of the grave with rather more vigour. They shovelled together in silence.

A robin hopped about the growing pile of soil looking for worms. The morning sounds of Thrush Green were muffled by the height of the earth walls about them, but in the distance they could hear the children playing on the two swings on the green. There was a rhythmic squeaking as the chains swung to and fro, and occasionally the thud of the see-saw and the cries of excited children.

The two men worked steadily until St Andrew's clock struck twelve above them.

'That's it then,' said Albert, clambering painfully out of the grave. Sam followed him.

'Time for a quick 'un?' asked Sam.

'Who pays?'

'We goes Dutch.'

'Humph!' snorted Albert, but he quickened his pace, never-theless, as he shambled towards the open door of The Two Pheasants.

But his thirst was not to be slaked immediately for, directly in his path, stood Dotty Harmer.

'I shan't keep you,' said Dotty briskly, eyeing the pair, 'but I want you to let me know if you hear of anyone wanting a kitten.'

'Well now, miss –' began Albert.

'I know you have a cat,' cut in Dotty. Her tone implied, rightly, that she felt sorry for it. She looked at Sam Curdle with distaste. 'And I know you haven't room for one in the caravan,' she told him dismissively. 'The thing is, I have five to dispose of.'

Sam's face lit up. 'I'd be pleased to drown 'em for you, miss. Any time.'

Dotty looked at him sharply. 'Out of the question. They are far too big to drown.'

'You wouldn't catch 'em anyway,' gloomed Albert. 'Them wild cats never gets caught. Where've you got 'em?'

Dotty told him.

'Never get 'em out o' there,' said Albert, with relish. 'Why, I recollect that there was a widder woman over Lulling Woods way who had two – *just two*, mark you – livin' in her logs, and within the year she'd got *eighteen* kittens!'

'That's why I intend to tame them,' said Dotty firmly. 'I am going to get the mother cat spayed as soon as she has confidence in me.'

'You'll be lucky!' growled Albert. 'Best by far have a cat shoot and get done with the lot.'

'Disgraceful!' snapped Dotty.

'You won't never tame 'em, miss,' Sam said, hoping for five shillings, if not by drowning, then by a little erratic marksmanship.

'I should set a dog on 'em,' advised Albert. 'Rout 'em out, like, and then shoot 'em as they run away.'

'Have you thought,' asked Dotty severely, 'that they might simply be *maimed*, and not killed outright?'

'They'd die eventual,' said Albert casually.

'I am not proposing to harm these kittens, in any way whatsoever,' said Dotty, now dangerously calm. 'I shall do my best to get them tame enough to be accepted into good homes. *Good* homes!' she repeated firmly.

'I am on my way to Mrs Young to see if she will be able to have one,' she added, nodding to one of the five houses behind the chestnut avenue. 'All I wanted to ask you was to let me know if you hear of anyone needing a kitten.'

'Right, miss,' said Albert with rare deference. His dirty finger rose of its own volition to his greasy cap. Plain potty Miss Harmer was, and no doubt about it – but she was still gentry, and some innate, long-stifled instinct to acknowledge the fact had twitched Albert's hand to its unaccustomed position.

'Yes, miss,' added Sam meekly. 'I'll bear it in mind, miss.'

They entered The Two Pheasants for their long-awaited drink, the kittens already forgotten.

But Dotty, striding purposefully towards Joan Young's house, seethed with indignation. 'Drowning! Shooting! Setting a dog on them! A pity those two have never heard of reverence for life. I should like to have introduced them to Albert Schweitzer.'

She thought again.

'Or better still, my dear father. He'd have given them the horse-whipping they deserve!'

She reached the Youngs' gate.

'How I do hate cruelty!' said Dotty aloud, making for the front door.

Joan Young was the wife of a local architect. Her sister Ruth, who was lunching with her that day, was married to Doctor Lovell who, at that moment, was attending a cantankerous old bachelor of ninety-two to the south of Lulling.

Lunch was set in the large sunny kitchen. Paul Young was already at the table, waiting impatiently with the voracious hunger of a young schoolboy for the chicken which had just been lifted from the oven.

Opposite him, in his own old high chair, sat his baby cousin Mary banging lustily with her spoon.

'What's that?' asked Paul, as the bell of the front door rang sharply.

'Wozzat?' echoed his cousin, not caring particularly, but glad to try out a new expression.

'Oh, damn!' said Joan, tugging the fork from the bird. 'You carry on, Ruth, while I see to this.'

'You shouldn't swear,' reproved her son. 'Miss Fogerty made

Chris wash his mouth out with soapy water once because he swore.'

'Sorry, sorry!' cried his mother, struggling with her apron strings. 'It slipped out.'

'Oh, damn!' echoed the baby thoughtfully. 'Oh, damn!

The two sisters exchanged resigned looks, but had the wisdom not to comment. The bell split the air again, and Joan hurried to the door.

'Oh, do come in, Miss Harmer,' she cried, doing her best to sound welcoming. Who else but Dotty, she wondered, would call at twenty past twelve, and be clad, on a boiling hot day, in a tweed coat with a fur collar, topped by a purple velour hat, thick with dust, and decorated with a fine diamond brooch which, as Joan knew, had been in the family for generations and, amazingly enough, had not yet been lost by its present scatter-brained owner.

'Will you have a glass of sherry?' asked Joan, ushering her guest into the drawing-room.

'No, thank you, dear. I shall have a glass of rhubarb and ginger wine with my lunch. I find I get so sleepy if I mix my drinks midday.'

She looked sharply about the room.

'No cat?' said Dotty.

'No. Just Flo, the old spaniel, you know.'

'Well,' began Dotty, undoing her coat and settling herself. 'I'll tell you why I've come.'

Joan listened patiently to the saga of the kittens, half her mind on the fast-cooling lunch.

'And so it is essential that I wean the kittens, first and foremost,' she heard her visitor saying. 'Mr Fortescue says he can't possibly operate until the mother cat is *absolutely dry*.'

Dotty embarked on an involved obstetrical account about nursing felines, showing a remarkable grip on the subject for a spinster, thought Joan.

Her attention wandered again, only to be riveted suddenly when she heard Dotty putting a straight question.

'So how many kittens would you like?'

'Heavens!' exclaimed Joan. 'I must think about this! I don't know that Flo would care about a kitten –'

'Be a companion for her,' said Dotty firmly. 'What about Ruth? She'd like one, wouldn't she?'

'I'll ask her,' promised Joan meekly.

To her relief, Dotty rose, and began to make her way to the door.

'Well, dear, I hope that's two kittens settled. It's quite a problem. I refuse to allow them to go to any but the nicest homes.'

'Thank you,' said Joan faintly.

'They won't be ready for a month or so,' continued Dotty, now on the doorstep.

Joan rallied her failing senses. 'I will ring you before the end of the week,' she promised, 'and let you know if Ruth and I can have one each.'

'And tell your friends,' shouted Dotty from the gate. 'Those that are *definite cat-lovers*.'

Joan nodded her agreement, and watched the eccentric Dotty trotting briskly homeward to her rhubarb and ginger wine.

'What was all that about?' asked Ruth, when she returned to the kitchen.

'I'll tell you later,' said Joan. 'Little pitchers, you know.'

'Have big ears,' said her son. 'It was Miss Harmer, wasn't it? Did she tell you about her kittens? Chris told me. Isn't it smashing?'

He paused, and his mother watched, with mingled amusement and dismay, the light which suddenly broke out upon his countenance.

'Did she say we can have one, Mummy? Did she? Oh, *please* let's! Oh, Mummy, *do* let's have one! Please, please!'

Albert Piggott, much refreshed, set out from The Two Pheasants to his nearby cottage. An aroma of boiling bacon wafted towards him as he approached.

Mellowed already by a pint of bitter, Albert's spirits were cheered still further by the thought of pleasures to come. Maybe Nell wasn't such a bad sort, after all!

At that moment, a clattering van appeared at the top of the steep hill from Lulling, and Albert's heart turned once more to stone.

'Oilmen!' He spat viciously into the hedge.

'Women!' He spat again.

Albert Piggott was back to normal.

5. A PROBLEM FOR WINNIE

A rare spell of superb harvest weather was broken early in September by a day of violent rainstorms. Naturally enough, it was the very day on which Mrs Prior and her son moved into Tullivers.

Gusts of wind shook veils of rain across Thrush Green. Sheets of water spread across the ground which was baked hard by weeks of sunny weather. A small river gurgled down the hill to Lulling, and the avenue of chestnut trees dropped showers of raindrops and blown leaves.

Those unfortunate enough to have to brave the weather, routed out long-unused mackintoshes, umbrellas and wellington boots, and splashed their way dejectedly across the green, sparing a sympathetic glance for the removal men, staggering from their van into Tullivers with rain-spattered furniture.

Within the little house Jeremy and his mother did their best to create order from chaos. It was no easy task, for as fast as they wheeled an armchair to its allotted place, a tea-chest would arrive to be dumped in its way.

'Where d'you want this, ma'am?' was the cry continuously, as the men appeared, far too quickly for the poor woman's comfort, with yet another bulky object.

She had thought, when packing up the belongings in Chelsea, that each tea-chest and each large piece of furniture had been labelled. As in most moves, only half seemed to bear their place of destination, and soon the kitchen was beginning to become the resting place of all those boxes needing investigation.

'It's like a shop,' said Jeremy happily, surveying the scene.

'Or a lost property office,' said his mother despairingly.

At that moment, Mrs Bailey appeared.

'I'm not even going to offer to help,' she said. 'I should be quite useless. But do please both come to lunch. It's only cottage pie, but I'm sure you'll be ready for a break when the men have gone.'

She put up her umbrella again in a flurry of raindrops, waved cheerfully, and set off through the downpour.

By one o'clock the removal van had rumbled away, and Mrs Prior and Jeremy sat thankfully at the doctor's hospitable table.

'I feel as if I'd been through a washing machine,' said the girl. 'Thoroughly soaked, then tumble-dried. I'll never move again!'

'Goody-goody!' commented her son. 'I don't ever want to move away from here.'

'I certainly hope you won't,' replied Mrs Bailey, handing vegetable dishes. 'Runner beans? They're from the garden.'

'That's something I must do,' said the girl. 'I intend to grow as many vegetables as possible. There are some currant and gooseberry bushes in the garden at Tullivers, I see.'

'You may have to replace them,' said the doctor, toying with his tiny helping. 'They must be pretty ancient.'

'Do fruit bushes cost much?'

There was a note of anxiety in the girl's voice which did not escape the doctor's ear.

'More than they used, no doubt. If I were you, I should clear away all those weeds and long grass around them, fork the ground and put in plenty of bone meal. Then see if they give you a decent crop next season. If they do, well and good. If not, out with 'em!'

The girl nodded thoughtfully, acknowledging his advice. Mrs Bailey, watching her eat her cottage pie, noticed how exhausted she looked. It was understandable: the two had made an early start, and a moving day was always bone-wearying. But she seemed thinner, and there were shadows under the lovely eyes, as though she had slept poorly for many nights. Mrs Baileys' motherly heart went out to this quiet young woman in her trouble – for trouble she guessed, correctly, that she had in abundance. But this was no time to force any confidences. Perhaps, one day, the girl would feel ready to speak, and then would be the time for understanding.

At the end of the meal, the girl and her son rose to go.

'It has been simply lovely. You've really restored us both. But now we must go back and tackle the muddle.'

35

'Thank you for having us,' said Jeremy politely. He stood soberly eyeing the doctor's wife for a few moments, then flung his arms round her waist and gave her a tremendous hug.

'You *are* nice!' he cried. 'Like my granny!' His face was alight with happiness.

Mrs Bailey ruffled the flaxen hair, more touched than she cared to admit.

'Then I *must* be nice,' she agreed. 'Come and see me whenever you like. And put up your umbrella in the porch, or you'll be washed away before you reach home.'

She watched them splash down the path, and then caught sight of Willie Marchant, the postman, tacking erratically back and forth uphill. His black oilskins ran with water, and drops fell from the peak of his cap on to the mackintosh which covered his parcels.

He pulled in to the kerb, propped up his bicycle amidst a shower of drops, and extracted a letter from a bundle.

'One for you, Mrs Bailey,' he grunted gloomily. 'Marvellous, ain't it? Got twice as many this afternoon just because it's raining cats and dogs. That's life, ain't it?'

Mrs Bailey agreed, accepting the letter and studying it with drooping spirits.

Richard again! Now what on earth did he want?

Richard was her sister's boy, and Winnie Bailey had to confess that he was her least favourite nephew. He had always seemed mature, self-centred, and rather smug. Perhaps if he had been blessed with brothers and sisters this unchildlike quality of self-possession would have been mitigated. As it was, as an only child, Winnie Bailey found him uncannily precocious, and at times a trifle supercilious.

As he grew from babyhood to childhood, it was apparent that Richard would make his mark in the world. He was highly intelligent, hard-working, and as efficient on the games field as in the classroom. His school reports were glowing. His parents adored him, and he appeared to be popular with his school fellows. But secretly to his aunt, he was always 'that odd boy'.

To Winnie and her husband he was always punctiliously polite when he saw them. But, thought Winnie, surveying the envelope in her hand, Richard had never given her a warm-hearted hug as young Jeremy had just done!

He had obtained a First in Physics at Oxford, and spent a year or two in America collecting further honours. As he grew older, his manner had become rather more sociable, and his somewhat anaemic looks had blossomed into wiry sparseness as maturity and a passion for walking grew upon him.

He was now a man of thirty-two, engaged upon research so divorced from the ordinary scheme of things that Winnie Bailey and her husband found themselves unable to comprehend the language, let alone the aims, of Richard's studies. They saw little of him, for his travels and lecturing commitments were extensive. Doctor Bailey heard of each academic success with coolness.

'Nothing wrong with his head,' was his comment, 'but he's no heart.'

Perhaps, thought Winnie, making her way to the drawing-room and her reading glasses, that is why she had never really warmed to Richard, but she kept these feelings to herself.

The doctor slept in the afternoon, and it was almost tea-time before she could hand him Richard's letter. The rain still fell relentlessly, drumming upon the roofs of Thrush Green, and drenching the school children as they straggled from the school porch. Their cries mingled with the spatter of rain on the window-panes of the quiet room, as the doctor read the letter.

'Wants something, as usual,' he commented drily.

Winnie remembered that this had been her own first unworthy reaction.

'What do you think?'

'It's up to you, my dear. If you feel that you would like to have him here while he is engaged on this particular work at Oxford, then go ahead. But it all means more for you to do, and I'm enough of a burden, I feel.'

'I don't like to refuse him,' began Winnie doubtfully. 'And we've plenty of room.'

She wandered to the window and looked out upon the rain-lashed garden. A few leaves, torn from the lime tree, hopped bird-like about the grass in the onslaught. On the flagged path, shiny with rain, a tawny dead sycamore leaf skidded about on its bent points, like some demented crab. The garden was alive with movement, as branches tossed, flowers quivered, grass shuddered, and drops splashed from roofs and hedges.

Winnie Bailey gazed unseeingly upon its wildness, turning over this problem in her mind. Richard, after all, was her nephew, she told herself – probably rather hard up, and simply asking for a bed and the minimum of board. Perhaps, for a little while –?

'Shall I invite him for a fortnight to see how we all manage?' she asked her husband, now deep in *The Times* crossword puzzle.

'By all means, if you would like to.'

'It wouldn't be a nuisance to you?'

'Of course not. I don't suppose I shall see much of the fellow, anyway, and he was always a quiet sort of chap about the house.'

Winnie sighed, partly with relief and partly because she had a queer premonition that something unusual – something disquieting – might come from Richard's visit.

Time was to prove her right.

During the next week or so the inhabitants of Thrush Green observed their new resident with approval. They watched her tackling Tullivers' neglected garden with considerable energy. The smoke from her bonfire billowed for two days and nights without ceasing, as hedge-trimmings, dead grass, long-defunct cabbage stalks and other kitchen-garden rubbish met their end.

The flagged path was sprinkled with weed-killer, and the hinge mended on the gate which had hung slightly awry for three years, wearing a scratched arc on the flag-stone each time the gate was opened or shut.

The gate was also given a coat or two of white paint, and the front door as well. The girl's efforts were generally approved, and Jeremy too was considered an exceptionally well-brought-up little boy.

But the continued absence of Mr Prior was, of course, a cause of disappointment and considerable speculation among the newcomer's neighbours at Thrush Green. He was obliged to be abroad for a few months, went one rumour, getting orders for his firm – variously described as one dealing in French silk, Egyptian cotton, Italian leather and Burmese teak.

Others knew, for a fact, that he was a specialist in television equipment, computers, road-surfacing, bridge-building and sewage works. Betty Bell, however, had it on the highest authority (her own) that he had something to do with advertising, and went overseas to show less advanced countries the best way to sell ball-point pens, wigs, food-mixers, plastic gnomes for the garden, and other necessary adjuncts to modern living.

Albert Piggott, on the other hand, thought that he was probably in hospital with a lingering complaint which would keep him there for many months to come. He said as much to his fat wife Nelly, whose response was typical.

'Trust you to think that, you old misery! More like he's run off with some lively bit. That wife of his don't look much fun to me!'

It certainly seemed nearer the target than some of the wild rumours. Winnie Bailey, who knew her neighbour better than the rest of Thrush Green's inhabitants, had come to much the same conclusion, but kept it to herself.

Young Doctor Lovell, who occasionally caught a glimpse of the newcomer from his surgery window, also wondered if the girl had parted permanently from her husband, and felt sorry for her vaguely forlorn appearance.

He spoke about her to Ruth, his wife, and she pleased him by replying: 'Joan and I are going to see her this afternoon. Paul and her little boy would probably get on very well together, and she might be lonely, even if she is up to her eyes in getting that place straight.'

The two sisters were not the only people to welcome Phil Prior. The rector, of course, called a few days after she had arrived, his chubby face glowing with the warmth and kindness he felt for all he met, even such stony-faced parishioners as his own sexton. Ella Bembridge called, bearing a bunch of Michaelmas daisies tied with what appeared to be a length of discarded knicker elastic, and an invitation to 'blow in any time you feel like it'. Harold Shoosmith spoke to the girl over the wall while she was hacking down some formidable stinging nettles, and offered a hand with any heavy clearing up which she might encounter.

Within a fortnight she found that she knew quite well at least two dozen people nearby, and was on speaking terms, country-fashion, with every other soul who passed. When Dimity Henstock called to invite her to a small dinner party, she looked forward to getting to know her Thrush Green neighbours even better.

'But I shall have to find a baby-sitter,' she said, after thanking Dimity. She looked completely at a loss.

'It's all arranged,' Dimity told her. 'Doctor Bailey does not go out these days, and dear Winnie usually stays in, too. However, she would be more than happy to spend the evening at Tullivers, keeping an eye on Jeremy.'

'You are all so kind. I shall look forward to it,' the girl said.

And Dimity, who had brought her modest invitation half-expecting to find someone used to much more sophisticated entertainment, went away knowing positively that young Mrs Prior was quite sincere in her expressions of pleasure.

On her way back to the rectory, she called into her former home to see her old friend Ella, whom she found standing on a chair far too frail to support her bulky twelve stone of solid flesh. She was struggling to hang a curtain.

'Shan't be a minute, Dim,' she puffed. 'Got too many hooks for the rings, as usual.'

'I'll do it,' said Dimity automatically.

Ella thumped heavily to the floor, and Dimity took her place on the chair. As her neat fingers worked quickly at the muddle created by her friend, she told her about her visit to Tullivers.

'And it really looks a proper home,' she added.

'What d'you expect?' cried Ella, a note of truculence in her voice. 'A single woman can make a comfortable home just as well as a married one. Don't need a man cluttering up the place to make *a home*!' she boomed.

From her perch, Dimity gave an all-embracing glance at yesterday's ashes in the grate, a vase of withered roses and the soft veil of dust upon the furniture.

'You're quite right, dear,' she said meekly, threading the last hook into place.

6. A DINNER PARTY AT THRUSH GREEN

The Fuchsia Bush, which stands well back from the road in Lulling High Street, prides itself on its home-made cakes and artistic furnishings. It is Lulling's only tea-shop, and having no competitor it tends to be a trifle smug.

Ella Bembridge, smoking one of her untidy hand-rolled cigarettes as she waited for her coffee to cool, looked with lack-lustre eye upon the Fuchsia Bush's décor.

The walls had been freshly painted in an unhappy shade of lilac, and the new curtains were purple. The two waitresses wore the habitual garb of the establishment, overalls of pale mauve, with collar, lapels and belt in a dreadful shade of puce. These garments, faded from much washing, now clashed sadly with the new furnishings, and a pot of real fuchsias, on the table by the door, struggled to make the point that what Nature can do successfully cannot always be copied by Man.

A plastic tumbler, pretending to be made of glass, held a sheaf of mauve paper napkins a few inches from Ella's nose. Disgusted, she moved it to a neighbouring table, just as Dotty Harmer entered.

'Come and have a cup of this ghastly drink – coffee I *will not* call it,' shouted Ella cheerfully. The waitresses exchanged supercilious glances. How common could you get? You'd have thought a lady like Miss Bembridge would have had better manners, their look said clearly.

'Thank you, dear. Yes, a cup of coffee,' said Dotty, pulling up one thick speckled stocking which was forming a concertina over the lower part of her skinny leg. A commercial traveller, coffee cup arrested half way between table and moustache, watched with fascinated horror.

'Was going to bob down and see you,' said Ella.

'Eggs?' queried Dotty.

'No, no. Milk.'

'Why, hasn't the milkman called?'

'He's called all right,' said Ella grimly, grinding the stub of her cigarette into the Benares brass ashtray. 'But he won't be calling again.'

'Why not?'

'Because it's not milk he's delivering, but muck!'

Ella began to throw a small heap of tobacco upon a cigarette paper and roll yet another cigarette.

'Whitewash!' she continued vehemently. 'He calls it "Homogenized – ma'am".' Ella's voice rose to a squeaky falsetto as she mimicked her terrified milkman's tone. 'No cream on it at all. What's a woman to put in her coffee?'

'I take mine black,' said Dotty.

Ella brushed aside this irrelevancy.

'It's perfectly horrible. No proper taste of milk, fiendishly white, like liquid paper! No! More like that stuff they make you drink in hospital, to see your innards. Begins with S.'

'Barium,' said Dotty, inspecting the plate of cakes.

'That's it – barium! Well, I'm not standing for it. I want milk that *is* milk, with cream on top and honest milk all the way down to the bottom of the jug. Can you spare some?'

'I can't make up my mind,' said Dotty thoughtfully, 'which is less indigestible – a Danish pastry or a doughnut.'

'Danish pastry,' said Ella promptly. Indecision nearly drove her mad.

Dotty took it reluctantly.

'I prefer the doughnut,' said Ella, transferring it swiftly to her own plate. 'I'm slimming.'

'Then you shouldn't be eating at all,' replied Dotty tartly, justifiably irritated by Ella's manoeuvres.

'Shock treatment,' Ella informed her blandly. She lodged her smoking cigarette across the ashtray, and attacked the doughnut energetically.

'I've only got goat's milk,' said Dotty, after a few minutes munching. 'I could spare you a pint a day. Dear Daisy is producing splendidly at the moment, but I have one or two regular customers, as you know, and the kittens are heavy drinkers just now. I'm trying to wean them.'

'I thought you had two goats,' said Ella, wiping sugar from her mouth with a man's khaki handkerchief.

'Dulcie is too young yet,' began Dotty primly. 'She hasn't been mated. After the kids are born –'

'Oh, spare me the obstetric details!' begged Ella. 'A pint of Daisy's daily would be a godsend, Dotty, if you can spare it. I'll collect, of course. When can we start?'

'This afternoon? After tea?'

'Fine,' said Ella, thrusting her wheel-back chair from the table with an ear-splitting grating on the flagged floor.

'Have you got some milk to go on with?' asked Dotty solicitously.

'Half a pint of hogwash,' said Ella. 'I'll do.'

The two ladies collected their parcels, paid their bills to the less disdainful of the waitresses, and emerged into Lulling High Street.

'If them two wasn't ladies,' said one waitress to the other, 'they'd both be in the mad-house, and that's the honest truth.'

'You can say that again,' agreed her colleague, dusting a plate languidly against her lilac hip, as she watched the two customers disappearing into the distance.

St Andrew's church clock was striking six as Ella crossed the green to fetch the goat's milk.

In her basket lay a clean bottle, a copy of last week's *Punch* and a copy of *The Lady*. There was also a paper bag containing half a pound or so of early black plums from the ancient tree in Ella's garden.

The air was warm and soft. The gentle golden light of a fine September evening gilded the Cotswold stone buildings, and turned the windows of the church into sheets of dazzling flame.

Albert Piggott stood motionless in the church porch. With his head out-thrust and his drooping mouth he reminded Ella of a tortoise she had owned as a child.

'Lovely day!' she called.

'Swarmin' with gnats,' responded the sexton gloomily. 'Sign of rain.'

Ella did not pursue the conversation, but strode rapidly down the narrow alley beside the Piggotts' abode to the field path which led to Dotty's cottage some half a mile away.

As she approached the garden gate she became conscious of a voice – Dotty's voice – keeping up a relentless monologue.

'Come on, boys, out you come! Come and get your good suppers! It's no use skulking in there. How d'you expect to get anyone to give you a good home if you behave so foolishly? Be brave now. Show yourselves. No food for cowardly cats. Come out and feed properly, or back it goes into the house!'

Ella waited, out of sight, irresolute.

Dotty's slightly hectoring tone changed to one of maudlin encouragement. Obviously, one brave kitten had emerged from its hiding place.

'Sweet thing!' murmured Dotty. 'Brave puss! Now, don't run away again. There's a *good* little cat.'

There was a sound of lapping, and Ella approached cautiously. Her shadow fell across the dish of milk, the kitten vanished with a squawk, and Dotty gave a startled squeal of exasperation.

'There now, Ella, you've scared them! Just as they were coming out. What on earth brings you here at just this particularly awkward time?'

'Goat's milk,' said Ella mildly. 'And, dammit all, Dot, I had to come *some* time. How long do you spend here squatting on that uncomfortable log?'

'I try and have half an hour in the morning and another about this time,' replied Dotty, dusting her skirt sketchily. She peered through her steel-rimmed spectacles into the depths of the log shack, but nothing stirred. She sighed sadly.

'Well, that's ruined this evening's session. Come along, Ella, and fetch the milk.'

She led the way into the kitchen, and Ella thought, yet again, what a perfect film set it would make for a witch's background. Bundles of drying herbs hung from the rafters. A dead chicken, waiting to be plucked, hung upside down against the back of the door. A pungent reek floated from a large copper preserving pan bubbling on the stove, and the kitchen table was crowded with jars, bottles, newspaper cuttings, an enormous ledger with mottled edges, and a butcher's cleaver still sticky with blood.

Add a few living touches, thought Ella, such as frogs and bats, and the place would be complete.

The milk, mercifully, was already bottled, corked, and standing on the cool brick floor in Dotty's larder.

'That looks fine,' said Ella warmly, surveying the beautiful rich colour admiringly. What were a few germs anyway? 'Makes my homogenized muck look pretty silly. Thank you very much, Dotty dear. And what do I owe you?'

'Say sixpence,' said Dotty vaguely.

'Make it a shilling,' replied Ella, slapping the coin down upon the laden table. 'Suits me, if it suits you.'

'Very well,' responded Dotty. 'I must admit the kittens are costing me quite a bit to feed. I'm having to buy tins of stuff called "Pretty-Puss" and "Katsluvit". I don't approve of the names, but the kittens seem to eat everything ravenously. Such a relief! It means that I can take the mother cat to the vet next week.'

'Got homes yet?' asked Ella.

'The Youngs are having one. Paul was persistent, I gather, sensible child. And Dimity is dithering. Frightened of the traffic, I think.'

'I'll speak to her,' said Ella ominously. 'Cats must take their chance these days.'

The two ladies made their farewells, one moving off to Thrush Green, and the other setting out yet again, to try her luck with the interrupted cat-taming in the log shed.

Dimity Henstock's dinner party was an outstanding success right from the start.

Betty Bell was in charge of the kitchen that evening. She was a first-class cook, even if her cleaning and dusting were sketchy, having been trained in a ducal establishment in the north, under a dragon of a cook who had terrified young Betty but had taught her supremely well.

To be able to engage Betty Bell for the evening was a sure foundation for the success of a dinner party, as Thrush Green and Lulling hostesses knew well.

As Dimity looked at the seating arrangements in the dining-room, she could hear Betty singing cheerfully as she coped with leg of mutton, onion sauce, roast potatoes, cauliflower, peas and young Brussels sprouts. She had also made some attractive shrimp and grapefruit cocktails and set them in place, and insisted on adding a vast apple pie to the delicate orange mousse, which Dimity had made and privately thought quite adequate, for the sweet course.

'You wants more than that for men,' maintained Betty stoutly. 'No *body* to mousse. Men likes a bit of pastry.'

'There will be cheese and biscuits,' Dimity pointed out, 'if they are still hungry.'

'Not the same,' asserted Betty. 'Mrs Furze,' she added, referring to the she-dragon who had taught her all she knew, 'wouldn't dream of putting but the one sweet on the table.'

'Very well,' agreed Dimity. She knew when she was beaten. 'Certainly make an apple pie. I'm sure it will be delicious.'

The dinner table pleased even her over-anxious eye. She had polished the rector's silver candlesticks herself and the light of six candles fell upon the bowl of orange dahlias which formed the centrepiece. For once, the bleak lofty room looked warm and inviting. The carpet was thin and worn, the furniture shabby, but the kindly candlelight hid these things, and Dimity felt proud of her arrangements.

Dimity longed to furnish the rectory as she knew it should be furnished. It needed thick velvet curtains at the tall narrow windows to mitigate the draughts and the gauntness of design. It was a house which cried out for soft carpets and central heating, but there was no money for such luxuries on the rector's stipend, and Dimity loved him far too well to ask him for the impossible. The floors of the bedrooms and the long draughty passages were covered with the dark brown linoleum chosen by a predecessor of Charles Henstock's. It was badly worn, but gleamed with years of polishing. Nevertheless, it wrung Dimity's heart to see her beloved Charles walking barefoot on a winter's morning upon such an inhospitable surface. The few small rugs available lay like tiny rafts upon the glassy sea. Sometimes Dimity envied her husband his spartan attitude to their surroundings, and there were times when she thought, with secret longing, of the small cosy bedroom under the thatched roof opposite, where she had slept snugly for so many years.

Eight people sat down to enjoy the leg of mutton. The guests were Edward and Joan Young, Doctor Lovell and his wife Ruth, Harold Shoosmith and the newcomer, Phil Prior.

Dimity had selected her visitors with considerable care. She wanted to introduce Mrs Prior to people much of her own age. The Lovells and Youngs were in their early thirties, but try as she might Dimity could find no unattached male of that age to balance her dinner table.

'What a *blessing* Harold is single,' she said to her husband whilst making her preparations. 'We could do with half a dozen more men really in Thrush Green. I mean, if one were going to have a really big affair it would be simple to find a dozen single women – Ella, Dotty, the three Lovelock sisters and so on – but where are the *men*?'

'Safely married,' replied Charles smugly. 'Like me. You can't have it both ways, my dear.'

'And even dear Harold is a little older than I really wanted,' mused Dimity to herself.

'He's no older than I am,' the rector pointed out mildly, and was amused to see the contrition on his wife's face as she strove to make amends.

In any case, thought Dimity, looking happily about her dinner table, Harold was easily the most handsome man there, and by far the best dressed. Why was it, she wondered, that young men these days appeared so scruffy compared with their elders? Their wives looked so pretty in their silk frocks; one sister in green and the other in striped grey and white, while the new-comer wore a softly-draped frock of very fine wool starred with tiny flowers. A Liberty print, guessed Dimity correctly, thinking how beautifully it set off the girl's dark looks.

She was more animated than Dimity had ever seen her. Among these old friends, so easy with each other, she showed no shyness.

'And how many committees do you find yourself on?' asked Harold.

'Why, none yet.'

'Amazing! I was on *five* before I'd been here a month,' said Harold. 'You see, your turn will come. Which reminds me, Charles, I haven't been able to type the minutes of the Entertainments Committee. My typewriter has collapsed.'

'What's the matter with it?' asked Mrs Prior with genuine interest.

'Asthma, I should imagine, from the rhythmic squeaks it gives out. It's gone in for an overhaul. Poor old thing, it's well over thirty years old and spent most of its life in the tropics, so it's not done too badly.'

'I could type the minutes, if you'd like me to,' offered the girl.

'Do you type too?' asked the rector, in open admiration. 'How clever of you! Without looking at the keys?'

'Of course,' she said, laughing. 'I should have been thrown out of my typing class pretty smartly if I'd dared to look at the keyboard.'

'Well, I've never been able to master a typewriter,' confessed the rector. 'I once tried to type "How doth the little crocodile" on Harold's machine, and it made an awful lot of 8s and halfpennies, I remember. Do you use yours much?'

'I do a column for a girls' weekly,' said Mrs Prior. 'About five hundred words. And a few book reviews.'

This modest disclosure brought forth a buzz of excited comment. Thrush Green had no writers among its inhabitants, and to meet someone who not only wrote, but who actually had those writings published was indeed thrilling.

'I've always thought I could write,' observed Edward Young, adding predictably, 'if I only had the time.'

'I couldn't,' said his brother-in-law honestly. 'It's quite bad enough writing prescriptions. Anything imaginative would floor me completely.'

'When you say "a column",' said Dimity, 'do you mean a short story?'

'A brief article,' answered the girl, 'on some topical matter which would interest girls. Sometimes I make one of the books the subject of the column – that's cheating, I feel, but the editor approves.'

'You must enjoy it.'

'Not always – but it's well paid, and the editor is a sweetie.'

'Mary has just learnt to hold a crayon properly,' said Ruth Lovell proudly, 'and has scribbled on *every page* of the laundry book.'

The company agreed that this might, conceivably, show literary promise.

The orange mousse and the apple pie were eaten to the exchange of news about children, and no more was said about the writing until the company were enjoying Dimity's excellent coffee by the drawing-room fire.

Harold Shoosmith, who settled himself next to the girl, asked if she would find it a nuisance to type the minutes.

'Or I could do them myself, if I might borrow the typewriter for half an hour,' he said. 'Whichever is simpler for you. They only take up a page of quarto-size.'

'Bring them in tomorrow,' said the girl. 'I shall be in all day.'

And so the matter was left, and the evening passed very pleasantly in general conversation, except for ten minutes of television news which Edward Young asked if he might see as he had heard that a house he had restored for a wealthy pop singer had just been burned out and it might be shown on the screen.

The company obligingly sat through a student demonstration, plentifully sprinkled with bleeding noses and blasphemies, a multiple car crash on a motorway from which a stretcher, ominously blanketed, was removed, an interview with a distracted mother whose child had been abducted, and the arrival at London airport of a half-naked film star whose long unkempt hair was something of a blessing in view of her neck-line. But Edward Young's burned-out masterpiece was not included among the attractions, and everyone was thankful when the set was switched off.

'I don't call that news, do you?' said Charles Henstock. 'Not by Thrush Green standards anyway. What I mean by news is hearing about Dotty Harmer's kittens, or Albert Piggott's prize onions or meeting a charming newcomer to the village,' he said, bowing slightly to his guest of honour.

'And why should one be subjected to all these horrors on one's own hearth rug?' agreed Doctor Lovell. 'To think we *pay* for it too! It's galling.'

'Too bad about your house,' said Dimity to Edward. 'It probably wasn't ghastly enough to compete with all that violence. I suppose nobody was burned?'

'No one, as far as I know.'

'That accounts for it,' said Dimity reasonably. 'An item of news like that, without so much as a few charred bones, or firemen falling screaming into the blaze, wouldn't stand a chance.'

At eleven o'clock the guests began to make their farewells. Only the Lovells drove home, for their house was a mile away. The rest of the guests lived round the green and walked across the grass together.

Already most of the houses were in darkness, for country people have to be up betimes and midnight is considered a very late hour indeed for going to bed.

But a light shone still at Tullivers, where Winnie Bailey sat sewing, her young charge fast asleep in the bedroom above. She heard his mother's light footsteps on the path, and put down her needlework.

'My word,' she said, looking at the girl's glowing face in the doorway, 'I can see you've had a lovely evening. And so, my dear, have I!'

7. A QUESTION OF DIVORCE

The next morning Harold Shoosmith crossed the green to Tullivers. He found Mrs Prior alone, her typewriter already on the table and an appetizing smell of steak and kidney casserole floating from the kitchen.

'Jeremy gets home at twelve,' she said, 'and we have our main meal then. It gets cooking over and done with for the day, and I boil an egg or have some cheese and biscuits when Jeremy's in bed.'

'I do much the same,' said Harold, 'though Betty Bell is always willing to come and fatten me up, if given half a chance.'

He put the hand-written minutes on the table.

'Are you sure it's not an imposition?' he asked.

The girl laughed. 'It will be a change from the perils-of-Pauline stuff I'm attempting at the moment. I'm trying to sell some short stories to magazines.'

'Here, or overseas?'

'Here, and in America. They pay most generously over there, but I doubt if my stuff will be suitable.'

Harold Shoosmith gazed thoughtfully through the window. 'I've an editor friend in one of these magazine combines. If I could be of any help –?'

'You're very kind. If I get too many rejections, I'll remember. I'm sorting out old material just now, and trying to bring it up-to-date.'

'Wouldn't it be better to start again?'

'I need some money pretty quickly,' replied the girl frankly. 'This house – as always – has cost far more to put to rights than I bargained for, and if I can sell some stories now, I can get down to some really new stuff while they are being considered. Editors

seem to take an unconscionable length of time to make up their minds.'

'If you think I could help by looking through any of your stories to see if they seem to be on the right lines for Frank, I would be only too happy to do so,' said Harold.

'I might be very glad indeed,' replied Phil, 'but let's see how my luck turns out in the next few weeks. In any case I've always got my column to keep the wolf from the door.'

'Yes, indeed,' said Harold, but there was doubt in his tone.

'And my husband is very generous,' the girl added, a shade too swiftly. 'But, of course, one likes to feel independent.'

'Of course,' echoed Harold, obviously bemused, but doing his best to cope with the situation. There was a slight pause. The clock struck eleven, and brought Harold to his senses.

'Well, I must be off. When shall I call for the minutes?'

'Oh, don't bother. I'll pop over after tea, if I may.'

'That would be very kind of you,' said Harold gravely, making for the door.

He crossed the green thoughtfully.

'That devil's left her!' he said to a startled blackbird on his gatepost.

Harold Shoosmith had guessed correctly, but it was Winnie Bailey who heard the truth first from the girl herself.

It was a fine October afternoon, clear and vivid, and Winnie noticed how auburn the chestnut avenue had become since the first few frosts. Her spirits were high as she breathed the keen air.

It was quite two weeks, she told herself, since she had talked to Phil, but this was not surprising. One's next-door neighbours, however dear, tend to be neglected for the plain reason that they *are* next door. It is the friends at a distance whom one makes the effort to meet. But she had caught a glimpse of her at the typewriter, and knew that she was busy.

She was calling now to see if she could persuade her to collect for Poppy Day. The Misses Lovelock who had quartered Lulling and Thrush Green between them for decades, had decided that their arthritis and general frailty would not allow them to continue the good work. To find one noble soul willing to turn out in November to rattle a collecting tin, is hard enough. To find *three* was proving a headache.

Full of hope, Winnie knocked with the late admiral's great brass dolphin on Tullivers' front door. It was opened by Phil herself, white of face and red of eye. Winnie Bailey, used as a doctor's wife to seeing men and women in misery, thought she had never seen quite such a tragic face.

'Phil, tell me!' she said impulsively, and then checked herself. 'No, my dear, let me creep away. You won't want to be bothered with callers just now.'

'Do *please* come in,' cried the girl. 'I need a friend badly.'

She led the way into the little sitting-room and motioned the older woman to take a seat. Winnie watched her as she put two logs on the dying fire. Her hands were trembling and tears were running unheeded down her cheeks.

'What is it?' begged Winnie. 'Someone ill? Or worse?'

'Worse,' choked the girl. 'It's my husband.'

'Not dead!' Winnie whispered.

'Oh no, thank God!' She gave a high, cracked laugh, frightening to hear. 'Though why I should thank God, I don't know. He's left me.'

'You poor dear,' said Winnie, patting the arm that was near her. She felt the gnawing pity and the tragic impotence which captures those who are in the presence of grief which they are powerless to assuage.

The girl fumbled for a damp handkerchief, mopped her eyes, and took a deep shuddering breath.

'He left me almost six months ago. Another woman, of course. A French woman – a buyer for one of the Paris houses. I met her once.'

She stopped, and mopped her eyes again.

'Perhaps it's just an infatuation,' said Winnie. 'Is she very attractive?'

'Not a bit,' cried Phil. She smiled damply. 'Well, I know I'm biased, but I don't think anyone – except John – would find her attractive. She's one of those bony French women with a long face like a disapproving horse. Marvellous figure, of course, and dresses superbly, but no glamour-girl, I assure you. When he wrote and said that they were in love, I laughed out loud. It seemed so ludicrous, I just couldn't believe it – like some awful unspeakable joke.'

She helped herself to a cigarette, and lit it shakily.

'But it was no joke, as you can imagine. He came back several times to the flat, and was more determined each time to break with me. I tried desperately to keep my head. I was sure he would get tired of her – that it was, as you said, an infatuation. But the day came when he told me flatly that he was going to bring her to live in our house, and I must get out. Then I really did grovel! I told him I loved him still. I pleaded for Jeremy's sake. I swore I'd never throw this affair in his face if he'd think again. All useless!'

She stood up and walked restlessly about the little room.

'When I saw it was hopeless, and that she'd won, we made a scratch agreement to part. He gives me a regular amount each month, and he let me take the things I wanted from the Chelsea flat. But I absolutely refuse to give him a divorce. I still hope that he will come to his senses – or she will. Meanwhile, I try to keep it all from Jeremy. He adores John. It turns the knife pretty keenly, as you can imagine, when he prattles on about Daddy.'

She rolled the damp handkerchief into a ball and thrust it into her cardigan pocket.

'But this morning I had another letter. It's so terrible – so terrible –' She shook her head desperately, and a tear flew into the fire and sizzled.

'It's brought it home to me. We simply can't go on like this. I think I must make up my mind to go forward with a divorce. I suppose I've been evading it really – hoping, just stupidly hoping. The very idea of solicitors and courts and settlements and all the other beastly details absolutely revolts me. But I see now I must face it. He's only too pleased to give me grounds,' she added bitterly.

She sat down beside Winnie on the couch and took her hand. 'What would you do? What would you do if you were wretched me?'

Winnie put a comforting arm round the girl's shoulders.

'I should wait until tomorrow before doing anything. You've been brave and patient for so long, keep it up for a little longer. By that time it won't hurt so much and you'll tackle things better.'

The girl nodded dumbly.

'Don't write,' cautioned Winnie, 'don't telephone, don't talk to anyone about it until you've slept on it. No one will learn anything from me, I promise you. Then why not talk it over with your parents?'

'They died some years ago. I was an only child.'

'Is there someone else? A cousin, say, or a family friend?'

'Not that I could discuss this with. I would sooner tell our old family solicitor. He's wise and kind . . . a real friend.'

'Then why not go to him?'

'I'll do that,' whispered Phil huskily. 'It's keeping up appearances before Jeremy which is so hard. I've cried all day. Thank God he didn't seem to notice much at dinner time.'

'Let me walk across to the school when the children finish,' said Winnie, 'and take him back with me to tea.'

'No, really –'

'Please. I should love it, and it will give you a chance to get over the shock a little. I'll bring him back before half past six.' She stood up and kissed the girl's pale cheek gently. 'Go and have a warm bath,' she advised. 'Hot water truly is the benison that Rupert Brooke said it was. And then give yourself a tot of something strong. You'll feel twice the girl.'

'You are an angel,' cried Phil, accompanying her to the door. 'I've done nothing but moan, and I haven't given you a chance to tell me what brings you here.'

Silently, Winnie held up the poppy tin.

'Of course I'll do it,' said Phil warmly. 'I can't weep for ever.'

Winnie's nephew Richard arrived the following week. He seemed genuinely grateful for his aunt's hospitality, and set himself out to be exceptionally charming to Doctor Bailey. To Winnie's eye he looked very fit and lively, having acquired a fine tan in America which set off his pale hair and blue eyes. But it was not long before symptoms of the hypochondria which had always been present showed themselves in strength.

Two small bottles of pills stood by his plate at the first evening meal, and naturally excited the professional interest of his uncle.

'I find them indispensable,' said Richard. 'Otto – Professor Otto Goldstein, you know, the dietician – prescribed them for me. The red ones take care of the cholesterol, and these yellow and black torpedoes check acidity and act as a mild purge. Constipation is a terrible enemy.'

'You need a few prunes,' said the doctor, 'and a bit of roughage.'

'Donald!' protested Winnie. 'Must you? At table?'

'Sorry, my dear, sorry,' said her husband.

'Too bad of me,' apologized Richard. 'Living alone such a lot makes one over-interested perhaps in one's natural functions.'

Winnie felt that this could lead to somewhat alarming disclosures which might be regretted by all. She changed the subject abruptly.

'You must meet our new neighbour,' she said brightly, passing her nephew Brussels sprouts.

He held up a stern denying hand. 'Not for me, Aunt Winnie. Not *cooked* greens, I fear. Quite forbidden by Otto because of the gases. You haven't two or three raw ones, by any chance?'

'Not washed,' replied Winnie shortly, passing the rejected

dish to her husband. She was keenly aware of the smile which hovered round the old doctor's lips.

'A pity,' murmured Richard, tackling pork chops *en casserole* with faint distaste.

'She plays bridge and whist, and is a very nice person to talk to. She writes.'

'Really?' replied Richard vaguely. Clearly his mind was concerned with his digestive tract.

'Will you have any spare evenings?' pursued Winnie.

Richard gave a gusty sigh, the sigh of one who, over-burdened with work, still enjoys his martyrdom.

'I very much doubt it. I shall be writing the notes on my experiments, of course, and I intend to spend as much time as I can refuting Carslake's idiotic principles. An obstinate fellow, if ever there was one, and a very elusive one too. I must thrash things out with him during the next few months.'

Winnie felt a wave of pity for the absent Professor Carslake. Richard, on the rampage, must be an appalling bore. She decided to put aside the idea of arranging Richard's social life at Thrush Green. Richard obviously did not want it, and was it really fair to her friends to inflict her nephew on them, she added reasonably to herself?

She watched him swallow a red pill and then a yellow and black one. It was quite apparent that he enjoyed them far more than the excellent dinner which Winnie had spent hours in preparing.

'Coffee?' she asked, rising from the table. 'Or does Professor Goldstein forbid that too?' There was an edge to her tone which did not escape her observant husband.

'No, indeed,' replied Richard, opening the drawing-room door politely. 'He approves of coffee, provided that the berries are really ripe, well roasted and coarsely ground. He doesn't agree with percolators, though. He always strains his through muslin. Do you?'

'Not with Nescafé,' said his aunt, with a hint of triumph, leading the way.

Richard was not the only one at Thrush Green suffering from indigestion. Doctor Lovell gave Albert Piggott a prescription, and then a few words of sound advice.

'Your wife's a fine cook, I know. But have small helpings. Don't forget your stomach was on short commons for years. It can't cope suddenly with all this bounty.'

Nelly tossed her head when Albert relayed this piece of advice.

'Good food never hurt nobody. Who does he think he is – the old Tin-ribs? He could do with a bit of flesh if anyone could. I bet he never gets his teeth into a decent steak and kidney pudding with that dreamy wife of his to do for him! Take them dratted pills, if you must, Albert Piggott, but you eat what's put in front of you and be thankful!'

She seemed to surpass herself in the days that followed. Cold fat bacon with pickled onions, fried cod cutlets with chips and peas, ox-tail soup, hot and glutinous, with swedes mashed with butter, all followed each other in succession, flaunting their richness and tempting Albert to fatal indulgences. His liverishness grew: his temper became more morose than ever. Nelly became aggrieved and nagged more and more bitterly.

The oilman began to figure largely in her conversation.

Albert, belching prettily after consuming a plate piled with pickled brawn, beetroot and bubble-and-squeak, spoke his mind.

'Can't you shut up about that ruddy oilman? Any more of it, and I'll tell 'im to stop calling. Givin' 'im cupsertea! Giggling like some fool-girl! I seen you at it – eggin' 'im on!'

'I'll thank you,' said Nelly haughtily, 'to mind your tongue. I only treat him civil. The poor chap's wife's left him.'

'Best day's work she ever done, I shouldn't wonder. You'd best take a leaf outer her book, my gal.'

'It's a pity if I can't have a friendly word with a gentleman without you getting filthy ideas into your head,' snapped Nelly, crashing cutlery about dangerously. 'The Lord alone knows I get little enough pleasure from your company. If you're not down the coke-hole you're in The Two Pheasants. Why I was ever fool enough to give in to your begging of me to marry you I *cannot think*!'

This complete travesty of the facts of Albert's wooing rendered him speechless. But not for long.

'I *could* say,' said Albert, with a hiccup which marred the heavy solemnity of his utterance, 'exactly the same words, my gal, and with a deal more truth.'

Rumbling dangerously, he left his kitchen for something to settle his stomach next door.

8. GOSSIP AND GARDENING

The rapid spread of news through a village is a natural phenomenon which is hard to explain. Phil Prior, after much inward wrestling, sought the advice of a London solicitor as a preliminary step to divorce from her husband.

She said not a word to anyone. Winnie Bailey, true to her promise, breathed not a syllable, not even to her husband. And yet the possibility of a divorce was generally known in Thrush Green.

How did such knowledge get around so swiftly? Winnie Bailey asked herself this, not for the first time. She supposed that someone originally made a shrewd guess, and passed on the surmise to a friend.

The friend then might say: 'I hear that there's talk of a divorce between the Priors.' And the next step would be: 'Have you heard about the Priors' divorce?' After that it was, of course, an accepted fact, despite the usual riders: 'Mind you, it's only what I've *heard*,' or 'It may be only idle gossip,' or 'Don't repeat it unless you hear it confirmed.' And, sure enough, the snippet *would* be confirmed within an hour or so. Thus easily does bush-telegraph work in a small community.

Fortunately, Phil Prior, new to country ways, was not conscious of her matrimonial affairs being common gossip. Now that the first wretched step was taken, she felt calmer, and renewed her writing efforts.

Harold Shoosmith proved a wise adviser in literary matters, and the girl frequently called on him to discuss possible markets. Frank, the editor friend, had received one of her stories with guarded enthusiasm, but after keeping it for some time, returned it with the excuse that it 'was not strong enough' but said he would consider it again if she felt she could amend it.

'What does he mean exactly?' asked Phil of Harold Shoo-smith. 'Not enough shooting and rape, do you think? I mean, I simply can't write about violence. The only person I ever saw shot was a neighbour who was peppered in his garden by the boy next door with an air gun. To make matters worse, the wretched boy's feeble excuse was that he thought he was a squirrel! He weighed eighteen stone,' added Phil reminiscently.

'Insult to injury,' agreed Harold. 'I hope the boy had a good hiding on the spot, and was not made the subject of psychiatric reports two months later, when everyone had forgotten all about it.'

'Lord, yes!' cried Phil. 'This was years ago before such refinements were thought of. He was a good friend of mine, and he said he had one beating from his father and was then handed over to the victim of his attack. He didn't seem to bear any grudge about it. He was always a resilient child.'

She turned again to her typescript.

'But how on earth can I make it *stronger*? I wish editors would either reject a thing outright, or take it as it is. I do loathe messing about with a piece of writing which, after all, you have made as near perfect in the first place as you possibly can.'

'I'd be inclined to send him another,' advised Harold, 'while the going's good, and mull over this one for a bit. Tell him you will let him have it later, when you've had a chance to revise it.'

He watched the girl turning the pages, a worried frown creasing her brow. Damn Frank, he thought suddenly! And that wretched husband too! Why should such a nice woman have all this confounded work and worry? She should be enjoying life, not fighting for existence.

'Come and see my last few roses,' he said, rising abruptly. Suddenly, he longed for fresh air and sunshine.

Harold's garden was quite six times the size of Tullivers' but was in a state of exquisite neatness.

'With no help at all?' queried the girl unbelievingly, gazing about her.

'Piggott comes for an hour or so when he needs a little extra drinking money,' said Harold, 'but I find I can keep it fairly trim now that it's in order.'

He snipped another rose to add to the bouquet he was making.

'I wish you would let me help you with your garden,' he continued. 'It would be such a pleasure to me, and if it is straightened up this autumn it should be so much easier to manage next year. As you see, I'm well ahead here, and could easily spare the time, if you would allow me to trespass.'

'You are very, very kind,' said Phil warmly, accepting the bouquet gratefully. 'And these are simply lovely. To be honest, I'd be terribly thankful for a hand with some bramble bushes which seem to have roots from here to Lulling.'

'I'll be over tomorrow afternoon, if that suits you,' said Harold briskly.

They walked together to the gate, and Harold watched her cross the green, the bunch of late roses making a splash of colour against her pale coat.

Another figure was advancing, in the distance, from his right. It was Dotty Harmer, struggling with a large cat basket. Heavy though it appeared to be, Dotty was making good headway, so that Harold, who felt unequal to Dotty's conversation at the moment, retreated strategically to the peace of his study, chiding himself for cowardice and lack of chivalry the while.

Dotty was bound for the Youngs' house, a bewildered tortoise-shell kitten mewing its protests as they made the uphill journey together.

She was glad to rest the basket on the doorstep as she rang the bell. The kitten, relieved that the motion had stopped, now sat mute among its blankets, but watched warily.

Paul opened the door, and fell upon his knees in front of the basket adoringly.

'You nice little puss! Are you coming to live here, then? Dear little cat, nice little –'

At this point, Dotty poked him sharply, bringing his ecstasies to an abrupt halt.

'Where are your manners, boy? What about speaking to me before you fuss with the cat!'

Scarlet with shame, Paul struggled to his feet and made apologies, just as his mother arrived.

'Please come in. I'd no idea you were going to bring the kitten. We intended to come and fetch it to save you trouble.'

'No bother,' said Dotty, about to lift the basket again.

'Let Paul do it,' said Joan. 'It really is very sweet of you to have carried it all the way here. What a very pretty one!'

They stood and admired the minute scrap, crouching among its bedding.

'Now, if I were you,' said Dotty, taking charge, 'I should put the basket in an empty warm room, and put its earth box and a saucer of milk there too. Then make sure it cannot get out of the room, open the door of the basket, and let it explore for some hours.'

'What about buttering its paws?' asked Paul, anxious to show his knowledge.

'Fiddlesticks!' snapped Dotty. 'You do as I say, and he'll soon settle down.'

'Do you think it is a he?' asked Joan, with some anxiety.

'That I can't be sure of. Cats are very difficult to sort out. But the vet will cope at six months either way.'

'But I should *like* it to have kittens!' protested Paul. He was on his knees again, one finger stroking the kitten's head through the wire door of the basket.

'Precocious, that child!' said Dotty to his mother, in a dark aside. 'Who said anything about kittens, young man?' she added forthrightly. 'We know what we're about, and what's best for that cat. Just you go and do as I said.'

'Take it up to the spare bedroom,' directed his mother, 'and I'll come up in a moment. Don't undo the door until I come.'

Paul picked up the basket. Without being prompted, he smiled upon Dotty and spoke his thanks.

'That's more like it,' said Dotty grudgingly. 'Remembered your manners after all! Now, take care of that mite. It's the tamest of the litter. It wants plenty of love, warmth and food, in that order. And if I hear you've tormented it *in any way*, I shall *take it back*!'

'Yes, Miss Harmer,' said Paul meekly, and began to mount the stairs with his treasure.

'Not a bad child,' conceded Dotty, watching his departing back.

'We find him fairly satisfactory,' agreed Joan drily.

The mild irony was lost upon her guest.

'It's because you haven't kept many animals,' said Dotty. 'Now, they are *completely* satisfactory. Which reminds me, I must return to mine. I've left a saucepan of fish simmering, and I don't want it to boil dry.'

'Nothing worse,' said Joan, 'than the smell of boiling fish, I agree.'

'It's not the smell I worry about,' cried Dotty, stepping out of the front door, 'but the dear cats won't touch fish if it's the slightest bit caught.'

She set off at a fast trot towards the pathway to Lulling Woods and her animal family.

True to his word, Harold Shoosmith made his way to Tullivers the next afternoon. The girl came to the door immediately, for she had seen him pass the window. Papers were spread upon the table, and her typewriter stood among the litter.

'Don't let me stop you,' said Harold. 'I think I know where the brambles are.'

He pointed to the wall which divided Tullivers' garden from the Baileys' orchard. A border lay at its foot, but was so overgrown with many weeds, including the brambles, that it was practically invisible.

'There are some tools in the shed at the back of the house,' said Phil. 'I'll get them for you.'

'No, no! I can find them,' said Harold. 'Don't let me interrupt the writing.'

He made his way round the house as the girl returned to her typing. He found the shed easily enough, but surveyed the tools with mingled dismay and pity. There were very few of them, and all looked hopelessly inadequate or outworn to Harold's sharp eye.

The only fork available was a very large, heavy old veteran with wide flat tines, meant for digging up potatoes. The spade was equally heavy, and coated with dried Cotswold clay. The handle was badly cracked and had been bound, in an amateurish fashion, with string. Two trowels, a rake with a wobbly head, a birch broom, and a rusty bill-hook comprised the rest of the gardening equipment, except for a lawn-mower whose newness simply threw the age of the other tools into sharp relief.

Very quietly, Harold went round the back of the house to the gate, so that he did not need to pass the worker's window, and went to collect his own shining equipment from across the green.

Half an hour with a swinging mattock loosened the worst of the roots, and Harold enjoyed piling up the rubbish on the ashy remains of earlier bonfires. Brambles, elder shoots, and lofty nettles removed, it was possible to see the remains of the border. Among the shorter weeds which clothed the earth, Harold found clumps of irises, peonies and pinks still surviving suffocation. At one time the border had been well-stocked. It would be very rewarding, thought Harold, to see it trim and colourful again.

With his light fork he loosened wild strawberry runners, groundsel, docks, chickweed and yards and yards of matted couch grass roots.

The pile of rubbish grew higher and higher, and Harold was just contemplating the possibility of lighting a bonfire, as he straightened his back, when Phil came out from the house to admire his handiwork.

'And I believe you've got some nerines among those clumps of bulbs,' said Harold enthusiastically. 'It's an ideal spot for them there. Don't disturb them. I'll put a marker by them next time I come.'

'But you can't spend too much time among my weeds,' protested Phil. 'Your own will sneak up on you.'

Harold, flushed with his exertions, looked contentedly at the first few yards of border revealed.

'I'd like to finish this job,' he said. 'Three or four afternoons should see it cleared.'

Phil was looking at his fork with envy.

'Is it stainless steel?'

He said, somewhat apologetically, that it was.

'One gets used to one's own tools, you know. When you replace, my dear, I do advise you to get stainless steel. It is well worth it.'

'I shan't be replacing for some time,' said Phil, laughing. 'But I came to tell you that I had made some tea.'

It was snug in the little house. Harold had been so happy and busy in the garden that he had not noticed the grey clouds scudding ominously from the west. A spatter of rain on the window heralded a wet evening.

Phil nodded at a large envelope, stamped, sealed and ready for the post.

'I've taken your advice,' she said, 'and looked out another story. I do hope he likes this one. I'm going to alter the one he's just sent back. I had a brain-wave last night in bed which might work, I think.'

'Any more luck?'

'A hopeful letter from a women's magazine in America. I sent an article about how to encourage children to take to books. So many don't, you know. Thank heaven Jeremy likes reading!'

'I must be off,' said Harold soon after, rising. 'Thank you for restoring me with tea. I'll be in London for the next two days, but I hope you'll let me tackle the border when I come back.'

'You know I shall be very, very grateful,' Phil replied, opening the front door.

The rain fell heavily, splashing from the admiral's brass dolphin upon the door mat.

Harold picked up his bundle of tools, neatly swathed in a sack.

'Here, give me your letters,' he said, eyeing the downpour. 'I'll put them in the box as I pass. You'll get drenched if you go out, and Willie's due to collect any minute now.'

She put the bundle of letters, including the large packet, into his outstretched hand.

'You really should spit on the big one, for luck,' she called after him as he hurried down the path.

With his tools across his shoulder and the letters in his hand, Harold made his way to the letter box at the corner of Thrush Green. The Cotswold stone glistened with rain around the red oblong.

Harold inserted the small letters, and then carefully threaded the large one into the aperture. It fell with a satisfying plop, and as it vanished Harold wished it luck.

Whistling cheerfully, he splashed beneath the chestnuts to his home, thinking gaily of work well done and the pleasure derived from a good-looking woman's company.

Little did he think that the packet he had so carefully posted would be the cause of much concern for the pair of them.

On that same rainy evening Sam Curdle, who had managed to conduct his affairs in a relatively honest manner for some months, succumbed to temptation.

It so happened that Percy Hodge, the farmer in whose yard the battered Curdle caravan was housed, had seen some fine wallflower plants going cheaply in Lulling market. He bought twelve dozen and left the twelve newspaper-shrouded bundles lodged against the corner of his back porch.

'If you get that lot put in for me tomorrow, Sam,' he told him, 'there's half a sack of spuds for you. Fill up the round bed in the front of the house, and the border under the greenhouse. You'll need the gross, I reckon, to make a tidy show.'

Sam agreed with alacrity. Half a sack of potatoes would be most welcome to the family, and planting out a few wallflowers was easy work.

It took Sam less than five minutes to plan how he could make a few shillings for himself on the deal. Percy Hodge would be out all day at a sheep sale, Sam knew. By planting the wall-flowers carefully, he reckoned he could keep two, or possibly three, dozen aside for sale elsewhere.

That new woman at Tullivers, he pondered, as he lay beside his snoring Bella that night. She looked the sort who might fall for a few plants, and Lord alone knew that garden of hers was in need of something. Sam surmised, correctly, that she would know little about prices, and would not be the type to haggle.

What should he ask now? Six shillings a dozen? Too steep, perhaps, even for a greenhorn such as that Londoner. He'd heard down at The Two Pheasants that most of the locals were getting twopence a plant. Maybe it would be best to settle for fivepence. After all, he reasoned happily to himself, if he swiped two dozen from Percy Hodge he'd make a clear ten bob. With any luck, though, he could appropriate three dozen. Fif-teen bob, now that really would be useful! He might even have a flutter on a horse in the afternoon, and make a bit that way too.

As for Percy Hodge, he'd never notice a few wallflowers missing once the beds were planted. It was a chance too good to miss, Sam told himself.

Well content with his plans, he turned on his side, wrenched rather more of his share of the marital blankets from his wife's recumbent form, and settled to sleep.

9. SAM CURDLE TRIES HIS TRICKS

On the whole, Winnie Bailey found Richard's stay with them less punishing than she had first feared. Nevertheless, she was becoming heartily sick of his preoccupation with his ali-mentary canal, and said as much to her husband one day when her nephew was safely in Oxford about his affairs.

'Ignore it,' advised Doctor Bailey.

'That's easier said than done,' said Winnie, knitting briskly. 'After all, I have to spend a great deal of time and thought on our meals, and it really is maddening to see him picking about like an old hen.'

'The boy wants more exercise,' said her husband. 'As far as I can see, the walk from the front door to the garage is about the sum total of his exertions. He's bound to be liverish.'

'Have a word with him,' begged Winnie. 'It really can't be good for him to be so introspective about his food, and honestly, it's driving me quite crazy.'

'I'll do my best,' promised her husband, but privately he had little hope of curing a hypochondriac so easily.

His chance came a day or two later when Winnie was out at an evening meeting of the Lulling Field Club, accompanied by her old friend Dotty Harmer. Winnie had left cold chicken and ham, and a fresh green salad for the menfolk, with a delicious orange trifle for their pudding. She herself would be dining on two Marie biscuits and a cup of weak tea, as the Lulling meeting began at 7.00 p.m. and these exciting refreshments would be served at half-time – somewhere about 8.15 p.m. This was the usual pattern of evening meetings in Lulling and Thrush Green, and accounted for the internal rumblings of hungry stomachs which invariably accompanied local lectures and whist drives.

Doctor Bailey helped his nephew to the meat which his wife had left neatly sliced on the dish.

'Oh, far less than that, please,' begged Richard. 'Somehow I seem to be averse to flesh these days.'

The doctor obligingly transferred two small slices to his own plate.

He watched Richard turning over the salad. Now that Winnie had made him aware of the young man's foibles, he noticed how anxiously he picked over the greenery, selecting a lettuce leaf here, a sprig or two of cress there and taking care to miss the sliced cucumber which hid among the leaves.

'Averse to cucumber too?' asked the older man pleasantly. 'I always enjoy cucumber, I must confess.' He helped himself generously.

'Aunt Winnie's food is always delicious, but I don't seem to get as hungry as I used to do. And then, of course, I like to keep to Otto's diet. I'm sure he's in advance of his time in these matters.'

'You need more exercise,' said the doctor.

'I agree, my dear Uncle. I couldn't agree more. As you know, I've had to cut down my walking time since I've been engaged on this Oxford project, and I certainly feel all the worse for it,' replied Richard vigorously. 'It's one of the reasons why I try to cut down on my intake of food.'

'You probably worry too much about your work at the moment. Nothing like worry to deaden the appetite. You should take life more easily.'

Richard, chewing his lettuce as conscientiously as Mr Gladstone, looked gratified. Rarely did he get any active encouragement to talk about his health. To have the attention of a medical man, even a medical man with ideas as antiquated as his uncle's, was wholly delightful. He became more confidential, encouraged not only by the doctor's interest but also by the absence of his aunt.

'I think you are quite right, Uncle. Otto seemed to think that I was a shade too highly strung. He suggested that marriage might help. It relieves tension, you know.'

'It can increase it,' observed the doctor drily, dabbing his lips with his napkin. 'A lot depends on one's wife.'

'I have been thinking about it,' continued Richard, brushing aside his uncle's comment. 'It looks as though I shall need to settle in London within the next year or so, and it would be wise, I think, to buy a small house. A wife would be very useful domestically. I'm no hand at cleaning and cooking, I'm afraid.'

'You could always get a housekeeper,' said Doctor Bailey, with a touch of asperity.

'I was thinking of Otto's advice. He seemed to think that I needed a comfortable settled background in order to do my best work. And although I don't consciously miss it, busy as I am with my research, he assures me that I am deeply deprived sexually.'

'You could always get a mistress too,' said Doctor Bailey, even more frostily. His thin fingers drummed on the edge of the table. Winnie would have known that he was becoming very angry indeed. Richard blundered on.

'I dislike the idea,' he said primly. 'And frankly, Uncle, I'm surprised that you suggest it. No, I feel sure that I'm ready for marriage. After all, I shall be thirty-three next birthday. I think it's time I found a wife.'

'You may have some difficulty,' said Doctor Bailey.

'Really?' Richard was genuinely surprised. 'I don't want to appear conceited, but I'm reasonably healthy and good-looking, and as for prospects – well, I think I can safely say that I shall be at the top of my particular tree within the next five years.'

The older man hit the table so sharply that the glasses jumped.

'Richard, will you never grow up?'

His nephew looked at him with startled blue eyes.

'You seem to view marriage purely as a panacea for your own ills,' continued the doctor, his cheeks flushed with exasperation. 'You talk as though a wife were a cross between a box of tranquillizing pills and a Hoover. *Not once* have you mentioned affection, respect or mutual happiness. D'you think any girl worth her salt is going to take you on, on your terms? Believe me, Richard, you're the one that will remain single if all you are offering are the attractions you've just mentioned.'

'Uncle –' began Richard, in protest, but he was ignored.

'I must say it, my boy, hard though it sounds. You are as bone-selfish now as you were at seven years old, and you've grown no wiser with the years. Marriage might well do you a power of good – heaven knows you need humanizing somehow – but I pity the girl who ever takes you on.'

The doctor raised his glass and sipped some water. Across the table his nephew sat transfixed, a slightly sulky look replacing the one of utter surprise.

'I'm sorry I should have upset you,' he said stiffly at last. 'I had no idea I was so objectionable.'

'Oh, tut-tut!' said Doctor Bailey testily. 'Don't get in a huff over a bit of straight talking. You've got your good points, my boy, as we all have – but unselfishness is not among them at the moment. You think over what I've said now.'

He reached for the trifle.

'Let me give you a helping of this, Richard. Dr Goldstein would approve, I feel sure.'

But Richard was not to be mollified by a helping of trifle or a quip about his medical adviser. He rose from the table, his whole demeanour expressing acutely wounded dignity.

'No, thank you, Uncle. My appetite has completely vanished after those remarks. If you'll excuse me, I will go for a walk.'

'You couldn't do better,' said the doctor cheerfully. 'And take an alka-seltzer before you go to bed. You'll be as right as a trivet in the morning.'

When Winnie returned, Richard was still out.

'Walking somewhere,' said her husband, in answer to her inquiries. 'Getting over the sulks. We had that little talk you suggested.'

'Oh, Donald, you haven't upset him, have you?'

'I rather hope so. We went from food to marriage. Richard seems to think that a wife might be a useful cure for his constipation and save him from doing his own chores.'

'Donald! Is that all?'

'That's what I asked him. He's out now, I fancy, trying to find the answer.'

Next door, at Tullivers, Harold Shoosmith continued his assault on the neglected border. Some days had elapsed since his first visit, and on his second he was surprised to see that the little bed just inside the gate had been planted with healthy wallflower plants.

'Your handiwork?' he asked.

'Yes. Are they put in properly? Not too close, are they?'

'No, they're just right. Very fine specimens too. They put my own to shame. Where did you buy them?'

'As a matter of fact,' said Phil, 'a sandy-haired man came to the door with them while you were in London. I can't remember his name – but he's often about. He helps old Piggott sometimes, I think.'

'Sam Curdle,' said Harold grimly.

Phil looked at him anxiously. 'Why, what's wrong?'

'What did he ask for them?'

'I paid him ten shillings for two dozen. Was that too much?'

'Much too much, my dear. Especially as he probably pinched them in the first place.'

'Damn!' said Phil softly, thrusting her hands into her coat pockets and surveying the border ruefully. 'I might have known.

What shall I do? If these have been lifted from someone else's garden, they'll be furious.'

'Leave it to me,' replied Harold. 'I'll have a word with Sam Curdle. He's no business to charge more than two shillings a dozen anyway, and well he knows it. Don't have any dealing with that chap. You'll be done every time.'

'I'll watch him in future,' promised Phil. 'How I do hate to be fooled!'

'Who doesn't?' smiled Harold, moving off to his digging.

Sam Curdle's peccadillo, as it happened, had already been discovered. Percy Hodge had a farmer's sharp eye, and a pretty shrewd idea of how twelve dozen plants would look in the garden beds allotted to Sam's care. It did not take him long to discover that they were fairly sparsely planted. He confronted Sam the morning after the sheep sale.

Sam denied the charge.

'You be allus down on us Curdles,' he complained, a gypsy whine creeping into his voice. 'Every blessed plant as was outside your back door I planted, as God's my Saviour.'

'Fat lot of saving you'll get,' said Percy Hodge roundly. 'There's a good score or more plants missing, and I want them back. Understand?'

'How'm I to get 'em? I tell you, sir, they're all set in, as you can see.'

'You get them back, Curdle, or tell me what's happened to 'em. You can take yourself and your missus off my land if I don't get the rights of this business. You had fair warning when I let you come into the yard.'

'You be a hard man,' whimpered Sam. In truth, he was more frightened of his wife's reaction to the news than his master's threats. Bella could be ferocious in anger, and Sam still bore the scars of marital battle from earlier engagements with his wife.

At that moment, the telephone rang and Percy Hodge strode indoors to answer it, leaving Sam to his thoughts.

For the rest of that day, and the next, Sam puzzled over his problem. Not for a minute did he consider telling the truth. Such a straightforward course was completely foreign to Sam's devious temperament. Somehow he must slide out of this tangle of trouble and, more important still, without Bella finding out.

Fate was against him. Percy Hodge and Harold Shoosmith met on the evening of Harold's discovery at Tullivers. Both men were on their way to the post-box at the corner of Thrush Green. After the usual greetings, and comment on the weather, Harold came to the point.

'Is Sam Curdle still with you?'

'Yes, indeed, the rogue. But he'll not be with me much longer, I fancy. He's up to his old tricks. Pinching wallflower plants this time.'

'I'll show you where they are,' said Harold, and led the way across the road to Tullivers.

It was beginning to get dark, but the sturdy plants, so carefully put in by Phil, were clearly to be seen. The two men gazed at them over the gate.

'D'you know what he got for them?' asked Percy, turning away. The two men moved towards the green.

'He fleeced Mrs Prior of ten shillings,' said Harold. 'It's despicable.'

'She must be a green 'un,' commented the farmer.

Harold's wrath kindled. 'She is a Londoner. One wouldn't

expect her to know the price of plants. And Sam Curdle knew that well enough!'

Percy Hodge looked at his companion curiously.

'No offence, old man. I'm not trying to excuse Sam. He's a twister right enough, and he'll get his marching orders in the morning.'

'I can let you have a couple of dozen plants,' said Harold, more coolly, 'if you're short. It seems a pity to worry Mrs Prior about this. She was upset when I told her my suspicions.'

'Well, that's very handsome of you, but I've got all I need really. Tell the lady to leave them where they are, and not to worry her head about the matter. I'll deal with our Sam, you mark my words.'

They walked across to the Land Rover which the farmer had left in the chestnut avenue, and bade each other a cheerful good night.

'That was a rum thing,' mused Percy Hodge to himself, as he drove up the shadowy lane to Nod and Nidden. 'I shouldn't wonder if old Harold Shoosmith isn't a bit sweet on that young woman. Ah well, no fool like an old fool!'

He trod on the accelerator, keen to confront Sam Curdle with the fruits of this chance encounter.

Suddenly, the thought of his farmyard, free of the Curdle tribe for ever, filled him with pleasurable relief.

Harold Shoosmith's flash of anger surprised the man himself quite as much as it surprised the observant farmer.

He returned thoughtfully to his quiet house and sank into an armchair. What exactly was happening to him? He didn't mind admitting that he was attracted to Phil Prior, but then he had been attracted to many girls in the past. He had always enjoyed the company of intelligent women, and if they were pretty, then so much the better. This protective feeling for Phil Prior, he told himself, was the result of her unfortunate circumstances. Anyone with a spark of humanity would want to help a poor girl left defenceless and hard up, especially when she had to cope with the rearing of a young child, single-handed.

Sam Curdle's was such a dirty trick! He grew warm again at

the very thought. It was small wonder that he flared up in Hodge's company. Any decent man would.

Or would he? Harold rose from the chair and walked restlessly about the room. Was he really becoming fonder of this girl than he realized? Damn it all, this was absurd! He was a steadfast bachelor and intended to remain so. He was old enough to be Phil's father. Well, nearly –

He walked to the end of the room and studied his reflection in the handsome gilt-framed mirror which lay above the little Sheraton side-table.

He was tall and spare, his eyes bright, and his hair, although silver, still thick. As a young man he had been reckoned good-looking. He supposed now, trying to look at himself dispassionately, he still had a few good points – but he was old, old, old, he told himself sternly. No young woman would consider him now, and quite right too!

He returned to his chair, dismissing these foolish thoughts, and opened the paper. It was as inspiring and exhilarating as ever. Four young men were appearing on charges of peddling drugs, an old lady had had her hand chopped off whilst attempting to retain her purse, containing two and eightpence, and a motorway to end all motorways was proposed which would wipe out six particularly exquisite villages and several hundred miles of countryside.

Harold threw it to the floor, leant back and closed his eyes. How pleasantly quiet it was! The fire whispered. The clock ticked. Somewhere, across the green, a car changed gear as it moved towards Lulling, and hummed away into nothingness. This was what he had looked forward to throughout those long hard years of business life in Africa. He would be mad to try and change his way of life now.

And yet Charles Henstock had found a great deal of happiness in later life since his marriage to Dimity. Charles, Harold pointed out to himself, had nothing to lose when he married. Ruled by that dreadful old harridan Mrs Butler, that desiccated Scotswoman who half-starved the poor rector, enduring the chilly discomfort of that great barn of a rectory all alone – of course marriage was attractive! Besides, Charles was the sort of man who *should* be married: he was not. That was the crux of the matter.

He took up the poker and turned over a log carefully. Watching the flames shoot up the chimney, he told himself firmly that marriage was out of the question. Once that poor girl's divorce was through he hoped that some decent, kind *young* man would appear to make her happy, and take some of her present burdens from her.

Meanwhile, he would do what he could to help her, and would frankly face the fact that her presence gave him enormous pleasure. But, for her sake, he must guard his feelings, he reminded himself. Thrush Green was adept at putting two and two together and making five, and she had enough to contend with already, without being annoyed by foolish gossip.

'Avuncular kindness!' said Harold aloud, and was immediately revolted by the phrase. He hit the flaring log such a hefty thwack that it broke in two. He dropped the poker, and went to pour himself a much-needed drink.

10. HAROLD IS IN TROUBLE

Regrettably, but understandably, Thrush Green folk tended to avoid Dotty Harmer when they saw her approaching. Few had the time to stand and listen to her diatribes against juvenile delinquency, the present-day teaching of history, air pollution, the exploitation of animals or whatever subject happened to be to the fore of Dotty's raggle-taggle mind.

Now that Dotty had kittens to find homes for, the pursuit of her neighbours was doubly frightening to them. Even she, unobservant as she was, began to notice how people hurried away at her approach.

'Can't understand it,' she told Ella, one gloomy November afternoon. She was carrying the daily bottle of goat's milk to her friend's house. 'Anyone'd think I'd got the plague,' she complained, putting the damp bottle down upon the freshly-polished dining table. 'What's wrong?'

'Kittens,' said Ella briefly. 'How many left?'

'Three,' replied Dotty. She looked accusingly at Ella. 'I was relying on you to help me find homes. What about Dimity? Although I still think that house is too draughty for cats. They need warmth, you know.'

'Better a chilly rectory than a watery death,' said Ella downrightly. 'Sam Curdle would drown them for you, I expect, if you're really stuck.'

Dotty blew out her papery old cheeks with indignation.

'The very idea, Ella Bembridge! If that's your idea of a joke, I consider it in particularly poor taste!'

'Don't be stuffy,' said Ella, 'and sit down, for Pete's sake, mopping and mowing about, with the door open too. It's downright unnerving.'

She slammed the door shut, and watched Dotty perch herself primly on the edge of a chair, the epitome of one who has taken umbrage and is rather enjoying it.

'To tell you the truth, Dotty, I clean forgot to ask Dim about the cat. Anyway, I've an idea that Charles is allergic to them. He certainly never had one while Mrs Butler was with him.'

'*That* woman,' said Dotty, 'wouldn't have had *anything* in the house if she'd had her way! I certainly shouldn't have let any cat of mine go there with *her* in charge of the domestic arrangements. It would have been fed on cold potato and bread crusts, I have no doubt – with watered milk to drink. A quite dreadful person! She once had the temerity to offer me a helping of bread pudding to take home. She got short shrift from me, I can tell you. "Throw it to the birds, Mrs Butler," I told her. "If they're strong enough to lift it from the ground they are welcome to it." She wasn't very pleased, I remember.'

'She's got a post as cook in a boys' school, I hear,' said Ella conversationally.

'Dotheboys Hall, no doubt,' commented Dotty sharply, unwinding a long woolly scarf from her skinny neck.

'Have a cup of tea,' suggested Ella, glad to see that her old friend's wrath was subsiding.

'Thank you, dear. That would be most acceptable,' said Dotty graciously, unskewering her hat and placing two formidable hat-pins upright in the arm of her chair, where they quivered like antennae.

'Tell you what,' said Ella, using one of her favourite phrases, as she returned from the kitchen with the tray. 'Let's go over to Dimity's when we've had this. And what about that Mrs Prior? She might like a kitten. Have you tried her?'

'Now, that's quite a good idea,' replied Dotty, picking over the biscuits thoughtfully. 'No, dear, not Petit Beurre. I find them rather too rich. Ah, an Osborne! Just what I love, and a happy reminder of dear Victoria!'

She nibbled happily, and Ella thought, not for the first time, that there was something infinitely endearing about Dotty's innocent pleasure in simple things. Anyone who could wax enthusiastic about an Osborne biscuit commanded Ella's respect.

When their light repast was over, the two ladies crossed to the rectory to find the rector and his wife sitting by their fire, winding wool.

'A new waistcoat for Charles,' said Dimity. 'Do sit down.'

Ella, as usual, came to the point at once. 'Forgot to ask you before, but do you want one of Dotty's kittens?'

To her surprise, Dimity looked distressed and gazed at her husband.

'Well –' she began timidly.

'I should simply love one,' said the rector. 'But Dimity –'

'But *I* should love one too,' cried his wife, 'but I always thought you disliked cats – that you had hay fever or something when they were in the house. Wasn't that why you never had one here?'

'Mrs Butler was the reason why I didn't have one,' said Charles robustly. 'Somehow, I've always thought *you* didn't really want one, and so I've never mentioned it.'

'For two grown people, you really are pretty stupid,' scolded Ella. 'All this sparing each other's feelings can only lead to misunderstandings, as you see. You should speak your mind.'

'Then I take it,' said Dotty, pulling out a crumpled notebook in a businesslike manner, 'that you want one.'

'Yes, please,' said Charles and Dimity in unison, smiling at each other.

'Male or female?'

'Do you know which is which?'

'Well, frankly, no!' confessed Dotty, suddenly becoming less businesslike.

'In that case,' said the rector, 'we'll be happy to leave it to the vet, when the time comes.'

'Now, I'm very glad to hear you say that,' said Dotty, lowering the indelible pencil which she had been sucking. Her blue-stained lips and tongue gave added piquancy to her appearance.

'I was so afraid you might have religious scruples, Charles, about interfering with nature. I'm glad to see you are more enlightened.'

'Better to give one doctored cat a home, than twenty kittens an untimely end,' said the rector philosophically.

'Quite, quite!' agreed Dotty, turning the pages of her note-book briskly. 'Well, which is it to be? Tortoiseshell, black with white paws, or plain tabby with exceptionally fine eyes?'

The rector and his wife exchanged amused glances.

'We'll come and see them tomorrow,' promised Dimity, 'and pick ours, shall we?'

'Very well,' said Dotty, stuffing the book untidily into her coat pocket. 'Come to tea – you too, Ella dear – and it will save me bringing up the goat's milk.'

'I think,' said the rector, making his way to the sideboard, 'that this transaction should be celebrated with a drink.'

And so it was.

Harold Shoosmith finished his labour of love on the flower border at Tullivers just before the first sharp frosts of winter arrived. There was still plenty of work in the garden to warrant many more visits, but he was beginning to wonder if it would be wiser to pay calls less frequently.

His heart-searchings had left him somewhat ruefully amused. He was certainly becoming extremely fond of Phil, and Thrush Green must not know it. Nor, of course, must the girl, particularly with divorce proceedings in the offing. Life, thought Harold, cleaning the prongs of his gardening fork, was quite complicated enough without tangling it even more.

He was admiring the tidy border as Willie Bond, the postman,

came with the afternoon letters. Phil came to the door to collect them, then crossed the grass to admire his handiwork.

'It really is splendid,' she said truthfully. 'So neat – and so lovely to find that it's got such a lot of good stuff in it already.'

She waved one of her letters.

'Do you mind if I open this now? It's from your friend Frank. Perhaps he's taken something after all.'

She ripped open the envelope and read the contents. Harold watched her growing pink with excitement. She thrust the letter towards him.

'There! Isn't that marvellous? Fifty guineas! I can't believe it.'

'Congratulations,' said Harold warmly. 'Which story is this?'

'Oh, the one about the two friends and the curate,' said Phil. 'I've a copy on the table if you're interested. When do you think they'll publish it? Shall I get paid on acceptance, do you think?'

'I should tell Frank that's what you want,' replied Harold, shouldering his tools. 'And, yes, please, I'd love to read the story.'

'You must have brought it luck,' said the girl when she handed it over. 'You posted it for me. Remember?'

'So I did,' said Harold. 'I've a strong share in this success.'

He made his way back across the green, warmed with the thought of the girl's pleasure. When he had changed, and was sitting by his fire, he settled back to read the story.

He turned the typed pages with growing dismay. It was not the telling of the tale which worried him. Phil's style was as crisp and lucid as always, and the suspense was well-sustained. But the characters, in this present story, were far too realistically portrayed for Harold's peace of mind.

Here, for all the world to see, were Ella and Dimity, in the guise of Jean and Phoebe, and Charles Henstock – though far less attractive – under the name of Tobias Fuller, a hearty curate.

Even, their appearance fitted. Jean was thickset, Phoebe skinny. Their determined pursuit of the innocent curate was told with a nice sense of the ridiculous which Harold would have appreciated in different circumstances.

He read it through to the end, let the typescript drop to his knees, and gazed thoughtfully at the fire. This simply must not be printed. He must go and see Phil immediately, before she wrote to accept the offer of payment.

But what a kettle of fish! What could have possessed the girl to lift two characters from life so inartistically! He looked through the story again, and sighing, went to the telephone.

Phil answered immediately.

'Do you think I might come over for a few minutes? It's about the story.'

'Of course. Something wrong with it?'

'Frankly, yes.'

There was a short silence. Then Phil spoke briskly.

'Well, bring it over with you, and we'll go through it. I expect it can be altered easily enough.'

She showed him into the sitting-room where a log fire crackled welcomingly.

'No Jeremy?' asked Harold.

'Early bed tonight. He's running a slight temperature. But he's quite happy reading a Paddington Bear book.'

'I'll go and see him, if I may, before I go.'

'He'd love that. But do tell me – you can guess how anxious I am – what's the matter with the story?'

Harold found her bright gaze very difficult to face.

'If you want to continue to live at Thrush Green,' said Harold, 'I'm afraid you'll have to scrap it.'

'Scrap it!' cried Phil, in horror. 'But why?'

'Jean and Phoebe are Ella and Dimity to a T. The curate, though not so near the knuckle, might be Charles Henstock.'

The girl looked aghast. 'I never thought of that,' she whispered. 'Here's a how-d'you-do.'

She looked swiftly at Harold and put a hand upon his arm.

'You surely don't think I did this knowingly? I wrote that story three years ago – long before I knew anyone here. Don't you remember? You said it would be a good idea to send a story I had by me while I altered the new one. This is it.'

'I remember very well.'

'What on earth shall I do?'

'Tell Frank to send it back.'

Phil's face took on a mutinous look.

'I don't really see why I should. I've got a clear conscience. This is pure coincidence. Frank's accepted it, and I'm damn glad to have earned fifty guineas. Besides, Frank won't be particularly anxious to take other things if I mess him about with this effort.'

Harold said nothing.

'Besides,' continued Phil, getting up and walking restlessly about the room, 'how many people in Thrush Green are likely to see this particular magazine? And what the hell does it matter if someone thinks I've written about Ella and Dimity? I wrote that story in good faith, and the money's honestly earned. And, believe me, it's needed. I've just had a further bill from the wretched builders for eighty-five pounds. This isn't the time to start being squeamish about possible hurt feelings.'

Harold let her argue herself to a standstill. Soon enough, he realized, she would be able to cope with this bitter disappointment, and he felt sure that she would decide, eventually, to withdraw the offending story.

'I really think you are fussing about nothing,' she went on, standing in front of his chair. 'Why must you be so maddeningly interfering? The implications would never have dawned on me – and I don't suppose, for one minute, that they ever will on any readers in Thrush Green – if there are any. Why did you have to meddle in this?'

'Because I don't want to see you leaving Tullivers,' said Harold drily.

Phil snorted. 'It would take more than a few wagging tongues to oust me from Thrush Green, I can assure you.'

She sat down abruptly in the armchair on the opposite side of the hearth. Harold could see that her fury was fast abating. Far more upsetting, to his tender heart, was the look of hurt bewilderment which began to creep across her countenance.

'What on earth shall I do?' she asked quietly. 'I could, I suppose, have it published under a pen-name.'

She sounded near to tears, and Harold began to feel alarmed about his own ability to cope with an emotional situation. If only she weren't so confoundedly pretty, it would be easier, he told himself.

'I feel partly to blame,' he said. 'Shall I have a word with Frank and say that I've noticed this likeness?'

'No, thanks,' replied Phil shortly. 'I can handle it.'

Harold refused to feel rebuffed.

'Very well. But you do see that it would be far wiser to scrap the story?'

'No, I can't say I do. And I'm not making up my mind one way or the other until the morning.'

'I'm glad to hear it.'

'I think you meant well –'

'Thanks,' interjected Harold grimly.

'But I don't relish your interference, I must say. I've nothing to blame myself for, and I need the money. Naturally, I don't want to upset good neighbours, but I'm not keen on upsetting Frank either.'

She stood up, and Harold rose to make his departure.

'No hard feelings?' he said with a smile.

'Of course not.' Her tone was warm.

'And can I see the boy?'

'Yes, indeed. Let's go up.'

But when they reached the bedroom the child was asleep with the open book lodged upon his chest.

Phil removed it quietly, put out the bedside light and they went downstairs.

'By the way,' said the girl. 'We're going to have a cat.'

'One of Dotty's?'

'That's right. Jeremy's thrilled.'

'And what about you?'

'Modified rapture. I love them, but I'm terrified of the traffic, and we're so horribly near the road.'

'Keep your fingers crossed,' said Harold, on the doorstep. He hesitated for a moment. 'Will you be kind enough to let me know how you decide to act?' he said diffidently. 'Perhaps I shouldn't interfere any more.'

'I shall let you know as soon as I've made up my mind,' said Phil stiffly.

She watched him make his way to the gate, raised her hand in farewell, and closed the door, with what seemed to Harold, unnecessary firmness.

'Damn!' said Harold, plodding homeward. A much-quoted dictum of his old nurse's floated into his perplexed mind. 'What can't be cured must be endured!'

Cold comfort indeed, thought Harold, turning the key in his front door.

Harold Shoosmith was not the only person in the neighbourhood to suffer a disturbed night.

Sam Curdle was receiving the lashing of Bella's tongue, as they packed their few poor belongings in the stuffy caravan. They were off at first light, making for a village north of Southampton.

Bella had learnt the bitter truth that they were to depart from the farmer's wife.

'I'm sorry to lose you, Bella,' Mrs Hodge said truthfully. 'You've been a good worker and we've got on well. But my husband won't be done, as you know, and Sam's a fool to try it on.'

Bella had pleaded for leniency, promising to keep an eye on her erring husband, although she knew, in her heart, that he was too slippery a customer even for her control. The poor woman was at her wits end. There were three children to bring up and she knew that Sam's chances of getting any kind of job in the Thrush Green area were slight indeed.

Mrs Hodge stood firm. It was as much as her life was worth, she said, to oppose Percy. Sam had known from the start that he was allowed in the yard on sufferance. He had flouted the master's demands, and there was an end to it.

A furious scene between Sam and Bella followed. The next day, Bella, slightly less heated, betook herself to the telephone booth at the corner of Thrush Green, a fine assortment of coins in hand.

Unknown to Sam, whom she had left sulking in bed, she put her pride in her pocket and decided to talk to her father who kept a country pub in a village in Hampshire. She had been his barmaid before marriage, and hoped that he and her step-mother would take pity on their plight now.

She disliked the idea of going there intensely, but there seemed to be no alternative. Her father had married some years after the death of Bella's mother, and her step-mother was a hard-working, but tight-fisted woman who had never taken particularly to her blowsy step-daughter. It wouldn't be a very comfortable situation for the Curdle family, Bella knew, remembering her step-mother's sharp tongue, but beggars couldn't be choosers, she told herself, as she dropped the coins in the box.

Her father was a tender-hearted man and responded kindly to her tearful call for help. Yes, they could all come, and the caravan could stand in the backyard. As it happened, his present barmaid was leaving to have a baby, though she would be back in a couple of months, Bella must understand.

And Maud herself, Bella's step-mother, was laid up with a sprained ankle, so Bella would be doubly welcome. Sam, said her father, with rather less warmth, could find himself a job nearby and could earn a few bob helping him in the evenings with the crates.

'But you can tell him straight, Bella, he's to behave himself. You know what I mean. You and the kids are welcome for a bit, just to tide you over like, but Sam had better get down to a steady job and make a proper home for you all. Tell him I said so.'

Bella promised, with some relish, thanked her father sincerely and went back to the caravan to face Sam with the ultimatum.

'Well, we ain't going!' said Sam roundly, when faced with the news.

A dangerous glint appeared in Bella's eye, and Sam began to quail inwardly.

'You speak for yourself, Sam Curdle. Go where you like – it don't trouble me, and that's flat. But me and the kids set off tomorrow for home. I can drive well enough to get us down there, and I reckons I own this caravan more than you do. It's my wages as keeps us going, and we'll all be a damn sight better off without you.'

'Now, Bella –' began Sam.

Scarlet in the face, Bella rounded upon him. 'Take it or leave it! We're off first thing tomorrow, come rain or shine. Come if you like, or clear off – one or the other!'

And so, next morning, the battered caravan clattered out of Percy Hodge's yard for ever. As it rattled by Harold Shoosmith's house, Willie Bond the postman watched it. At the wheel was a grim-faced Sam. Beside him, arms folded, sat an equally grim-faced Bella. The news that the Curdles were off had already flown around the neighbourhood, but Willie was the only witness to their departure.

'Good riddance to bad rubbish!' said Willie aloud, as the caravan slid out of sight down the steep hill to Lulling.

He echoed the general feelings of Thrush Green.

11. ALBERT HAS SUSPICIONS

Harold Shoosmith's bathroom was at the back of the house overlooking the little valley that lay to the west of Thrush Green. In the distance were Lulling Woods, a deep blue smudge against the winter sky.

As he shaved the next morning he gazed beyond the shaving mirror on the window-sill observing the bare trees and brindled hedges of winter. The elm trees, near Dotty Harmer's distant cottage, spread their fans of black lace, and a wisp of blue smoke, curling up towards them, showed that Dotty was already astir.

After his restless night, Harold felt out of sorts. He had gone over the irritating affair of Phil's story, time and time again, in the maddening way one does at night. He had almost decided, at one stage, to ignore Phil's request to cease meddling and to ring Frank and explain matters, swearing his old friend to secrecy. But with morning light, things could be seen more coolly, and Harold made up his mind to let this business work itself out, without worrying himself unduly. He had made his point. It was Phil's decision, and she had plenty of sense.

He determined to put it at the back of his mind, and went downstairs to brew his coffee and make toast. Nevertheless, he intended to keep within earshot of the telephone. Luckily, Betty Bell came that day to go through the house, like a mighty rushing wind, and she would answer the telephone if Harold were called away unexpectedly.

For the first part of the morning he worked at his desk, the telephone within arm's reach. It rang once and he snatched it up, only to be told that the exchange was testing his line.

Betty Bell burst in, without knocking, at eleven o'clock, bearing half a cup and half a saucerful of far too milky coffee, and two soggy gingernuts.

'Heard the news?' she asked.

'What about?'

'Them Curdles.'

'I heard Percy Hodge had asked them to leave,' said Harold guardedly.

'Fair old rumpus they had, Bella and Sam,' said Betty sitting down on *The Times* which Harold had left in the armchair. 'Willie Bond said they looked as black as thunder going off in that old van. Got a tin bath and the pushchair lashed on top. He said it sounded like Alexander's rag-time band.'

Betty burst into merry laughter, rocking back and forth to the detriment of *The Times*.

'Proper cough-drop old Willie is! You ever heard him sing "I Gotter Motter"?'

'No,' said Harold, pouring the coffee from the saucer into the cup. The biscuits he had wrapped in blotting paper and deposited in the waste-paper basket.

'You ought! You really ought! Brings the house down. Never fails. Always gets an encore, does Willie.' She got up bouncily. 'Well, this won't buy the baby a new frock, will it? I'm doing you liver and bacon for your dinner. All right?'

Harold nodded. Betty Bell, in full spate, after a poor night, was more than usually exhausting.

She whirled out, crashing the door behind her. Harold sipped his tepid coffee and looked across the green to Tullivers. What was going on there?

A pale wintry sun lit the scene. He decided that he would do some gardening. No point in moping about. Fresh air and exercise would do him good.

'Give an ear to the phone, Betty,' he said casually, as he dragged on his wellingtons. 'I'm expecting a call.'

But it did not come. The morning passed. The liver and bacon were cooked and eaten. Betty Bell departed, leaving her master hoeing the beds beneath the study window where the telephone bell could be heard should it happen to ring.

But it remained silent for the rest of the day, and when

evening came Harold shrugged aside the whole stupid incident and bent his energies to solving a much-crumpled crossword puzzle in *The Times*.

The departure of Sam and Bella Curdle had repercussions in the community. John Donne's dictum about no man being an island is truer in a village, perhaps, than in any larger community.

In the first place, Winnie Bailey was expecting him to come to the house to sweep the kitchen chimney. An odd quirk in this structure, necessitated by a by-gone architect's devious design, meant that it needed a sweep's ministrations twice a year. Doctor Bailey owned some stout brushes, which were frequently loaned to neighbours, for this purpose, and Sam was always ready to do the job for five shillings.

Albert Piggott was the second person to miss Sam. They had been instructed by the rector to take out some rusty and damaged iron palings from the churchyard fence.

'Children or animals could be injured so easily,' said the rector anxiously.

His sexton had snorted, but made no spoken comment. Children and animals, his expression implied, got what they deserved if they meddled.

'It's too bad,' said Mrs Bailey, when she heard that Sam had gone. 'That wretched boiler will start smoking as soon as the wind changes, mark my words. I shall have to get someone up from Lulling, I suppose.'

'No need,' said Richard, sprinkling wheat germ on his plate of Otto-recommended breakfast cereal. 'I'll do it this evening.'

Winnie surveyed her neat nephew with new respect. 'Do you know what to do?'

'Of course. I rather like sweeping chimneys. And cleaning drains. So worthwhile. Instant rewards, you know.' He poured himself some coffee. 'Think no more of it. I'll be ready for the job after dinner tonight, if that suits you.'

'Wonderful!' cried Winnie. 'I'm most grateful, Richard dear. I'll let the boiler out this afternoon.'

True to his word, Richard tackled the job that evening. He was clad in ex-RAF overalls, once white, but now mottled with the stains of many a year and many a job, from creosoting fences to cleaning out wells.

'They go everywhere with me,' said Richard, stroking his filthy overalls fondly. 'Such a useful rig-out.'

This practical side of Richard's nature was new to his aunt, and she found her respect for the young man growing considerably as she watched him tackling the flue. He was quick and clean. He had had the forethought to spread newspapers at strategic points, and he wasted no time in idle conversation as Sam Curdle did.

While the flue brush was rattling away inside the chimney, Phil Prior called.

'My goodness,' she said, with admiration. 'You're making a splendid job of that.'

'A minor accomplishment,' replied Richard, with a rare smile. 'It's more useful than painting water-colours these days.'

'It certainly is,' agreed the girl. She turned to Mrs Bailey. 'I hate to bother you, but would you come and have a look at Jeremy? He's looking so flushed. He went to sleep as usual, but he's woken up again so crotchety. I don't like to bother Doctor Lovell, but if you think –'

'Let me slip on my coat,' said Mrs Bailey, making for the stairs.

'Ah!' said Richard, with enormous satisfaction. A sizeable piece of hardened soot rattled down the chimney and splintered on the waiting newspaper.

'I think Aunt Winnie wants a different sort of fuel for this contraption.'

He picked up the soot in a blackened hand and studied it with close attention. Phil watched, amused. At last, this young man had come to life! Until then, she had found him cold and a trifle supercilious.

'Do you often sweep chimneys?' she asked lightly.

'If I'm asked I do,' replied Richard. 'I like mucky jobs. It makes a change from my finicky figure work.' He looked at her swiftly. 'Do you want anything done?'

'Not chimneys, alas. They were done when we moved in, but –' She hesitated. 'No, nothing really,' she finished lamely.

'It's a waste-pipe,' said Richard shrewdly.

Phil laughed. 'You're clairvoyant! As a matter of fact, it is.'

'Well, I love a good stuffed-up waste-pipe,' said Richard, with relish. 'I'll be over tomorrow evening, if that suits you.'

'There's no hurry – it's the spare room waste-pipe, but I'd be eternally grateful, if you really mean to do it.'

'Mean to do it? Of course, I mean to do it,' said Richard indignantly. 'If not tomorrow, then one evening soon. I'll ring first to see if it's convenient.'

'You are kind,' said Phil gratefully.

Mrs Bailey reappeared and the two women hurried next door. After inspecting Jeremy, Winnie suggested a little milk of magnesia.

'And if he still seems feverish in the morning, send for Doctor Lovell. He'll pop in before morning surgery, no doubt.'

'You've relieved my mind,' said the girl. 'I seem to worry unnecessarily.'

'How are things going?' Winnie ventured.

'Worse,' said Phil. 'By that I mean that the wheels are grinding along. What I *cannot bear* is the thought of Christmas for Jeremy without his father. I must screw myself to telling him before long. I can't tell you how I dread it.'

'Do you hear from him?'

'Sometimes he writes a short note when he sends my cheque. He's in France, at the moment. With her, I imagine.'

The girl sounded dog-tired and hopeless. Winnie felt powerless to help.

'And the writing?' she asked, hoping to find a more cheerful topic.

Phil laughed mirthlessly. 'All in a muddle. I've had an acceptance, but I'm not sure if I want it to be published now. There are plenty of stories, by me, waiting to be read by editors. Something may turn up.'

'I'm sure it will,' said Winnie robustly. 'Now have an early night, and by morning both you and Jeremy will be fighting fit again.'

She kissed her gently, and returned home, shaking her head.

'Poor young thing!' she murmured, opening the kitchen door.

Richard was taking up the newspapers. The stove was back to rights and freshly washed.

'That's a nice young woman,' observed Richard thoughtfully. 'Is her divorce through yet?'

My goodness, thought Winnie, in some alarm, Richard's touch may be sure enough with chimneys and waste-pipes, but it was surely rather too heavy and direct in his dealings with women!

Albert Piggott did not find help as easily as Winnie Bailey. He surveyed the cold November day through his cottage window. It was going to be proper bleak tugging up them old railings. Been stuck there, in Cotswold clay, for a hundred years. They'd take some shifting – and no Sam to give him a hand.

He said as much to Nelly, who was whirling about behind him with a tin of polish and a duster. He got short shrift from her.

'A good day's work won't hurt you, Albert. Make a nice change,' she puffed, rubbing energetically at the top of the table. 'Do that liver of yours a power of good.'

Fat lot of sympathy she ever gives me, thought Albert morosely, lifting his greasy cap from the peg behind the door. He dressed slowly, watching his buxom wife attacking the furniture with zest.

All right for some, Albert grumbled to himself, crossing to the windy churchyard. She'd never had a day's illness in her life – strong as a horse, she was – and still game to make eyes at that oilman.

The pain which gnawed intermittently at Albert's inside seemed worse today. Doctor Lovell's pills helped a little, but Nelly's food was too rich, no doubt about it, and he was that starved with hunger when it came to meal times, he ate whatever she provided, dreading too the lash of her tongue if he refused to eat.

He set about the broken railings and found the job as difficult as he had feared. As he tugged he contemplated his marriage. What a fool he'd been! A clean house and good cooking was no exchange for peace and quiet, and that was what he missed. The only times he had the house to himself were Tuesdays and Fridays when Nelly took herself to Bingo at Lulling.

Or did she? A sudden suspicion made Albert straighten his

back and look across Thrush Green. Come to think of it, Bingo was on Saturday night. It dawned, with horrible clarity, on Albert's dull mind, that Nelly must be meeting the oilman on Tuesdays and Fridays.

That was it! Tuesday was the oilman's half-day, he remembered, and Friday was his pay-day. It all fitted together.

He bent to his task again, half relishing the scene when he confronted Nelly with his discovery. The pain in his stomach seemed worse, and there was a tight feeling across his chest which he had not suffered before, but he continued tugging with the vigour born of righteous indignation.

He saw Nelly whisk out of the cottage, a basket on her arm, bound for the butcher's down the hill. He gave her no greeting, but watched sourly as her ample back vanished in the distance.

'You wait, my gal,' said Albert grimly. 'You just wait!'

Young Jeremy Prior was no better the next morning and Doctor Lovell called at Tullivers when morning surgery, next door, was over.

'There's measles about,' he told Phil when they were downstairs again, 'but it doesn't look like it at the moment. No rash yet, of course. But keep him in bed, and I'll look in tomorrow.'

He eyed the girl sympathetically. She looked wretchedly tired.

'Did you sleep last night?'

'Not much.'

'Would you like a few tablets?'

'Not really, many thanks. I've a horror of pills, and I know I'll have a good night tonight. It works out that way, I find.'

'Good,' said the doctor briskly. 'But if I can help, do just say. And don't worry about that young man upstairs. I think we'll find his temperature's down tomorrow.'

Throughout the day the child was unusually demanding and fractious. He wanted his mother with him most of the time, and she was content to shelve her writing and sit beside him reading stories or helping with a gigantic ancient jigsaw puzzle of the Wembley Exhibition, bequeathed to him by Winnie Bailey.

The affair of the story niggled at the back of her mind, but she had little time to give it attention that day. Harold Shoosmith's attitude she still found high-handed, and was annoyed that she

cared so much. The fact that he might expect to hear about her decision that day, never entered her head. She had told him that she would let him know what she would do, and this she intended to do in time.

Meanwhile, she kept Jeremy company and watched the activities of her neighbours through the bedroom window. She saw Albert Piggott attacking the church railings, and his fat wife waddling down the road. She saw Charles Henstock walking across the green, bent against the wind, to speak to Albert. Her friend, Joan Young, emerged from the fine house nearby, and battled her way towards Lulling, and across the green she watched the children pour into the playground at mid-morning, shouting and leaping, whilst little Miss Fogerty stood sipping her tea among the tumult.

It reminded Phil that she must let Miss Watson know why Jeremy was away. She would telephone during the dinner hour. She did not want to be out of earshot if Jeremy called.

But in the afternoon, when he fell into a peaceful sleep, she ventured into the garden to get a breath of the cold blustery air. A rose or two still starred the bushes and she picked them to enjoy indoors. The winter jasmine was in bud and already one or two bulbs were poking their green shoots through the earth.

Elsewhere winter held sway. The chestnut trees were bare now, in the avenue, and the dead leaves of the Baileys' beech hedge rustled drily in the wind. The skeletons of dead plants rattled together like castanets, and the matted ivy on the old wall flapped up and down like a loose curtain.

The Cotswold stone was as grey as the November sky above it. In the distance, the girl could see the dun-coloured meadows of winter and the faraway smudge of Lulling Woods. The grey coldness seemed to echo her own life just now. Would she ever know light and warmth, colour and excitement again? Would this desolation last for ever?

She was tired of the struggling, tired of keeping up a bright front for Jeremy, for the neighbours and for herself. If only something, however insignificant, would happen to give her hope.

12. ALBERT IS STRUCK DOWN

The wind increased to a gale during the night, screaming down the hill to Lulling, rattling windows and even shifting some of the heavy stone roof tiles of the town. The few remaining leaves were wrenched from the trees, and an old oak crashed across the road near Percy Hodge's farm, bringing down some telephone wires, and causing more than usual confusion in the Lulling exchange.

It was no better in the morning. Willie Marchant could make no headway on his bicycle in the face of this fierce northerly blast. Even his tacking methods were no use against it, and he was forced to wheel his bicycle up the steep hill, his eyes half shut against the cigarette ash which blew dangerously against his face from the inevitable stub in his mouth.

It was useless to try to prop a bicycle against the kerb in this wind, and when he reached Tullivers he prudently lodged it against the wall while he battled his way up the path.

There was no one about, and he thrust the letters through the flap beneath the admiral's dolphin and continued on his erratic course.

Everywhere he met tales of damage. A flying tile had broken the glass in Joan Young's greenhouse. The school dustbin had been found in the hedge at the end of the playground. Albert Piggott's cat was missing, 'blown to kingdom-come', its owner surmised gloomily.

Little Miss Fogerty did not tell Willie about her own troubles, but they had been severe. Two pairs of sensible long-legged knickers, of a style which she had been brought up to know as 'directoire', had blown from the discreet little clothes line hidden by laurel trees, over the hedge into her neighbour's garden.

Much agitated, she had watched until the man of the house had gone to work, and then had knocked timidly at Mrs Bates' door to explain about her embarrassing loss. Mrs Bates, a kind-hearted woman, forbore to show any coarse amusement, as some less refined Thrush Green folk might have done, rescued the garments from the roof of her hen-house and returned them gravely, wrapping them first in a piece of brown paper. Miss Fogerty was much touched by the delicacy of this gesture, but the horror of the incident haunted her for the rest of the day.

Harold Shoosmith heard about the havoc in the Lulling Woods area when Betty Bell burst into his house at half past nine.

'I found Miss Harmer's letters all twizzled up in her string bag in the road. Soaking wet, of course, but it never bothered her. "They'll dry, dear," was all she said when I took 'em in to her. Willie won't be best pleased, I'll lay. And the roof blew off the hen-house at The Drovers' Arms and landed in the pond! My, what a night! Any damage here?'

Harold had to admit that he had found none. Betty looked disappointed. She thrived on daily drama.

It was later that morning that the telephone rang, and Harold's spirits soared when he heard the excitement in Phil's voice.

'Wonderful news! Frank's taken the latest story, and for more money.'

'I'm so glad. Well done!'

'Isn't it splendid? And he wants me to meet him "with a view

96

to further work", so his letter says. I'm going to ring him in a few minutes.'

'You'll find him very easy to talk to,' said Harold. 'What's more, he can explain the sort of thing he wants done, which saves a lot of time and temper.'

He paused, wondering if the girl would tell him about the awkward story. As if she knew his thoughts, she spoke of it next.

'I've decided to scrap that other thing. You were quite right.'

'That's extremely generous of you.'

'Not at all. It could have upset people here – though I still think the chances were slight, particularly if I'd used a pen-name. Anyway, this second acceptance takes care of most of the builder's bill, and I don't feel so hard-pressed.'

'I can't tell you how pleased I am,' said Harold warmly. 'You deserve to succeed. You've worked so hard lately.'

'I hope you weren't expecting a call yesterday,' said Phil suddenly. 'Jeremy was off-colour and I didn't really bother much about the other problem. He's much better this morning, thank goodness, but won't go to school until next week.'

'Well, give the young man my regards,' said Harold. 'Now, I'm not going to hold you up – you must be anxious to get in touch with Frank. Remember me to him, if it enters your head. I hope he'll come down here one day. Meanwhile, the best of luck with all your ploys.'

He put down the receiver, feeling unusually elated. It was a relief to know that the story would never appear, and even more gratifying to know that the girl was having some success. Frank would treat her right, thought Harold robustly!

He went into the windy garden, whistling like a boy, and Betty Bell, well-versed in affairs of the heart, winked at her reflection in the hall mirror as she polished it.

Richard was as good as his word and appeared some evenings later dressed in his working overalls and carrying his drain-clearing equipment. His expression was animated, and when Phil opened the door to him she was struck by his good looks, which she had not noticed before.

'Got plenty of newspaper?' asked Richard, mounting the stairs. 'I like lashings of *really thick* paper to spread about.'

'About a dozen *Telegraphs* and great fat wads of *Sunday Times*,' said Phil. 'And all those lovely Business Supplements no one reads. Absolutely unopened, they are.'

'Good, good! Pity you don't take the *Sunday Express* though. Wonderful powers of absorption for this sort of job.'

He spread the papers busily, patting them down happily, and humming to himself. It was quite obvious to Phil that he would be better alone with his passion.

'I'll get out of your way,' she said diplomatically, 'but shout if you want anything.'

She heard nothing for the next twenty minutes but the sound of running water and Richard's footsteps up and down the stairs as he hurried outside to make sure that the water was flowing without interruption. When he finally appeared in the sitting-room, he looked triumphant.

'As I thought, simply the U-bend. No difficulty at all. Some-one has been using a disintegrating face-flannel, I suspect.'

'Not guilty,' smiled Phil. 'Perhaps the admiral's sister? I believe she used that room.'

She indicated a tray of drinks on a low table by the fire.

'What will you have? My goodness, you've earned a drink! I'm so very grateful.'

Richard looked at the pale chair covers, and with rare thoughtfulness began to step out of his filthy overalls. It seemed to Phil, watching him, that this young man wasn't the ogre that Winnie, despite her tact, had portrayed.

'My aunt tells me that you write,' said Richard. He sipped his dry sherry appreciatively. Otto allowed one small sherry a day if it were a dry one, Richard remembered happily.

'Not as successfully as I should like,' admitted Phil, 'but it all helps. I'm hoping for some more work next Wednesday.'

She told him about Frank.

'Wednesday,' repeated Richard. 'I'm going to town myself that day. Let me run you up. What time do you have to meet him?'

Phil told him that she was lunching with Frank and that she had planned to catch the 10.10 train from Lulling, changing at Oxford, as her car was needing attention.

'It will give me time to see Jeremy safely to school and to tidy up here,' she said. 'Joan Young is having him to lunch and tea, and I shall collect him about six.'

'I was proposing to leave about 10.30,' said Richard. 'I am spending the night with the Carslakes, so I'm afraid I can't bring you back, but do please give me the pleasure of your company on the journey up.'

'I should love to,' said the girl, and thought how pleasant it was to be talking to a man of her own age again. A jaunt to London would be something to look forward to after the recent drab weeks at Thrush Green, and Richard she found surprisingly interesting.

He stayed for over an hour and was at his most charming. As he returned to the Baileys' house, carrying his impedimenta, he sniffed the frosty air with relish.

He put his head round the sitting-room door. His uncle and aunt surveyed him mildly over their spectacles.

'It's a wonderfully bright night,' said Richard. 'Do you mind if I take a brisk walk?'

'Not at all, dear boy,' said Winnie. 'But don't get over-tired.'

'Tired?' echoed Richard in amazement. 'My dear aunt, I could walk ten miles without stopping tonight!'

He vanished, and they heard the front door slam.

The doctor lowered his newspaper and looked across at his wife. 'Would you think,' he asked pensively, 'that our Richard is putting some of Otto's theories into practice?'

International crises always seem to occur at weekends. Domestic crises appear to follow the same pattern.

Certainly, there was a crisis at Albert Piggott's home on the Sunday. Nelly had dished up a boiled hand of pork, broad beans, onions and plenty of parsley sauce. She had also excelled herself by providing a Christmas pudding for the second course with a generous helping of brandy butter.

'I made six full-size ones,' said Nelly, surveying the pudding fondly, 'but this little 'un was for a try-out before Christmas. What d'you think of it?'

'All right, if your stummick's up to it,' replied Albert dourly, turning his spoon about in the rich fruitiness.

'Lord love old Ireland!' cried Nelly, in exasperation. 'Ain't you a misery? Small thanks I gets for slaving away over the stove day in and day out. Wouldn't do you no harm to have bread and water for a week.'

'You're right there,' agreed Albert sarcastically. 'You knows full well the doctor said I was to go easy on rich food. I believes you does it apurpose to upset me.'

Nelly rose from the table with surprising swiftness for one of her bulk. She whisked round the table behind her husband, and before he knew what was afoot, she had thrust his head sharply into his plate of pudding.

'*You besom!*' spluttered Albert emerging with a face smothered in the brown mess, and with a badly-bumped nose. He picked up the plate and threw it at his wife. It clattered to the floor, pudding side down, but miraculously did not break.

Nelly, who had dodged successfully, now broke into peals of hysterical laughter as she watched her husband grope his way to the sink to wash off his dessert.

'You wait till I get my hands on you,' threatened Albert. 'I'll beat the living daylights out of you, my gal! Pity I never done it before. You and that oilman!'

Nelly's shrieks of laughter stopped suddenly.

'You can leave him out of this, Albert Piggott. He knows how to treat a lady.'

'Humph!' grunted Albert, from the depths of the roller-towel on the door. 'I'll bet he knows! I could have the law on him, if I'd a mind, carrying on with another man's wife.'

Nelly adopted a superior aloofness.

'I'm not stopping here to listen to your filthy insinuations,' she said loftily. 'I shall go and have a lay-down, and you can clear up this mess you've made with your tantrums.'

'That I won't!' shouted Albert to her departing back. 'I'm due at church at 2.15 for christenings, and you can damn well clear up your own kitchen!'

The door, slamming behind Nelly, shook the house, and a minute later Albert heard the springs of the bed above squeak under his wife's considerable weight.

Growling, he flung himself into the chair by the fire, picked up the *News of the World*, and prepared to have a quarter of an hour's peace before going across to St Andrew's for his duties.

Hostilities were not resumed until the early evening. Nelly remained upstairs, but ominous thumps and door-bangings proclaimed that she was active. When she reappeared, she was dressed in her best hat and coat, and was carrying a large suitcase which she set upon the table, taking care to miss the dirty dinner plates and cutlery with which it was still littered.

'Well, Albert, I've had enough,' said Nelly flatly. 'I'm off!'

If she expected any pleading, or even surprise, from her husband she was disappointed. Albert's morose expression remained unchanged.

'Good riddance!' said Albert. 'You asked yourself here and you can go for all I care. But don't come here whining to be took back when that fancy-man of yours has got fed up with you.'

Nelly drew in an outraged breath. 'Come back here? Not if you went down on your bended knees, Albert Piggott, and begged of me! No, not if it was with your dying breath! You've seen the last of me, I can tell you. I'm going where I shall be appreciated!'

She hoisted the case from the table and struggled to the door. Albert remained seated by the fire, the newspaper across his knees, his face surly and implacable.

He remained so for several long minutes, listening to his wife's footsteps dying away as she walked out of his life for ever. He had no doubt that Nelly spoke the truth. Their ways had parted.

He looked at the kitchen clock. Time he went to ring the bell for Evensong. But when he came to stir himself, the pain across his chest seared him like a red-hot knife. He fell to his knees, his head pillowed on the *News of the World* on the hearth rug, and was unable to move. The last thing he saw, before the blackness engulfed him, was the remains of the Christmas pudding spattered, dark and glutinous, across the kitchen wall.

The rector, robing in the vestry, realized with alarm, that Piggott was absent.

'You'd better ring the bell,' he told the largest choir-boy. 'Mr Piggott seems to have been held up.'

Privately, Charles Henstock feared that his verger might be the worse for drink. It had happened before, but he did not wish to be uncharitable, and he told himself that he must postpone judgement until he had seen the fellow.

Albert did not appear during the service, and as soon as his few parishioners had departed, Charles put out the lights himself, saw that things were in order, and then crossed to Albert's cottage.

The windows were dark, and the rector feared that Albert was indeed in a stupor. Really, drink was a great nuisance!

He knocked and got no reply.

'Anyone at home?' called the rector, opening the door. The sight that met his eyes, in the gloom, frightened him exceedingly.

He found the light switch and surveyed the chaos. Albert's huddled body lay before the dying fire, but his heavy breathing showed that he was still alive.

'Thank God!' said the rector from his heart, kneeling beside the man. He turned him over, into a more comfortable position and put the cushion from the armchair beneath his head.

'Piggott!' he cried sharply. 'Can you hear me, Piggott?'

A growling sound came from Albert's pale lips, and his eyelids fluttered spasmodically.

'Stay there,' cautioned the rector, thinking, as he said it, how idiotic it was. There was small chance of Albert moving far. 'I'm going for help,' he said, making for the door. The man must have a doctor. Should he telephone from home, or run along to Harold Shoosmith's? There was nothing in it as to distance, and he did not wish to alarm Dimity. Harold it should be.

He ran through the darkness, past The Two Pheasants, and was soon banging Harold's knocker.

'My dear chap,' said Harold to his breathless friend. 'What is it? Come in, do.'

'It's Piggott. A seizure or something,' puffed Charles. 'Can I use your telephone?'

'I'll ring Lovell,' said Harold, taking command, 'while you go back. I'll follow as soon as I've got through. And don't worry,' he shouted to his retreating friend, 'it's probably only the drink!'

'Not this time, I fear,' called back the rector, hurrying away.

Twenty minutes later Doctor Lovell agreed with the rector as he surveyed his patient.

The three men had carried Albert up the narrow stairs to his bed. He was conscious now, but very weak and pale.

'We've got an ambulance on the way for you, Albert,' said Doctor Lovell. 'I want to have a proper look at those innards of yours. Where's your wife?'

'Gorn,' said Albert, in a whisper. 'For good.'

None of the three men tried to dispute the statement. The signs of a fight downstairs, the empty clothes cupboard in the bedroom, and the general disorder, were plain enough. There had been plenty of talk about the Piggotts' differences, and about the oilman's advances. Albert, they knew, was speaking the truth.

'We'd better let her know anyway,' said the doctor. 'Know her address?'

'No,' said Albert shortly. 'Nor want to.' He closed his eyes.

An hour later he was asleep between the sheets at Lulling Cottage Hospital, and Harold and Charles were telling Dimity what had happened.

'She's bound to come back,' she said. 'She wouldn't leave him just like that – not in hospital, not when she hears that he's ill!'

'I agree that most women would bury the hatchet when they heard that their husbands had been taken ill, but somehow,' said Harold, admiring his whisky against the light, 'I don't think Nelly will return in a hurry.'

'But what will he do?' asked the rector, looking distressed. 'He must have someone to look after him when he comes out of hospital!'

'I know,' said Dimity suddenly. 'I'll write to Molly, his daughter. She married Ben Curdle, the man who owns the fair,' she told Harold. 'She left here just before you came to live here. A dear girl – we all liked her so much. She should know anyway, and perhaps she will come and look after him.'

'He wasn't very nice to her when she did live with him,' ventured the rector doubtfully. 'And now she has Ben and the child to look after, I really can't see –'

'Never mind,' said Dimity firmly. 'I shall let her know what has happened, and it is up to her to decide. I must ring Joan Young for her address. I know she keeps in touch. They were such friends when Molly used to be nursemaid to Paul.'

She made her way briskly to the study, and the two men heard her talking to Joan.

The rector gave a loud yawn and checked himself hastily. 'I'm so sorry. I'm unconscionably tired. It's the upset, I suppose. Poor Albert! I feel very distressed for him.'

'You'd feel distressed for Satan himself,' replied Harold affectionately. 'Poor Albert, indeed! I bet he asked for it. I don't blame Nelly for leaving that old devil.'

'I married them myself,' said the rector sadly, gazing at the fire. 'I must admit, I had doubts at the time.'

Dimity returned, a piece of paper fluttering in her hand. 'I've got the address. If I write now, then Willie can take it in the morning.'

'Well, I must be off,' said Harold rising. 'Many thanks for the drink.'

'I've just thought,' cried Dimity, standing transfixed. 'Did you see Albert's cat? I'd better go across and feed it.'

'You leave it till the morning,' advised Harold, patting her thin shoulder. 'It won't hurt tonight. There's plenty of Christmas pudding lying about the kitchen to keep it going.'

13. CHRISTMAS PREPARATIONS

Signs of Christmas were beginning to appear in Lulling and Thrush Green.

The squat Butter Market cross, beloved by residents and anti-quarians from further afield, was being wreathed in coils of wire ready for its garland of coloured lights later on.

In the shops, gifts were on display. Puddocks, the stationers, decked one of their windows with Christmas cards and the other with a fearsome array of table mats arranged round a scarlet typewriter. Ella found the juxtaposition of these articles extremely annoying, and said so to the manager.

'If you're going to show table mats put something like a large dish, or a vase with Christmas decorations in it,' Ella told him, in a voice audible to all his customers. 'Or if you want the ruddy typewriter on show – though who on earth you imagine is going to pay over thirty quid for one Christmas present these days, I'm blessed if I know – then put office stuff round it. Blotters, say, or calendars, or pens and pencils. But to mix up the two just isn't good enough!'

The manager made perfunctory apologies. As a young man he had dreaded Ella's comments. Now that he was grey and tubby he was hardened to this awkward customer's remarks. Ella Bembridge was a byword in the town. No one was going to worry about her little foibles, he told himself.

He directed her attention to the other window.

'I've done my own,' said Ella, scrutinizing the crinolined ladies, the churches in the snow, and the kittens in paper hats, with obvious disgust.

'Appalling, aren't they?' she said cheerfully, and departed before the manager could think of a cutting reply.

The window of the electricity showroom was much admired by the young if not by their elders. It showed an all-electric kitchen with the oven prominently displayed. The oven door stood open, the better to show a dark brown shiny turkey and some misshapen roast potatoes. At the kitchen table, a smiling woman stirred something which seemed to be Christmas pudding mixture, while a dish of mince-pies stood on the top of the refrigerator beside her.

Quite rightly, the good wives of Lulling found this scene as exasperating as Ella found Puddocks' window.

'Bit late mixin' the pudden,' one said sourly to another.

'And that bird won't get done with the door open,' agreed her friend tartly. 'I shouldn't care to try them spuds either.'

'Nor them mince-pies,' observed another. 'Plaster-a-Paris as plain as a pike staff. Bet some fool of a man arranged that window. I've a good mind to go in and tell 'em.'

The Fuchsia Bush had excelled itself with rows and rows of silver bells, made from tinfoil, which were strung across the ceiling and rustled metallically every time the door opened.

'Come in handy for keeping the birds off the peas later,' observed one practical customer, speaking fortissimo above the din of the dancing bells.

The bow-shaped windows were studded with dabs of cotton-wool to represent snowflakes, and two imposing flower arrangements of dried grasses, seed-pods and fern, all sprayed with silver by the ladies of the Lulling Floral Society, took pride of place in each window.

Thrush Green's preparations were less spectacular, but Dimity took out the figures for the Christmas crib and washed them carefully in lukewarm water well-laced with Lux.

Miss Watson and Miss Fogerty were in the throes of rehearsals for the annual Christmas concert. Miss Fogerty, who was the more realistic of the two and knew the limits of her infants' powers, had wisely plumped for simple carols, sung in unison by the whole class, with 'growlers' tucked strategically at the back of the stage and warned to 'sing very quietly'. A few percussion instruments in the hands of the most competent few, who included young Jeremy Prior, were going to accompany the infant choir.

In fact, Miss Fogerty's main concern was to get the children to pronounce their vowel sounds correctly. Constant repetition of:

'Awy in er-er mynger'

was causing her acute distress.

Miss Watson, who was more ambitious, had decided rashly to stage a nativity play. The ten-year-olds who were the most senior of her pupils and who, it might be supposed, would be competent to play the leading roles, were at the self-conscious stage, and tended to giggle and look sheepish, which Miss Watson found both irritating and irreligious.

She found herself speaking with unusual sharpness.

'Don't mumble into your beard, Joseph. The parents want to hear you, remember. And if you three wise men keep tripping over the rector's spare room curtains I shall be returning them in shreds. Pick your feet up, do! As for you beasts in the stall, for pity's sake stop nodding your masks in that inane way. You'll have them off, and I'm not made of cardboard!'

With such travail was Christmas being welcomed at the school.

'I suppose it will be all right on the day,' said Miss Watson resignedly to Miss Fogerty.

'Of course it will,' Miss Fogerty replied stoutly, watching her

children paste paper chains with frenzied brushes, and more chatter than was usually allowed. She dived upon one five-year-old who was twirling his paste-brush energetically in his neighbour's ear, removed the brush, slapped the offender's hand, and lifted the malefactor to the corner where he was obliged to study the weather chart for December, with his back to the class. Throughout the whole incident, Miss Fogerty's face remained calm and kindly.

Miss Watson sighed. Dear Agnes's methods were hopelessly old-fashioned, and she knew quite well that corporal punishment was frowned upon by all enlightened educationalists. Nevertheless, thought Miss Watson, returning to her own boisterous class, a sharp slap seemed to work wonders now and again, and at times, like this, one surely could be forgiven.

In the houses round the green, more preparations were going on. Ella had looked out half a dozen lumpy ties, ear-marked for male friends such as Charles Henstock. The Christmas cards, a stack of bold woodcuts with a certain rough attraction, waited on the dresser for dispatch later.

Her present to Dimity remained to be finished. She was

sewing a rug, in a stitch called 'tiedbrick stitch', in gay stripes of scarlet, grey and white. It gave her enormous satisfaction to do, but its bulk was difficult to hide in a hurry, on the occasions when Dimity called unexpectedly to see her.

Harold Shoosmith, efficient as ever, had bought book tokens for all his friends, and had a neat pile waiting in his desk to be written in, and posted on the correct day. Betty Bell had made him a Christmas pudding large enough for a family of ten, and was upset when her employer told her firmly that he refused to countenance her proposal to make him a dozen mince-pies, two trifles and a couple of jellies 'to keep him going'.

'My dear Betty,' he said kindly, 'I'm going to Christmas dinner with the rector and his wife. I have invited them here for Boxing Day evening, as you know, and that delicious Christmas pudding will be ample.'

'You'd best have a trifle as well,' said Betty mutinously. 'Miss Dimity likes trifle.'

'Very well,' sighed Harold capitulating. '*One trifle!* And thank you.'

Across the green, Phil Prior wrapped a few presents for Jeremy and hid them among her clothes, but her heart was not in the coming festivities. The prospect for her was bleak, and any day now she must steel herself to break the news to Jeremy that his father would not be there at Christmas time. The boy would have to know the truth before long. If only she could get it over!

Meanwhile, she worked hard at her writing, and prepared a batch of stories, articles and ideas, which might interest Frank when she met him for the first time on the Wednesday.

The day dawned clear and bright. Phil watched Jeremy eat his breakfast egg, and felt surprisingly excited by the prospect of a day in London.

'And I go straight to Aunt Joan's, don't I?' he said, for the third time. 'She's having sausages because I told her I liked them. Paul said so.'

'Then you're very lucky,' said his mother. 'Don't forget to thank her when you go back to school.'

'And you'll be back to put me to bed?'

'Of course. Probably by tea-time, but it just depends how long I have to spend with the editor, and how the trains run.'

'Can't you come back with Richard?'

'No. He's staying in London.'

'D'you like him?' Jeremy's gaze was fixed upon her intently.

'Of course.'

Jeremy drained his cup of milky coffee, and wiped away his wet moustache. 'I don't.'

'Why not? He's very kind. He cleared our drain for us, you know.'

'He did that for *you*,' said Jeremy shrewdly. 'Not for me. He doesn't notice me.'

Children! thought Phil, clearing the table swiftly. Too quick by half!

'Why should you mind that?' she answered reasonably. 'Grown-up people have a lot to think about. They don't always take notice of children.'

Jeremy made no reply, but bent to tie his shoe-laces. This was a new accomplishment, and gave him great satisfaction.

'Miss Fogerty gave me two sweets the first time I tied my laces,' he said, surveying his shoes proudly.

'Two? Why two?' asked Phil, glad to have the subject changed.

'Dolly mixture,' replied her son briefly.

She helped him on with his coat, and gave him a hug. His soft face smelt sweetly of Morny pink lilac soap, as he kissed her.

'Have a lovely time,' he said cheerfully.

'You too,' said Phil, opening the front door. 'Have a lovely time,' she echoed, when he reached the gate.

She watched him run across the grass and turned back to make her preparations, turning over in her mind the child's comments on their neighbour.

She enjoyed the drive with Richard. He was quick and competent in traffic, and quite unruffled by the antics of bad drivers around him.

They talked of Thrush Green, of books, and of music.

'There's a concert at Oxford just before Christmas,' said Richard. 'Will you come?'

'Thank you,' said Phil. 'If I can get someone to mind Jeremy, I should love to.'

'Aunt Winnie would sit-in, I'm sure,' said Richard. 'I'll ask her.'

'No, please don't. She's been so kind –'

'She's always kind. Looks after me too well,' said Richard, and began to tell her about his dietary difficulties.

For the first time, Phil began to see why Winnie Bailey found her nephew something of a trial. It seemed incredible that an intelligent grown man should be quite so worried about himself.

'But who is this Otto?' asked Phil, when the great man's name cropped up yet again.

'The wisest dietician of our time,' pronounced Richard solemnly, swerving to evade a cyclist bent on suicide. He went on to explain Otto's theories, his methods and his astounding successes. Phil did her best not to yawn.

'Where can I drop you?' asked Richard as they drove along Piccadilly. 'I have to go up Regent Street, if that's any help.'

'Yes, please. Somewhere near Hamleys if it's possible. I want to buy a gadget for Jeremy's train set.'

'Good luck with the editor,' called Richard, when she left the car. He gave her one of his disarming smiles, and Phil momentarily forgot the boredom of his digestive troubles as she thanked him and said goodbye.

The sausages were splendid – crisp and very dark brown – exactly as Jeremy and Paul liked them. As an added attraction, Joan had tucked them into an oblong of mashed potato with only the ends showing.

'Sausages-in-bed,' she told them. Jeremy was entranced with this gastronomic refinement, and determined to tell his mother how much better sausages tasted when so served.

The Youngs' tortoiseshell kitten greeted the boys affectionately.

'We're having one too,' Jeremy told Paul, proudly. 'It's coming at the weekend and I'm making a bed for it out of a cardboard box. I've got a piece of a rug to put at the bottom. A car rug my Daddy bought.'

'What's he giving you for Christmas?' asked Paul, a direct child.

'My daddy? I'm not sure.'

'He'll probably bring you a surprise,' said Paul.

'Yes,' agreed Jeremy. There was a slight doubtfulness in his tone which did not escape Joan, who knew the sad circumstances. 'If he comes,' he added thoughtfully.

'Of course he'll come,' scoffed Paul robustly. 'Bound to at Christmas.'

The school bell began to ring, and Joan held up a finger.

'A quick wash, Jeremy, and then off you go. We'll see you after school, my dear.'

Truly saved by the bell, she thought!

She spent the afternoon engaged in her own Christmas preparations. Her sister Ruth Lovell and her husband and baby were coming for Christmas Day. Her parents were arriving on Christmas Eve and would spend several days at Thrush Green. Mr Bassett, father of Joan and Ruth, had now retired, and was always threatening – in the kindest possible way – to turn out the Youngs from their Thrush Green house. It had been left to him on the death of his parents, and one day, he promised himself, he would go there to live.

She busied herself in preparing their room and sorting out bed-linen and blankets. The time passed so quickly that she was surprised to hear the shouts of the school children as they emerged at half past three.

She hurried downstairs to meet young Jeremy who was rushing up the garden path, unbelievably grubby after two hours in school.

'Let me wash your face,' she said, 'and then we'll go down to Lulling to pick up Paul. And shall we buy some crumpets for tea?'

Sitting beside his hostess in the car Jeremy spoke decidedly.

'Next to my house,' he told her, 'I like yours best. If I hadn't got a home, could I live with you?'

'Anytime,' said Joan sincerely. 'Anytime, Jeremy.'

Travelling back alone, in the train, Phil closed her eyes and pondered on the day's happenings, well content.

She had liked Frank the moment she saw him. He was tall, heavily-built, with a beautiful deep voice and very bright eyes of that true brown which is so rare. She found him remarkably easy to talk to, and found herself telling him far more about her circumstances than she intended, over a splendid lunch.

The work he had in mind, he told her, was similar to that which she already did for young girls. Would she be interested in writing a half page for a monthly for slightly younger children of both sexes? He told her the payment he had in mind, which was extremely generous.

'And more stories, please,' he said, 'for the women. I like your touch. Tell me more about the one you want me to suppress.'

She told him the details.

'Harold is far nicer than I am,' she admitted. 'I would have gone ahead, but it would have upset him, I'm sure.'

'He's a very fine chap,' said Frank. 'And most meticulous. But I can see no real reason why you should stand to lose your proper reward.'

He went on to tell her that his company owned two Scottish evening papers which printed a short story daily.

'No possible chance of Thrush Green eyes seeing them,' he told her. 'And we'll use a pseudonym. Think one up, and let me have it. I liked that tale. You handled the two old ladies beautifully.'

After lunch, they returned to the office where he gave her a number of back copies of the young people's magazine to study at home. They discussed things very thoroughly, and Phil was surprised to find how quickly the time flew past.

'It's so good to be doing something again,' she said. 'You shall have the copy very quickly.'

'Tell Harold I will come and see him when Christmas is over. You will be spending it at home, I suppose?'

'Yes.'

'I'm going to my son's. He's farming in Wales and there are four children, under ten, so I shall be lively enough. It's rather flat being on one's own at Christmas. My boy Robert understands that.'

They wished each other goodbye and Phil set off for Paddington feeling happier than she had done for many a long day.

14. Sudden Death

When Albert Piggott came round in hospital, he was bewildered and resentful. Where was his comfortable feather pillow, familiarly sour-smelling and crumpled? Where was the sides-to-middled sheet, soft with age? And worse still, where was the cane-bottomed chair beside the bed, with the glass for his teeth and his tin of extra strong peppermints?

Everything was wrong. The light was too bright. The ceiling was too clean and too far away. And now that he could focus his aching eyes, why were there other beds around him?

He tried to sit up, but a pain in his head felled him like a log. After a little while, he managed to turn his head on the hard starched pillow and surveyed the occupant of the next bed through half-shut eyes. Outlined against the bright window, the man appeared simply as a dark hulk to Albert, but he was aware that he was being watched closely.

'Comin' round then, Bert?' he said kindly, and Albert's heart sank still further. If it wasn't Ted Allen, who kept The Drovers' Arms at Lulling Woods! And could he talk? Just his luck to be beside an old gas-bag like Ted Allen! Albert shut his eyes tightly.

'Nurse!' shouted Ted, in a bellow that set Albert's head throbbing. 'Mr Piggott's come round. Looks a bit poorly.'

He felt a cool hand on his hot forehead, and another hand holding his wrist. He opened one eye – the one furthest from Ted Allen – with extreme caution.

A fresh-faced young girl smiled down at him beneath her starched cap. 'Feeling better now?' she asked.

'No,' said Albert.

'Like a drink?'

'What of?' asked Albert, with a flicker of interest.

'Water? Cold milk?'

'No thanks,' said Albert disgustedly.

'He could do with a pint of bitter, Nurse,' said Ted with hearty jocularity.

Albert winced.

'Now, Mr Allen,' said the nurse severely, 'don't be a tease.

Mr Piggott needs his rest. I'm going to put a screen round his bed for an hour or two.'

'Thank God for that,' said Albert, and meant it.

Later, after some hours of fitful dozing, the nurse came back, removed the screen, and lifted him against the pillows.

'Like some supper?' she said brightly.

'What is it?' asked Albert suspiciously.

'You'll see,' said the nurse, with an archness that annoyed Albert.

She whisked away. Bet it wouldn't be anything as good as Nelly cooked him, he thought morosely.

Nelly! What was it about Nelly, that he ought to remember? Something to do with Christmas pudding and shouting and a row. He groaned with the effort of thinking.

'You all right, old chap? Anything I can do?' asked Ted solicitously.

'Shut yer gob,' said Albert rudely.

'Thanks, I'm sure,' said Ted, offended.

Blessed silence fell, and Albert tried out his powers of memory again.

Nelly shouting at him. Banging down a suitcase on the table. The oilman! Now he'd got it!

She'd gone!

With horror, Albert found his eyes were wet. Within a minute two tears were rolling down his cheeks. What had come over him? He was damned if he was crying about Nelly, he told himself fiercely. Good riddance to bad rubbish, that was! Nothing but everlasting rows and nagging ever since she'd caught him!

Too proud to wipe the tears away with Ted's sharp eyes upon him, Albert watched the tears splash down upon the snowy sheet top, making neat round stains.

The nurse came back bearing a small bowl full of some milky substance.

'Now, now, now!' she scolded him. 'What are we getting upset about?'

She whisked a paper tissue from a box nearby and mopped Albert's face painfully.

'Upsadaisy now!' she said, heaving him a little higher in the

bed. 'Cheer up, cheer up! Worse troubles at sea! Have some supper. That'll put new heart into us.'

Albert surveyed the contents of the bowl sourly. 'Don't eat slops,' he said flatly.

'It's all you're going to get for a bit,' said the nurse firmly, 'so you may as well get used to it.'

'Why?' asked Albert, with some spirit. 'What's up with me? What you been doin' to me while I was unconscious?'

'You've had an operation for a very nasty ulcer,' said the nurse primly.

'Bin *cut*, 'ave I?' yelped Albert, outraged.

'Our Mr Pedder-Bennett performed the operation,' said the girl reverently. 'A beautiful bit of work, the theatre sister said.'

'That ol' butcher?' cried Albert indignantly. 'I'll have the law on the lot of you! Letting that ol' saw-bones loose on a chap as is unconscious. I'll –'

'You'll eat your supper,' said the nurse, deftly thrusting a spoonful into Albert's protesting mouth. 'And stop talking nonsense.' She lodged the bowl in front of him and bustled out of the ward.

Albert removed the spoon from his mouth and pushed it about in the bowl gloomily. He became conscious of other people eating in the ward, and looked at his companions with some interest.

Ted Allen kept his eyes sedulously upon his tray. His expression was lofty. He wasn't going to waste his time being pleasant to an old misery like Albert Piggott. Let him stew in his own juice!

'What've they given you?' asked Albert, trying to make amends.

Ted Allen, good-hearted, quickly forgave his neighbour.

'Some sort of mince,' he said. 'Could be anything from rat to rabbit. You name it – this is it!'

'Looks a sight better than this muck,' said Albert, with considerable self-pity.

'You wants to take things careful,' advised Ted. 'You was pretty bad when you come in. And a proper ghastly colour when they brought you back from the operation. Lay there groaning, you did, and snoring horrible.'

'Did I now?' said Albert, brightening. 'Bet you thought I wouldn't come round.'

'That never worried us,' said Ted ambiguously. 'But you kep' us all awake.'

Albert tried another spoonful tentatively and pondered Ted's last remark.

'What you in for?' he asked at length.

'Appendix. Caught me while I was lifting the crates. Good thing Bessie was nearby. She got Doctor Lovell double quick and here we are. I goes out sometime this week.'

'You're lucky,' growled Albert.

Ted Allen looked about him reflectively.

'I don't know. I've quite enjoyed meself, being waited on. Makes a nice change. And people comin' to see you with fruit and papers. I'll be quite sorry to go, what with one thing and another.'

'Don't suppose anyone'll come and see me,' said Albert.

'What about Nelly? She'll be down with a steak and kidney pud hidden in her pocket, I'll bet.'

'That she won't,' replied Albert, putting the spoon and bowl on the locker top. 'She's cleared off!' No point in trying to keep secrets in Lulling, he told himself.

'You don't say!' gasped Ted, registering acute surprise. Bessie had told him the news twenty-four hours earlier. She had also told him about the oilman. 'What did she do that for?'

'Gone off her chump over some fellow that's no better than he should be,' replied Albert austerely. 'That's why.'

'She's a fool then,' said Ted. 'Throwing over a steady chap like you.'

Albert looked mollified. There was one thing about Ted Allen, blab-mouth though he was. He was a good judge of character, thought Albert.

The nurse came scurrying down to his bed, and peered into his bowl.

'That's better. Next time you must finish it all up, but we'll let you off tonight. Feeling happier now, are we?'

'No,' said Albert.

'Well, you will when I tell you the news,' said the girl, undeterred. 'Your daughter's here to see you.'

'What? Molly?'

'Yes, and her husband. Now, you be nice to them. They've come a long way.'

She beckoned to two figures at the end of the ward. They advanced shyly. For one terrible minute, Albert thought that the tears would come again. Weakness it was, just weakness, he told himself, fighting for control.

'Dad,' said Molly. 'How are you feeling now?'

'Middlin',' said Albert huskily. She put a small posy of anemones on the bed.

'They must have cost a pretty penny,' commented Albert ungratefully.

'Never mind that,' said Ben. 'You look better than I thought you would.'

'Been at death's door, I have,' Albert said with pride. 'Ain't I, Ted?'

'Mr Allen!' cried Molly, turning round. 'And how's your wife, and The Drovers' Arms? Those were happy times!'

They talked for a minute or two, for they were old friends.

Molly had worked there as barmaid before her marriage, and the Allens had always been good to her.

'You heard about Nelly?' asked Albert.

'Yes, Dad. Miss Dimity told me when we got here. I'm sorry. What'll you do?'

'Same as I did before, of course. Look after meself. I ain't helpless, you know.'

'We know that,' said Ben diplomatically. 'But best see how you get over this operation. Maybe, Molly can look after you for a bit until you're on your legs again. I can spare her for a week or two.'

The two young people smiled at each other. It was plain to Albert that they had been making plans before they paid this visit.

Suddenly, he felt ineffably tired. It had been a long day. Seeing the look of exhaustion, Molly rose and nudged Ben.

'We'll be off now, Dad, and come and see you tomorrow before we go back home.'

She kissed his unresponsive face. Ben shook his hand gently, and they departed.

'She's a grand girl,' said Ted Allen, watching them go. 'Always bright and cheerful, as Bessie says.'

'Takes after her old dad,' said Albert drowsily, and fell into a deep sleep.

In the week that followed Phil's trip to town, she worked hard at the writing. It was always difficult to begin a new type of work, and she had never written for children of ten to fourteen for whom the new column was intended.

Nevertheless, she had experience with slightly older readers, and she was comforted by the thought that Frank was the sort of person who would say exactly what was right, or wrong, with a piece of work, and also give her sound advice.

She had passed on his message to Harold who looked pleased at the thought of entertaining his old friend.

'And I think I ought to tell you,' she added, after some hesitation, 'that the story about the two village ladies is to be published after all.'

She explained about the Scottish papers and the pen-name. Harold was elated.

'I'm so glad. I've felt rather wretched over the whole affair. I'm afraid you must have thought me unspeakably stuffy.'

'Well, I was horribly rude. I was so cross,' laughed Phil. 'Still, all's well that ends well, and I really am most terribly grateful to you for introducing me to Frank and all this lovely work. I shall be quite rich in the New Year.'

The next morning, while Phil was tapping busily at her typewriter, Harold appeared at the window, waving a pair of secateurs.

'Would you like me to prune those roses at the end of the garden? We missed them earlier, you remember. I've just finished mine, and thought I'd ask while it was in my mind.'

'I'd be very thankful,' said Phil, 'I'm particularly dim about pruning. I'll give you a call when I'm making coffee. I just want to finish some alterations.'

'Don't disturb yourself on my account,' said Harold cheerfully, departing down the garden.

It was a clear mild December day. Against the house, a flourishing winter jasmine was breaking into yellow stars. A robin eyed Harold speculatively from the top of the wall, hoping for upturned worms. Nearby, a fat thrush jabbed rhythmically at a rotting apple in the grass.

Harold got on with the job, humming happily to himself. It was a relief to know that all was well between himself and Phil, and an even greater relief to know that she was getting steady work which was decently rewarded.

He was making a neat job of the neglected bushes, and stacking the prickly shoots in a pile ready for burning, when he heard the gate click, and looked up.

Stepping up the path was the local policeman, Constable Potter. He hailed him gaily. The officer walked across the grass towards him.

'And what brings you here?' asked Harold lightly. 'Traffic offences?'

The constable remained unsmiling, and Harold felt a sudden constriction in his chest. 'Not bad news, I hope?'

'Afraid so, sir. But I must tell Mrs Prior first. Is she alone, d'you know?'

'Yes. The boy's at school. But can I help?'

'Not yet, sir. But will you be around?'

'Yes, of course. I'll be here, in the garden.'

He watched the burly blue back advance towards Tullivers' front door with heavy foreboding.

For Harold, there followed the longest ten minutes he could remember. Mechanically he snipped at the rose bushes, while the robin whistled to him. He collected handfuls of dried grass which were caught about the lower shoots like grey lace, and added them, unseeing, to his pile of rubbish. What could have happened? Was it something to do with the divorce? Wouldn't her solicitor cope with all that? Why on earth would young Potter want to call?

At length, the front door opened and the two emerged. Constable Potter replaced his cap, and made his farewells in a low voice. He gave one swift anxious look in Harold's direction, raised a hand, and stumped heavily down the path.

Phil, looking pale and stunned, walked across the grass to Harold who hurried towards her. She looked ready to faint, but when she reached him she held up her arms like a bewildered child and clung to him.

'There, there,' Harold heard himself say, as he patted her back. 'Come into the house, my love, and tell me.'

They entered the house, hand in hand, and in silence. When he had settled her in an armchair, he stood waiting, his back to the fire.

'Brandy?' he asked gently.

She shook her head. At last she spoke.

'I can't believe it. He's dead.' She raised her eyes slowly, and looked mutely at Harold. 'That policeman. He brought a message from Paris. John's been killed in his car.'

'Oh no!' whispered Harold. 'This is terrible news. Terrible!'

'I must go. I must get over there.' She rose unsteadily and leant against the mantelpiece. 'I told the policeman I must go. He left a piece of paper with the times of the flights.'

She began to wander distractedly about the room, searching

in an aimless way. Harold saw a piece of paper protruding from her cardigan pocket. He took it out and studied it.

'The next one is at two o'clock,' he told her. 'Let me take you over this afternoon.'

'No, no!' The girl faced him more steadily. 'I'd sooner go alone. I must go alone on this journey.'

'Then let me take you up to Heathrow.'

'I'd be grateful for that. I'll go and get some things together.' She stopped suddenly.

'But Jeremy? I must arrange something for Jeremy.'

'I'll take charge of that,' said Harold. 'I'll call and see Joan Young, and go and get the car, while you pack.'

He looked at her white face anxiously.

'Have that drop of brandy before you begin,' he said.

She nodded, and he fetched her a tot in a glass, standing over her while she gulped it down, shuddering.

'I'll be back in a quarter of an hour,' he told her. 'Wrap up well, and don't forget your passport.'

She nodded again, dumbly, and he hurried across the green on his errands. Still dry-eyed, Phil went upstairs very slowly, like an old, old woman, to prepare for the saddest journey of her life.

She scarcely spoke on the way to the airport but sat with her hands clenched tightly upon the handbag in her lap.

They had some time to wait and Harold fetched coffee and sandwiches as they sat in the crowded waiting area.

Beside Phil sat two women with the most clownish make-up that Harold had ever encountered. He found his eyes straying to the green eyelids, the black-rimmed eyes, and the curiously luminous lips. His father would have made no bones about labelling them 'strumpets', thought Harold, but apart from their outlandish faces, they seemed normal enough. Their dress was plain, their speech quiet, their apologies sincere when they accidentally jogged Phil's coffee cup. Harold was baffled.

The food seemed to revive Phil. She smiled tremulously at him, as though she were seeing him for the first time.

'I can never thank you enough for today,' she told him softly. 'You understand how I feel about going to John alone, though?'

'Of course,' he told her.

'I don't really believe it's happened,' she said wonderingly. 'I don't want to cry, because I just don't believe it.'

She turned to him suddenly.

'Look after Jeremy, won't you? Tell Joan what's happened. I'll tell Jeremy later.'

He patted her arm comfortingly.

'Are you all right for money?' he asked.

'I've a cheque book, and about five pounds.'

He took out his wallet and gave her some notes.

'It's simpler to have ready money. You don't know what expenses you'll find. If you want me to come over, just ring. I'm absolutely free to come at any hour, as you know.'

'I'll remember.'

'And I'll meet you here, in any case.'

'Dear Harold,' said Phil softly.

A booming voice above, nasal and distorted, announced that passengers for the flight must now depart. Phil rose hurriedly, and went with Harold to the door.

'Don't wait, please,' she told him. 'You've done so much. Get back to dear Thrush Green.'

She was swallowed up in the crowd of travellers and vanished from his sight.

But Harold did not return to Thrush Green until he had gone to the roof of the building and watched the plane take off. He watched until its greyness merged into the greyness of the December sky, before turning to go home.

15. HAROLD TAKES CHARGE

The departure of Nelly Piggott from Thrush Green may not have upset her husband unduly, but it certainly distressed Miss Watson and Miss Fogerty.

Every morning and evening Nelly had cleaned Thrush Green school with all the vigour of her thirteen stone. The classrooms, lobbies, windows – even the dingy old map-cupboard – were kept spotless. Nor had Nelly chided the children for stepping in snow or mud.

'So good-hearted,' mourned Miss Watson. 'And so *thorough*.' She lowered her voice. 'Did you know, Agnes, that she scoured the outside drains every morning? Scrupulously clean – scrupulously!'

'I can't think how poor Albert Piggott will manage without her,' said Miss Fogerty compassionately. 'He'll need someone there when he comes out of hospital.'

'Well now,' began Miss Watson, looking important, 'I heard a rumour that Molly might be back for a bit.'

'Splendid!' cried Miss Fogerty, clapping her small hands together. 'Dear Molly!'

'It's not *definite*, Agnes dear,' said Miss Watson severely. 'Don't repeat it, until we've had it confirmed. As you know, I cannot abide idle gossip. But certainly, that's what I heard.'

'I shan't breathe a word,' promised Miss Fogerty solemnly. 'But I do so hope you heard aright.'

She turned her attention to the hymn book in her hand. 'What shall we have this morning?' she asked her headmistress. ' "Jesus bids us shine"?'

'I am afraid it had better be a carol, dear. They still need plenty of practice before the concert "Away in a manger", perhaps?'

Miss Fogerty winced. 'Not again, please. I have to go through it so often.'

'Very well,' said Miss Watson indulgently. 'You choose, Agnes dear.'

'What about "Once in royal"?'

'Splendid,' said Miss Watson, looking about for a bell-ringer. Her eye lit upon Ben Lane who was engrossed in cleaning the doorknob with a spat-upon handkerchief.

'You may ring the bell, dear,' she said graciously. A tag from her well-worn college notes came into her mind.

'Always direct the child's energies into useful channels.'

Of course, she thought, a minute later, as the school bell rang out its warning to latecomers, we may need the children's labour to keep the school clean now that Nelly's gone. But Ben Lane's methods, of course, *would not* be countenanced.

Nothing had been heard from the departed lady. The oilman had left Lulling without giving anyone an address, so that neighbours put two and two together, as always, and this time came to the right conclusion. The love-birds had flown together.

The local paper had Albert Piggott's story in it. Not, of course, the story of his broken marriage, but a sensational one about his dramatic collapse.

'St Andrew's Sexton Found Unconscious' it said boldly. And in smaller print below: 'Timely Aid by Vicar'.

'I do wish,' said Charles Henstock, quite waspishly for such a kindly man, 'that papers would get their facts right. Everyone here knows I'm a *rector*.' He read the rest of the story with an expression of marked distaste on his chubby countenance, but his comment was typically Christian.

'Perhaps Nelly will see this, wherever she is, and come back to him.'

'More fool her if she does,' said Ella who was present.

She voiced the general sentiments of Thrush Green.

But the drama of the Piggotts was soon overshadowed by Phil Prior's sad news. Despite the fact that her husband seemed to be 'a proper fast one', as they had observed to each other, Thrush Green folk were sincerely shocked by the tragedy which had befallen the newcomer, who had so quickly become one of the community.

Harold Shoosmith, on his return, had gone at once to see Joan Young. The little boys were playing in the garden with Flo, the old spaniel, and he could speak openly.

'She's in a pretty bad state of shock, naturally,' he said, 'but wanted to go through this business alone. She'll ring tomorrow to let us know what's happening. I've told her to telephone me. I hope you don't mind? I'm there alone, and it might be awkward for you if the boys were within earshot.'

'By far the best thing,' agreed Joan. 'I hope she won't feel that she must hurry to get back to Jeremy – though I know she'll want to, of course. But he's a dear child, and fits in so happily.'

'There'll be a few formalities to go through, no doubt, but I should think she'll be back in about two or three days. It depends on the funeral arrangements.'

He walked to the window and stood staring across the

chestnut avenue to the green. Joan could see how worried he was and, woman-like, knew why without being told.

'Would you like to come and have dinner here tonight with us?' she asked impulsively. 'Edward and I would love it, if you are free.'

As though he knew what was in her mind, he turned quickly and smiled.

'You're very kind, but I ought to write a letter or two, and I want to let the Baileys know about this. Winnie will wonder what's happened when she sees the house in darkness.'

'I understand,' said Joan.

A little later she saw him crossing to the doctor's house, and thought what an attractive man he was.

'Phil could do a lot worse,' she thought, then chided herself for thinking of such things, when poor John Prior was not yet in his grave.

Jeremy had asked only a few questions about his mother's absence, for which Joan was truly thankful.

'Why has she gone to France? To see Daddy?'

'Yes,' said Joan.

'Why so quickly? Why didn't she take me?'

'Daddy had an accident in the car, so she went straight away.'

'He always drives fast,' said Jeremy, proudly. 'Once we did *ninety! Ninety!*' he repeated.

'My uncle,' said Paul, 'once did a hundred and thirty. And my friend Chris says his father did *two hundred* on a straight road in Norfolk!'

'Don't boast,' said Joan. But she was glad to have had the subject changed, nevertheless.

Harold found the Baileys, and Richard, taking their ease and watching, in a lack-lustre way, a programme on television. Winnie rose to switch it off as he entered.

'Oh please, don't let me interrupt anything you want to see,' cried Harold.

'It's a relief to switch it off,' said the doctor. 'We've been too idle to do so. It's one of those tiresome interviews where the interviewer is obsessed with the importance of prepositions. You know the sort of thing – "The Minister is here, AT this moment, to answer questions ON our policy IN regard TO our commitments." Dreadful stuff!'

'I'm so glad you've come in,' said Winnie. 'I was going to ask you about the garden next door. Do you think there is room for a rose bush or two? We thought we might give Phil a couple for Christmas.'

Harold looked at her quickly, and then at the doctor. 'Yes, I'm sure there's room for the roses. A lovely idea. As a matter of fact, it's Phil I've come about.'

He stopped, and the doctor thought how unusually exhausted he seemed.

'Richard, get us all a drink, there's a good fellow. Sherry, or whisky?'

'Sherry, please,' said Harold.

He sat in silence while Richard handed glasses, and then began again.

'I'm afraid she's had bad news of her husband.'

'The divorce is through?' Winnie looked puzzled.

'No. He's had a car crash. In France.'

'Dead, I suppose,' said the doctor quietly.

Harold nodded.

'Poor, poor girl!' said Winnie, her face puckered with distress. 'I must go round at once.'

'No,' said Harold, 'that's what I came to tell you. She's over there already.'

'On her own?' said Richard sharply. 'Surely not on her own.'

'She preferred it that way,' Harold replied.

'Did she fly?'

'Yes. I took her to Heathrow this morning.'

'I'll meet her when she returns,' said Richard. 'I don't like the idea of her being alone through an ordeal like this. I wish I'd known earlier.'

Harold felt some irritation at Richard's assumption that his presence was necessary to Phil's well-being, but he tried to speak calmly.

'The arrangements are settled about her return,' he said. 'Of course, no one knows yet which day it will be.'

'I can be free at any time,' said Richard.

Harold decided to ignore the remark, and turned to Winnie.

'Joan is taking care of Jeremy. He seems very cheerful there, and doesn't know the truth yet, of course.'

Doctor Bailey turned his glass thoughtfully round and round in his thin old hands.

'It is a dreadful affair. A young fellow like that. In his thirties, I suppose. She will be badly shaken, despite these last few months of separation.' He looked up at Harold. 'What about the practical side? This must mean the end of her allowance from him. Is there anything to leave, do you know?'

'I've no idea. They probably hadn't much between them. After all, they haven't been married very long – not long enough to amass much in the way of savings.'

'What about her writing?'

'Chicken feed, I should think,' interjected Richard, who was now walking about, hands in pockets, looking extremely agitated.

'How I wish she had parents to turn to!' cried Winnie. 'She's so alone in the world.'

It was the feeling which was uppermost too in Harold's mind, but he felt unable to speak about it at the moment.

'I thought you should know the news,' he said, rising to go. 'Do you have a key to Tullivers, by any chance? I thought I might go round the house and make sure the switches are off, and the windows closed, and so on. We left pretty hurriedly.'

'I know where one is hidden,' said Winnie. Country folk invariably know where 'the secret key' is kept by their neighbours. On occasions such as this, it is a useful piece of knowledge.

'It's in the garden shed,' continued Winnie, 'on the ledge on the right-hand side of the door, by the plant labels.'

'Good,' said Harold. 'I'll go and see to it now before it gets dark.'

'I'll come with you,' said Richard.

There was no earthly reason why he should be prevented, so that the two men walked together through the chilly dusk to Tullivers.

'My God,' said Richard, 'this is a fine thing! How will she manage? D'you think she'll move?'

'I've no idea. I don't think she'll want to.'

They plodded across the grass to the little shed which housed Phil's splendid new mower and the few poor broken tools which had distressed Harold by their uselessness. The key was carefully lodged behind the packet of plant labels, and they made their way to the front door.

Apart from a bathroom heater which had been left on, and a tap dripping at the kitchen sink, everything was in order. The scent of freesias hung about Phil's bedroom, bringing memories of her sharply to Harold.

'I know they didn't get on,' Richard said, as they descended the stairs, 'but this is a real blow for her. So damn final, death, isn't it?'

Harold made a noise of agreement. Richard's obvious agitation was surprising. He had not met the fellow very often, and had no idea that he knew Phil as well as this concern for her seemed to show. Harold found his anxiety a trifle alarming.

'We can't do anything yet,' he observed reasonably. 'We know nothing. One thing, she's a girl with plenty of courage and good sense. I'm sure she'll do nothing silly, or in a hurry.'

'She'll need advice,' said Richard.

'I understand she has a good solicitor,' replied Harold shortly.

He locked the front door, and put the key in his pocket. He intended to be the one to take charge of Tullivers while its owner was absent.

'If you'll excuse me,' he said politely, to Richard at the gate, 'I must get back.'

He set off homeward at a brisk pace, turning over this new development in Phil's affairs in his mind.

'And to think,' he said to himself as he opened his front door, 'that I chose to come to Thrush Green for a simple life!'

Winnie Bailey was taking coffee with Ella Bembridge the next morning when Dotty arrived bearing a large bundle of magazines, and the daily pint of goat's milk for Ella.

Thrush Green had a very sensible institution, started in wartime, called the magazine club. A number of residents each took a weekly or monthly magazine. They were collected together by one of the members and passed round in turn. In this way everyone saw a dozen or so journals regularly for the price of one. The rota had remained the same for years, only removals, or deaths, altering the system.

Ella took *Punch* although, as she said: 'It ceased to be funny after 1920.' The Baileys took *Country Life*, Harold *The Field*, Charles Henstock *The Church Times*, the Youngs weighed in with the *Spectator* and *The Listener* and Dotty contributed *The Lady* and *History Today*. Less intellectual matter was supplied by Ruth Lovell and various ladies at Lulling, and included 'really readable stuff', according to Dimity, who was no highbrow, such as *Woman*, *Woman's Own* and *Homes and Gardens*. It was interesting to note that these last three magazines were always the most well-thumbed when they came to be passed on. *The Field*, *The Church Times* and the *Spectator* remained immaculate for quite a time.

'Heard the news?' inquired Dotty, unwinding a long scarf from her stringy neck, and dropping the bundle of magazines in the process.

The ladies bent down to put the bundle together again, Dotty uttering little cries of self-reproach the while.

'No harm done,' said Ella, straightening up. 'Have some coffee, Dot?'

'Thank you. I must say I was very surprised to hear about it.'

'About what?' asked Winnie carefully. She had just told Ella the sad news about John Prior, but had not realized that it might have reached as far as Lulling Woods already.

'A very good thing really,' continued Dotty. 'It had to come some time.'

'How d'you mean?' asked Winnie cautiously.

'Well, I mean, we're all getting older every day. Can't expect to carry on for ever. Taking the long view we'll all be the better for it.'

'What on earth,' said Ella downrightly, 'are you maundering on about, Dotty?'

Dotty looked hurt. 'Albert Piggott, of course. His wife's gone off with the oilman, though how she could I just don't know. Such a vulgar fellow. Always talking about "the ladies", and "the fair sex", and "being a mere male". If it weren't for the fact that he comes right to the house with the paraffin, and carries very good old-fashioned wax tapers, I shouldn't allow him to call. Father would have shown him the door.'

'Yes, we had heard,' said Winnie.

There was an ominous hissing sound from the kitchen.

'Blast! The milk!' cried Ella, stumping off.

'I'm having mine black just now,' Dotty informed her when she returned.

Ella, speechless for once, exchanged a meaning glance with Winnie.

'And had you heard that Molly may be coming back?' asked Dotty. 'I do so hope that she and that nice Curdle boy settle here. Did you know that she taught him to read and write after they were married? He didn't have much schooling, shifting about with the fair. I thought it was so clever of her to do that.'

'And brave of him to try,' agreed Winnie. 'Some men would have been too self-conscious to admit their ignorance.'

The ladies sipped their coffee and Winnie was about to let Dotty know Phil Prior's news when Dotty herself mentioned the girl.

'I'm taking the last of the kittens to Tullivers this weekend. I must say I shall miss them sorely. They've all turned out remarkably well-behaved and intelligent. How's Tabitha doing?'

Dimity and Charles had chosen the tabby with exceptionally fine eyes. Dotty kept a vigilant eye and ear open for news of the various kittens.

'Scoffing down ox liver at four-and-six a pound,' said Ella, 'last time I saw her.'

'Oh, I do so hope dear Dimity isn't over-doing the protein,' cried Dotty. 'A little raw liver is *excellent*, of course, but too much can be rather heating. I must have a word with her.'

She rose to make her departure. Winnie got up too. This seemed the time to break the news.

'I should leave the kitten for a little longer,' said Winnie. 'Phil Prior is away for a few days. In France, in fact.'

'At this time of year?' protested Dotty. 'If anything, the weather's worse than in England.'

'It's no pleasure trip,' Winnie said gravely. 'Her husband had an accident there. I'm sorry to say he has died. She's gone over to see about things.'

Dotty stood transfixed for a moment at the enormity of the news.

When she spoke, it was with her usual breathtaking directness. 'Sad, of course,' she said, picking up the disreputable scarf, 'but it simplifies things a lot. Harold Shoosmith will be able to go ahead now, won't he?'

She preceded a stunned Winnie Bailey to the door, thanked Ella for the coffee, and bustled away down the path, her skinny legs, in their thick speckled stockings, twinkling energetically.

'Sometimes,' said Winnie faintly, 'I wonder if Dotty is clairvoyant.'

'She's an old witch,' responded Ella roundly.

16. HAROLD THINKS THINGS OUT

Phil Prior was away for four days. She rang Harold and Joan on alternate evenings and was mightily relieved to hear how little Jeremy appeared to miss her.

Everyone was being incredibly kind and helpful, she told

them. Formalities had been hurried through, and she would return immediately after the funeral. John's parents had met her out there, and they were doing their best to comfort each other. Her plane was due to arrive at five-thirty, and she was longing to get back to the haven of Thrush Green and all her friends.

During her absence, Harold had plenty of time for thought. This tragedy had quickened his affection and admiration for the girl, and his determination to do all in his power to help her. Whether, in the distant future when she had recovered from the blow, she could ever contemplate marriage again, he had no idea. Whether he himself really wanted to give up his serene bachelorhood, he was not sure. But one thing he did know – if he ever should marry, then the only person he wanted was Phil.

He took several long solitary walks in the few days of Phil's absence, trying to come to terms with this new surprising feeling which so strangely moved him. The weather was mild and quiet, overcast and vaguely depressing, as though the world were in waiting for some momentous happening. Away from the domestic bustle of Christmas, the countryside was infinitely soothing, Harold found.

He found himself noting things with newly-awakened observation and sensibility. Tiny spears of snowdrop leaves were pushing through. Already the honeysuckle showed minute leafy rosettes, and in the still morning air, a thousand droplets quivered on the spikes of the hawthorn hedge.

Percy Hodge's black and white cows gazed at him over the gate, their long eyelashes rimed with mist, their sweet breath forming clouds in the quiet air. A thrush, head cocked sideways, listened intently to the moving of a mole just beneath the surface of the grass verge. In Lulling Woods the trees dripped gently, their trunks striped with moisture, while underfoot the damp leaves deadened every footfall.

He returned from these lonely walks much refreshed in spirit, even if any sort of decision still evaded him. It was good to escape from people, now and again, and a positive relief to be away from Betty Bell's boisterous activities. The coming of Christmas seemed to rouse her to even greater energy, and carpets were beaten within an inch of their lives, pillows shaken until the feathers began to escape, paint was washed, windows polished and all to the accompaniment of joyful singing which Harold had not the heart to suppress.

'Got all your presents tied up?' asked Betty, busily winding up the Hoover cord into an intricate figure-of-eight arrangement, which Harold detested. It was useless to tell her that this was a strain on the covering of the cord cable. Figures-of-eight Betty Bell had always done, and would continue to do until her hand grew too frail to push the Hoover. Harold averted his eyes from the operation.

'Yes, Betty. I think everything's ready.'

'Want a Christmas tree?'

'No thanks.'

'Holly? Ivy? Anythink o' that?'

'Well, perhaps a little holly –'

'Fine. I'll send the kids out. Don't want to waste good money in the market, do you?'

'No,' agreed Harold. 'But only a sprig or two, Betty, please. I can't cope with a lot of stuff.'

'I'll see you right,' Betty assured him, flickering his desk energetically, and knocking his fountain pen to the floor.

Harold retrieved it patiently.

'I suppose there's nothing 'eard from that Nelly Tilling? Piggott, I should say.'

'Not as far as I know.'

'Miss Watson's in a fine old taking,' said Betty conversationally. 'Talking of getting that Mrs Cooke back as lives up Nidden way. Must be hard up to want her to take over the school cleaning. Proper slummocky ha'porth, she is. Ever seen her?'

'I don't think so.'

'Once seen never forgotten.' Betty burst into a peal of laughter, as she picked up the Hoover, ready to depart to the kitchen. 'Ugly as sin, and could do with a good wash. You wouldn't fancy anything as she'd cooked, I can tell you. Ham omelette do you?'

'Beautifully,' said Harold.

Betty bore away the Hoover, and slammed the study door with such vigour that it set a silver vase ringing on the mantelpiece.

Harold wandered to the window and looked out upon empty Thrush Green and the quiet countryside beyond. The lines of a hymn floated into his mind.

> Where every prospect pleases
> And only man is vile

Perhaps not 'vile', Harold thought forgivingly, but distracting certainly.

Two days before Albert Piggott's release from hospital, Molly Curdle arrived at her old home with her little son, George, an energetic toddler.

Ben, who had brought her, was obliged to return to his work, but promised to spend Sunday with his family. It was the first time the couple had been parted since their marriage, and Molly felt forlorn as she watched him drive away.

However, there was plenty to do at the neglected cottage, and she set to with her customary vigour. In the afternoon she was delighted to receive a visit from Joan Young, who was bearing a pretty little Christmas decoration of holly, Christmas roses and variegated ivy, set in a mossy base.

The two young women greeted each other affectionately, and George was admired by Joan, as much as the posy was admired by Molly.

'I can't tell you how lovely it is to have you back,' said Joan sincerely. 'How long can you stop?'

'Well, Ben and I hope it won't be for longer than a fortnight, but it depends on Dad. You know what he's like. He'd sooner manage on his own, I know, but he can't do that just yet.'

'No news of Nelly?'

'None. But she won't show up again, I'm positive. And frankly, I don't blame her. We never thought it would last.'

'Bring George to tea tomorrow,' said Joan. 'Paul's longing to see you and to show you off to his new friend Jeremy.'

Molly agreed with pleasure. She had always loved the Youngs' house, and had been very happy working there. She had learnt a great deal about managing children from looking after Paul as a young child, and this experience was standing her in good stead in bringing up George.

The tea party was much enjoyed. There was a rapturous reunion between Paul and Molly, and George enjoyed being the centre of attention.

It was the last day of Molly's freedom, for the next morning her father arrived from the hospital and was put comfortably to bed.

She had expected him to be a demanding patient, but was surprised by his docility. Hospital discipline seemed to have improved Albert's manners. At times he was almost grateful for Molly's attentions. It couldn't last for ever, Molly told herself philosophically, but while it did, she enjoyed this rare spell of good behaviour.

His first short walk was across to St Andrew's church. It was not being cared for in the way he thought proper, as he pointed out to the rector when he called, but nevertheless he admitted grudgingly that it could be a lot worse. This was high praise indeed, from Albert, and the rector was suitably impressed.

'I really feel that affliction has mellowed Albert,' he told Dimity on his return to the rectory.

'Don't speak too soon,' his wife replied sagely.

Phil's plane was due to arrive at half past five and Harold set off from Thrush Green soon after three o'clock.

The same quiet grey weather continued, with a raw coldness in the air which the weather-wise said was a sure sign of snow to come. But despite the bleak outlook, Harold was in good heart. To be driving to meet Phil again was enough to raise anyone's spirits. How would she be, he wondered? He thought of the numbed silence of the drive to the airport, with the pale girl suffering beside him.

He remembered the two ladies 'painted to the eyes' who had sat beside Phil as they drank their coffee. Out of the blue came the verse which Phil's parents must have had in mind when they chose their daughter's name.

> The ladies of St James's!
> They're painted to the eyes,
> Their white it stays for ever,

Their red it never dies:
But Phyllida, my Phyllida!
Her colour comes and goes;
It trembles to a lily, –
It wavers to a rose.

Sentimental, maybe, thought Harold as he threaded his way through the traffic, but how light and elegant! He turned the lines over in his mind, relishing their old-fashioned charm. It didn't do, he told himself, to dwell too long on 'trembling to a lily' and 'wavering to a rose'. One might as well say, 'it wobbles to a wallflower –'.

Harold checked his straying thoughts. Whatever the merits of the poem, without doubt his favourite line was:

But Phyllida, my Phyllida!

The years fell from him as he said it silently to himself.

The plane was punctual, and Phil smiled when her eyes lit upon him. She looked wan and somehow smaller than when she left, but her voice was steady when she greeted him.

He tucked a rug round her protectively when they reached the car.

'Heavens, how lovely! It's colder here than in France. My parents-in-law are flying back tomorrow and wanted me to stay on for another night, but now that all has been done – all the *awful* things – I wanted to hurry back to Jeremy.'

Harold told her that the boy had been wonderfully cheerful, but was longing to have her back.

'Do you know,' said Phil, as they neared Thrush Green, 'that when the constable told me the ghastly news, my first thought was: "I shan't have to tell Jeremy about the divorce." And then, "Thank God, I shan't have to go through all that wretched court business." It's a shameful thing, I suppose, to admit, but I felt I must tell someone, and you are just about the most under-standing person to confess to.'

'It strikes me as a reasonable reaction,' replied Harold soberly. 'You've been dreading breaking the news for months now. It didn't mean that your grief was any the less. That, if I may say so, was quite evident.'

There was a long pause before the girl spoke again.

'It seems as though I've died twice. Once when he left me, and then when I heard of his death. Even now, after all this time apart, I can't imagine life without John. Whatever happens, you simply can't wipe away years of married life. The sense of loss is far, far greater than ever I imagined it would be. It's like losing an arm or a leg – some vital part. I suppose one grows numb with time, and other things happen to cover the scar, but I'm sure it will always be there. Thank God I've got Jeremy, and work to do!' she added. 'Without those two things I think I should sink.'

'Never!' said Harold stoutly. 'You'll never sink. You're far too brave for that.'

They climbed the steep hill to Thrush Green. It was dark, and the lighted windows looked welcoming to the tired girl. The lights were on at Tullivers, and she looked inquiringly at Harold.

'Betty Bell and Winnie between them have made you and Jeremy a little supper, I believe. We all thought you'd prefer to be alone the first night, but if you would sooner have company, then do, please, spend the evening with me.'

Phil shook her head, smiling.

'You've thought of everything. I'll never be able to thank you properly. I couldn't have got through this week of nightmare without you, Harold dear.'

He helped her in with her case. In the hall Jeremy and Winnie met her. After painful hugs from her son, Phil stood looking at the welcoming flowers, the fire and the table set for two.

'Something smells delicious,' she said, sniffing the air.

'Chicken casserole,' said Winnie. 'Betty's left it all ready to serve.'

'I didn't know, until this minute, how hungry I was,' confessed Phil. 'Stop and share it, both of you.'

'No indeed,' said Winnie, 'I'm off to see to my two menfolk.'

'I'll call in the morning,' said Harold. 'Sleep well!'

Phil and Jeremy watched them depart down the path before returning to the firelit dining-room.

'It's so lovely to come home,' said Phil. 'I've missed you so much.'

'Me too,' said Jeremy cheerfully, and began to tell her about the wonders of Paul Young's electric railway. The saga continued all through the meal, leaving Phil free to consider the terrible problem of when to break the news. She felt that she really could not face any more that day. It must wait until morning, she decided.

She took the boy upstairs to the bathroom and left him in the bath while she unpacked her case.

When she returned to give him a final inspection, she found him sitting very still, gazing into the distance.

'He's dead, isn't he?' he said softly.

There was no mistaking his meaning, and Phil made no pretence.

'Yes, Jeremy,' she answered.

There was silence, broken only by the plopping of water dripping from a tap.

'Tell me, darling,' she said, very gently, 'how did you know?'

He looked up at her, wide-eyed and tearless.

'I saw it in your face.'

17. Richard Contemplates Matrimony

The mild quiet weather continued over the Christmas season, and the inhabitants of Thrush Green were divided in their feelings towards the such unseasonably balmy weather.

The pessimists pulled long faces. 'A green Christmas means a full churchyard,' they pointed out. 'A nice sharp frost or two is what we want. Kills off the germs.'

'Kills off the old 'uns too,' retorted the warmth-lovers. 'Give us a nice mild winter – germs and all!'

The church had been lovingly decked by Winnie, Dimity, Ella and other Thrush Green ladies. Albert Piggott was still kept in bed for most of the day by Doctor Lovell, and his temper was fast deteriorating to its normal stage of moroseness. His condition was not improved by seeing fat Willie Bond, the postman, looking after St Andrew's, while he himself was laid up. There had never been any love lost between the two men since the time that Willie's vegetable marrow had beaten Albert's, by a bare inch in girth and length, at Lulling Flower Show two years earlier.

Molly was beginning to wonder how long she would have to stay with her trying old father. Ben came every weekend, but it was obvious that he was becoming impatient at the delay, and resentful of the old man's carping attitude to his poor hard-working Molly.

'It can't be helped,' Molly said, doing her best to pour oil on troubled waters. 'It won't be much longer, Ben. The minute the doctor says he can be left, I'm flying back to you and our caravan.'

And with such limited consolation Ben had to be content.

Christmas, for Phil Prior, was made less painful by the kindness of her neighbours. Jeremy's natural joy in the festivities found fulfilment at the Youngs' house, where a children's party and innumerable presents helped to put his father's tragedy into the background. The arrival of the long-awaited kitten added to his excitement. But inevitably, it was more difficult for his mother. Memories of past Christmases were inescapable.

She saw again John lighting the red candles on the Christmas tree, with wide-eyed two-year-old Jeremy gazing with wonder at each new flame. John pulling crackers, and showing Jeremy the small fireworks inside – setting fire to the 'serpent's egg', waving a minute sparkler, making a flaming paper balloon rise to the ceiling, whilst Jeremy applauded excitedly. John wrapping her in a scarlet cashmere dressing gown, which she considered madly extravagant, but adorable of him. John had always been at his best at Christmas, gay, funny, sweet, considerate. It was more than Phil could bear to think that he would never again be there to make Christmas sparkle for her.

It was strange, she thought, how the bitterness of the last year was so little remembered. The humiliation, the misery, the wretched effort of keeping things from Jeremy, were all submerged beneath the remembrances of earlier shared happiness. She marvelled at this phenomenon, but was humbly grateful that her mind worked in this way. When the subject of his father cropped up, which was not very often, Phil found that she could speak of him with true affection, keeping alive for the little boy his early memories of a loving father.

She was relieved when the New Year arrived and things returned to normal. Jeremy started school during the first week in January, and she was glad to see him engrossed in his own school affairs and friendships again. Meanwhile, she set herself to work with renewed determination.

It was plain that she must work doubly hard. John's affairs had been left tidily, with a will leaving his wife everything unconditionally. But when all had been settled, it seemed that Phil could expect a sum of only about six thousand pounds which included one or two insurances, and the sale of the furniture at the Chelsea flat. The flat itself was rented, and the firm for which he had worked had no pension schemes for dependants. There was no doubt about it – things were going to be tight if she decided to continue to live at Tullivers.

But she was determined to stay there. She loved the little house and she loved Thrush Green. The friends she had made were the dependable, kindly sort of people whose company would give her pleasure and support in the years to come, as their affection towards her, in these last few terrible weeks, had shown so clearly. She had settled in Thrush Green as snugly as a bird in its nest, and so had Jeremy. Whatever the cost, Tullivers must remain their home.

Winnie Bailey had grown particularly dear to Phil since John's death. Quiet and loving, unobtrusive, but always available, Phil found herself looking upon her as the mother she unconsciously missed. Winnie lived with anxieties herself. She knew, only too well, that her husband could not live much longer. Only constant care and rest had kept him alive so long, and the doctor himself was well aware of the fact.

'I'm living on "borrowed time", as dear old Mrs Curdle used to say,' he said matter-of-factly. 'And very lucky I am to have these few extra years.'

His complete absence of self-pity made things more bearable for Winnie, but the secret sadness was always there, and made her doubly sympathetic towards the young widow next door.

Richard, too, was unusually attentive, and made himself

useful by mending a faulty lock, an electric kettle, and a pane of glass broken by Jeremy's football. He would like to have taken Phil to the theatre one evening in Oxford, but decided against it.

'The pantomime is at the New until heaven knows when,' he told his aunt impatiently, 'and the Playhouse have three weeks of something translated from the Czech by a Frenchman, which is set in near darkness with long sessions of complete silence. I don't think Phil would find it very cheering, at the moment.'

'Take her out to lunch,' said Winnie. 'I think she'd prefer that. I know she likes to be at home when Jeremy gets back after school. He can come here for his lunch that day.'

Richard brightened. 'Kingham Mill, perhaps? The Old Swan at Minster Lovell? The Shaven Crown at Shipton-under-Wychwood?'

'Ask Phil,' advised Winnie. And so he did.

The day of their jaunt together was clear and cold. There had been a sharp frost, and the grass was still white in the shade when Phil went to the Baileys for a drink before setting off. She found Winnie and the doctor alone, but sundry thumps overhead proclaimed that Richard was getting ready.

'He's becoming quite a Beau Brummell,' said Winnie. 'You are a good influence, Phil.'

'I don't know about that,' said her husband lightly. 'He's taking the day off for this spree.'

'Heavens!' exclaimed Phil. 'I hope I'm not taking him from his work!'

'Do him good to have a break,' said his aunt firmly.

There was a particularly heavy crash above, as though a drawer had been pulled out, too abruptly and too far, and had landed on the floor.

'It reminds me,' said the doctor ruminatively, 'of the remark made by Dr Thompson, of Cambridge, sometime in the last century. He said of Richard Jebb: "The time that Mr Jebb can spare from the adornment of his person, he devotes to the neglect of his duties." I hope that our Richard will appear as elegantly turned out as his namesake when he *does* appear.'

He certainly looked uncommonly spruce, Phil thought, when at last he arrived, full of apologies.

'And so bad for the system, fussing and fuming,' he added.

'Otto's paper on the consequences of an overflow of adrenalin upon the digestive system is always present in my mind when I begin to get worked up. Truly horrifying, his findings were! Remind me to lend the pamphlet to you sometime.'

Ella was stumping up the path as the pair made their way to the car. They greeted each other, and Ella watched the car drive away.

'Where are they off?' asked Ella abruptly.

'They're having lunch at The Swan,' replied Winnie. 'Come in, Ella.'

'They're not making a match of things, are they? "Going steady", as they say?'

'Really!' expostulated Winnie. 'How ridiculous you are, Ella! Richard is simply showing a little kindness to the poor girl!'

'That's a change for Richard,' observed Ella. 'What's he hoping to get out of it?'

Winnie drew a long breath, and then let it out slowly. She had known Ella long enough to forgive her behaviour.

'What can I do for you, dear?' she asked mildly. Winnie's self-control was admirable.

The departure of the two together had been observed by several other people on Thrush Green.

Little Miss Fogerty, taking a physical education period with the infants, noticed Jeremy's mother entering the car. The children were ostensibly playing in four groups with suitable apparatus. Jeremy's group was nearest the playground railings, each child struggling to ply a skipping rope. Most of the little girls were twirling theirs adroitly enough, with expressions of smug superiority on their infant faces.

The boys, including Jeremy, were bouncing energetically but becoming hopelessly entangled with their ropes. It was whilst he was engaged in extricating himself from the loops round his ankles that Jeremy noticed his mother, and rushed to the fence to wave enthusiastically. Miss Fogerty, following his gaze, noted that Mrs Prior was accompanied – and by a bachelor!

'And so soon,' thought Miss Fogerty, sadly shocked.

'There's my mummy!' shouted Jeremy excitedly. 'And

Richard! They're going to Minster Lovell. And Mrs Baileys' giving me lunch.'

'Lovely, dear,' said Miss Fogerty primly. But there was something in her tone which made Jeremy look up quickly at her little button mouth.

He resumed his clumsy skipping thoughtfully.

Harold Shoosmith was equally thoughtful. He had waved his hat cheerfully at the distant pair, as he crossed the green on his way to see Charles Henstock, but he could not ignore the involuntary spasm of concern which gripped him. Damn that fellow, Richard! He was making a confounded nuisance of himself.

As for Betty Bell, strategically placed for observation by cleaning the inside of the bedroom windows, her reactions were as straightforward as Ella's.

'*She's* not losing much time!' said Betty tartly.

The keen-eyed watchers of Thrush Green would have been singularly disappointed if they could have witnessed the innocent happenings at Minster Lovell.

The village, peaceful in its winter emptiness, showed little movement. A few wisps of blue smoke curled from the honey-coloured stone chimneys. An aged cocker spaniel, white round the muzzle, ambled vaguely along the green verge, sniffing here at a gatepost, there at a drystone wall.

The river Windrush purled placidly along, dimpling under the bridge, the current criss-crossed by the willow branches trailing on its surface. The ancient inn drowsed in the winter sunlight, and welcomed them with a great log fire which whispered, rather than roared. A white-haired old lady, dozing in a leather chair, scarcely stirred as they entered.

The entire village seemed to be wrapped in dreams – an atmosphere which Phil found wholly in keeping with her present state of suspended animation. Since John's death, she had gone about her daily life automatically, as though she were enclosed in an invisible shell which cut her off from everything around her. Her senses were still numbed, her reactions slow, her thoughts, when she wrote or spoke, seemed to drop from her with deadly deliberation, as slowly and stickily as cold treacle from a spoon.

If Richard could have known he would have been surprised and hurt to realize that it was this apathy which had made Phil accept his invitation in the first place. It was easier to accept than to produce an excuse when the young man had pressed her, but in truth she would have been happier getting on with a story which she had in mind.

Nevertheless, she was grateful for Richard's kindness, and believed that Winnie was glad to see them both having a brief break. She would hate to hurt Winnie, after all her concern.

The lunch was excellent, and Phil was content to let Richard do the major part of the talking. She found him interesting and remarkably astute when talking about his work, but incredibly naïve in his attitude to people.

'He's just not interested in them,' thought Phil to herself, watching him demolish caramel custard with a few swift movements. In fact, the only person he ever seemed to mention with any sort of feeling was the redoubtable Professor Otto Goldstein. And on this subject, Richard was, without any doubt, the most crashing bore, Phil decided.

They had coffee alone by the whispering log fire, which shed a few white flakes of ash every now and again, as if to prove that the natural laws of gravity still held good even in this spellbound lotus-land. Afterwards, they strolled up the somnolent village street towards the ruined priory. The cocker spaniel, exhausted by his morning exercise, lay sprawled on his side in the shelter of a sunny wall. He did not stir as they passed.

Walking across the shorn grass and ancient stone paths of the ruins, a wonderful sense of peace crept over Phil. Richard stopped to study a map of the site, and she walked alone into the roofless hall and gazed at the tracery of the empty windows framing the pale blue skies of winter. A lone blackbird was perched upon one of the stone vaultings, and piped a few melancholy notes, as clear as the river water that ran nearby, and as round as the washed pebbles beneath it.

What had these venerable walls witnessed in their time, Phil wondered? Passion in plenty, bloodshed without doubt: but also piety, perseverance and simple happiness. How many people had stood here, as she did now, puzzled, unhappy, numb with pain and perplexity? And how many had found comfort in the knowledge of the continuity of life, of being but one link in a long chain of human experience, in this old, old setting?

Somehow, thought Phil, feeling the grey roughness of the ancient stones with her bare cold hand, one's own sufferings were put into perspective in the face of this survivor of the centuries. For the first time, since John had left her, a tiny tremor of hope ran through her – the faint stirring of life renewed.

They drove back slowly. Although it was barely three o'clock, the sun was low on the horizon, and the shadows of the trees lay long and straight across the bare winter fields.

'I've enjoyed it so much,' said Phil. 'It was kind of you to give me such a treat. I feel better for it.'

'I hope we can do this again,' replied Richard. 'But, of course, I shan't be at Thrush Green much longer.'

'Why, is the work nearly finished?'

'Practically. I shall have to go back to London within two or three months.'

There was a pause, while he negotiated a sharp double bend expertly, and then he spoke again.

'Would you think of coming to live in town?'

Instantly, Phil was on her guard. From his tone it was clear that the two words 'with me' might well have been added. The happy daze engendered by Minster Lovell and the sunshine fled instantly, and Phil was suddenly alert. This was a possibility of which she had not really been aware.

'I want to settle in Thrush Green,' she replied carefully. 'Both Jeremy and I are very happy there.'

'I should think you might get bored. Not many people of our age there. Besides, if you were in town you'd be on the spot for meeting your editors, wouldn't you?'

'I go up about once in three weeks to discuss things with Frank,' said Phil. 'It seems quite often enough to plan the work ahead. I'm sure I shouldn't want to call into the office more frequently, even if I were nearer.'

Richard did not reply, and Phil sensed that he was a little put out. The car's speed increased considerably, and a muscle twitched in his cheek.

Really, thought Phil, emotions of any kind were very tiresome. What was more, they were horribly exhausting. She hoped that she was wrong in imagining that Richard was interested in her – or rather, in matrimony.

She pondered on the subject as they neared Thrush Green. No doubt Richard had reached the stage when domesticity had its appeal. She suspected that anyone reasonably attractive and companionable would be eligible to Richard just now, and did not delude herself by thinking that her own personal charms had fired the young man. To be honest, would *anything* fire him?

She recalled Doctor Baileys' words. 'Richard's a cold fish,' he had said to her once. 'I'm afraid the only person Richard considers is – Richard!'

They drove up the hill from Lulling to Thrush Green. The sun had vanished behind Lulling Woods and a sharp little wind reminded the world that it was still January.

Phil sighed. It had been a lovely day, despite this small cloud between them. And whatever happened, she had Richard to thank for taking her to the tranquil ruins of Minster Lovell, and that sudden miraculous glimpse of life again after the long months following John's desertion. For that, she would always be grateful to him.

She thanked him sincerely at her gate, and he did his best to smile in return.

But there was something tight-lipped about the smile, which made it plain that Richard had been crossed, and did not like it.

Albert Piggott was one of those who saw the return of the couple. He was standing at his cottage window gazing gloomily across the green.

Willie Bond had just entered St Andrew's with a slightly pompous air of ownership which Albert found intensely irritating. What was that fat lump going to muck up now, he wondered?

He looked beyond the church to the car from which Phil emerged, his mouth curving downwards with distaste.

'Fine goings-on,' grunted Albert to Molly, who was trying to dress her fidgety son for his afternoon's outing.

'Hold still, do!' said Molly sharply. 'What goings-on, Dad?'

'That young widder-woman. Setting her cap at Mrs Baileys' young fellow. Not that he's much catch, Lord alone knows, but it ain't hardly decent to go running after the men with her own poor chap scarce cold in 'is grave.'

'Maybe he's just given her a lift up from the shops,' said Molly reasonably, controlling her temper.

Albert gave a disbelieving snort. 'That's a likely tale!'

Molly buttoned George's coat with unnecessary violence.

'The trouble with you, Dad, is you always thinks the worst of folks. You can't wonder you haven't got any friends.'

Albert bridled. 'Whatcher mean, no friends? What about them next door?'

'They sell beer,' said Molly roundly. 'You're a good customer. They're kind-hearted, I know, but you look around – there's not one true friend to your name!'

'That's right!' said Albert, adopting a quavering tone. 'You pitch into your poor ol' dad, just when he's too weak to stand up for hisself. I don't know what the world's comin' to when children turn on their parents. I does my best – ill though I be – to give no trouble, but you've got no proper feelings in you, you wicked hussy!'

Molly bit back the flow of words which she would willingly have poured forth, dumped George from the table to the floor, and tugged him smartly outdoors into the blessed calm of Thrush Green.

This couldn't go on, she fumed to herself, watching George stagger across to the steps which supported the statue of Nathaniel Patten, Thrush Green's famous missionary son. Jumping from the steps was the little boy's favourite activity, and Molly was glad to see him engaged so happily while she studied her problem.

When Ben had come the weekend before, Albert appeared to be rather worse, but whether this was wholly physical, or simply a way of drawing attention to himself, it was difficult to say. In any case, Molly had discussed with Ben the possibility of making their home at the cottage, in order to look after the old man.

Ben's face had clouded. 'Can't be done,' he said slowly. 'I know how you feel, but it's not right for you or George – or me, for that matter.'

He had looked across at the churchyard where his redoubtable old grandmother lay at rest.

'And Gran,' he added, 'wouldn't have let me give up her fair. And quite right too.'

'Perhaps just for the winters?' pleaded Molly, torn both ways. 'When the fair's laid up?'

'Well, I'll think about it, my love, but I don't like the idea and that's flat. You'll be nothing but a skivvy, and I'm not having that.'

Now, watching George clambering up the steps on all fours, she knew that Ben was right. She could stand it no longer. Plans would have to be made to see that the old man was provided for, and she would have a good talk with Doctor Lovell to make sure that he was not being left too soon. But go, eventually, she must.

And so, unwittingly, Phil and Richard's jaunt had brought matters to a head, in the cottage across the green, nudging into motion Albert Piggott's particular wheel of fortune.

18. Harold Entertains an Old Friend

One morning in February, Willie Marchant tacked up the hill to Thrush Green and delivered a letter to Harold Shoosmith.

Later that day Harold walked across to see Phil.

'Frank's coming down for the weekend,' he told her. 'I'm so pleased. Now I shall have a chance to repay the dozens of times I stayed at Frank's house when his wife was alive. They were so good to me when I came home on leave.'

'Bring him over for a drink,' invited Phil.

'Thank you. I know he'd love to see the cottage. But I really came to ask you and Jeremy to lunch one day, while he's here. I must get Betty Bell to whip up something rather special. He's thoroughly spoilt by Violet who housekeeps for him.'

'So Richard tells me,' said Phil.

'Richard?' exclaimed Harold. 'How does he know?'

'They belong to the same club, I gather,' said Phil, picking the kitten out of a box of new typing paper in which it was settling for a nap.

'I didn't realize they knew each other,' said Harold, looking a little put out. 'Well, well! Shall we say about twelve o'clock on Saturday?'

'That would be lovely,' agreed Phil. 'And what's more I'll give him my week's work to take back with him, and save postage.'

'That's admirably thrifty,' commented Harold with approval.

'Needs must,' laughed Phil. 'By nature I'm rather like the Flopsy Bunnies, "very improvident and cheerful", but I have to discipline myself these days.'

'How are things going, seriously?' asked Harold, emboldened by her own introduction of ways and means.

'Not too badly. I've had an introduction, through Frank, to an editor who's in charge of a number of local papers in the Midlands, and I'm starting a series of articles for him. Pretty good pay, too.'

'That's cheering news,' said Harold, rising to go. 'But don't work too hard. You ought to be having some fun now and again. What about a day out soon? Jeremy too, of course, if you'd like to bring him.'

'There's nothing I'd enjoy more,' said Phil, and meant it.

Jeremy had found a new interest since the arrival of the kitten. He had called on Dotty Harmer to report the cat's progress, and discovered the wholly delightful mode of life at the old lady's cottage.

There was no nonsense about wiping feet before entry, or having clean hands, or respectable clothing. If you arrived in the middle of one of Dotty's sketchy meals, it didn't seem to matter. As likely as not, she would be consuming a light repast as she stood at her stove or walked about the house on other affairs. As far as Jeremy could see, the meal usually consisted of a piece of brown bread, liberally spread with butter, a rough lump of cheese, and some unidentifiable leaves, by way of a salad. This seemed to be eaten at any time, followed by the crunching of a home-grown apple. Jeremy was always offered one too, and found this largesse much to his liking.

But better by far than the informality of Dotty's welcome, and the present of the apple, was the large number of animals which made up Dotty's family. The goats, in particular, fascinated the boy and he even drank the milk whilst it was still warm from the animal, with uncommon relish, which Dotty heartily approved.

One spring Saturday morning he bounded down the path by Albert Piggott's cottage and gained the path leading to Dotty's and finally to Lulling Woods. The air was balmy, his spirits high, and he carried a large bunch of grass and greenery from the hedges as a present for Daisy, the milker, and Dulcie, the younger goat.

Charles Henstock privately thought that Dulcie was poorly named – neither sweet nor gentle, and very quick to use her horns on unsuspecting visitors, as he had found to his cost one wet day. His clerical grey trousers had never completely recovered from their immersion in the puddle in which Dulcie's sly butting had landed him. Jeremy, however, was rather more alert to Dulcie's wiles, and his passion for her was unclouded.

On this particular morning he found Dotty in a somewhat agitated mood. She was having difficulty in fixing a chain to

Dulcie's collar. Daisy, taking advantage of the disturbance, was adding gleefully to the chaos by bleating continuously, and rushing round and round in circles so that her tethering chain was soon shortened to a couple of feet. This gave her the opportunity to bleat even more madly, puffing noisily between bleats to prove how sorely she was being tried.

Dulcie, unduly skittish, kicked up her heels every time that Dotty approached her. Dotty, red in the face, greeted Jeremy shortly.

'Get Daisy undone, boy, will you? And give her some of that stuff you've brought to stop her row.'

Jeremy obediently accomplished this task. In the comparative peace that followed, Dotty captured the younger goat, and sighed noisily with relief.

'Where's Dulcie going?' asked Jeremy.

'To be mated,' said Dotty flatly.

'What d'you mean – *mated*?' queried Jeremy.

'Married, then,' said Dotty, hitching up a stocking in a preoccupied way.

'*Married*? But only *people* get married!' exclaimed Jeremy.

'I know that,' said Dotty, nettled. Dulcie began to tug powerfully at her lead.

'But you said –'

'Here, you clear off home,' said Dotty forthrightly. 'I'm up to my eyes this morning, as you can see.'

The boy retreated very slowly backwards. 'Will she have baby goats when she's been mated?'

'*Kids*, you mean,' said Dotty pedantically. 'Do use the right expressions, child.'

'Well, will she?'

'What?' said Dotty, stalling for time.

'Have baby goats. Kids, I mean?'

'Maybe,' said Dotty, with unusual caution. Difficult to know how much children knew about the facts of life these days, and anyway it wasn't her business to enlighten this one.

'Can I have one when they come, Miss Harmer?' begged Jeremy longingly. '*Please* can I?'

Dotty's slender stock of patience suddenly ran out at her heels like gunpowder. Her voice roared out like a cannon.

'Look, boy! I don't know *if* she'll have kids, *when* she'll have kids, or if your mother would let you have one if she *did* have kids! You're far too inquisitive, and a confounded nuisance. Get off home!'

She raised a skinny, but powerful, arm, and Dulcie, sensing joyous combat, lowered her head for action. In the face of this combined attack, Jeremy fled, but even as he ran determined to come again as soon as things at Dotty's had returned once more to their usual chaotic normality.

Meanwhile, he decided, slackening his pace as the distance between Dotty's and his own breathless form increased, he must set about persuading his mother that a little kid would be very useful for keeping Tullivers' grass down. But, somehow, he sensed that that would be an uphill battle.

Frank arrived the following weekend, in the midst of a torrential rainstorm. Ella Bembridge, struggling to shut an upstairs window to keep out the deluge, was the first to see the beautiful sleek Jaguar creep through Harold's gateway. She knew whose it must be, for Dimity had told her all about Harold's friend, his redoubtable Violet, and the fact that he was a busy editor. If Frank had been aware how much was known about him already at Thrush Green he would have been very surprised.

'What a welcome for you!' exclaimed Harold, opening the front door. 'Come in, my dear fellow, before you are wet through.'

He showed his friend to his bedroom and went downstairs again to prepare drinks. From the kitchen, delicious smells of lunch emanated.

'Not quite up to Violet's standards, I'm afraid,' said Harold, when his friend reappeared, 'but pretty good, nevertheless. By the way, Mrs Prior and her boy are joining us for lunch.'

'How nice!' said Frank. 'Whereabouts is her house?'

Harold pointed out Tullivers through the veils of slashing rain.

'If this doesn't stop, I must fetch her,' said Harold. 'It will save her getting out her car. She could get soaked just going to her garage.'

It occurred to Frank that Harold was rather unduly solicitous.

'Mine's out already,' he said. 'We'll fetch her together.'

But, as it happened, the storm swept away before Phil and Jeremy needed to set out, and by the time they arrived, the sun was turning the puddles on Thrush Green to dazzling mirrors.

Betty Bell, who had heard quite enough of the paragon Violet to be put on her mettle, brought forth a superb steak and kidney pudding swathed in a snowy napkin. The Brussels sprouts, the braised celery and the floury potatoes were all at the peak of perfection, and a truly enormous orange trifle, decorated with almonds and crystallized orange segments made Jeremy sigh with ecstasy.

'And if that Violet can do better than that,' said Betty grimly to herself as she returned to the kitchen, 'I'll eat my hat!'

After lunch, the three friends sat and talked over coffee, while Jeremy lay on the floor with volumes of *Punch* around him. It was a happy relaxed little party, mellowed by Betty's superb cooking and Harold's good wine, but Frank was alert enough to notice the attentions which his old friend Harold gave to the young woman, and thought that they were perhaps a trifle warmer than ordinary civility dictated. Could this confirmed bachelor, now approaching sixty, have designs on his promising new contributor?

It looked highly probable, thought Frank, sipping his coffee, but who would have suspected it?

Just before three, Phil and Jeremy departed.

'We'll look forward to seeing you both tomorrow about half past six,' said Phil. 'I've asked the Baileys to come in to meet you. And Richard.'

When they had gone, the two friends settled by the fire again.

'An attractive girl,' said Frank cautiously, 'and very sound as a writer. I have you to thank for introducing her to me, Harold.'

'We're all very fond of her here,' replied Harold. 'I can't make up my mind if her husband's sudden death was a good thing or not. She was dreading the court proceedings, and telling the boy, of course. A messy business – but she was terribly shocked by his death. I wonder if she'll ever get over it.'

'Be married in six months,' said Frank robustly, producing a pipe and ramming home a generous pinch of tobacco. 'Got any eligible young men nearby?'

A faint look of distaste crept over Harold's face, and was observed by the wily Frank.

'There's Richard. You know him, I believe?'

'Slightly. I see him at the club, but he's such a crashing bore about his insides I give him a wide berth, I don't mind admitting.'

'Phil seems to like him, nevertheless.'

'Does she?' said Frank thoughtfully.

They leant back in their armchairs, pondering on the idiosyncrasies of women.

'I shouldn't think he stands a chance,' said Frank, at length. 'She's too much sense to take on a fellow like that. Why, he thinks of no one but himself!'

Harold brightened a little. 'That's how I feel. How I *hope*, perhaps I should say. But then, after all, they are much of an age, and she might think that marriage would improve Richard.'

'Any woman who marries a man expecting to improve him,' said Frank tartly, 'deserves all she gets – and that's disappointment. No, Phil won't be so foolish, I feel positive.'

He tapped his pipe briskly on the bars of the grate.

'But you say you *hope* she won't marry Richard, Harold,' he went on. 'Perhaps I shouldn't ask, but tell me, are you at all interested?'

There was a little silence before Harold replied. Outside, the rooks cawed above the chestnut avenue, and the sound of distant church bells told of a Saturday afternoon wedding.

'Yes, I am,' said Harold very quietly, looking down at his clasped hands. 'But to be truthful, I find it hard to sort out my feelings. I love my present way of life. I'm not at all sure that marriage would suit me, and in any case, I can't see that it would be fair to ask a young woman like that to take on a man of my age.'

'You're only five years my senior,' pointed out Frank. 'I still look upon myself as a spry young-middle-ager.'

'You've always been young for your years, anyway,' answered Harold. 'I've knocked about such a lot, I sometimes feel older than mine.'

'Try your luck,' said Frank spontaneously.

'Too early yet,' replied Harold. 'Let her get over her tragedy first, I think. Besides, do I really want to get married? That's the test, I think. Surely I should be more wholehearted about this affair? What do you think, Frank? You know I value your opinions.'

Frank took a long pull at his pipe.

'I hate to give any advice in a case like this. But I do just wonder, Harold, if your kind heart and old-fashioned sense of chivalry are rather pushing you into this offer of marriage. To my mind, you are a perfectly-balanced person on your own – self-sufficient without being self-satisfied, a truly rare combination. You may well find that matrimony complicates your well-ordered existence, and puts more of a strain on you than you had imagined. On the other hand, as I know full well, marriage can make a man. I miss Margaret more than I can say.'

'That I can understand. She was a fine woman in every way. But not having been so blessed, I've no experience. No, Frank, reason tells me that it would not be fair to Phil – she'd probably spend the last few years of my life as a nurse – appalling thought! And I don't think I really want to give up my selfish way of life.'

'Put the whole affair out of your mind for a month or two,' said Frank. 'You'll both know your feelings better by then.'

'Good old Time,' agreed Harold quietly. 'I'm sure you're right.'

He got up and fetched a map from his desk, closing the subject of Phil Prior.

'I thought we'd drive out to Lechlade for a meal tonight,' he said. 'Which way shall we go?'

The two friends held the map between them and plans for the distant future were forgotten in making those for the evening.

The tiny sitting-room at Tullivers just held the six grown-ups comfortably, and Jeremy, as the important seventh, made himself useful in passing salted nuts and other delicious morsels to his seniors whilst managing to dispatch a generous selection on his own account.

Frank found Doctor Bailey a fascinating companion. They were both fishing enthusiasts, and the doctor regaled the younger man with tales of past exploits on the Windrush.

'You must come down again and try your luck on the Lechlade stretch,' said the doctor. 'I've several old friends there who would be delighted to give you a day's sport.'

He nodded across the room to Richard.

'Our nephew there,' he continued, 'isn't interested, more's the pity.'

Richard was making himself particularly charming to Phil. Since their outing, she had taken care not to meet him alone, but was glad of this opportunity to repay his invitation in the company of others.

There was no doubt about it, thought Frank privately, Richard showed up to greater advantage here than in town. And he was a personable young man, and certainly going to be a very successful one. Harold seemed to have a rival here.

He watched his hostess's reaction to Richard's attentions, but could perceive nothing more than ordinary politeness on her part.

The cottage he found charming, and delighted Phil by saying so when she showed him round.

'It's the perfect place to work,' she told him. 'Small enough to keep tidy easily, and gives me a peaceful base when Jeremy's at school.'

'I think I've got an American magazine interested in a longish short story from you, sometime in the future. Perhaps a Christmas story? Like the idea?'

'*Rather!*' cried Phil warmly.

'I'll tell you more when you come up next week,' promised Frank.

That evening he said farewell to his old friend Harold, being careful not to mention the confidences which he had been given earlier.

'Come to me for a weekend in April,' were his last words before setting off, and Harold promised that he would.

Frank drove home speedily, his thoughts full of Thrush Green and its inhabitants.

What did the future hold for them, he wondered?

Spring seemed a long time in coming to Thrush Green, and people were getting heartily sick of being housebound.

Keen gardeners, such as Harold, fretted at the delay in planting early potatoes and vegetable seeds. The lawns were as tousled and rough as unshaven old men, and the mowers, oiled and waiting to be used, had to wait still longer as snow showers and cold rain kept the ground soggy.

Molly's father developed a mild attack of bronchitis which meant that her departure must be delayed.

'Done it a-purpose, I shouldn't wonder,' commented Ben, who was chafing at Molly's enforced absence from her own home.

'Just till he's over this,' Molly pleaded. 'I must stay till he's back on his feet, Ben. I don't relish it, you know that, but who's to do for him?'

At the school, Miss Watson and Miss Fogerty looked forward to the end of term. Measles and mumps had taken their toll in February and March, and the bitter weather had meant that play outside was impossible. Tempers became frayed, and the fact that the school was most sketchily cleaned did not help matters.

Mrs Cooke of Nidden, who had come back temporarily 'to oblige', was no Nelly Piggott when it came to elbow grease, and Miss Watson and Miss Fogerty were often to be seen sweeping up the classrooms which, in theory, had already been done by Mrs Cooke.

'But what else can we do?' asked Miss Watson despairingly of Miss Fogerty, two days before term ended. 'I had a word with Molly Curdle. She'd be perfect, of course, living so near and being such a good worker, but she's too tied with George and that dreadful old father to consider it. In any case, it would only be a temporary arrangement again.'

Matters came to a head when Mrs Cooke arrived on the last day of term. She wore a look of smug importance, as she carried her broom into Miss Watson's room. The children had departed, excited at the thought of three weeks' holiday, and bearing home their term's drawings to show their resigned mothers. As most of these were executed in chalk, and were being clutched face down against winter coats, their reception at home might be expected to be bleak indeed.

'I thought I'd tell you straight off,' said Mrs Cooke cheerfully, 'that I'm not to do any more work. Doctor's orders.'

'Good heavens!' exclaimed Miss Watson. 'What's the matter?'

'Another little stranger on the way,' replied Mrs Cooke, with immense satisfaction.

Miss Watson's mind was in confusion. Could Mrs Cooke's pleasure really come from the thought of yet another addition to her large, dirty and unruly family? Or was she simply pleased to have a good excuse to leave the school in the lurch? Miss Watson, a realist, was inclined to think that the latter reason caused Mrs Cooke's evident smugness.

'Will you be able to cope with the holiday scrubbing?' asked Miss Watson, knowing the answer before the question was finished.

'Not a hope,' replied Mrs Cooke triumphantly. 'I'm inclined to miscarry if I does too much. It's a weak sort of uterus, you might say. Doctor said something about a prolapse. You know what that is?' asked Mrs Cooke darkly.

'No, I don't,' replied Miss Watson shortly. What a blessing to be a spinster, was her heartfelt thought! 'Well, that's that, I suppose, Mrs Cooke,' she continued resignedly. 'I must thank you for stepping into the breach. You'll sweep up now, will you?'

'I'll oblige,' said Mrs Cooke, inclining her head regally, and set about her limited labours.

'Would you have thought it?' asked Miss Watson of Miss Fogerty later. 'I gather she's still feeding that last baby – Adrian, or Clifford, or whatever it is. Frankly, I lose count of them.'

'It's quite a common fallacy,' pronounced Miss Fogerty importantly, 'that a woman who is feeding a child cannot fall again.'

Miss Watson looked at her assistant in astonishment.

'Agnes, dear,' she protested, 'how on earth do you know such things?'

'I always read the mothers' page under the dryer at the hairdresser's,' answered little Miss Fogerty imperturbably.

She skewered her good velour hat to her skimpy bun, and the two ladies made their way outside.

'But this doesn't solve our problem, does it?' said Miss Fogerty, pausing in the chilly porch.

Next door, Harold Shoosmith's gate clanged as Betty Bell set off home on her bicycle. Rosy and bright-eyed, as fresh as when she had arrived at work some hours earlier, she waved energetically to the two ladies in the school porch, before pedalling away briskly down the hill.

Miss Watson looked at Miss Fogerty, rather as stout Cortez looked upon the peaks of Darien, so long ago.

'Dare we?' she whispered.

'Why not!' said little Miss Fogerty robustly.

It was in April that Richard's work at Oxford came to an end, and as the time approached, Winnie Bailey was mightily relieved.

In all fairness, she admitted, that although Richard had stayed longer than was at first intended, he had really been very little trouble, and had more than pulled his weight by tackling little jobs about the house which were beyond her own understanding and the doctor's strength.

Nevertheless, the thought of having the house to themselves again was heart-lifting. She wondered, sometimes, about the relationship between her nephew and the young widow next door. She had noticed that the outing *à deux* had not been repeated, and that since that day Richard had been unduly restless, but nothing had been said, and in any case, Winnie would not have expected to hear about such a personal matter from Richard.

It was all the more surprising, therefore, when he broached the subject one Sunday morning at breakfast time. The doctor was still in bed, having had a restless night, and Winnie and her nephew lingered over their coffee.

Richard was busy grating a raw apple into a bowl of rolled oats, pine kernels, sultanas and milk – a mixture which he concocted each morning for himself from a recipe of Otto's.

It was a messy business, and Winnie watched the operation resignedly.

'Why don't you eat the apple separately?' she asked.

Richard looked up from his work in some surprise.

'My dear aunt, that would quite defeat Otto's object. The enzymes in the saliva react in a truly magical way upon the mixture of minerals in this bowl. Wonderfully purging, and marvellously toning to the lining of the digestive tract. A friend of Otto's claims to have cured dyspeptic ulcers with this mixture alone.'

He continued to grate energetically, stirred up the mash, and ate it with much relish.

Winnie watched him as she sipped her coffee.

'I've been meaning to tell you about my immediate plans, Aunt Win,' he said, when at last the bowl was empty. 'I really do appreciate your hospitality. You've both been so kind. I hope I haven't been too much of a nuisance.'

Winnie reassured him on this point.

'Well now, I ought to be off in a week or two's time. The point is that the Carslakes have offered me their house while he has a year at Harvard as a visiting professor. They're asking only a nominal rent – they really want someone to keep an eye on things, I gather, and of course it would suit me perfectly.'

'And you are going to accept?'

'It all depends.'

'What on? It seems straightforward enough to me.'

For once in his life Richard appeared discomfited. The vestiges of a blush were apparent to Winnie's sharp eyes.

'The point is,' said Richard, pushing back his chair and walking to the window, 'I've been thinking of getting married, and I suppose the girl would like to see the house first. Hardly fair to take her there if she loathed the place.'

'Quite so,' agreed Winnie. 'And who have you in mind?'

'Why, Phil Prior!' exclaimed Richard. 'Surely you realized that I was interested?'

'I knew you liked her,' said Winnie guardedly, 'but not that you hoped to marry her.'

'Aunt Winnie,' said Richard, returning to the table and looking down at his aunt pleadingly, 'do you think I've a chance? Has she said anything to you about me?'

'Nothing at all,' confessed Winnie, 'except to say how beautifully you'd cleaned out the drain.'

'Hardly a sufficient basis for marriage!' observed Richard, with a wry smile. 'But I suppose I can count it as half a point in my favour.'

He wandered back to the window, hands in his pockets. Something about the slouched back, the ruffled fair hair and general air of desolation, touched Winnie's kind heart.

'You could always ask her,' she pointed out.

'But what hopes, d'you think?'

'Who knows?' said Winnie. 'But why not try your luck?'

She began to pile the coffee cups on to the tray. Richard continued to stand, glooming out upon the garden with unseeing eyes. She wondered what effect this preoccupation with love would have upon Richard's fickle digestion.

He was certainly not her idea of a husband, thought Winnie, bearing the tray towards the kitchen.

Nor, she thought with some satisfaction, Phil Prior's, if she knew anything about that sensible young woman.

*

'Here,' cried Betty Bell to her employer one morning. 'Got something to tell you! I've got a new job!'

'Betty!' exclaimed Harold, dumbfounded. As everyone knows, one of the most heinous crimes which can be committed in a small community is inveigling someone else's domestic worker into coming to work for oneself. Many a deep friendship has been wrecked by such perfidy, and Harold could not believe that Betty Bell would be a party to such treachery.

'You're not going to leave me?' pleaded the stricken man.

Betty's hearty peal of laughter set the silver ringing on the sideboard.

'Now, would I do a thing like that? No, I was just pulling your leg. Made you sit up though, didn't it, eh?'

'It certainly did. But, tell me, what's all this about?'

Betty settled herself comfortably on the edge of the dining-room table. Harold, forewarned, shifted the remains of his breakfast out of harm's way.

'Well, it's like this. Mrs Cooke's expecting again –'

'No!' broke in Harold.

'Strue! Like rabbits, ain't it? Well, as I was saying, she's off work for a bit – if she was ever *on*, if you take my meaning – and them two poor old things next door are up to their hocks in dirt in that school, so they've asked me if I'd help 'em out.'

'Oh,' said Harold, 'and what have you replied?'

Betty suddenly became rather distant and adopted the air of one-who-knew-her-place.

'I said I must ask your permission, sir. They was going to come and have a word with you themselves, but I said let me sound you out. If you was going to be funny about it, I said I'd turn the job down.'

'What does it mean – from my point of view?' asked Harold cautiously.

'If you was willing, I'd come to you half an hour earlier, as soon as I'd done in there in the morning.'

'Humph!' said Harold, considering the matter. It seemed reasonable enough, and he knew Betty could do with the extra money which the school job would provide.

'Very well,' he agreed. 'Let's see how it works out.'

'You're a real gentleman!' cried Betty, bouncing off the table energetically. Harold retrieved a spoon which had been whisked to the floor by her skirt. 'I'll call in next door on my way home and tell the poor old soul!'

'I'll call on Miss Watson myself,' said Harold. 'I'm glad to be of some help to the lady.'

'You'll be mentioned in her prayers tonight,' said Betty heartily. 'And to tell you the truth, in mine too, Mr Shoosmith. Money's not easy to come by these days, and I'm thankful to get a bit of extra work.'

She whirled from the room and very soon Harold heard her voice raised in song as she polished the bathroom floor.

Harold smiled to himself. She really was a wonderful girl. He supposed he must be prepared to share his good luck with Thrush Green School. If Betty Bell took on the job, she would certainly do it splendidly.

It was, in fact, the school's luckiest day, for Betty Bell was to keep it spotless and shining for many a long year.

Two days after Richard's breakfast conversation with his aunt, the young man dressed himself with some care and made his way next door.

Dusk was falling, and although the weather still remained cold, a few early daffodils had braved the April winds, and the sticky buds in the avenue of chestnut trees were beginning to break into leaf.

The birds were busy struggling with wisps of dry grass, feathers, and other nesting material. It seemed a propitious time for a young man to go a-wooing, and Richard approached the late admiral's dolphin knocker in the appropriately nervous condition brought on by mingled hope and ardour.

Phil answered the door with a bath towel thrown over one shoulder, her hair in a state of disarray and a blue streak across one cheek, which had been made, Richard guessed correctly, by a ball-point pen, and would, he had no doubt, be the very devil to remove.

'Do come in,' she said somewhat distractedly. 'I'm just giving Jeremy a quick once-over before he puts on his pyjamas. He's rather like a cat in his ablutions – terribly busy working on one or two square inches, and completely neglecting the rest.'

She led the way to the sitting-room and handed him a decanter and a glass.

'Help yourself, Richard. I'll be back in a tick.'

Richard poured himself an inch of dry sherry. Otto did not approve of alcohol, but Richard felt that on this occasion even the stern Otto would have relaxed his rules. And as he had once said to his disciple, 'If you *must* drink such liver-rotting poison as sherry, then drink a small glass of the driest you can find.'

He sat there twirling his little glass disconsolately. Having girded himself for the endeavour, it was doubly hard to have the event postponed, even for a few minutes. He realized that he must approach the delicate proposal with some preliminaries, but he had decided that they must be as short as ordinary civility demanded. He was no speech-maker, and he had wisely made no rehearsals. He felt it best to rely on the spontaneous prompt-ings of his feelings.

When Phil returned, she had combed her hair, miraculously removed the blue streak, and generally looked her usual neat and attractive self.

'May I pour you one?' asked Richard.

'Thanks. I can do with it. I always think that the time between tea-time and bed-time is the most exhausting for mothers. Just when one is most tired is the time when most is demanded.'

She accepted the sherry gratefully, put her feet up on a footstool, and sighed happily.

'But what brings you here, Richard? I hear from Winnie you are leaving us very soon. Will you be sorry?'

Such an abrupt approach to the matter in hand took Richard off his guard. He swallowed awkwardly, and set himself spluttering, as a drop of sherry went down the wrong way.

'Let me get you some water,' said Phil, getting to her feet, and viewing her scarlet-faced visitor with concern.

'All right now,' he gasped huskily, still fighting for breath. What a way to go about a proposal of marriage, thought Richard!

Phil resumed her seat.

'I always think it's extraordinary,' she remarked, 'how violently the body reacts to something in the windpipe.'

'Good thing it does,' responded Richard. 'You'd soon croak if it didn't!'

An amicable silence fell. A tiny jet of flame hissed from a crack in the coal in the fireplace. The clock ticked companionably above it, and outside the birds shrilled and piped before going to roost for the night.

Richard, now recovered, felt that he must return to the subject of his departure. He put down his glass carefully.

'You asked if I should miss Thrush Green, and I certainly shall. Uncle Donald and Aunt Winnie have been very patient, and so good to me.'

'They're absolute darlings,' agreed Phil warmly. 'Don't you agree?'

Richard refused to be side-tracked. 'But the person I shall miss most of all,' said Richard firmly, 'will be you.'

'Me?' cried Phil, with mingled surprise and dismay. 'But we've had very little to do with each other, after all.'

'I should like to think,' said Richard, warming to his theme, 'that we could be a great deal together in the future.'

'How do you mean?' asked Phil, her heart sinking. She rose and poured herself another glass of sherry. If this were to be a proposal of marriage, she could do with a little support, she told herself.

Richard launched into a long explanation of the Carslakes' offer of their house for a year, and before he was half way through the saga, Phil could foresee the outcome.

'And there is no one in the world,' declared Richard, with more warmth in his voice than Phil had ever heard before, 'I should like to share it with, more than you yourself. It may seem a roundabout way of asking you to consider marrying me, but if you could –?'

His voice faltered to a halt, and his blue eyes were full of pleading.

At that moment, Phil found him more alive, more attractive, more lovable than she would ever have thought possible. It was a pity that his Uncle Donald could not see the 'cold fish' now.

For this one fleeting moment, Richard was a warm human being. Rare emotion had shaken him into life at long last.

'Could you?' he asked earnestly.

'Oh, Richard!' exclaimed Phil, genuinely moved. 'I hate to upset you – I really do. But it would never work, you know. We're not in the least – what's the word I want – *compatible*.'

'We could try,' said Richard.

Phil shook her head. 'No, we couldn't,' she said gently. Already, the mutinous little-boy-crossed look had come into Richard's face. 'In some ways, I'm so much older than you are. I'm a lot further along the road of experience, for one thing, with a marriage behind me and a boy to bring up. And then, in so many ways, you are much cleverer than I am. I'm afraid you would soon be impatient of my shortcomings. I know nothing of your work. You know nothing of mine. There's so little to hold us together, Richard.'

Richard's gaze was downcast. The hissing coal fell from the fire and smouldered, unheeded, on the hearth. Somewhere, on the other side of Thrush Green, a child called to another, and a man went by Tullivers, tapping rhythmically with his walking stick.

These little outside noises seemed to break the spell of silence.

'Well, that's that, I suppose,' said Richard mournfully. 'I'm disappointed, but I'm not surprised. I suppose I'm not what Aunt Winnie would call "much catch". I've never had anyone to consider but myself. It makes a man selfish, but if you had felt you could marry me, I think it would have been the making of me.'

And what about me? was Phil's silent rejoinder. She surveyed the young man for a few moments, wondering if she should speak her mind or not.

She made her decision. She had nothing to lose. Richard, and perhaps another girl one day in the future, had much to gain.

'Richard, of course I'm grateful for being asked to think of marrying you, but do you realize that not once have you said you want me to marry you because you love me? I'm not a romantic woman, heaven knows, but you'll meet a great many who are, and *any* woman will want to be assured that she is loved before she enters marriage. Who on earth is going to get married without it?'

'But you must know that I shouldn't have asked you if I didn't love you!' protested Richard.

'Then say so,' said Phil, with some asperity. 'I think you will marry eventually – probably very soon, but you'll have to put your under-worked heart, as well as your over-worked head, into persuading any normal girl to take you on.'

She paused, and Richard rose to depart. Had she gone too far?

'I'm sorry to hurt you,' she said impulsively, 'but someone must tell you. No hard feelings?'

'Of course not,' said Richard. 'I'll think over what you've said.'

He held out a hand. 'I probably shan't see you again. I'll move into Carslake's place as soon as I can.'

Phil ignored the hand, and kissed him gently on the cheek.

'Dear Richard! Don't take it too badly, and look out for someone who really will make you a good wife one day. Thank you for being so kind, always, to me and Jeremy.'

Richard's blue eyes blinked rapidly as he turned away.

Phil accompanied him to the front door. The green was dark now, and the light at the corner by the pillar box silhouetted the writhing branches of the chestnut trees.

At the gate he turned and raised his hand to his fair hair in the semblance of a salute.

It was to be a very long time before Phil Prior ever saw Richard again.

20. AN ENGAGEMENT

It was May before Molly managed to rejoin Ben. The fair had come as usual to Thrush Green on the first day of that month, but, as the doctor said to Winnie, it wasn't the same without Mrs Curdle to run it.

'And I still expect a bouquet of artificial flowers,' confessed Winnie. 'Embarrassingly large though it was, and really quite hideous, I loved her for bringing it.'

All the children of Thrush Green had spent a hilarious few hours on the simple swings and roundabouts, the coconut shies and side-stalls of Ben Curdle's little fair. Jeremy and Paul had tried everything, and Jeremy had presented his mother with a hard-won vase of shocking pink with heavy gilding, and a very small goldfish in a jam jar. These treasures she had accepted with praiseworthy, if mendacious, expressions of delight.

When the fair closed down that night, after its one-day stand, Ben and Molly sat in Albert's kitchen and talked of their plans. Upstairs, Albert snored noisily. In the next bedroom young George, thumb in mouth, slept just as soundly.

'Doctor Lovell says he can manage pretty well on his own, and I've made arrangements for him to have a hot dinner at The Two Pheasants next door every day,' said Molly. 'At least for a bit.'

'And who pays for that?' asked Ben.

Molly looked confused. 'Couldn't we do that, Ben? You know how he's placed and –'

Ben cut her short with a hug. 'Anything to get you back,' he told her cheerfully. 'I'll go round and settle things with them. But knowing your dad, I reckon it would be best to do this a month at a time. See how things go with him. If he gets hitched up again, he won't need it!'

'I can't see anyone being fool enough to take him on,' admitted Molly. 'He's nigh on killed me this last few months.'

And so it was arranged. A week later Molly was ready to go. The cottage was spruce, the larder well stocked, with a fruit cake in the cake tin, and a steak and kidney pie in the larder. Her father's linen was washed, ironed and mended, and Molly said goodbye to him thankfully. She set out with little George on her lap and with Ben at the wheel, to go back to her own life.

They drove slowly across the green, Molly waving to the bent figure of Albert standing pathetically in the cottage doorway. Thrush Green had its newly-washed, innocent, early morning look – the wide grassy spaces bare of figures, the rooks circling lazily above the church.

Molly felt a pang at leaving it all. There was nowhere as dear as Thrush Green, and despite her father's niggardly ways, she felt a certain sympathy with the old man.

Ben, knowing her gentle heart, put a comforting hand on her knee as the car slid down the hill to Lulling.

'He'll do,' said Ben, and added wickedly, 'the devil looks after his own.'

Later that day, the rector found Albert Piggott walking briskly around the churchyard. He carried no walking stick, and although he was thinner and paler than usual, he seemed remarkably spry. He was inspecting old Mrs Curdle's grave. Ben had decked it with tulips and daffodils. At every visit he had thus honoured the memory of his much-loved grandmother, and even Albert's flinty heart was touched.

'Why, Albert,' cried the rector, with genuine joy, 'how well you look! I'd no idea you were getting on so famously!'

Albert acknowledged the kindness with a perfunctory nod.

'Got to do for meself now, sir, so I'd best get used to it. I was thinking I might manage the church again if you're so minded.'

'But, of course!' exclaimed the rector, delighted. 'If you are sure you feel up to it.'

Albert's face took on its usual woebegone and cautious look. 'I don't say as I could do the graves. I'm past that sort of work – but the boiler, now, and any little inside jobs as I used to do, well – I reckons I can struggle along with they.'

'I'm sure we can come to some arrangement with Willie about the heavy work,' Charles Henstock assured him. 'Now look after yourself, Albert, and don't stay out too long in this treacherous wind.'

He returned to the rectory in high spirits.

'Dimity, my dear,' he declared to his wife, 'Albert Piggott's made a truly remarkable return to health. He was actually walking without a stick! Think of that!'

'I am,' said Dimity drily. 'Now that Molly's gone he can finish with his acting.'

The rector made his way thoughtfully to his study. As a student of human nature, he gave his keen-eyed wife full marks. But who would have thought it?

Sometime later that month, Ella Bembridge strode across the green to collect her goat's milk from Dotty.

At last the weather had relented. May, the loveliest of months, was warm and sunny, and as if to make up for lost time, the leaves and flowers burst out of their sheaths and filled the air with glory.

Butterflies and tortoises emerged from their long hibernation. Bees hummed among the wallflowers, and the cats of Thrush Green sunned themselves on the warm stone walls.

Ella found Dotty watching the antics of Dulcie's new twin kids. They were a skewbald pair, white and brown, and already as nimble and wicked as their proud mother. They skittered away, prancing sideways, their eyes upon Ella as she approached.

'A handsome pair,' commented Ella, wisely keeping her distance from Dulcie. She knew, from painful experience, that Dulcie had a way of running rapidly round a person's legs, trapping them in her chain, and bringing them heavily to the ground. It was a pastime which never palled for Dulcie. The unwilling victims failed to see the joke.

'Got homes for them?' asked Ella.

'I shall keep one,' said Dotty, 'and that Prior child wants one, but whether his mother does, I don't know.'

'Not much room at Tullivers,' observed Ella.

'Well, I suppose she may well be at Harold Shoosmith's before the year's out,' said Dotty reasonably. 'Now Winnie's Richard has left the coast clear, I can't think why Harold doesn't move in for the kill.'

Ella, forthright as she was, could not help feeling that Dotty's expressions were rather stronger than necessary.

'Maybe he doesn't want to get married. And anyway, they may prefer to live at Tullivers, if they do make a match of it.'

'Doubtful,' said Dotty, taking out a man's red and white spotted handkerchief from her skirt pocket, and blowing her nose with a resounding trumpeting. 'Too pokey for Harold. All those cups and things he's got. And he's used to large rooms, living out in Africa, with all those natives fanning him.'

'Got any goat's milk?' asked Ella abruptly. The conversation seemed to be getting out of hand, and Dotty, once started, was deucedly difficult to stop.

'Well, for the kid's sake, I hope they make up their minds quickly,' continued Dotty, leading the way through a rabble of hopeful hens to the house, 'and plump for Harold's place. Plenty of good grass there, and a nice hazel hedge. I shall rely on you, Ella, to do your best to further this affair.'

'Who do you think I am?' cried Ella. 'Dan Cupid? If you ask me, Harold Shoosmith's quite capable of doing his own work. He knows his own mind, mark my words!'

But, if the truth were known, Harold was only now coming to know his own mind.

He had been at Frank's when Richard departed, and learnt from the Baileys about the young man's haste to go, after his visit to Tullivers.

'Sent him away with a flea in his ear,' said the old doctor, with some relish. 'Can't blame her, can you?'

'I think you're misjudging her,' said Winnie. 'She's too kind to deal over-ruthlessly with Richard. But you know how he is – hates to be crossed. He's been hopelessly spoilt ever since he was a child. He was bound to take this badly.'

'How is she?' asked Harold.

'As cheerful as ever. Very busy writing for your friend, as you know. She's said nothing to me about Richard's proposal. Probably thinks I don't know, but he burst in here that night, looking as black as thunder, and simply said: "She won't have me. I'm off next week!" And that was it.'

It certainly brought matters to a head for Harold, and as the days slipped by he studied his feelings as dispassionately as he could. There was no doubt about it. The girl was very dear to him, but the longer he postponed his decision to speak, the more certain he became that marriage was not for him.

All the arguments that he and Frank had discussed, when his friend visited Thrush Green, were gone over again. When Harold had stayed with Frank, only a week or so before, little had been said on the matter, except that Harold had intimated that he felt that he could not expect an attractive young woman like Phil to take him on, and that his own feelings were, perhaps, as Frank had once suggested, a compound of pity and protectiveness.

The more he thought about it, the stronger grew his conviction that he would never be accepted, even if he were brave enough to ask her. Time, his old ally, seemed to be slow in coming to his aid, and he was still troubled in his mind when he called at Tullivers, one fine morning at the end of May, to help Phil in her kitchen garden.

Their combined efforts had made it one of the tidiest and most attractive gardens at Thrush Green. Harold surveyed, with pleasure, the double row of sturdy broad beans, and the neat labels which showed where carrots, early potatoes and beetroot had been planted. The currant and gooseberry bushes, which he had rescued from suffocation last autumn, were making vigorous growth, and Phil's fruit trees had plenty of blossom. The walnut tree which grew at the end of the garden, by the Baileys' wall, was in young auburn leaf.

Everything, Harold thought, looked in good heart, and when Phil came from the house to join him, he thought how well she looked too. There was a radiance about her which was new.

Of course, he told himself, he had never known the girl when she had been free of worry. Now, with the winter and its tragedy behind her, she seemed to be responding to the spring with all the natural joy of young things. How easy it would be to take the plunge, to ask her to marry him, to leave it to the gods – and to Phil – to arrange his future!

He realized that she was looking at him, as though she read his thoughts.

She put out a hand and touched his arm, speaking quickly as though she had just come to a decision.

'Come and sit down for a minute. I've something to tell you.'

He followed her to an old garden seat which the admiral had placed years ago in a sunny corner against a southern wall. At Harold's feet an early bee was rolling over and over, its striped furry body entwined with a wallflower blossom from which it was zealously extracting the honey.

'I've some wonderful news,' said Phil, 'and I want you to be the first to know. Can you guess?'

Harold looked at her. He had always thought that poets grossly overstated things when they talked of eyes like stars. Now he began to understand.

'I was never good at guessing,' he confessed.

'I only knew myself yesterday. Frank has asked me to marry him. Say you're pleased.'

Harold took a deep breath. If he felt a pang of jealousy, it vanished at once. Wholeheartedly, he congratulated her.

'He's the luckiest devil in the world,' he told her sincerely, taking her hands in his.

'He's coming here tomorrow to arrange things with the rector,' said Phil. 'We had the longest telephone talk ever known to the Lulling exchange last night. We shall get married this summer.'

She leant forward and kissed Harold on the cheek.

'And will you give me away?' she asked.

'It's like asking me to part with my heart,' replied Harold, half-meaning it, 'but since you ask me, I shall count it an honour, my dear.'

They stood up and gazed across the garden.

'Will you leave Thrush Green?' asked Harold.

'We haven't got that far,' smiled Phil. 'But I don't think I could ever leave Tullivers. We could build on, I suppose.'

She looked about her vaguely, trying to envisage the future, and suddenly became conscious of the wonder of a life which contained such a precious element as sure joy to come.

She turned to Harold wonderingly. 'What is it about Thrush Green which makes it so special? Is it the air, or the green, or the people?'

Harold considered the question seriously before he spoke. In the silence between them they could hear the distant sounds of a Thrush Green morning. Miss Fogerty's children called to each other in the playground, the rooks cawed above St Andrew's elms, and Winnie Baileys' voice could be heard as she opened a window to the sunshine.

'All those things make Thrush Green,' said Harold, 'and much, much more.'

He thought of his own restless wanderings abroad, and his present joy. Here he had found a home and deep happiness. He knew he shared this feeling with the girl beside him. Thrush Green seemed to have some magic quality which they both recognized instinctively.

'The power of healing,' said Harold softly, as if to himself.

Gossip from
Thrush Green

Miss Read

To
Janet
With love and thanks

CONTENTS

* * *

1	Afternoon Tea	1
2	Friends and Relations	12
3	Jenny Falls Ill	22
4	Dimity Gets Her Way	34
5	The Henstocks Set Off	44
6	A Turbulent Tea Party	55
7	The Fire	67
8	At Young Mr Venables'	79
9	Trouble at Tullivers	88
10	A Golden May	99
11	A Sea-Side Interlude	111
12	Bessie's Advice	122
13	Jenny Decides	132
14	After the Storm	143
15	Dotty Faces Facts	154
16	Sunday Lunch at the Misses Lovelock's	165
17	Housing Plans	175
18	Help Needed	185
19	Charles Meets his Bishop	195
20	Looking Ahead	207

1. Afternoon Tea

In far too many places in England today, the agreeable habit of taking afternoon tea has vanished.

'Such a shocking waste of time,' says one.

'Much too fattening a meal with all that dreadful starch,' says another.

'Quite unnecessary, if one has had lunch or proposes to eat in the evening,' says a third.

All very true, no doubt, but what a lot of innocent pleasure these strong-minded people are missing! The very ritual of tea-making, warming the pot, making sure that the water is just boiling, inhaling the fragrant steam, arranging the tea-cosy to fit snugly around the precious container, all the preliminaries lead up to the exquisite pleasure of sipping the brew from thin porcelain, and helping oneself to hot buttered scones and straw-berry jam, a slice of feather-light sponge cake or home-made shortbread.

Taking tea is a highly civilized pastime, and fortunately is still in favour at Thrush Green, where it has been brought to a fine art. It is common practice in that pleasant village to invite friends to tea rather than lunch or dinner. As Winnie Bailey, the doctor's widow, pointed out one day to her old friend Ella Bembridge, people could set off from their homes in the light, and return before dark, except for the really miserable weeks of mid-winter when one would probably prefer to stay at home anyway.

'Besides,' said Ella, who was fond of her food, 'when else can you eat home-made gingerbread, all squishy with black treacle? Or dip into the pounds of jam on the larder shelves?'

'I suppose one could make a sponge pudding with jam at the

bottom,' replied Winnie thoughtfully, 'but Jenny and I prefer fresh fruit.'

'Jenny looks as though a sponge pudding might do her good,' said Ella, naming Winnie's home-help and friend. 'She seems to have lost a lot of weight recently. She's not *dieting*, I hope?'

Winnie proffered the dish of shortbread, and Ella, who was certainly not dieting, took a piece.

'I've noticed it myself,' confessed Winnie. 'I do hope she's not doing too much in the house. As you know, we've offered to look after Tullivers when Frank and Phil are away, and Jeremy will stay with us. So I'm determined that Jenny shall not overwork then.'

Tullivers was the attractive house next door to Winnie Bailey's. Built of the local Cotswold stone, it faced south, standing at right angles to her own home, and their gardens adjoined. Since the death of her doctor husband, Donald, she had been more thankful than ever for her good neighbours, the Hursts.

Frank Hurst was an editor, and his wife Phyllida a freelance writer. They had met when Phil was busy submitting work some years earlier. Her first husband had been killed in a motoring accident, and she had been left to bring up her young son Jeremy with very little money.

This second marriage had turned out to be a very happy one, and the inhabitants of Thrush Green thoroughly approved of the Hursts, who played their part in village life, supplying prizes for raffles, jumble for the many rummage sales, and consenting, with apparent cheerfulness, to sit on at least half a dozen local committees. Jeremy was a happy child, now in Miss Watson's class at Thrush Green village school, and due to start at his new school, in nearby Lulling, next September.

In April, Frank and his wife were off to America where he was to spend six weeks lecturing. It was too long a period to keep Jeremy from school, and Winnie had offered at once to look after him.

'It would give me enormous pleasure,' she assured the Hursts, 'and the boy is never any bother. Just the reverse in fact. It would be such a comfort to have a man about the place again.'

And so it was arranged.

On this particular February afternoon, when Winnie and Ella were enjoying their modest tea-party, the weather was as bleak and dreary as any that that wretched month can produce.

A few brave snowdrops had emerged under the shelter of Winnie's front hedge, and the winter jasmine on the wall still made a gallant show, but the trees remained gaunt and bare, and the prevailing colour everywhere, from heavy clouds above to the misty fields below, was a uniform grey.

'The winters get longer,' commented Ella, craning her neck to look out of the window, 'and the summers shorter. Dimity and Charles don't agree, but I'm going to keep a weather diary next year to prove my point.'

Charles Henstock was the rector of Thrush Green, and had married Dimity, Ella's lifelong friend, a few years earlier. They lived contentedly in the most hideous house on the green, a tall, badly proportioned Victorian horror, covered in peeling stucco, whose ugliness was made more noticeable by the mellow beauty of the surrounding Cotswold architecture.

Most of the Thrush Green residents were resigned to this monstrosity, but Edward Young, the local architect, who lived in the most splendid of Thrush Green's houses, always maintained that a glimpse of the Henstocks' rectory gave him acute pains in the stomach. His wife Joan, a cheerful down-to-earth person, dismissed this as quite unnecessary chi-chi, and hoped that he was not going to grow into one of those tiresome people who affect hyper-sensitivity in order to impress others.

This trenchant remark had the effect of restoring Edward's good humour, but he still stuck to his guns and was the first to attack the unknown and long-dead architect of Thrush Green's great mistake.

'Dimity,' went on Ella, 'was wondering if she could persuade Charles to move his study upstairs. It's so cold and dark at the moment, and they could easily turn that little bedroom over the kitchen into a nice snug place for the writing of sermons. Heaven alone knows, there are only about two rooms in that house which get any sun.'

3

'I gather he doesn't like the idea,' commented Winnie.

'Well, he's not being *too* obstinate, but suggests that they wait until after their holiday.'

'That should put it off nicely,' agreed Winnie, pouring her guest a second cup of Darjeeling tea. 'Now tell me the rest of the news.'

Ella frowned with concentration. 'Dotty is toying with the idea of adopting a little girl.'

Winnie put down the tea pot with a crash.

'She can't be! The way she lives? No adoption society would countenance it!'

Dotty Harmer, an elderly eccentric friend, beloved of both, lived some half a mile away in a dilapidated cottage, surrounded by a garden full of chickens, ducks, geese, goats and any stray animals in need of succour. Indoors lived several cats, kittens, dogs and puppies. Occasionally, a wounded bird convalesced in a large cage in the kitchen, and once an ailing stoat had occupied the hospital accommodation.

'He is rather smelly,' Dotty had admitted, 'but it's handy for giving him scraps when I'm cooking.' Even her closest friends had

found hasty excuses for declining invitations to meals whilst the stoat was in residence. At the best of times Dotty's food was suspect, and a local ailment, known as Dotty's Collywobbles, was quite common.

'I don't think Dotty has thought about that side of it. She told me that now that she was getting on it might be a good idea to train someone to take over from her, and look after the animals and the house.'

'The mind boggles,' said Winnie, 'at the thought of dear Dotty training *anyone*.'

'Well, she said it seemed a shame that she had no one to leave things to when she died, and it really could provide a very nice life for someone.'

'I am shocked to the core,' confessed Winnie. 'But there, we all know Dotty. She's probably forgotten about it by now, and is full of some other hare-brained scheme.'

'Let's hope so,' said Ella beginning to collect her bag and gloves. 'And that reminds me that I must get back to collect my goat's milk from her. She promised to call in about five-thirty with it, and I want her to choose some wool for a scarf. I've dug out my old hand loom, and I warn you now, Winnie dear, that all my friends will be getting a handwoven scarf next Christmas.'

'You are so kind,' said Winnie faintly, trying to remember how many lumpy scratchy scarves of Ella's making still remained unworn upstairs. Sometimes she wondered if fragments of heather and thistle remained in the wool. It was impossible to pass them on to the local jumble sales for Ella would soon come across them again in such a small community, and Winnie was too kind-hearted to inflict them upon such distant organizations as Chest and Heart Societies. Their members had quite enough to put up with already, she felt.

'By the way,' said Ella, turning at the front door, 'are you going to Violet's coffee morning? It's in aid of Distressed Gentlefolk.'

'I should think those three Lovelock sisters would qualify for that themselves,' observed Winnie.

'Don't you believe it,' said Ella forthrightly. 'With that treasure house around them? One day they'll be burgled, and then they

5

really will be *distressed*, though no doubt they're well insured. Justin Venables will have seen to that.'

She set off down the wet path, a square stumpy figure, planting her sensible brogues heavily, her handwoven scarf swinging over her ample chest.

Winnie watched her departing figure affectionately.

'Yes, I'll be there,' she called, and closed the door upon the bleak world outside.

The Misses Lovelock, Violet, Ada and Bertha, lived in a fine old house in Lulling High Street, less than a mile downhill from Thrush Green.

Here the three maiden ladies had been born at the beginning of the century, and here, presumably, they would one day die, unless some particularly forceful doctor could persuade them to end their days in one of the local hospitals.

They had been left comfortably off by their father, which was as well, as the house was large and needed a great deal of heating and maintenance. Not that they spent much on these last two items, and prudent visitors went warmly clothed when invited to the house, and could not help noticing that walls and woodwork were much in need of fresh paint.

The amount spent on food was even more meagre. The sisters seemed able to survive on thin bread and butter, lettuce when in season, and the occasional egg. Guests were lucky indeed if meat appeared on the table, not that the Lovelocks were vegetarians, but simply because meat was expensive and needed fuel and time to cook it. Most of their friends consumed a substantial sandwich before dining with the Lovelocks, or faced an evening of stomach rumblings whilst sipping weak coffee.

The extraordinary thing was that the house was crammed with valuable furniture, and with glass cabinets stuffed with antique silver and priceless porcelain. All three sisters had an eye for such things, and were shrewd bargainers. They were also quite shameless in asking for any attractive object which caught their eye in other people's houses, and this effrontery had stood them in good stead as a number of exquisite pieces in their collection proved.

There were several people in Thrush Green and Lulling who cursed their momentary weakness in giving way to a wheedling Miss Ada or Miss Violet as they fingered some treasure which had taken their fancy.

On this particular afternoon, while Winnie was tidying away the tea things and Ella was unlocking her front door, the three sisters were sorting out an assortment of articles already delivered for the Bring and Buy stall at the coming coffee morning.

'I wonder,' said Violet pensively, 'if we should buy this in, dear?'

'Buying things in' was another well-known way of acquiring some desirable object. It really meant having first pick, as it were, at the preview, and many a donor had looked in vain for some pretty knick-knack on the stall when one or more of the Misses Lovelock had had a hand in the preparations.

Violet now held up a small silver-plated butter dish in the form of a shell.

Ada scrutinized it shrewdly. 'I think Joan Young sent it. Better not. It's only plate anyway.'

Violet replaced it reluctantly.

'Would you say fifty pence for these dreadful tea-cosies?' asked Bertha.

'Mrs Venables crocheted those,' said Ada reprovingly, 'and you know how her poor hands are crippled with arthritis. At least seventy pence, Bertha, in the circumstances.'

Bertha wrote three tickets for that amount. Ada always knew best.

A circular biscuit tin bearing portraits of King George V and Queen Mary proved to be a treasure chest of buttons, buckles, beads and other trifles. The three white heads met over the box. Six skinny claws rattled the contents. Six eyes grew bright with desire.

'And who sent this?' inquired Bertha, anxious not to offend again.

'Miss Watson from the school,' replied Violet. She withdrew a long piece of narrow black ribbon studded with jet. 'How pretty this would look as an edging to my black blouse!'

'It would look better as a trimming on my evening bag,' said Bertha. She took hold of the other end.

'Miss Watson,' said Ada dreamily, 'will not be able to come to the coffee morning. These things were left her among a lot of other trifles, she told me, by her aunt in Birmingham.'

'Well, then—' said Violet.

'In that case—' said Bertha.

Both ladies were a little pink in the face.

'Put it on one side,' said Ada, 'and we'll think about buying it in later. I see there are some charming jet buttons here too. They may have come from the same garment. A pity to part them, don't you think?'

Scrabbling happily, the three sisters continued their search, while outside the lamps came on in the High Street of Lulling, throwing pools of light upon the wet pavements, and the damp figures of those homeward bound.

One of the figures, head bent, and moving slowly towards the hill which led to Thrush Green, was that of St Andrew's sexton, Albert Piggott, who lived alone in a cottage facing the church and conveniently next door to The Two Pheasants, Thrush Green's only public house.

Albert was always morose, but this evening his gloom was deeper than ever. Cursed with habitual indigestion which his diet of alcohol, meat pie and pickles did nothing to help, he had just been to collect a packet of pills from Lulling's chemist.

Dr Lovell of Thrush Green, who had married Joan Young's sister and had served as a junior partner to Donald Bailey, was now the senior partner in the practice, and Albert Piggott was one of his oldest and most persistent patients. It was vain to try to get the irritable old man to change his ways. All that he could do was to vary his prescription now and again in the hope that Albert's tormented digestive tract would respond, at least temporarily, to new treatment.

'Plain bicarb again, I don't doubt,' muttered Albert, slouching homeward. 'What I really needs is good hot meals.'

He thought wistfully of Nelly's cooking. Nelly, his wife, had left him – twice, to make it worse – and both times to share life with the oil man whose flashy good looks and honeyed words had attracted her on his weekly rounds.

Nelly now lived with her new partner on the south coast, and it was he who now enjoyed her superb steak-and-kidney puddings, succulent roasts and well-spiced casseroles. The very thought of that chap's luck brought on Albert's indigestion.

Not that Albert lacked attention. In many ways, he was better off.

Nelly's cooking had tended to be rich, even by normal standards. She excelled with cheese sauces, fried potatoes and creamy puddings. Her cakes were dark and moist with fruit, her sponge cakes were filled with butter icing, and more icing decorated the top. Dr Lovell's pleas to her to provide plainer fare for her husband fell on deaf ears. Nelly was an artist. Butter, sugar and the best quality meat and dairy foods were her materials. She cooked, and Albert ate. Dr Lovell hadn't a chance.

But since Nelly's departure, presumably for good this time, his daughter Molly had done her best to look after the old man. She was married to a fine young fellow called Ben Curdle, and the couple lived nearby with their little boy George in a flat at the top of the Youngs' house. Ben was employed in Lulling, and Molly helped Joan in the house. The arrangement worked well, for Molly had been known to the Youngs for all their lives. They had rejoiced when Molly had finally succeeded in escaping, through marriage, from the clutches of her selfish old father. Now that she was back in Thrush Green they only hoped that she would not be so kind-hearted as to fall into the trap again.

Molly, wiser than Nelly, cooked with prudence for her father, leaving him light dishes of fish or eggs as recommended by the doctor. More often than not these offerings were given to the cat by Albert, in Molly's absence. He dismissed them as 'pappy stuff' and either went next door for his pie and beer, or used the unwashed frying pan to cook himself another meal of bacon and eggs.

At times Molly despaired. Ben took a realistic attitude to the problem.

'Lord knows he's old enough to know what's good for him. Let him go his own way. Don't upset yourself on his account. He never put himself out for you, did he?'

There was truth in this. Molly had enough to do with looking after Ben and George, and the housework. She loved being back in Thrush Green. The only snag was her obstinate old father. At times she wished that Nelly would return to look after him. Although she disliked her blowsy stepmother, at least Albert's cottage had been kept clean and he had been looked after.

Albert trudged up the hill, the rain slanting into his face from the north. Lights glowed from the cottage windows. A car swished by, splashing the old man's legs. The bulk of St Andrew's church stood massively against the night sky.

'Best lock up while I'm on me feet,' thought Albert, changing course towards the building. The door was ajar, but no one was inside. Albert stood in the dark aisle looking towards the three shadowy windows behind the altar. The familiar church smell compounded of damp and brass polish met his nostrils. Somewhere a scuffling and squeaking broke the silence.

'Dratted mice!' exclaimed Albert, kicking a pew end.

Silence fell again.

Albert withdrew, clanging the heavy door behind him. From beneath the door mat he extracted the enormous key. He locked the door, and stuffed the key into his pocket to take across to the house for the night.

Standing in the shelter of the porch, he surveyed the view through the rain. His own cottage, directly opposite, was in darkness. The Two Pheasants was not yet open, although he could see the landlord moving about in the bar. Beside the pub stood the village school, the playground now deserted and swept by gusts of rain. A light was on in the main schoolroom which meant that Betty Bell was busy clearing up the day's mess. There was a light too downstairs in the school house where Miss Watson, the headmistress, and Miss Fogerty, her assistant, were sitting snugly by the fire discussing school matters in the home they shared.

Almost hidden from Albert's view by the angle of the porch

was the fine house which stood next door to the school. Here lived Harold Shoosmith, a bachelor until his sixties, but now newly married, and very content. There were lights upstairs and down, and the porch light too was on.

Albert grunted disapprovingly. 'Waste of electric,' he said aloud. 'Money to burn, no doubt.'

He hauled his large watch from his pocket and squinted at the illuminated dial. Still a quarter of an hour to go before old Jones opened up. Might as well go home and hang up the key, and take a couple of these dratted pills.

Clutching his coat around him, Albert set off through the downpour.

2. FRIENDS AND RELATIONS

An hour or two later, as Albert Piggott sipped his beer and warmed his legs by the fire at The Two Pheasants, his daughter Molly tucked up young George, and then went to the window to look out upon Thrush Green.

Rain spattered the glass. The sash window rattled in its frame against the onslaught of the wind. The lights of the pub were reflected in long puddles in the roadway, and the leafless trees scattered drops as their branches were tossed this way and that.

It was a beast of a night, thought Molly, but she loved Thrush Green, whatever the weather. For the first few years of her marriage she had accompanied Ben on his tour of towns and villages with the small travelling fair which had once been owned by his grandmother, the redoubtable Mrs Curdle, who had also brought up the boy. She now lay in St Andrew's churchyard, her grave lovingly tended by her grandson.

It grieved Ben to part with the famous fair, but it was the only thing to do. Customs and fashions change. A small family fair could not compete with bingo halls and television, and in the end Ben had sold it, and had taken a job with a firm of agricultural engineers. Molly's happiness was a joy to see, and Ben was content.

Or was he? Molly pondered upon this question as she gazed upon the dark wet world. Never by word or sign had he shown any regret for the life he had given up, but Molly sometimes wondered if he missed the travelling, the change of scene, the renewing of friendships in the towns where the fair rested.

After all, he had known nothing else. His home, as a child, had

been the small horse-drawn caravan which now stood, a permanent reminder of Mrs Curdle and that way of life, in the orchard
of their present home. He had played his part in the running of
the fair, willing to do whatever was necessary at any time of the
day or night.

Surely, thought Molly, he must sometimes find his new mode
of living irksome. To leave home at the same time, to learn to
watch the clock, to put down his tools when a whistle blew and
to return to Thrush Green at a regular hour. Did he find it dull?
Did he ever hanker for the freedom he once had? Did he feel tied
by so much routine? Was he truly happy?

A particularly vicious squall flung a sharp shower against
the glass by her face, making the girl recoil. Well, no point in
worrying about it, she told herself. She was lucky to have such a
good-tempered husband, and maybe he was just as happy as she
was.

She left the window, looked at her sleeping son, and went to
cook Ben's supper.

Over the way, at Tullivers, Frank and Phil Hurst also had a
problem on that stormy night.

Robert, Frank's son by his first marriage, was farming in
Wales. He rarely rang up, and still more rarely wrote a letter,
although father and son were fond of each other, and Frank was
proud of the way in which the youngster had tackled life in
Wales, a tough hill farm and four boisterous children.

'I've got a proposition for you, Dad,' said the cheerful voice on
the telephone. 'When do you set off on the lecture trip?'

Frank told him.

'And you'll be away all through May?'

'That's right. Back the first week in June, if all goes well.'

'It's like this. A friend of mine, just married, is coming up to his
new job in an estate agent's, somewhere in your area, near
Oxford. He's got to be out of his house in April, and I just
wondered if you'd feel like letting him have Tullivers for a few
weeks.'

'Hasn't he got anywhere to go this end?'

'Their place isn't ready, and won't be until the summer. I wouldn't ask, Dad, if it weren't for the fact he's been good to me in the past, and there's a baby on the way as well. He's a nice chap. Very musical. You'd like him.'

'I can't say yes or no until I've talked it over with Phil. In any case, I'd need some sort of references. And I really don't know if I'd like a stranger in the house – or have any idea what to charge him.'

'Well, he hasn't much cash, that I do know, but he'd want to pay his whack obviously.'

There was silence for a moment, broken at last by Frank. 'I'll have a word with Phil, and ring you tomorrow.'

'Oh good! It would help him enormously if he knew there was somewhere to go when he leaves here. Give him time to look around, and chivvy the workmen your end.'

There was a crackling sound and Frank replaced the receiver.

Phil looked at him inquiringly. 'What's the problem?'

Frank told her.

I'm not keen on the idea,' she said eventually. 'We don't know him from Adam, and I don't want to have someone here who might turn out to be a nuisance to the neighbours.'

'I should turn it down flat,' agreed Frank 'if it weren't for Robert. He speaks well of him, says he's musical, known him for some time evidently, and he's been a good friend to him in the past. I must say it is all rather complicated.'

'Well, say we must know more and would like to meet him and his wife,' suggested Phil. 'And if we have any doubts, we harden our hearts.'

And on this sensible note the problem was shelved for twenty-four hours.

The storm blew itself out during the night, and Thrush Green woke to a morning so sweet and pearly that spirits rose at once.

Even Willie Marchant, the gloomy postman, noticed the sunshine as he tacked purposefully on his bicycle back and forth across the hill from Lulling.

'Lovely morning, Willie,' said Ella, meeting him at her gate.

'Ah!' agreed the postman. As usual, a cigarette end was clamped to his lower lip. Was it pulling the skin, or did he essay a rare smile? Ella could not be certain.

The Reverend Charles Henstock met Willie as he returned from early service, and collected his post from him.

'This makes one think of spring,' commented the rector, sniffing the air appreciatively.

'Long way to go yet,' said Willie, as he pedalled away on his rounds. He was never one to rouse false hopes, and whatever his secret pleasure in the change in the weather, he intended to show his usual dour countenance to those he met.

General optimism greeted him.

Joan Young pointed out the bulbs poking through in her shrubbery. Little Miss Fogerty, who took in the letters at the school house, said that a blackbird had begun to build in the hedge. Harold Shoosmith next door could be heard singing in a fine resonant baritone voice, and his new wife gave Willie such a ravishing smile when she opened the door that he almost forgot himself and smiled back.

The Thrush Green post delivered, Willie set off in a leisurely way along the narrow lane which led westward to Lulling Woods. Once out of sight of Thrush Green eyes, Willie propped his bicycle against a stone wall, put his canvas mail bag on the grass to keep out any dampness, and sat himself upon it, leaning back comfortably in the lee of the wall. Here the sun was warm, a lark soared above him, greeting the morning with the same rapture as his clients, and Willie took out a fresh cigarette.

It was a good spot, Willie admitted, looking at the distant smudge of Lulling Woods against the sky line. Definitely a smell of new grass growing, and that was a fresh mole hill over there, he noted. Tiny buds like beads studded the hawthorn twigs nearby, and an early bemused bumblebee staggered drunkenly at the edge of the track.

Willie blew a cloud of smoke, and stretched luxuriously. Not a bad life, he told himself, especially with the summer ahead. Could do a lot worse than be a postman on a fine morning.

The barking of a dog reminded him of his duties. Dotty Harmer's cottage, a quarter of a mile distant, was his next call. Obviously, she was up and about, as the barking dog proved. No doubt the old girl was feeding the hens and goats and all the rest of the menagerie she kept in that ramshackle place. Nutty as a fruit cake, thought Willie, rising stiffly from the crushed mail bag, but got some guts. You couldn't help liking the old trout, and when you think of what she put up with when her wicked old dad was alive – well, you had to hand it to her.

Willie himself had been a pupil for a short time under the redoubtable Mr George Harmer, headmaster of Lulling Grammar School. The memory of that martinet, his rigid rules and ferocious punishment if they were broken, was still fresh in the minds of those who had suffered at his hands, although the old man had lain in the churchyard for many years now, leaving his daughter to enjoy the company of all those animals which had been forbidden whilst he lived.

Good luck to her, thought Willie, clambering on to his bicycle again. She deserved a bit of pleasure in her old age.

As he had guessed, Dotty was in the chicken run. She was trying to throw a rope over a stout bough of the plum tree which leant over the run. For one moment of alarm, Willie wondered if she were contemplating suicide, but Dotty would be the last person to take an easy way out of anything.

'Ah, Willie! How you startled me! I'm having such a job with these Brussels sprouts.'

She pointed to five or six leggy plants which were attached to one end of the rope. All became plain.

'You want 'em hauled up? Give it here,' said Willie. With one deft throw he cast the other end over the plum branch and pulled. Up went the plants.

'How high?' asked Willie, his head level with the dangling sprouts.

Dotty surveyed them, frowning with concentration. 'Not *quite* as high as that, I think, Willie. You see, I want the hens to get some exercise in leaping up to reach the greenstuff. They lead rather a sedentary life, and I'm sure their circulation and general good health would be improved by a little more exercise.'

'Ah,' agreed Willie, lowering the plants a trifle.

'On the other hand,' went on Dotty, 'I don't want them *too low*—'

Willie gave a slight hitch. The plants rose three inches.

'Or, of course, that defeats the object. But I don't want them so high that they lose heart and *don't try* to jump. Or, of course, too high for them to jump in *safety*. I don't want any *injuries*. Hens have funny little ways.'

Not the only ones, thought Willie, patiently lowering and raising the sprouts before Dotty's penetrating gaze.

'Right!' shouted Dotty suddenly, hand raised as if about to stop traffic. 'I think that will do splendidly. What do you think?'

'That's about it, I reckon,' said Willie, tying a knot.

Dotty beamed upon him. 'Most kind of you, Willie dear. Now if you'll just come in the kitchen I'll let you have two letters I wrote last night.'

He followed her towards the back door, stepping over three kittens who jumped out at him from the currant bushes and dodging a goat which was tethered to a post on the way.

The kitchen was in its usual state of chaos. Willie was quite familiar with its muddle of bowls, saucepans, boxes, string bags, piles of newspapers and a hundred assorted objects overflowing from the table, shelves and chairs. A vast fish kettle, black with age, simmered on the stove, and from it, to Willie's surprise, came quite a pleasant odour of food cooking.

'Now where did I put them?' enquired Dotty, standing stock still among the muddle. 'Somewhere safe, I know.'

She shifted a pile of newspapers hopefully. Willie's eyes raked the dresser.

'They'd be on top, most like,' he suggested, 'seeing as you only wrote them last night.'

'Very astute of you,' said Dotty. She lifted the lid of a vegetable dish on the table, and there were the letters.

'Safe and sound,' said Dotty happily, pressing them into Willie's hand. 'And now I mustn't keep you from the Queen's business. A thousand thanks for your help with the hens. I'm sure they will be much invigorated after a few jumping sessions.'

She picked up a slice of cake which was lying on the table beside a small brown puddle of unidentified liquid. Coffee perhaps, thought Willie, or tea? Or worse?

'What about a little snack?' suggested Dotty. 'You could eat it on your way.'

'I'd best not, much as I'd like to,' replied Willie gallantly. 'It'd take the edge off my appetite for breakfast, you see. Thank you all the same.'

'Quite, quite!' said Dotty, dropping it down again. This time it was right in the puddle, Willie noticed.

He escaped before Dotty could offer him anything else, and moved briskly down the path towards his bicycle.

The hens, as far as he could see, were ignoring the sprouts completely. You'd have thought they would have done the decent thing and had a look at them anyway, thought Willie resentfully, after all the trouble they had gone to.

He went on his way, in the golden sunshine, suitably depressed.

Little Miss Fogerty and her headmistress, Miss Watson, were breakfasting in the sunny kitchen of the school house. Each had a boiled egg, one slice of toast and another of Ryvita and marmalade.

It was their standard breakfast on schooldays, light but nourishing, and leaving no greasy frying pan to be washed. On Saturdays and Sundays, when time was less limited, they occasionally cooked bacon and egg or bacon and tomato, and now and again a kipper apiece.

Dorothy Watson loved her food but had to be careful of gaining too much weight. Agnes Fogerty, who had lived in lodgings nearby for many years, had discovered an equal interest in cooking since coming to live with her friend, and enjoyed watching her eat the dishes which she made. Agnes's weight never varied, whatever she ate, and had remained about eight stone for years.

Miss Fogerty had never been so happy as she was now, living with Dorothy and next door to another old friend, Isobel Shoosmith, who had been at college with her years before. Although she had not realized it at the time, looking back she could see that her life at Mrs White's had been quite lonely. True, she had had a pleasant bed-sitting-room, and Mrs White had cooked for her and always been welcoming, but on cold evenings, sitting in her Lloyd loom armchair by a gas fire, turned low for reasons of economy, Agnes had experienced some bleakness.

It was such a pleasure now to wake each morning in the knowledge that she was near to her friends, and had no need to make a journey, in all weathers, to the school. She was usually down first in the kitchen, happy to see to the kettle and the eggs and toast in readiness for Dorothy, who was still rather slow in her movements since breaking a hip.

It was that accident which had led to Agnes being asked to share the school house, and she looked forward to several years together before retirement age. What happened then, Miss

Fogerty sometimes wondered? But time enough when that day loomed nearer, she decided, and meanwhile life was perfect.

Willie Marchant had brought two letters, one from the Education Office obviously and one which looked as though it were from Dorothy's brother Ray. Miss Fogerty sipped her tea whilst her headmistress read her correspondence.

'Ray and Kathleen are proposing to have a week or ten days touring the Cotswolds next month,' she told Agnes, as she stuffed his letter back into the envelope.

'How nice,' said Agnes. 'Are they likely to call here?'

'A call I should like,' said Dorothy, with some emphasis, 'but Ray seems to be inviting himself and Kathleen to stay here for a night or two.'

'Oh!' said Agnes, somewhat taken aback. The school house had only two bedrooms. The one which had once been the spare room she now occupied permanently. Before then, she knew, Ray had sometimes spent the night there on his travels as a commercial salesman. Since Dorothy's accident, however, things had been a little strained. She had confidently expected to convalesce with her brother and his wife, but they had made no offer, indeed nothing but excuses. If it had not been for Agnes's willingness to help, poor Miss Watson would have been unaided in her weakness. It was quite plain to Miss Fogerty that she had not forgiven or forgotten.

'I could easily make up a bed in the sitting room,' offered Agnes, 'if you would like to have mine. Then they could have the twin beds in your room.'

'It won't be necessary, Agnes dear,' said Dorothy, in the firm tones of a headmistress. 'We are not going to put ourselves out for them. They have quite enough money to afford a hotel. They can try The Fleece if they must come and stay here. Frankly, it won't break my heart if we don't see them at all.'

'Oh Dorothy,' begged gentle little Miss Fogerty, 'don't talk like that! He is your own flesh and blood – your own brother!'

'No fault of mine,' said Dorothy, briskly, rolling up her napkin. 'I didn't choose him, you know, but I do choose my *friends*!' She glanced at the clock. 'Better clear up, I suppose, or we shall be late for school. I really ought to look out some pictures for my history lesson this morning.'

'Then you go over to school, dear,' said Miss Fogerty, 'and I'll see to the breakfast things.'

'You spoil me,' said Miss Watson, limping towards the door.

And how pleasant it was to have someone to spoil, thought Agnes, running the tap. More often than not she did stay behind to do this little chore, but never did she resent it. Looking after others, children or adults, was little Miss Fogerty's chief source of pleasure.

Miss Watson, making her way carefully across the playground, thought fondly of her assistant. She was the soul of unselfishness, as her ready offer to vacate her bedroom had shown yet again. But Miss Watson was determined that Agnes should now come first. She had been a loyal colleague for many years, respected by parents and children alike, and since the accident had proved a trusted friend and companion.

All that stuff about blood being thicker than water, thought Miss Watson robustly, was a lot of eyewash! She had had more help and affection from her dear old Agnes than ever Ray and Kathleen had shown her. It had to be faced, they were a selfish pair, and she had no intention of upsetting Agnes's comfort, or her own, to save them a few pennies.

'You can come and help me to carry some pictures, George dear,' she said to young Curdle who was skipping about the playground. It was by way of being a royal command.

She swept ahead to enter her domain, followed by one of her willing subjects.

3. JENNY FALLS ILL

That halcyon spell of weather lasted exactly two days, and then bitter winds lashed the area and continued into March.

During this bleak period, the problem of letting Tullivers to Robert's friend was resolved. Frank discovered that he knew the young man's father. He and Dick Thomas had worked together on a west country newspaper for some time. He had an idea he had even met this son, Jack, when he was a babe in arms.

Robert had got the local vicar to send a letter to his father vouching for the young man, which Frank found rather touching. Obviously, Robert wanted everything to go smoothly. Frank was impressed too by a letter from Jack Thomas, and by the fact that he had managed to get his landlord to extend his stay until the end of April, which would mean just one month at Tullivers if Frank were willing to let.

The young couple came to lunch at Tullivers one boisterous March day and seemed enchanted by all that they saw. They discussed dates and terms, and Frank promised an agreement in writing. He was obviously much taken with them.

Phil was more cautious.

'They seem a sensible pair,' was Frank's comment as the Thomases drove away.

'I hope so,' said Phil. 'She didn't seem to know much about cooking, I thought.'

'Never mind! She'll soon learn,' replied Frank indulgently.

'That's what I'm afraid of! With my kitchen equipment!' retorted Phil. 'Anyway, they both looked clean, and were polite. We forgot to ask him about his music, by the way. Does he play an instrument?'

'A guitar,' said Frank.

'Well, that sounds reasonably quite,' conceded Phil. 'I shouldn't like dear Winnie and Jenny disturbed with drums and cymbals.'

'Oh, I'm sure they wouldn't be so thoughtless as to upset the neighbours,' said Frank reassuringly, 'but I will mention that when I write.'

'It might be as well,' agreed Phil. 'After all we don't really know them, and they may not realize that most of us go to bed around ten at Thrush Green.'

And so the matter was left.

Across the green, at the rectory, Ella was visiting Charles and Dimity Henstock. The question of the rector's holiday was being discussed, and Dimity, always anxious for the health and happiness of her husband, was doing her best to get him to make a decision.

Ella, forthright as ever, was giving vociferous support. 'Don't be such an ass, Charles. Of course, you need a holiday. Everyone does. You'll come back full of beans, and with some new ideas for sermons.'

Charles looked wounded. 'My dear Ella, you speak as though you hear the same sermon time and time again. I assure you—'

'Oh yes, yes!' said Ella testily, fishing out a battered tobacco tin and beginning to roll herself a cigarette. 'I know it sounded like that, but I didn't mean anything so rude. You manage very well,' she continued kindly.

She licked the cigarette paper noisily.

'And I can truthfully say,' she continued, 'that I have only heard that one about the Good Samaritan three times, and the one about arrogance twice. Mind you, as you well know, I don't go *every* Sunday, but still, it's not a bad record on your part, Charles dear.'

The rector's chubby face was creased with distress, but he remained silent. Dimity flew to his support.

'Those sermons, Ella, were *quite different*. Charles approached the subject from a fresh way each time, and in any case, those themes are universal, and can stand being repeated. But you have a point, dear, about returning refreshed from holiday, and I wish Charles would see it.'

'If it's money you need,' said Ella bluntly, 'I can let you have some.'

'We're quite accustomed to being short of money,' said Charles, with a smile. 'But thank you, Ella, for a kind offer. The difficulty is to find the time.'

'Well, what's wrong with nipping away for a week or so between Easter and Whitsun? I can quite see that you've got to fix a holiday in a slack period. Like farmers.'

'Like farmers?' echoed Charles, bemused.

'They have to go away after hay-making or after harvest, you surely know that? And they usually get married in October when the harvest's in, and they have some corn money for a honeymoon.'

'What a grasp you have of agricultural economy,' commented Charles, 'but now I come to think of it, I do seem to marry young farmers in the autumn.'

'I think Ella's suggestion of a May break is very good,' said Dimity, bringing the subject to heel again. 'Why not write to Edgar? Better still, ring him up one evening. Yorkshire would be lovely then, if he could spare the house.'

Charles looked from one determined woman to the other. He knew when he was beaten.

'I'll do something this week,' he promised. 'In any case, I have neglected Edgar sadly for the last few months. That living of his in Yorkshire keeps him very busy, and I really should be the one who writes. But where do the weeks go, Ella? Do you know?'

'They turn into months far too quickly,' said Ella, 'and that's because we're all getting old and can't pack as much into a month as we used to. I'm sure Edgar will understand. What do you propose to do? To have a straight swap of livings for a week or two?'

'Probably. I must say, we both love the Dales, and Edgar and Hilda seem to enjoy the Cotswolds. It's just a case of arranging dates.'

'Which is where I came in,' said Ella, heaving herself to her feet. She ground out her cigarette end in the earth surrounding Dimity's choicest geranium plant on the window sill. Dimity caught her breath in dismay, but, as a true Christian, forbore to comment.

'And of course I'll feed the cat,' continued Ella, making for the door. 'Does she still live on pig's liver?'

'I'm afraid so,' replied Dimity. 'Such dreadful stuff to chop up.'

'No worse than tripe,' said Ella, and vanished.

It was towards the end of March that Winnie Bailey crossed from her house into the surgery which had been her husband's, and was now occupied by John Lovell, the senior partner in the practice since Donald's death. He was a quiet conscientious young man who had learnt a great deal from Winnie's husband, and was liked by his Thrush Green patients.

He glanced up from his papers as Winnie entered, and went to fetch a chair.

'I saw that the waiting room was empty,' said Winnie. 'Are you just off on the rounds?'

'In a few minutes, but no great hurry. Any trouble, Winnie?'

'It's Jenny. She's been off her food for a week or so, and has a horrible cough. But you know Jenny. She won't give up, and says it's nothing. Do come and have a look at her, John dear.'

'I'll come now,' said the young man, picking up his stethoscope. 'There's a particularly vicious flu bug about. It may be that.'

Together they returned to the hall, and thence to the kitchen, where Jenny stood at the sink peeling potatoes. She was unusually pale, John Lovell noticed, but her eyes were inflamed, and her forehead, when he felt it with the palm of his hand, was very hot.

'Sit down,' he directed. Jenny obeyed, but cast an accusing look at Winnie.

'Mrs Bailey,' she croaked. 'There wasn't no need to bother the doctor.'

'Unbutton your blouse,' he directed, arranging his stethoscope, 'and open your mouth.'

Gagged with a thermometer, and immobilized with the stethoscope dabbed here and there on her chest, poor Jenny submitted to a thorough examination.

When it was over John Lovell pronounced sentence. 'Bed for you, and lots to drink. You've a fine old temperature and your lungs are congested.'

'But I'm doing the potatoes!' protested Jenny.

'I can finish those,' said Winnie. 'You must do as Dr Lovell tells you. Up you go, and I'll bring you a hot water bottle and some lemon barley water.'

'I'll go back to the surgery,' John told Winnie, 'and let you have some inhalant and pills.'

Jenny departed reluctantly, and Winnie looked at John.

'I don't think it's much more than an infection of the lungs, but it could be the first stage of something catching. I suppose she's had all the childish ailments?'

'I'm not sure. She was brought up in an orphanage, you know, until she came to her foster-parents here. She was about ten or twelve, I think. No doubt she had all the catching things at the orphanage, but I'll find out from her.'

John went to fetch the medicine, and Winnie put on the kettle for Jenny's bottle.

Later, with two pills inside her, a hot bottle at her feet, and the jug of inhalant steaming on the bedside table Jenny tried to remember if and when she had had whooping cough, scarlet fever, measles, chickenpox, and all the other horrid excitements of childhood.

'I can't honestly recall all of them,' she confessed. 'There was always something going the rounds at the orphanage with so many of us. I know I didn't get ringworm,' she added, with some pride.

'Anyway, don't worry,' said Winnie. 'Let me drape this towel over your head, and you get busy with the Friar's Balsam.'

'Is that what it is?' said Jenny, from beneath her tent. 'I thought it was some new mixture of Dr Lovell's.'

'It's probably got a long and different name,' agreed Winnie, 'but I wouldn't mind betting it's basically dear old Friar's Balsam.'

'Well, *that* can't harm me,' agreed Jenny with relief, and bent to her task.

The next day was one of those windy blue and white March beauties when great clouds scudded eastward, and the sunshine lifted everyone's spirits at Thrush Green.

Everyone, except Albert Piggott.

He was wandering morosely round the churchyard, billhook in hand. If challenged, he would have said that he was busy cutting away the long grass which grew near the tombstones and the surrounding low wall. In fact, he was killing time until ten o'clock when the pub opened.

A small van drew up near him on the other side of the wall, and Percy Hodge, a local farmer, clambered out.

'Ah, Albert!' he began. 'D'you want a little job in the garden?' Occasionally, Albert 'obliged' locally with odd jobs, but latterly he had preferred his leisure to this extra drinking money. Still, Percy was an old friend . . .

'What sort of job?' he enquired cautiously. 'I don't mind telling you, Perce, I ain't the man I was since my operation.'

'Nothing too heavy,' Percy assured him. 'But I've been given a sack of seed potatoes, and I ought to get 'em in. My dear Gertie always put the spuds in. I miss her, that I do.'

Albert was embarrassed to see tears in the eyes of the widower. Mind you, he could sympathize. By and large, wives were kittle-kattle, more trouble than they were worth, but when it came to cooking or gardening they had their uses.

'I suppose I could give you a hand,' said Albert grudgingly. 'But I don't reckon I'm up to digging trenches for a hundredweight of spuds.'

'Oh, I'd be with you,' said Percy, blowing his nose, 'and of course there'd be a few for your garden, Albert. Or don't you bother to cook spuds, now your Nelly's gone?'

'Molly does some for me, now and again,' replied Albert,

secretly nettled by this reference to his truant wife. 'I don't go hungry, and that's a fact.'

'Your Nelly was a good cook, that I did know. Same as my dear Gertie. A lovely hand she had with puff pastry. I miss her sorely, you know.'

Albert grunted. Who would have thought old Perce would have been so sorry for himself? Other men had to make do without a wife to look after them. He began to move slowly away from the wall. With Perce at a loose end like this he'd have him there gossiping all day.

'When d'you want me to come up?' he asked, slashing at a dock.

'Tomorrow night suit you? About six, say? Or earlier.'

'Say five,' said Albert. 'Gets dark early still.'

A welcome sound fell upon his ears. It was the landlord of The Two Pheasants opening his doors. Percy Hodge turned to see what was happening. Albert put down his hook on a handy tombstone and looked more alert than he had since he awoke.

'Come and have a pint, Albert,' invited Percy.

And Albert needed no second bidding.

Hard by, at the village school, little Miss Fogerty was enjoying the exhilarating morning. The view from the large window of her terrapin classroom in the playground never failed to give her exquisite pleasure. For years she had taught in the north-east-facing infants' room in the old building, and had pined for sunlight.

Now, transposed to this modern addition, she looked across the valley towards Lulling Woods and relished the warmth of the morning sun through her sensible fawn cardigan.

How lucky she was to have such an understanding head-mistress, she thought. Headmistress and good friend, she amended. Life had never been so rich as it was now, living at the school house, and teaching in this delightful room.

She glanced at the large wall clock, and returned to her duties. Time for the class lesson on money, she told herself. There was a great deal to be said for the old-fashioned method of teaching the class as a whole, now and again, and some of these young children seemed to find great difficulty in recognizing coins of the realm.

She bent to extract a pile of small boxes from the low cupboard. Each contained what Miss Fogerty still thought of as the new decimal money in cardboard. Time was, when she taught for so many years in the old building, that those same tough little boxes held cardboard farthings, halfpennies, pennies, sixpences and shillings. There was still the ancient wall chart, rolled up at the back of the cupboard, which showed:

4 farthings make	1 penny
12 pennies make	1 shilling
20 shillings make	1 pound

Miss Fogerty remembered very clearly how difficult it had been to trace the real coins and cut them out of coloured paper to fix on to the chart. But it had lasted for years, and these children's parents had chanted the table hundreds of times. She felt a pang of nostalgia for times past.

There had been something so solidly *English* about farthings and shillings! And feet and inches, come to that. She hoped that she was progressive enough to face the fact that with the world shrinking so rapidly with all this air travel, and instant communication methods, a common monetary unit was bound to come some day. But really, thought Miss Fogerty, putting a box briskly on each low table, it seemed so *alien* to be dealing in tens when twelve pence to the shilling still haunted the back of one's mind.

'My granny,' said young Peter in the front row, 'learnt me a new song last night.'

'Taught, dear,' replied Miss Fogerty automatically.

'Called "Sing a song of sixpence". Shall I sing it?'

'Later, dear. Now, all sit up straight, and listen to me.'

'What is *sixpence*?' asked Peter.

High time we got on with the lesson, thought Agnes Fogerty, and directed her class to open the boxes.

*

Next door, Harold Shoosmith and his wife Isobel were admiring some early daffodils in their garden. From the house came the whir of the vacuum cleaner as Betty Bell, their helper, crashed happily about her work.

'One thing about our Betty,' observed Harold, 'she tackles everything with a will. Lord alone knows how many glasses she's smashed since she's worked here.'

'Not many since I came,' replied Isobel. 'You haven't noticed but I do the glasses now.'

'Ah! That accounts for the fact that I haven't had to buy any more for eighteen months! Marrying you was the best day's work I ever did.'

'Of course it was,' agreed Isobel matter-of-factly. 'How lucky for you that I took you on.'

A window opened near them and Betty's voice hailed them. '*Telephone!*' she roared.

While Harold was engaged with his caller, Betty caught at her mistress's arm.

'Is it all right if I go a couple of minutes early? Dotty – I mean Miss Harmer – wants me to give her a hand moving out her dresser. Lost some letter or other down the back as ought to be answered today.'

'Of course you can go,' said Isobel. Betty Bell was in great demand, she well knew. Dotty Harmer had employed her long before Isobel, or even Harold when a bachelor, had appeared on the scene. As well as these duties, Betty also kept the village school clean. Isobel was wise enough to recognize that a certain amount of flexibility in Betty's employment was inevitable.

'I must say,' went on Betty, attacking a windowsill with flailing duster, 'its a sight easier working here than at Miss Harmer's. I mean it's clean to start with. And tidy. Always was, even when Mr Shoosmith lived here alone. You don't expect a man to keep himself decent really, let alone a house, but he was always nicely washed and that, and the house always smelt fresh.'

Isobel said gravely that she was pleased to hear it.

'But down Miss Harmer's it's a fair old pig's breakfast, I can tell you. Can't never find nothing, and the dusters is old bloomers of hers like as not. Washed, of course, but you can't get the same gloss on things with 'em like this nice one.'

Isobel felt unequal to coping with this conversation, and said she would get on and see to lunch.

An hour later, Betty entered Dotty's kitchen to find her other employer sitting at the cluttered table studying a form.

'Oh, how nice of you to come, Betty! As a matter of fact I managed to reach this wretched letter by inserting a long knitting needle in the crack. It fell down, and I was able to get it by lying on the floor, and wriggling it out with a poker.' Her wrinkled old face glowed with pride.

'Well, you won't want me then,' said Betty, swatting a fly on the table. 'Filthy things, flies.'

'Oh, do wait while I just fill this in,' said Dotty, 'and perhaps you would be kind enough to post it as you go past the box.'

'Sure I will,' said Betty, lunging with a handy newspaper at another fly. 'You've got some real nasty flies in here.'

'Poor things,' said Miss Harmer, putting down her pen. 'So persecuted. I often wonder if they are as dangerous to health as modern pundits suggest. My grandmother used to sing a charming little song to my baby brother when flies were *quite accepted*.'

She began to sing in a small cracked voice, while Betty watched her with mingled exasperation and amusement.

> *Baby bye, there's a fly,*
> *Let us watch it you and I,*
> *There it crawls, up the walls,*
> *Yet it never falls.*

> *I believe with those six legs*
> *You and I could walk on eggs.*
> *There he goes, on his toes,*
> *Tickling baby's nose.*

'Well,' said Betty, 'fancy letting it! Downright insanitary!'

Dotty tapped the neglected form with her pen. 'Now, how did it go on?'

> *Round and round, on the ground,*
> *On the ceiling he is found.*
> *Catch him? No, let him go,*
> *Do not hurt him so.*

> *Now you see his wings of silk*
> *Dabbling in the baby's milk*
> *Fie, oh fie, you foolish fly!*
> *How will you get dry?*

'Did you ever?' exclaimed Betty. 'I mean, flies in the *milk*!'

'Well, it only goes to show how kind-hearted the Victorians were. And really so much more sensible about disease. My brother grew into a splendid specimen of manhood, despite flies.'

Betty looked at the clock. 'Tell you what, Miss Harmer, I'll come back for that form this afternoon. It'll give you time to work it out, and anyway Willie don't collect till five o'clock.'

Besides that, she thought privately, there was her shopping to do, and heaven alone knew when that would get done if she stayed listening to old Dotty.

'Perhaps that would be best,' agreed Dotty, turning again to her task, while Betty made her escape.

4. DIMITY GETS HER WAY

As the Hursts' departure for America drew nearer there was much speculation about the temporary residents who were going to stay at Tullivers.

'Well, for your sake, Winnie,' said Ella Bembridge, 'I hope they're a quiet lot. Don't want a posse of hippies, or a commune, or whatever the "in-thing" is.'

'Good heavens,' said Winnie reassuringly, 'Frank and Phil would never let the place to people like that! I have every confidence in their judgement. They both liked the young couple, I know, and Frank knew his father years ago.'

'That's not saying much,' said Ella, lighting a ragged cigarette. 'I know a lot of respectable people of my age with the most *extraordinary* children.'

'Jenny says Phil is putting away her best glass and china, which is only prudent, but she seems quite happy to leave everything else as it is. And if she's content, I don't think we need to worry.'

'And how is our Jenny now?'

'She's still got this wretched cough, but won't stay in bed. She's up in her room now, in her dressing gown, dusting the place. I'm getting John to look at her again today. She's still so flushed, I feel sure she's running a temperature.'

'Will she need to do anything at Tullivers?' asked Ella.

'Phil won't hear of it,' replied Winnie. 'She offered, you know, but now that these young people are coming, they can cope, and I intend to dust and tidy up before they arrive, to save Jenny's efforts.'

'You'll be lucky! You know Jenny. A glutton for work!'

She was about to go when Dimity and Charles entered.

'We did knock,' said the rector, 'but I expect you had something noisy working.'

Winnie looked blank.

'Like the vacuum cleaner, or the fridge, or the washing
machine,' enlarged Charles.

'Or the mighty wurlitzer,' added Ella.

'No need to knock anyway,' said Winnie, returning to normal.
'Do sit down. We were just discussing our new neighbours-to-be.'

'I shall call as soon as they have settled in,' said Charles. 'It will
be so nice if they turn out to be regular churchgoers.'

'He plays the guitar,' said Ella.

'I trust that does not preclude him from Christian worship,'
commented Charles.

'I heard that they met at Oxford, but didn't finish their
courses,' contributed Dimity.

'Perhaps they preferred to get out into the world and earn their
livings,' was Ella's suggestion. 'Bully for them, I'd say.'

'Well, he's an estate agent now,' said Winnie. 'Or at least, he
will be. He's joining a firm somewhere near Bicester, I believe, so
Robert said. Frank mentioned it.'

'Dotty intends to supply them with goat's milk,' said Dimity.

'Do they like it?' asked Winnie.

'They will after Dotty's called on them,' forecast Dimity.

'Well, I'm sure they will be very welcome here,' said the
rector. 'We must see that they have an enjoyable stay at Thrush
Green.'

Later in the day, Dr Lovell mounted the stairs to see Jenny. She
had insisted on dressing, but lay on her bed, trying to read. Her
flushed face and hot forehead bespoke a high temperature.

'Let's have a look at your chest,' said John Lovell, after studying the thermometer.

Jenny cautiously undid the top button of her blouse.

'I shall need more than that, Jenny,' observed the doctor. 'You
needn't be shy with me.'

Jenny undid two more buttons with reluctance, and John
studied the exposed flesh. 'Ever had chickenpox?'

'I can't remember,' said Jenny. 'We had all sorts up at the orphanage.'

'Well, you've got it now,' said John. 'So no stirring from this bed until I tell you. Keep on with the tablets, and I'll see you have a cooling lotion to dab on the spots.'

'But what about Mrs Bailey?' cried poor Jenny. 'Won't she catch it?'

'If she had any sense,' replied the doctor, 'she caught it years ago, and is immune. Now, into bed with you.'

Jenny's illness made a pleasurable source of discussion at The Two Pheasants that night.

'No joke getting them childish ailments when you're grown up,' said the landlord, twirling a glass cloth inside a tumbler. 'My old uncle caught the measles when he was nigh on seventy, and we all reckoned it carried him off.'

'Affects the eyes, measles does,' agreed Albert Piggott knowledgeably. 'Got to keep the light low, and lay off the reading. I met a chap in hospital when they whipped out my appendix—'

Meaning glances, and a few groans, were exchanged among the regular patrons. Were they going to go through that lot again from old Albert?

'And he'd had measles a few months before and had to have his spectacles changed after that. Proper weak, his eyes was. Watered horrible.'

'Mumps is worse,' contributed Willie Marchant. 'Can upset all your natural functions. Rob you of your manhood, they say.'

'Well, we don't want to hear about it in here,' said the landlord briskly. 'There's two ladies over there, so watch what you're saying.'

Willie Marchant did not appear abashed, and continued. 'But chickenpox is nasty too. Mixed up with shingles, and that's a real killer, I'm told.'

'Only if it meets round your ribs,' Albert assured him. 'You can have spots all over, but if they meets round your middle you're a goner.'

At this moment, Percy Hodge entered, and was informed of Jenny's illness.

'Poor old girl,' commented Percy, looking genuinely upset. 'I got it when I was about twenty. Got proper fed up with people telling me not to scratch. As though you could stop! Well, she's got my sympathy, that's a fact.'

'One thing,' said one of the regulars, 'she's in the right place. Got the doctor on the premises, as you might say, and you couldn't have anyone better than Mrs Bailey to look after you.'

And with that, all agreed.

The next morning Winnie was surprised to open the front door to Percy Hodge. He was holding a basket with a dozen of the largest, brownest eggs that she had ever encountered.

'Thought Jenny might be able to manage an egg,' said Percy.

'Won't you come in?'

'Well, that's nice of you. How is she?' he asked, following Winnie down the hall and into the kitchen.

'She seems a little easier now that the rash has come out,' replied Winnie, unpacking the basket and placing the superb eggs carefully in a blue and white basin. 'Percy, I've never seen such beauties as these! I shall take them upstairs to show her later on. I'm sure she will be so grateful. What a kind thought of yours.'

Percy suddenly looked shy. 'Well, I've known Jenny since we was at Sunday School together. She's a good girl. I was sorry to hear she was poorly. Give her my regards, won't you?'

He accepted the empty basket, and retraced his steps to the front door.

'Of course, I will,' promised Winnie, and watched Percy cross the green towards the lane leading to his farm.

What a very kind gesture, thought Winnie, toiling upstairs with the eggs, and Percy's message, for the invalid. She suddenly remembered that Percy was a recent widower. Could it be . . . ? But no, she chided herself, of course not. She must not put two and two together and make five.

'Just look what someone's sent you,' she said to the invalid, holding out the blue and white bowl.

'Good heavens!' cried Jenny. 'We'd best have an omelette for lunch!'

It was a sparkling April morning when the Hursts drove off from Tullivers to Heathrow. Harold Shoosmith had offered to drive them there, and Jeremy and Winnie Bailey accompanied them in the car to see them off.

Much to everyone's relief, Jeremy was cheerful and excited. Winnie Bailey was quite prepared to cope with some tears at parting, but was pleasantly surprised when the final kisses were exchanged without too much emotion all round.

'Not very long before we're back,' promised Phil, producing a small parcel for her son. 'Don't open it until you get back to Aunt Winnie's, darling.'

Jeremy waved vigorously to his departing parents and was quite willing to return to Harold's car, clutching the present. It had been arranged beforehand that there would be no waiting about at the airport to see the aeroplane leave the ground.

'God knows how long it will be before we finally get away,' Frank had said to Winnie. 'You know how it is these days: "Regret to say there is a mechanical fault." That's a two-hour job while they solder on the wing. Then the tannoy goes again: "Regret there is an electrical fault", and off you go for your forty-third cup of coffee while they unravel the wires for another hour. No, Winnie dear, you and Harold make tracks back to Thrush Green with the boy, and then we shall be able to ring you to ask if you would mind fetching us back until the next day.'

Luckily, Frank's prognostications were proved wrong, and their flight actually departed on the right day, and only a quarter of an hour behind schedule.

'What do you think it can be?' asked Jeremy shaking the parcel vigorously, when they were on their return journey. 'It doesn't rattle.'

'Try smelling it,' suggested Harold. 'Might be bath cubes.'

'*Bath cubes?*' said Jeremy with disgust. 'Why *bath cubes?*'

'Right shaped box. Long and thin.'

'It might be sweets,' said Winnie. 'Some rather gorgeous nougat comes in boxes that shape.'

Jeremy's small fingers pressed round the edge of the wrapping paper. 'Anyway, I'm not to open it until we get home,' he said at last, 'so put your foot down, Uncle Harold. I'm *busting* to see what's inside.'

He sat in the front passenger seat, parcel held against his stomach, and babbled happily to Harold about car engines, motor boats, his kitten, what Miss Fogerty said about tadpoles and a host of other interesting topics upon which Harold commented briefly as he drove.

In the back, Winnie Bailey, much relieved at the good spirits of her charge, dozed gently and did not wake until the car stopped at Thrush Green.

'Now I can open it, can't I?' begged Jeremy.

'Of course,' said Winnie and Harold together.

The child ripped away the paper, and disclosed a long red box. Inside, lying upon a cream velvet bed lay a beautiful wrist watch. Jeremy's eyes opened wide with amazement.

'Look!' he whispered. 'And it's mine! Shall I put it on?'

'Why not?' replied Harold.

He helped the child to slide the expanding bracelet over his wrist. The three sat in silence while the child savoured his good fortune.

At length, he gave a great sigh of supreme satisfaction. 'I can't believe it's really mine,' he said to Winnie. 'I'm so glad I've had chickenpox.'

'Chickenpox?' said Winnie, bemused.

'I can go straight up to Jenny and show her,' said the boy, getting out of the car, and making for the Baileys' gate without a backward glance.

'I must thank you on behalf of us both,' said Winnie to Harold with a smile.

Over at the rectory Charles and Dimity were poring over a letter from their old friend Edgar. There was nothing that he and Hilda would enjoy more than two weeks at Thrush Green in the near future.

He had already made tentative arrangements with obliging neighbouring clergymen who would undertake his duties while he was away, so that Charles and Dimity would be quite free. He suggested the first two weeks in May, with Easter behind them and Whitsun well ahead.

Charles thought of Ella's remark about farmers taking their break between haytime and harvest. How well it would fit in, two weeks away between the great church festivals!

'I must get in touch with Anthony Bull at Lulling, and see if dear old Jocelyn feels up to coming out of retirement at Nidden,' he told Dimity, naming the Lulling vicar, and a saintly eighty-year-old who occasionally held the fort for local clergymen in times of emergency.

'Of course they'll help,' said Dimity, 'and they know full well that you will be happy to do the same for them at any time.'

'I'll go and see them both today,' replied Charles, 'and we'll ring Edgar about tea time.'

'Make it after six, dear,' said Dimity. 'Yorkshire is a long way off, and the phone call will be so much cheaper.'

'How right you are,' agreed the rector. With his modest stipend, it was a blessing to have Dimity to remind him of the need for frugality.

He looked round his study when his wife had departed to the kitchen. Since his marriage, Dimity had done her best to mitigate the austerity of this sunless room where so much of his work was done. She had put a rug down by the desk, to keep his feet from the inhospitable cold linoleum which covered the floor of the room. She had bought some shabby but thick curtains from a village jumble sale, to take the place of the cotton ones which had draped the study windows ever since he had taken up residence years ago.

There was always a small vase of flowers on the side table, at the moment complete with pheasant-eye narcissi and sprigs of young greenery from the garden. An electric fire had been installed, and although Charles himself never thought to switch it on, used as he was to a monastic chill in the room, Dimity would tiptoe in and rectify matters on icy mornings.

He was a fortunate man, he told himself, to have such a wonderfully unselfish wife, and one who had the gift of making a home in the straitened circumstances in which they lived.

He thought of her suggestion about transferring his things from his present room to the upstairs one above the kitchen. Frankly, he disliked the idea. The very thought of carrying all his books up the steep stairs, of getting new shelves built, of sorting out his archaic filing system, and of asking someone to help him to manhandle his desk and armchair and all the other heavy furniture which was needed in his work, appalled him.

And yet Dimity was quite right, of course. That room was certainly much lighter and warmer. They would not need the electric fire as they did here. In the end, he supposed, they would save money. But what an upheaval! Could he face it?

He looked again at the results of Dimity's labours on his behalf. How it would please her to have him safely ensconced in

that pleasant back room! Surely, it was the least that one could do, to give way to one who was so unselfish and loving!

Charles leapt to his feet on impulse, and traversed the dark wind tunnel of a corridor to find Dimity in the comparative warmth of the kitchen at its end.

'My dear,' he cried, 'I've decided that your idea of moving the study upstairs is a wonderful one! As soon as we get back from Yorkshire we'll transfer everything, and meanwhile I'll think of someone to ask to make some shelves while we're away.'

Dimity left the onion she was chopping on the draining board and came to hug her husband.

'What a relief, Charles dear! It will be so much better for you, I know. You really are a good man.' Her face was radiant.

'I ought to be a lot better,' replied Charles. 'One can only go on trying, I suppose.'

That afternoon, when Charles had mounted his bicycle to go down the hill to Lulling to visit the vicar, Dimity went across the road to see Ella at the cottage which she had shared for many years with her redoubtable friend. She found her threading her ancient handloom on the table in the sitting room window.

'Hello, Dim,' she greeted her friend. 'Look at this for organization! I'm getting ahead with my scarves for Christmas. Any particular colour you fancy?'

Dimity swiftly went over the plentiful supply of Ella's scarves which were already stocked in a drawer. Pink, fawn, yellow, grey – now, what *hadn't* she got?

'I think a pale blue would be lovely,' she said bravely. 'It goes with so many colours, doesn't it? Thank you, Ella.'

She sat herself on the well-worn sofa, and watched Ella's hands moving deftly at her task.

'I've brought some good news,' she began.

'Won the pools?'

'Alas, no. But Charles has agreed to move his study upstairs.'

'Well, it's about time too. I wonder he hasn't had double pneumonia working in that morgue of his. Want a hand shifting stuff?'

'Well, not at the moment, Ella dear. But perhaps later. We don't propose to do anything until we come back from our holiday.'

'Tell me more,' demanded Ella.

Dimity explained about Edgar and Hilda, and the hoped-for help of Lulling's vicar and old Jocelyn.

'Thrush Green will be empty for most of May then,' said Ella. 'What with the Hursts away, and you two gallivanting in Yorkshire.'

'Oh come!' protested Dimity. 'That's only four of us. And in any case, the new couple will be at Tullivers then. Think how nice it will be to have some fresh faces here.'

'Depends on the faces,' replied Ella. 'Frankly, I prefer old friends. For all we know, these two outsiders are going to cause more trouble than Thrush Green bargains for.'

And as it happened, Ella was to be proved right.

5. THE HENSTOCKS SET OFF

The last day of April closed in golden tranquillity. Warm and calm, from dawn until sunset, there had been promise of the summer to come. The daffodils and early blossom in the Thrush Green gardens scarcely stirred all day, and the bees were already busy, their legs powdered with yellow pollen.

Joan Young, wandering about their small orchard, thought that she had never seen such drifts of daffodils there before. They surged around the wheels of Mrs Curdle's ancient caravan, and she remembered, with a sudden pang, that this would be the first year without Curdles' Fair to enliven May the first.

What must Ben be thinking? He never mentioned the fair in her presence, but she knew that Molly wondered if he grieved over the loss. For that matter, all Thrush Green mourned the passing of their much-loved fair. Now Mrs Curdle lay at rest across the green she knew so well, and this reminded Joan of something else.

She returned to the house and called upstairs to Molly.

'Help yourself to daffodils. There are masses just now, and if Ben wants some for his mother's grave, tell him to pick all he wants.'

Later that evening she saw Ben carrying a fine bouquet across to the courtyard. He had paid his tribute to his grandmother every May Day since the old lady's death, and Joan liked to think that his loyal affection was shared by all Mrs Curdle's friends at Thrush Green.

Much to the consternation of everyone, the question of Dotty adopting a child cropped up once more. She broached the subject

44

herself one morning when she called at the rectory.

'You know its weeks now since I wrote to four or five reputable adoption societies, and still no result. Isn't it dilatory? Here I am, hale and hearty, and all prepared to share a good home with some child in need – male or female – and all I've had have been acknowledgements of my letters.'

'But, Dotty dear,' began Dimity, 'these things always take time.'

Charles, more bravely, spoke his mind. 'I think you should reconsider the whole question of adoption, Dotty. You may be hale and hearty, but you are getting on, and I don't think any adoption society would allow a child to settle with you. And naturally, a home that can offer *two* parents is going to be preferred.'

Dotty snorted impatiently. 'I have filled in a form or two, come to think of it, and of course I had to put my age and status on them. And a rather strange fellow came to see me.'

That, thought Dimity, would be enough to put anyone off. Dotty's kitchen alone would strike horror into the heart of anyone trying to find a home for a stray cat, let alone a young human being.

'Are you sure he was from one of the societies?' asked Charles. 'Some very odd people call at houses these days to see if they are worth burgling later.'

Dotty dismissed this alarmist suggestion. 'Oh, he showed me some papers and a card which guaranteed his claims. I rather forget which society he represented, but I gave him a cup of coffee. He left most of it,' she added. 'Rather a waste of Dulcie's good goat's milk, I thought, but dear old Flossie finished it up when he had gone.'

She patted the cocker spaniel at her feet with affection. Flossie's tail thumped appreciatively on the rectory floor.

'I feel obliged to say this,' said Charles. 'I am positive that this idea of yours – though well-meant, and typical of your generosity, Dotty my dear – is quite wrong, and I can't help feeling that no adoption society would find you a suitable person to bring up a child.'

'And why not?' demanded Dotty, turning pink with wrath. 'I should put the child's interest first every time. There is plenty of room in my cottage, and all those lovely animals to enjoy. And of course I intend to leave my possessions, such as they are, to the child when I die.'

The kind rector sighed, but stuck to his guns. As Dimity, and all his parishioners knew well, his gentle manner cloaked an inflexible will when it came to doing his duty.

'Give up the idea, Dotty. Why not invite a younger relative or friend to share the cottage and to help you with your charges. What about Connie? You enjoy her company.'

Connie was Dotty's niece, a cheerful single woman in her forties, who lived some sixty miles west of Thrush Green and occasionally called on her aunt.

'Connie has quite enough to do with her own smallholding,' replied Dotty. 'And now she has taken up breeding Shetland ponies, and could not possibly find time to move in with me – even if she had the inclination.' She reflected for a moment. 'Of course, if I could buy that small paddock of Percy Hodge's, there might be an incentive for Connie to bring the ponies there. I must say I should enjoy their company.'

'And Connie's too, I trust.'

Dotty shrugged her thin shoulders. 'Oh, Connie's quite a reasonable gel. David brought her up very sensibly without too much money to spend, but I don't want *Connie*. And I'm quite sure Connie doesn't want *me*!'

She rose to her feet, hitched up her wrinkled stockings, and set off for the door, followed by the faithful Flossie.

'I'm quite sure all your advice is for the best, Charles,' she told him. 'But I know what I want, and I don't intend to give up my plans just yet. Have a good holiday in Yorkshire. I shall call on Edgar and Hilda when they have settled in, and bring them a goat's cheese which is already maturing nicely in the larder.'

And on this gruesome note she left them.

*

46

The possibility of some poor unfortunate child finding itself adopted by Dotty was an absorbing topic of conversation for the residents of Thrush Green and Lulling. All agreed that the idea was typical of Dotty – generous but outrageous. However, the general feeling was summed up by Willie Bond, Willie Marchant's fellow postman.

'No one in his right mind's going to let the old girl have a child living in that pig sty. Stands to reason, these adoption people know what they're up to. She doesn't stand a snowball's chance in hell.'

It gave his listeners some comfort.

Equally absorbing was the strange behaviour of Percy Hodge during the indisposition of Winnie Bailey's Jenny.

The present of eggs was followed by some lamb chops, a box of soap, a large tray of pansy seedlings which Winnie felt obliged to bed out in pouring rain, and several bunches of flowers.

Jenny was bewildered by these attentions, and somewhat scornful. 'What will people think? Silly old man! Making me look a fool.'

'Not at all,' replied Winnie. 'It's most thoughtful of him. I'm sure it's all done in a purely friendly spirit.'

'Well, I'm not so sure he isn't missing his Gertie's cooking,' said Jenny bluntly. 'Looking around for a housekeeper, I'd say. I'm half a mind to snub him soundly, cheeky old thing! As if I'd ever leave you!'

'Don't worry about it,' begged Winnie. 'Just accept the situation, and be polite to him. Time enough to worry if he pops the question.'

But despite her calm exterior, Winnie herself was a little perturbed. Jenny, she suspected, had summed up the position very neatly. If, of course, her feelings changed, marriage to Percy might be a very good thing for dear unselfish Jenny. He was a kindly fellow, affectionate and thoughtful. He had a sizeable farm and a pleasantly situated farmhouse which Jenny would enjoy cherishing. No, thought Winnie, of course she would not stand in Jenny's way if that was what she wanted one day in the future, but how she would miss her if that situation arose!

Comment at The Two Pheasants was less polite.

'No fool like an old fool,' quoted one of the customers.

'You'd think old Perce would count his blessings being a peaceful old widower,' said another sourly. It was well-known that his own marriage was fraught with acidity, acrimony and the results of too much alcohol.

Albert Piggott grunted his agreement. He knew about wives too.

'Not that Jenny wouldn't do well for herself,' he conceded. 'Percy's a warm man. Got a bit in the building society, and some in the post office. He told me so himself one day. And then his Gertie was a rare one for managing. I bet she left a nice little nest-egg. No, if Jenny's got any sense she could do worse than plump for old Percy.'

'What Jenny does is one thing,' announced the local dustman, pushing across his glass for a refill. 'What I hates to see is a chap of Percy's age making sheep's eyes at a gal. Looks a right fool he does, mincin' along with a ruddy bunch of flowers in his hand. Don't seem to care what people say, neither. I told him straight: "You be a bigger fool than you look, Perce Hodge, and that's sayin' something!" But he only smirked. Hopeless, that's what he is! Absolutely hopeless!'

'Ah! He's got it bad,' agreed Mr Jones, the landlord. 'But there, that's love. Takes you unawares like. Now drink up, please gentlemen! You can all see the clock!'

And the affair of Percy and Jenny had to be discussed later in the night air of Thrush Green.

Jeremy, naturally, was an interested observer of Percy's attentions, and frequently enquired about them. Winnie did her best to evade his questions, but he was a persistent young man, and sometimes caught her off guard.

'What will you do if Jenny goes to live at the farm?' he asked one evening, looking up from an ancient jigsaw puzzle which Winnie had unearthed for his pleasure.

'I don't suppose she will go,' answered Winnie equably. 'Jenny seems very happy here.'

'But it may be the last chance she gets of getting married,' pursued Jeremy. 'I mean, she's quite *old*. Do you think she'll have any babies?'

'Was that the door bell?' asked Winnie, playing for time.

'No. You see, you have to be pretty young to have babies. Paul told me all about having them last holiday.'

He searched among the box of pieces and held up a bit of blue sky triumphantly.

And how much, wondered Winnie, did Paul Young impart to his friend of this particular subject? And had Phil been informed?

'Do you think Jenny knows about babies?'

'I'm quite sure she does,' said Winnie hastily.

'Well, it all sounded pretty odd to me when Paul told me, but I was jolly glad to know what that button in your stomach was for at last.'

'Really?' said Winnie, much intrigued.

'Didn't you know? It blows up like a balloon, and when it pops, a baby is there.'

'Indeed?' observed Winnie politely.

'I'm surprised you didn't know,' said Jeremy severely. 'I should have thought Uncle Donald would have told you, him being a doctor. He must have seen it happen.'

'Probably,' said Winnie, 'but he was always very careful not to discuss his patients with me.'

'Ah! That's it, of course! But you will let Jenny know what happens, won't you? She might not be sure.'

'I am positive that Jenny knows all that is necessary,' said Winnie, 'and in any case, arrangements between Mr Hodge and Jenny are entirely their affair. It's something we should not discuss.'

Jeremy looked at her in mild surprise. 'But *everyone*, absolutely *everyone* is talking about it in Thrush Green!' he told her.

And that, thought Winnie, could well be believed.

'Time for supper,' she said briskly, and made her escape to the kitchen.

The day of the Henstocks' departure for Yorkshire dawned bright and windy. Great clouds scudded across the sky before an exhilarating south-wester.

Dimity and Charles packed their luggage into the car in high spirits. The ancient Ford had been polished the day before, and gleaned with unusual splendour. Before they set off, Dimity called at Ella's to give her the key and a number of agitated last-minute directions.

'There are six tins of evaporated milk in the larder for the cat, but there is one opened in the fridge which should be finished up. And there's *plenty* of pig's liver in the freezer, Ella dear, if you don't mind taking out a *small* packet the night before you need it. I've left scissors as well as a knife and fork with her plates, and perhaps—'

'My dear Dim,' said Ella, 'calm down! I know where everything is, and that cat won't starve, believe me. Now, you two go and have a real break, and forget all the duties here. They'll be waiting for you when you get back – you know that.'

'We really will relax,' promised Dimity. 'You can't imagine how we've been looking forward to it. You know the house will be empty until Wednesday? Hilda and Edgar are breaking their journey at Coventry to see a cousin in hospital.'

'I'll keep my eye on things,' Ella assured her, ushering her firmly down the garden path. 'Now off you go, and I'll see you the minute you get back. Have a lovely time.'

She watched Dimity flutter across the road and enter the gloomy portal of the Victorian rectory, then turned back to tackle the daily crossword.

'Poor old Dim,' she said aloud, as she searched for a pencil. 'Do her a world of good to see the back of that dreary house.'

She little thought that her words would prove to be a prophecy.

The bright breezy weather continued in the early days of May, much to the satisfaction of Thrush Green gardeners, zealous housewives who rushed to wash blankets, and Miss Fogerty and Miss Watson who had the inestimable relief of seeing their charges running off steam in the open air at playtimes.

'I think I really must find some new toys for the wet day

cupboard,' observed Agnes to her headmistress. They were enjoying their morning coffee in Agnes's new classroom, and the infant mistress was surveying a pile of torn comics and incomplete jigsaw puzzles which were due to be deposited in the dustbin.

'They've done very well,' conceded Miss Watson, scrutinizing the top comic. 'I see this one is dated 1965. Pity dear old *Rainbow* is now defunct. Did you have it as a child, Agnes?'

'Alas, no! My father thought comics an unnecessary indulgence, but I sometimes saw *Rainbow* at a little friend's house. I particularly enjoyed Marzipan the Magician, and a little girl with two dogs.'

'Bluebell,' said Miss Watson. 'At least, I think it was. It's some time since I read the paper, but how I *loved* Mrs Bruin! I wonder why she always wore a white cap, and that same frock with a poached-egg pattern?'

'Easy to draw, perhaps,' suggested Agnes practically. 'Do you think I could transfer some of the boxes of beads to the wet day box?'

'An excellent idea,' said Miss Watson. 'And remind me to look out some old *Geographical* magazines when we go home. Plenty there to amuse them. Such beautiful pictures – and if you like they could cut some out and start scrap books.'

'That's most generous of you,' said little Miss Fogerty, pink with pleasure at the thought of such riches. With such small joys are good infants' teachers made happy, which may explain why so many remain ever youthful.

Later that evening, Miss Watson routed out the magazines from the landing cupboard, and the two ladies were busy leafing through them when the telephone rang.

Miss Watson retired to the hall and was there for some time. Agnes was just wondering whether a splendid picture of an African family wearing only long ear-rings and a spike through the nose was quite suitable for her infants, when her headmistress returned. She was breathing rather heavily.

'That was Ray,' she said. 'They are just about to set off on this Cotswold tour they had to postpone because of that wretched dog of theirs.'

'Is it better?' asked Agnes.

'Unfortunately, yes! They propose to bring it with them – which I consider a mistake, and told Ray so – but, as you know, they are quite besotted with the animal and fear that it might pine in kennels.'

'Won't it be difficult to find hotels willing to take a labrador? I mean, it's such a large dog.'

'It is indeed, and this one is completely untrained, as you know. That is why Ray asked if they could stay here for two or three nights.'

'Oh! Can we manage?'

'We *cannot*!' said Dorothy Watson firmly. 'I told him so last time he mooted the question, and I suppose he thinks that I may have changed my mind. Well, I haven't. I have invited them to tea on the day they arrive in Lulling, and the dog can stay in the car while they eat it.'

'But, Dorothy, it may be a cold afternoon,' pleaded Agnes. 'Perhaps it could stay in the kitchen?'

'Well, we'll see,' said Dorothy, relenting a little, in the face of her friend's agitation. 'But I make no rash promises.'

And with that little Miss Fogerty had to be content.

She spent the night comforting herself with the thought that dear Dorothy's bark was always worse than her bite, and with another thought, equally cheering, that blood was thicker than water, and even if The Fleece forbade animals, The Fuchsia Bush always allowed pets to accompany their owners at lunch or tea.

The last of Agnes Fogerty's hopes was somewhat dashed the next morning by Willie Bond, the fat postman who shared the Thrush Green post round with gaunt Willie Marchant.

'Heard the latest?' he inquired, passing over three manilla envelopes obviously from the Education Office, and a postcard from America which, no doubt, was from the Hursts.

'No, Willie. What is it?'

Agnes could hear the kettle boiling, and was anxious to return to her duties.

'They say the old Fuchsia Bush is packing up.'

'Never!' gasped Agnes. 'I can't believe it! It always seems so busy.'

'Well, there it is. Can't make it pay, seemingly, and them girls wants the earth for wages, no doubt, so it'll have to put up its shutters.'

'We shall all miss it,' said Agnes.

'Your kettle's boiling from the sound of things,' said Willie, making slowly for the gate. 'Be all over the floor by the time you gets there.'

'Yes, of course, of course!'

Agnes hurried down the hall and met Dorothy entering the kitchen. She told her the dread news.

Miss Watson took the blow with her usual calm demeanour. 'I've no doubt that the story is greatly exaggerated, Agnes, and I shan't waste my time believing it until I have heard officially. Willie Bond was always a scaremonger, and I remember that he was always given to tall tales, even as a child.'

'But I wonder how he came by the story?' wondered Agnes, tapping her boiled egg.

'Time alone will tell,' responded her headmistress. 'Could you pass the butter, dear?'

6. A Turbulent Tea Party

As Miss Watson had surmised, Willie Bond's tidings were grossly exaggerated, although, even in the modified version, the truth was quite upsetting enough to the inhabitants of Lulling and Thrush Green.

The Fuchsia Bush, it seemed, was going to be open from 10 a.m. until 2.30 p.m., catering as usual for exhausted shoppers needing morning coffee, and local businessmen and women needing a modest lunch. The premises would then close until 6.30 p.m. when it would offer dinner to those who required it. The time-honoured afternoon tea was now a thing of the past, and regret and acrimony were widely expressed.

'Never heard such nonsense,' said Ella Bembridge to Winnie Bailey. 'The Fuchsia Bush was always busiest at tea time, and they've got that marvellous girl in the kitchen who knocks up the best scones in the Cotswolds. Why, those alone bring in dozens of travellers between four and five every afternoon.'

'They say it's a staffing problem,' replied Winnie. 'Evidently they can get part-timers to come in the morning and to cope with the lunches, and more to appear in the evenings, when the husbands are home to look after the children.'

'Well, it's a scandal,' replied Ella, blowing out a cloud of acrid smoke. 'It was just the place to meet after shopping or the dentist, and I must say their Darjeeling tea took some beating. As for trying to compete with The Fleece and The Crown and Anchor for dinners, it's plain idiotic.'

'Well, Jenny tells me that she knows two women who are going to do the evening stint there, and everyone feels it might work, so we must just wait and see.'

Miss Watson, proved right yet again, was inclined to be indulgent about the lost tea time at The Fuchsia Bush. In any case, teachers were usually buttoning children's coats, and exhorting them to keep out of trouble on their homeward journeys at the relevant opening time.

As she remarked to little Miss Fogerty: 'It won't affect us greatly, dear, but I think it is very foolish of these tea shops to close at such a time. American tourists alone must miss experiencing a truly English tea with attentive waitresses in those pretty flowered smocks to serve them.'

Miss Fogerty, whose purse had seldom allowed her to indulge in even such a modest repast as tea at The Fuchsia Bush, agreed wholeheartedly. She disliked change.

The Misses Lovelock, whose Georgian house stood close to the premises, were the only ones who seemed to favour the project.

'We shall have a little peace on summer afternoons now,' said Bertha. 'Why, I've even seen coaches stop there and drop *hordes* of people – some of them *not* quite out of the top drawer – and, of course, quite a few wandered about while they waited to go in, and one day a most dreadful man, with a squint, pressed his face to our window and very much frightened us all.'

'Good job it was downstairs,' Ella had remarked. 'Upstairs you might have been in your corsets, or less.'

Bertha chose to ignore such coarseness. Really, at times one wondered about Ella's upbringing!

'No,' said Violet, hastening to Bertha's support, 'we shan't mind The Fuchsia Bush closing for teas, whatever the rest of Lulling is saying.'

'You'll just get the racket later in the day,' observed Ella, stubbing out a cigarette in a priceless Meissen bon-bon dish at her side. 'Be plenty of cars parking, I expect, when they open in the evening.'

And, happy to have the last word for once, Ella departed.

The visit of Miss Watson's brother Ray and his wife occurred about this time. Although little Miss Fogerty was glad to see that Dorothy's sisterly feelings had prompted her to invite Ray and Kathleen to tea after school, nevertheless she had inner forebodings about their reception.

There was no doubt about it. The unfortunate coolness which had arisen dated from Dorothy's enforced stay in hospital with a broken hip some time before. Agnes, who had been a devoted visitor, realized that Dorothy's assumption that she would be invited to convalesce at Ray's was misplaced, to say the least of it. Luckily, she had been in a position to offer immediate help, and took up residence at the school house to look after the invalid. Dorothy, ever grateful, had reciprocated by asking her old colleague to make her stay a permanent one, and very happily the arrangement had turned out.

But Ray and Kathleen would never, it seemed, be quite as dear to her headmistress. Agnes could only hope that the proposed tea party would pass off pleasantly, and that bygones would remain bygones.

It was a perfect early May afternoon. Agnes had taken her little brood for a walk along the track to Lulling Woods, passing Dotty

Harmer's house, and waving to that lady as she tended a large and smoky bonfire of garden rubbish near the hedge.

The grass was dry enough for the children to sit on before they returned, and Agnes leant back against a dry stone wall out of the light wind and admired some early coltsfoot across the track, and some young ferns, curled like sea horses, against the Cotswold stone. The children seemed content to lie on their backs, chewing grass, and gazing at the sky above. It was a well-known fact that little Miss Fogerty had the happy knack of keeping children quiet and contented. The present scene would have proved this to any onlooker.

Agnes allowed her mind to dwell on the approaching confrontation. Dorothy had made a superb three-tier sponge cake, using five eggs and the best butter, and Agnes herself had cut cucumber sandwiches during the lunch break, and carefully wrapped them to keep fresh. Home-made scones with plum jam, and some delicious chocolate biscuits filled with marshmallow completed the meal provided. It was particularly unselfish of dear Dorothy to add the last ingredient to their afternoon tea, thought Agnes, as she adored marshmallows but was obliged to resist such temptation in the interest of watching her weight.

Agnes looked at her watch. 'Time to be going!' she called, and shepherded her charges back to Thrush Green.

The two ladies were back in the school house by a quarter to four. Dorothy had changed into a becoming blue jersey two-piece, and Agnes had put on her best silk blouse with her mother's cameo brooch at the neck.

The tea tray waited in the sitting room, and on a side table were all the festive dishes. Some golden daffodils scented the air, and the ladies waited expectantly. The visitors were due at four o'clock, but at ten past they had not appeared.

Dorothy began to get restive, wandering to the window to look down the road, and then back to the kitchen to make sure that the kettle was ready. Agnes viewed her growing impatience with some apprehension. Dear Dorothy was a stickler for punctuality.

'Isn't it extraordinary,' exclaimed her headmistress, 'how people never arrive on time? I mean, if I say between seven and seven-thirty, it's usually a quarter to eight before the bell rings. Why not seven-fifteen? Why not seven, for that matter?'

Agnes assumed that this was a rhetorical question and forbore to answer.

The little clock on the mantel piece struck a quarter past four, and Dorothy plumped up a cushion with unnecessary force.

'Of course, Ray never had any idea of time, nor Kathleen, come to that. Ray was even late for his own wedding, I remember. The whole congregation waiting for the bridegroom! You can imagine! One expects some delay before the bride appears but—' She broke off suddenly. 'Here they are at last! And about time too. Would you switch on the kettle, Agnes dear, while I let them in?'

Polite kisses were exchanged in the hall, and Miss Watson led the way into the sitting room. No apologies were made for their late arrival, she noticed, although it was now twenty-five minutes past the hour, but she decided to ignore the omission. As she had remarked to Agnes, time meant nothing to this pair.

'And how are you finding The Fleece?' she enquired.

'Rather run down,' said Ray. 'Under new management, I gather, and not very competent.'

At that moment, a ferocious barking broke out, and Agnes, coming in with the teapot, very nearly dropped it in her alarm.

The two visitors had rushed to the window, so that Agnes put down the teapot without being greeted.

'Oh, *poor* Harrison!' cried Kathleen. 'He's seen a horrid cat. So upsetting. We'd better bring him in, Ray.'

Ray began to make for the door.

'By all means go and calm the dog,' said Dorothy, with a touch of hauteur, 'but I think it would be wise to leave him outside while we enjoy our tea.'

'He always has tea with us,' said Ray. 'He usually has a saucer on the hearth rug. With plenty of milk, of course.'

'But not today,' replied Dorothy firmly, the complete headmistress. 'Now do say hello to dear Agnes who has been looking forward to seeing you so much.'

Reminded of their manners, Ray and Kathleen greeted her warmly, and did their best to ignore the persistent whining and yelping issuing from their car. But clearly their minds were elsewhere, and conversation had to be carried on at a high pitch to overcome the appalling din made by the unhappy animal.

'I take it that the management at The Fleece welcomes animals?' ventured little Miss Fogerty.

'I wouldn't say *welcomes*,' said Ray. 'Harrison is being allowed to sleep in his basket in one of the stables. No dogs in the hotel. That's the rule, we were told the minute we arrived.'

'Why "Harrison"?' asked Dorothy, passing the cucumber sandwiches.

Kathleen looked momentarily pleased. 'Well, you see, he is the image of the butcher who used to come round when we were first married. Isn't he, Ray?'

'Exactly. Same brown eyes, same expression—'

'Same black coat?' murmured Dorothy.

The visitors laughed politely.

'Almost,' agreed Kathleen, 'and certainly interested in *meat*.'

Agnes, who began to feel that the dog would be better ignored, if such a happy situation should ever be possible with the ear-splitting cacophony engulfing them, asked after Kathleen's health. At once, Ray's wife assumed a melancholy expression.

'I'm having some new treatment for my migraine attacks,' she told them, accepting a second cup of tea. 'It's terribly expensive, and I have to make two trips a week, but I think it may be doing me good.'

'I am so glad,' said kind Agnes.

'And I've been having attacks of vertigo,' volunteered Ray, with a hint of pride. 'Something to do with the middle ear. Very disconcerting.'

Agnes wondered if the dog's powerful voice could contribute to this discomfort, but thought it wiser to remain silent. Not once, she noticed, with rare warmth, had they enquired after poor Dorothy's broken hip – a much more serious business, surely!

'But there,' continued Kathleen, with sad recognition, 'I suppose we can't expect to be as spry as we were twenty years ago.'

'Indeed no!' agreed Dorothy, rising to cut the splendid sponge. She walked across to Kathleen, plate in hand. Was her limp rather more pronounced than usual, Agnes wondered? A little stiff from sitting perhaps, she decided.

'And how is the leg?' enquired Ray, somewhat tardily.

'I do my best to ignore it,' replied Dorothy. 'No one wants to hear about the troubles of the elderly.'

Kathleen greeted this pointed remark with a swiftly indrawn breath, and a meaning glance at her husband. He, man-like, pretended to be engrossed with his tea cup.

'And where are you proposing to go tomorrow?' asked Agnes hastily.

Before Ray could answer, Kathleen spoke. 'It's amazing how quickly people get over these hip operations these days. Why, a young curate we know was actually *dancing* six months after he fell from his bicycle.'

'He was fortunate,' said Dorothy.

'Oh, I don't know,' said Kathleen, shouting above the racket from the imprisoned dog. 'I'm sure it's a matter of attitude of mind. He *intended* to get better, just as quickly as possible. I think some people enjoy being invalids.'

Agnes noted with alarm that a pink flush was suffusing Dorothy's face, a sure sign of temper, and really, thought her loyal assistant, she had every right to be cross under the circumstances.

'I don't,' said Dorothy shortly.

'Of course not,' agreed Ray. 'It was exactly what I said to Kathleen when she was so worried about you in hospital.'

'Indeed?' replied his sister icily.

'Kathleen was a martyr to her migraine at the time, as you know, otherwise we should have invited you to stay with us when you were discharged. But we knew you wanted to get home and pick up your normal life again. I said so at the time, didn't I, Kathleen?'

'You did indeed, dear,' said Kathleen, dabbing her mouth with a spotless linen napkin and leaving lipstick as well as jam upon it.

Before any civilized reply could be made, there was a rapping at the front door. Agnes, glad to escape, hurried to open it, and was confronted by Dotty Harmer with her spaniel, Flossie, on a lead. A battered metal milk can dangled from the other hand.

Without being invited, Dotty pushed past Agnes and entered the sitting room. She was in a state of considerable agitation, and burst into speech.

'Oh, Dorothy my dear, there is a poor dog *absolutely stifling to death* in a car outside. No window left open, and it is in a terrible state of anxiety. Aren't people thoughtless? Really they need a horse-whipping, and my father would have administered it, I assure you, if he had come across such fiends! Someone calling at The Two Pheasants, I suppose, or at the Shoosmiths.'

'The dog belongs to my brother here,' said Dorothy, with a hint of smugness in her tone. 'I'm sorry it upset you so, Dotty dear. I'm afraid it must have upset a great many people at Thrush Green during the past hour.'

Dotty was not the slightest bit abashed. 'I don't think I have had the pleasure of meeting you before,' she said, transferring Flossie's lead to her left hand and entangling it dangerously with the milk can, whilst proffering her right.

'My sister-in-law Kathleen. My brother Ray. My friend Miss Harmer,' intoned Dorothy.

Ray bowed slightly, Kathleen gave a frosty smile, and Dorothy waved at the tea tray.

'Let me give you some tea, Dotty. Do sit down.'

Outside, the barking changed to a high-pitched squealing, even more agitating than before. Ray began to make for the door.

'Excuse me, I'd better bring Harrison in,' he said. He was through the door before anyone could stop him.

'So kind of you, Dorothy, but I'm on my way to Ella's and mustn't delay.'

Dotty began to make her way to the door. Flossie's lead was now hopelessly tangled around her wrinkled stockings.

At that moment, Ray's labrador, slavering at the mouth, burst into the room, gave a demented yelp, and rushed at Flossie.

The noise was indescribable. Flossie, the meekest of animals, screamed with alarm. Harrison charged into the table, knocking the sponge cake, chocolate biscuits, two tea cups, milk jug and a flurry of knives and teaspoons to the floor.

Dotty, pulled off balance, fell across Agnes's chair, driving her mother's cameo brooch painfully into her throat. Dorothy, ever quick-witted, sat down abruptly before her own precarious balance added to the confusion, and Kathleen, cowering in her chair, gave way to hysterics.

This scene of chaos confronted Ray when at last he regained the sitting room. With commendable promptitude he caught Harrison by the collar, and held him firmly, while Agnes and Dotty recovered their balance. The milk can had rolled under

Agnes's armchair and was dispersing a rivulet of goat's milk over the carpet.

'I apologize for this mess,' said Dotty. 'You must let me pay for any cleaning you have to have done. Goat's milk can be so very *pervasive*. I'd better return home and fetch some more for Ella. Luckily, Dulcie is giving a splendidly heavy yield at the moment.'

Quite in command of herself, she smiled politely in the direction of the hysterical Kathleen, now throwing herself about alarmingly in her chair, waved to Ray, and took the shaken, but now well-behaved, Flossie into the hall. Agnes accompanied her, hoping that the blood on her throat from the brooch's wound would not stain her best silk blouse.

'Are you *sure* you would not like to rest for a little?' enquired Agnes. 'The dining room has a most comfortable armchair, if you would like a few minutes' peace.'

'Thank you, my dear, but I am quite all right. The air will refresh me.'

Agnes watched her walk to the gate, as spry as a sparrow, and none the worse it seemed for her tumble. She returned, full of foreboding, to the scene of battle.

'Who *is* that interfering old busybody?' Ray was asking, as she returned.

'A dear friend of mine,' replied Dorothy, 'and a true animal lover. I absolutely agree with her that it was *monstrous* of you to leave that dog shut in the car.'

Kathleen's hysterics were now slightly muted, but had turned to shattering hiccups.

'If you remember,' she began, and gave a mighty hiccup, 'you yourself refused to have poor Harrison indoors.'

'I should have thought that *even you* knew better than to leave the car hermetically sealed. Calling yourselves animal lovers,' said Dorothy, with withering scorn. 'And the poor thing so badly trained that it cannot be brought into a Christian household.'

She bent down to retrieve the best china from the floor, whilst Ray picked up teaspoons with one hand and dabbed at the goat's milk with the other holding his handkerchief.

'*Please*, Ray,' said Dorothy, 'leave the mess to Agnes and me. We don't want it made worse by the use of your handkerchief.'

Agnes felt that, provoked though she might well be, such a slur on the cleanliness of her brother's personal linen was carrying things rather far.

'I will fetch some clean water and a cloth,' she said hastily, and made her escape. A wild wailing noise followed her. Obviously, Kathleen was off again!

'I think,' Ray was saying, when she returned with her cleaning materials, 'that we had better be going.'

'I wholeheartedly agree,' said Dorothy, standing facing him.

'You have thoroughly upset poor Kathleen,' he went on, 'and you know how she suffers with migraine.'

'When it suits her,' responded Dorothy.

'Are you implying,' cried her incensed brother, 'that Kathleen *pretends* to have these dreadful attacks?'

A terrible hiccup arrested Kathleen's wailing. She was now on her feet, eyes blazing.

'How dare you say such things? You know I'm a martyr to migraine! Not that I've ever had the slightest sympathy from you. You are the wickedest, most callous, unfeeling—'

Another hiccup rendered her temporarily speechless. Ray took the opportunity to put his arm about his wife, and to shepherd her and the panting Harrison to the door.

'Come along, my dear. We'll go straight back to The Fleece, and you must lie down with one of your tablets.'

'But poor Harrison hasn't had his tea,' wailed Kathleen. 'You know he likes it on the hearth rug!'

'There is plenty for him,' observed Dorothy, 'wherever he looks on the carpet.'

It was Agnes who saw them to the door, and then into their car.

'I shall never come here again,' cried Kathleen, still hiccupping violently.

'We are deeply wounded,' said Ray. 'I don't think I shall want to see Dorothy – sister though she is – for a very long time!'

They drove towards Lulling, Harrison still barking, and Agnes returned to break the dreadful news that Dorothy might never see the pair again.

'What a relief!' said her headmistress, with infinite satisfaction. 'Now, we'll just get this place to rights, and have a quiet evening with our knitting, Agnes dear.'

7. THE FIRE

After such a devastating experience it was hardly surprising that little Miss Fogerty slept badly. Usually, she read for half an hour and then was more than ready to plump up her pillows, put out the bedside light, and welcome deep sleep within ten minutes.

But on this occasion sleep evaded her. She went over, in her mind, all the terrible details of that catastrophic tea party. The noise of Kathleen's hysterical wailing still sounded in her ears. Ray's furious face, and Dorothy's tart retorts tormented her memory.

St Andrew's clock struck midnight, and she tossed back the bedclothes and went to survey Thrush Green by moonlight.

It was still and beautiful. No lights shone from the houses around the green, but the moonlight silvered the windows and dappled the young leaves of the chestnut avenue. Far away, along the lane to Nidden, an owl gave his wavering cry, and from the other direction came the distant sound of one of Lulling's rare goods trains chugging through the deserted station.

The air was cool from the open window and scented with the pheasant-eye narcissi which grew against the wall. Agnes took deep breaths, relishing the silence and the peaceful scene. Below her, and to her right, the empty playground stretched. In twelve hours' time it would be astir and strident with children running and shouting.

The thought made Agnes return to her bed. She must be fit to attend to her duties in the morning. At this rate she would have seven hours' sleep at the most. She must compose herself. She smoothed her sheets, straightened her winceyette nightgown, and put her head, with its wispy grey plait, down to the welcoming pillow. The party must be forgotten. She owed it to the children.

Within ten minutes she was asleep.

At about the same time, a little farther along the road, Albert Piggott sat up in bed and rubbed his rumbling stomach.

Should he, or should he not, go downstairs, take one of his indigestion tablets and make a cup of tea? It was on occasions like this that he missed a wife. It would have been the simplest thing to have aroused Nelly with a sharp dig of the elbow and to recount to her the overwhelming pain which he was suffering – pain which could only be assuaged by recourse to medicine and a hot drink – and which was too severe to allow him to fetch those ameliorations himself.

However, Nelly was not in his bed, but presumably in that of the oil man who had supplanted him in his fickle wife's affections. If he wanted medical attention he would have to supply it himself.

Muttering to himself, he climbed out of bed, a thin unsavoury figure clad in pants and vest, for Albert scorned such effete practices as changing from dayclothes into night attire, and stumbled down the stairs. His little cat, as thin, but far cleaner, than his master, greeted him with a mew, and was pleasantly surprised to be given a saucer of milk when Albert took the bottle from the cupboard.

The kettle seemed to take an unconscionable time to boil, and Albert gazed out of the kitchen window to the bulk of the church across the way. It was as bright as day now that the moon was high and nearly full. It shone upon the rows of tomb stones which now lined the stubby walls of the churchyard, and lit up the Gothic windows facing towards Lulling. Sharp black shadows fell across the dewy grass, and even Albert's meagre appreciation of natural beauty was stirred by the sight.

He made the tea, poured out a mugful and took it back to bed with the bottle of tablets. Propped up against the greasy pillow he sipped noisily, relishing the comfort of the hot liquid flowing into his tormented stomach. Two tablets were washed down, as he surveyed the moonlit bedroom.

He became conscious of the smell of smoke. It was very faint, and he dismissed it as coming from the last embers of the bonfire he had seen Harold Shoosmith making that morning. Nothing to do with him anyway, thought Albert, depositing his empty mug on the linoleum.

The pain was now lulled into submission. Albert belched comfortably, turned over, and fell asleep.

Below, in the kitchen, the cat licked the last delicious drops of Albert's bounty, washed his face, and then set out, through the open kitchen window, upon the business of the night.

An hour later, Harold Shoosmith smelt the smoke. Could his bonfire be responsible? Surely it had been out by tea time when he had conscientiously stirred the remnants? Nevertheless, bonfires occasionally had the disconcerting habit of resuscitating themselves and, apart from the danger, it was a pity if the beauty of such a night was being fouled by smoke of his making.

In the adjoining bed, his wife Isobel slept peacefully. He slipped quietly from his own, and made his way to the bathroom which overlooked the garden where the rogue bonfire had been lit.

All was peaceful. He could see the empty incinerator quite clearly in the light of the moon. Not even a wisp of smoke curled from it, he noted with relief.

But where then was the fire? Had Miss Watson or the landlord of The Two Pheasants been burning garden rubbish? As far as he could see, their gardens were as clear as his own, although some smoke began to drift across from some conflagration farther along the green towards the south, even as he watched.

He ran, now seriously alarmed, into the spare bedroom whose side window looked across to the church and rectory. To his horror, he saw that the smoke was pouring from the roof of the Henstocks' house, and before he could close the window a cracking report rent the air, the ridge of the vicarage roof dipped suddenly, and a great flame leapt into the air illuminating billowing clouds of thick smoke.

He ran downstairs, and Isobel woke to hear him crying: 'The fire brigade! And quickly! Thrush Green rectory is well ablaze!'

She heard the receiver slammed down, and within two seconds Harold was dragging trousers over his pyjamas and fighting his way into a pullover.

'I'll come and help,' said Isobel, reaching for her clothes.

Within five minutes a little knot of helpers was gathered at the blaze. The sight was awe-inspiring. The collapse of part of the roof had let in air which intensified the conflagration. Flames were now shooting skyward, and the upstairs windows showed a red glow. Smoke poured from the main bedroom window, and there were terrifying reports as the glass cracked in the heat.

Mr Jones, from The Two Pheasants, was organizing a chain of water carriers from the tap in his bar, and Albert Piggott, stomach pains forgotten, had trundled out an archaic fire-fighting contraption which had been kept in the vestry since the Second World War and had never been used since the time when a small incendiary bomb had set light to the tassels of the bell ropes, and an adjacent pile of copies of Stainer's 'Crucifixion', in 1942.

This relic, when attached to a nearby hydrant well-hidden in nettles in the churchyard, spouted water at a dozen spots along its perished length and saturated several onlookers.

'Get the damn thing out of the way!' yelled Harold Shoosmith. 'We'll have someone falling over it!'

He and several other men, including Edward Young and Ben Curdle, were busy removing furniture, books and papers, and anything they could grab downstairs, before the inevitable happened and the whole top floor collapsed. These were being piled, well away from danger, by willing hands. Ella Bembridge, for once without a cigarette in her mouth, worked as stoutly as the men, and would have forced her way into the building to collect some of Dimity's treasures, if she had not been forbidden to do so by Harold, who had taken charge with all the ready authority of one who had spent his life organizing others.

The welcome sound of the fire brigade's siren sent people scattering to allow its access across the grass to the blazing

house. It was a joy to see the speed and economy of effort with which the hoses were turned on.

'This started some hours ago, by the look of things,' said the captain to Harold. 'I can't think how it went undetected for so long.'

Harold explained that the house was empty, and at that moment a second fire engine arrived from Nidden, and started work at the side of the building where the flames seemed thickest.

A terrible roaring sound began to emanate from the doomed building, and the bystanders were ordered to get well away. With a thunderous rumbling the top floor of the rectory now collapsed. Sparks, smoke and flames poured into the air, and the heat became intense. People began to cough in the acrid air, and to rub eyes reddened with smoke and tears.

It was now quite obvious that nothing more could be rescued. The rector's modest possessions which were still inside the house must be consumed by the fire. It was a tragedy that few could bear to witness, and Winnie Bailey, in dressing gown and Wellingtons, led the redoubtable Ella away to her own house across the green. It was the only time she had seen her old friend in tears.

At first light, the people of Thrush Green gazed appalled at the havoc left by the events of the past twelve hours. Blackened stones and the gaunt charred remains of beams smoked in the morning air. Dirty rivulets of water moved sluggishly towards the gutters at the roadside, and puddles surrounded the remains of the Henstocks' home.

A tarpaulin had been thrown over the pathetic remnants which had been snatched from the blaze, and Harold had arranged for them to be stored in his garage and garden shed out of the weather's harm.

'I think Ella has Charles's telephone number,' he told Edward as the two begrimed and exhausted men were returning to their homes. 'But what about Hilda and Edgar? Aren't they due today?'

'Good Lord! I believe they are,' agreed Edward. 'I'll see if Joan knows anything about them. But first things first, old man. Bath and then coffee. Then a couple of hours' sleep for me – and you too, I recommend.'

'You're right. No point in ringing Charles and Dimity until about eight or nine. It's a tragic business, and particularly wretched when they are having one of their few breaks. Shall I ring or will you?'

'Do you mind tackling it? I'm supposed to be on the 9.30 train to London tomorrow – I mean, this morning – for a meeting.'

'Of course, I'll do it. Poor old Charles, it will break his heart, I fear.'

Four hours later, Harold sat in his study and rang the Yorkshire number. As he listened to the bell ringing so far away he wondered how on earth one could break such appalling news to a friend.

He was amazed to find how tired he was after the night's activities. Muscles he had never noticed before seemed to have

sprung into painful evidence. His eyes were still sore, and the hairs on his arms were singed. As for his finger nails, despite energetic use of the nail brush, he had not seen them so grimy and broken since his schooldays.

Luckily it was Charles who answered the telephone. Harold had already rehearsed what he should do if Dimity had lifted the receiver. Charles would have to be summoned. This was the sort of thing the men must cope with, thought Harold, true to his Victorian principles.

'Nice to hear you,' was the rector's opening remark. 'You're up early. Everything all right at your end?'

'I'm afraid not. Charles, I have to tell you some bad news. Are you sitting down?'

'Sitting down?' came the bewildered reply.

'Because this is going to be a shock,' continued Harold doggedly. 'There was a bad accident here last night.'

'No! Not anyone hurt! Not *killed*, Harold, don't say that!'

'Nothing like that. Perhaps *accident* was the wrong word. The fact is, your house has been badly damaged by fire.'

There was a brief silence.

'Hello!' shouted Harold. 'You there, Charles?'

'Yes, yes. But I can't have heard right. The house damaged by fire? How badly?'

'I hate to tell you – but it is completely gutted. I think it is quite beyond repair, Charles, as you will see.'

'I can't take it in. I really can't,' said the poor rector. 'How could it have happened? We switched off everything, I'm sure, and we hadn't had a fire in the grate for days. Surely no one would be so wicked as to set fire to the place?'

'I'm sure it wasn't that,' said Harold. 'I just felt you should know that our spare room is waiting for you and Dimity when you return, and could you tell us where to get in touch with Hilda and Edgar?'

'Oh dear, oh dear,' wailed Charles. 'How perfectly dreadful! Of course, they were due to arrive today, and I've no idea how we can get in touch. They were breaking their journey down to have a day or two in the Midlands. Wait now, they were going to visit a cousin in hospital. In Coventry, I think Edgar said. Beyond that, I know nothing, but we shall start for home—'

The rector's voice broke, and Harold distinctly heard a sniff before he resumed.

'We'll be back during the day, Harold, and our deepest thanks for offering us shelter tonight. What a terrible affair. I must go and break it to dear Dimity, and then we must clear up things here, and set off for Thrush Green without delay.'

'We shall look forward to seeing you,' said Harold.

'And Harold,' said Charles in a firmer tone, 'I very much appreciate your telling me the news so kindly. It couldn't have been easy. You have prepared us to face whatever awaits us there, quite wonderfully.'

He rang off, and Harold went to tell Isobel how well he had taken it, and to make another assault upon his finger nails.

Joan Young came over to the Shoosmiths' house as soon as Edward had departed for London.

'I thought I'd offer to track down Hilda and Edgar,' she said. 'In any case, they can stop with us until things get sorted out. If only we knew how to get hold of them!'

'I thought of ringing hospitals in Coventry and asking if Mr and Mrs Maddox were expected,' said Harold.

'Well, yes,' agreed Joan doubtfully, 'but do hospitals usually ask the names of visitors? It's such a shot in the dark.'

'Perhaps they could relay a message to the wards asking if anyone was expecting a visit from them. Is that possible, do you think?'

'It sounds highly unlikely,' said Joan, 'but I'll go back and put out a few feelers.'

The voice from the first hospital was brisk and rather impatient. Joan envisaged its owner as rushing, bedpan in hand, upon an urgent errand.

She embarked upon her message.

'Yes, yes!' said the voice. 'But if you could tell me the *patient's* name, I can get a message back to you.'

Joan said weakly that she did not know who the Maddoxes were visiting.

'In that case, I don't think I can help you. Visitors come at two o'clock until four here. I could get them to give their names at the reception desk, but as we have two hundred beds in this building alone, it would be rather a task.'

Joan said that she quite understood, thanked her and rang off. Obviously, this was going to be the pattern of any further investigations she might make. She decided that the project was impossible, and went to find Molly Curdle to help her with the beds for the unsuspecting Maddoxes, now, presumably, making their way to Thrush Green in expectation of a few carefree days in the rectory, poor dears.

Most of the inhabitants of Thrush Green went about their daily affairs in a state of shock that morning. Very few had slept throughout the night, and most had been helping to rescue the Henstocks' property until dawn arose and the firemen had departed.

Only the children, it seemed, viewed the wreckage with excitement. Little Miss Fogerty and Miss Watson had been far too upset to face their usual boiled egg at breakfast, and had nibbled Ryvita and marmalade simply to fuel their energies to get through their school duties.

Dorothy had given a short talk to the school at morning prayers, and told them how necessary it was to be of exceptionally good behaviour as so many people had been upset by the truly dreadful events of the night. She then composed a suitable prayer asking for comfort to be given to the rector and his wife, and offering thanks for the bravery of the firemen and helpers, and for the merciful lack of injury to any person involved.

Agnes was full of admiration for Dorothy's powers of extempore prayer, and led her infants across the playground still pondering upon this facet of her headmistress's varied ability.

It was young George Curdle who spoke first. 'But why did God let the fire happen?' he asked.

For once in her life, Agnes felt unable to answer.

*

As it happened, Dimity and Charles arrived first on the scene, having driven non-stop from Yorkshire. Hastily prepared sandwiches had sustained them as they drove, and they chugged up the hill from Lulling as St Andrew's clock struck three.

No one saw them arrive, and for that they were grateful. They halted the car on the edge of the battered and rutted grass which was still sprinkled with the ash and trodden cinders of last night's activities.

Dimity covered her face with her hands and her thin shoulders shook. Charles's face was stony as he gazed unwinking at the scene. He put his arm round his grieving wife, but was quite unable to speak. They sat there, silent in their distress, for five terrible minutes.

Then, sighing, Charles opened the car door and stepped into the desolation of what had once been Thrush Green rectory. He stirred the damp black ashes of the study floor with his foot. He could scarcely see for the blur of tears behind his spectacles, but he bent to investigate a glint of metal among the dust.

Turning it over in his hand, he recognized it. It was the silver figure of Christ which had been mounted on the ivory cross behind his desk. It was distorted and blackened by the heat, but Charles knew immediately what it was. He slipped it into his pocket, and turned to help Dimity over a low sooty wall which was all that was left of her kitchen.

And it was at that moment that Ella came from her cottage, and Harold and Isobel from their house, to give them what comfort they could.

That evening, when Edward Young arrived home, he found Hilda and Edgar, as well as Dimity and Charles, in his sitting room, still trying to get over the shock of the disaster.

It was as well that Joan had not continued with her efforts to trace them through Coventry hospitals and nursing homes, for their cousin, as it happened, had been sent home at the weekend and they had visited him in his own bedroom, finding him well on the way to recovery.

There was so much to discuss between all the old friends that it was beginning to get dark before the Maddoxes retired to an early bed. They proposed to leave after lunch the next day.

Joan and Edward walked back with the Henstocks to Harold's house, and hoped that they would be able to sleep, and so be released from their unhappiness for a few hours' oblivion.

They walked on together, past the silent school and the public house, until they rounded the bulk of St Andrew's church and stood facing the ruins.

The acrid stench which had hung over Thrush Green all day was almost unbearable here. Joan looked with pity and distaste at the mess which had once been the rectory.

She caught a glimpse of Edward's face in the dying light.

'Edward!' she said accusingly. 'You're *pleased*! How can you be so *heartless*!'

Edward hastened to explain himself. 'My darling, three-quarters of me grieves for dear old Charles and Dim, just as much as you do. But the other quarter – the professional bit – is so relieved to see the end of that ghastly place that it can't help rejoicing in a perverse sort of way.'

Joan gazed at him with disgust, and then began to smile. She took his arm, and they turned their backs upon the wreckage, and set off towards their home.

'I suppose you are already planning a new house, monster that you are,' she observed.

'How did you guess?' asked Edward.

8. AT YOUNG MR VENABLES'

It was hardly surprising that, with all this excitement at Thrush Green, the advent of Tullivers' temporary residents passed with very little comment.

They had arrived in a battered van. Young Jack Thomas and his wife Mary appeared to have only two suitcases, but a vast array of cardboard boxes which seemed to be full of electrical equipment of some sort. Winnie Bailey, watching shamelessly from her bedroom window, surveyed the writhing tangles of flex and plugs and supposed that they might have brought their own television set, or portable electric fires with them.

As she watched, a noisy motorcycle roared up and parked alongside the van. Two figures, clad in black leather, dismounted and took off their helmets. Both shook out long blond hair, but Winnie thought that one might possibly be a male. All four vanished into the house, and Winnie decided to let them remain undisturbed for an hour or so before calling to see if she could be of any help. Jeremy was due soon from school, and after tea he could accompany her.

The boy was excited at the idea of seeing the new occupants of his home.

'Do you think they'll mind some of the cupboards being locked? I mean, Mummy said my toys would be safer if I left them in the landing cupboard locked away, but they might need it for clothes and things, mightn't they?'

'I'm sure there's plenty of cupboard space for their needs,' Winnie assured him, thinking of the paucity of their travelling cases.

She lifted the heavy knocker which old Admiral Trigg had fixed

79

to the front door of Tullivers years ago. It was in the form of a dolphin, a suitably nautical object for the old seafarer to approve, and weighed several pounds. The door itself shuddered as the knocker thudded back into place.

Jack Thomas opened the door and gave Winnie such a dazzling smile that she was won over at once. She had handed the key earlier to his wife Mary, so that this was her first encounter with the new householder.

'Hello, you must be Jeremy,' said Jack, 'and, of course, you are Mrs Bailey. Do come in.'

They stepped into the sitting room where Winnie was surprised to see that several chairs had vanished and the remaining furniture was pushed back against the walls. The centre of the room was bare except for a number of the large cardboard boxes which Winnie had observed.

'Where are the chairs?' asked Jeremy.

'Oh, we've put 'em in the dining room. We'll probably live in there while we're here. You see, we need this space for the gear.'

He waved vaguely towards the tangle of wires in the boxes.

'Now, is there anything you need?' asked Winnie, returning to firmer ground. 'Bread, milk, eggs? Have you found out how to work the cooker and the lights? Do let me know if I can help.'

'Very sweet of you,' he said, with another heart-melting smile. 'I think we've all we need. We're going down to Lulling for a meal tonight.'

'I hear The Fuchsia Bush and The Fleece put on quite a good dinner,' replied Winnie.

'Oh, we'll fetch fish and chips,' said Jack. 'Much cheaper and less fag anyway than a meal out. And no washing up when you eat them straight from the paper.'

'Very true,' agreed Winnie.

'Shall I call the others?'

'No, no, don't trouble them. I'm sure you've all got enough to do moving in. But do come over if you want anything. I'm in most of the time. I hope you'll enjoy your stay with us,' she added politely, making for the door.

'I wish we could have fish and chips for supper,' said Jeremy wistfully as they walked home. 'But they'll have to wash up their plates, won't they? They won't really eat it all out of the paper with their fingers, will they? Won't they make dirty marks on the furniture?'

'Oh, I shouldn't think so,' said Winnie untruthfully. The same thought had gone through her mind, she had to admit.

But greasy fingers or not, thought Winnie, entering her own immaculate home, that smile of Jack Thomas's would forgive him anything.

The next few days were sad and busy ones for Charles and Dimity. The salvaged articles from the fire were pitifully small, and every hour brought a new loss to sight. Luckily, they had the clothes which they had packed for their Yorkshire holiday, and Harold and Isobel were able to lend them some immediate necessities, but there was the bewildering business of insurance and other matters to see to, and these things worried poor Charles very much.

Harold was a tower of strength, but so many necessary papers and documents had been consumed in the fire, and the fact that the property belonged to the Church with all sorts of legal and technical complications, made him advise Charles to see his friend Justin Venables, the Lulling solicitor.

Charles decided to walk down the hill to Twitter & Venables' office at the end of the town. His appointment was for four o'clock, and the May sunshine was at its warmest as he set off past the school and across the green.

He averted his eyes from the empty spot where once his beloved rectory had stood. As it happened, two large lorries were on the site loading the last remains of the rubble. Once they departed there would only be the scorched grass and the blackened soil to mark the place of the rector's home. The Church officials had been kind and sympathetic. He would be taken care of, supplied with a resting place very shortly, and would be kept informed, at every step, of the decisions of his ecclesiastical masters.

He had been severely upset to find that the investigation into the cause of the fire proved conclusively that faulty wiring in the airing cupboard was to blame. The immersion heater was housed in the lower part of this cupboard, and Charles could not forgive himself for not switching it off before they left the house. He said so to Harold.

'But, you see, Dimity said we must leave on the hot water because Betty Bell's cousin from Lulling Woods was coming in to do some spring-cleaning before Edgar and Hilda arrived. I fear I was greatly to blame. Of course, I confessed at once to the man who came about it.'

'Forget it,' advised Harold. 'That wiring should have been renewed years ago, and the Church is jolly lucky you two weren't burnt to cinders in your beds. Why, some of it is two-plug stuff, and some three, and you've got lead-covered wiring in your study and rubber stuff in the kitchen, and what looked like naked copper to me in that back kitchen of yours.'

'It is rather a hotch-potch,' agreed the rector. '*Was*, I mean. But then, you see, bits were added over the years, and I suppose they used whatever was in fashion. I know we had some trouble when we put in the refrigerator. All the lights blew out once when we opened the door. And the kettle used to snap on a red light sometimes, which frightened me very much, though Dimity assured me that it was a safety device. I'm afraid,' concluded the rector sadly, 'that I don't really understand electricity.'

'You'd have needed Faraday himself to sort out the system in your house,' said Harold. 'Just be thankful you weren't there when it finally blew up.'

'It wasn't so much *blowing up* as *smouldering*, they tell me,' replied Charles. 'You see the heat caught the lining paper on the shelves and that set light to the linen, and then the wooden slats, and then the roof timbers. And once the air got in everything became so much fiercer. I really can't bear to think of it. But, as you say, Harold, we must thank God that no one was hurt.'

He tried to put his anxieties out of his mind as he went down the hill to Lulling. The town was looking beautiful in its spring finery. The Cotswold stone garden walls were hung with bright mats of mauve aubretia and yellow alyssum. Daisies starred the lawns, and everywhere the heady scent of hyacinths and narcissi hung in the warm air. The lime trees lining Lulling High Street fluttered their young green leaves, and the ancient japonica which fanned across the Misses Lovelock's Georgian house was already bright with scarlet flowers. Outside The Fuchsia Bush, two tubs of splendid pink tulips flanked the door, and every window in the street, it seemed, held a vase of fresh spring flowers.

The rector's spirits rose as he strode along relishing the beauty around him. As expected, he was stopped several times by friends who commiserated with him and cheered him with their concern and sympathy.

He felt almost jaunty by the time he reached the solicitors' office, but the gloom of the entrance hall, a study in ginger-coloured grained paintwork, had a sobering effect upon the good man.

A plump middle-aged lady showed him into Justin's office on the left-hand side of the hall, and he was greeted affectionately.

'Just let me set you a chair, padre,' said Justin. 'Not that one. Take this, it has a padded seat.'

He levered up a heavy chair with a high Jacobean-type back and a seat upholstered in leather which was so old and rubbed that it resembled suede. It was, as Charles found, surprisingly comfortable.

'Tea now, I think, Muriel,' said Justin to the plump lady.

'Yes, sir,' she said, so humbly that Charles would not have been surprised to see her genuflect, or at least pull her forelock had she had such a thing. Obviously, Justin was the master in this establishment.

'Well now, just tell me the trouble,' began Justin, when the door had closed.

Charles gave a remarkably concise account of his actions before and after the fire, and explained his position as a tenant of Church property.

Justin listened carefully, his fingertips pressed together. He watched his client over his half-glasses and thought how rare and pleasant it was to be face to face with an absolutely honest man.

A discreet knock at the door heralded the arrival of Muriel with the tea tray. It was lowered reverently upon a vacant space on Justin's desk.

The good rector, had he given any thought to the matter, would have been grateful for a mug of ready poured out tea with perhaps a bowl of granulated sugar with a well-worn teaspoon stuck in it. He was much impressed with the elegant apparatus now before Justin. Two delicate china cups stood upon a snowy linen tray cloth. An embroidered satin tea-cosy covered a silver tea pot, and small cubes of sugar, accompanied by silver clawed sugar-tongs, rested in a matching bowl. Some excellent short-bread fingers were ranged alongside.

'Well!' exclaimed Charles happily, 'I really didn't expect such a beautiful tea! And what a handsome tea-cosy!'

'It is rather nice, isn't it?' agreed Justin, surveying it as though he had just noticed it. 'One of the girls in the office ran it up one Christmas. And the tray cloth too, I believe. Very good with her fingers obviously. A slice of lemon, Charles, or milk?'

'Milk, please. Do you usually have time for tea? I hope you haven't gone to all this trouble on my behalf.'

'From four to four-thirty is tea time,' replied Justin firmly. 'I only see old friends then whom I like to invite to share my tea tray. Try the shortbread. Muriel makes it for me weekly.'

The rector could not help thinking in what a civilized way Justin seemed to conduct his business. He had no doubt that just as much work got done in the leisurely framework of Justin's day as was accomplished by so many feverish young men rushing from one thing to another.

'Of course, we have always stayed open until six o'clock,' said Justin, submerging his lemon slice gently with his teaspoon. 'So many of our clients appreciate being able to call here after their work is over. One needs a cup of tea to refresh one towards the end of the day.'

'Very sensible,' agreed Charles, dusting shortbread crumbs as unobtrusively as possible from his clerical grey trousers.

Over the tea tray Justin dealt with the rector's anxieties, and assured him that all would be satisfactorily arranged with the insurance people, the Church authorities, and all other interested parties in this sad affair.

It was exactly twenty-eight minutes past four when he rose and shook his old friend's hand in farewell.

'By the way,' he said, on his way to open the door, 'I am retiring at the end of this year.'

'You can't be!' exclaimed Charles. 'Why, you know you are always referred to as "young Mr Venables"! Who will take over?'

'Young Mr Venables will be seventy next birthday,' smiled Justin, 'and the boys here are in their forties and fifties. Plenty of good fellows to carry on at Twitter & Venables, believe me.'

'I can't take it in,' confessed Charles. 'Of course, I shan't mention this until you give me permission to do so.'

'You have it now, my dear fellow. There's no secret about it. Now, I mustn't keep you.'

He opened the office door, and saw Charles out into the sunshine.

The rector retraced his steps in thoughtful mood, pondering on

Justin's decision to retire. Seventy next birthday, he had said. Well, perhaps he was right to leave the somewhat gloomy office and to feel free to enjoy his fishing and his golf when the sun shone. Certainly, Justin had served the little town well, as had his father before him. No doubt the middle-aged boys would carry on the good work, but it wouldn't please his old clients.

A car drew alongside the kerb just as Charles was approaching the Misses Lovelock's house. It was driven by the vicar of Lulling, the Reverend Anthony Bull, and his mellifluous voice floated across the warm air.

'Get in, Charles, if you are making for home. I'm off to Nidden.'

Charles was rather looking forward to walking home in the spring sunshine, but it would have been churlish to turn down this offer and, in any case, he always enjoyed Anthony Bull's company.

He was a tall handsome man with a fine head and expressive hands. As a single man he had fluttered many maiden hearts, and even now, happily married as he was to a rich wife, a steady supply of embroidered slippers, hand-knitted socks, and useful memo pads decorated with last year's Christmas cards, flowed into the vicarage from adoring members of his congregation.

'We only got back from a few days in Devon yesterday,' said the vicar, 'and were appalled to hear about your house. I gather you are at Harold's for the time being, but if you want to come to us, Charles, the vicarage has plenty of room, and we should both be delighted to put you up.'

Charles thanked him sincerely. The vicarage was an elegant Queen Anne house, overlooking Lulling's extensive green. It was common knowledge that Mrs Bull's wealth had contributed to the comfort of their establishment. The beautiful old house had flourished under her cosseting, and Charles could not think of anywhere more lovely to shelter, if the need arose. He tried to say as much to the generous vicar.

'You've heard the rumour, I expect,' said Anthony Bull, 'about the re-organization of the parishes around here? It's a case of spreading us rather more thinly on the ground, I gather. Nothing definite yet, but I shouldn't be surprised to hear that we are all going to play General Post before long.'

'Do you know,' said Charles, 'I haven't heard the game of General Post mentioned since I was a child! Nor Turn the Trencher, for that matter, nor Postman's Knock. Do you think people still play those party games?'

'I should like to think so,' responded the vicar, drawing up outside Harold's house on Thrush Green, 'but I fear they play rather more sophisticated games these days, with perhaps rather less innocent enjoyment.'

At that moment, Charles saw Dotty Harmer emerging from Ella's, milk can in one hand, and Flossie's lead in the other. He did not feel equal to coping with that lady, much as he admired and respected her. He hurriedly got out from the car.

'Thank you again, Anthony, for the lift, and your very kind offer of help.'

The vicar waved and drove off towards Nidden. What a beautiful glossy car it was, thought Charles, without a trace of envy. It was fitting that such a fine fellow as dear Anthony should travel in such style, and live in such a splendid house.

He opened Harold's gate, and walked with a thankful heart into his own temporary abode.

9. TROUBLE AT TULLIVERS

It was soon apparent to the inhabitants of Thrush Green that young Jack Thomas departed from Tullivers each morning at eight o'clock. The shabby van took the road north towards Woodstock, and presumably from there he went to the estate office where he was employed.

His wife Mary and the other two residents were not seen until much later in the morning. The more censorious of Thrush Green's housewives deplored the fact that only once had Mary been seen to shake the mats, and that was at eleven-thirty in the morning. As for the nameless pair with the motor bicycle, they seemed to be invisible most of the time, although Ella reported that she had seen them having coffee one morning in The Fuchsia Bush, and later had noticed their vehicle propped outside the Job Centre in Lulling High Street. Were they proposing to settle locally, people wondered?

About a week after the fire, the peace of Thrush Green was shattered between eleven and twelve one starlit night, by the raucous sound of pop music and the throbbing of drums. Occasionally an ear-splitting shriek broke the rhythm, and above it all was the wailing of a nasal voice which might have been a woman's or a banshee's.

The downstairs lights at Tullivers were still ablaze at that time, and the noise certainly came from that house. Ella Bembridge, some hundred yards or more away, was wakened by the din, and so were Isobel and Harold Shoosmith, equally far away.

'What the hell goes on?' muttered Harold, leaning out of his bedroom window. 'Thoughtless louts! They'll wake everyone at the Youngs' place, and I should think poor old Robert Bassett will be blown out of his bed at this rate.'

Robert Bassett and his wife were the elderly parents of Joan Young. Their home, converted from stables in the Youngs' garden, was one of the nearest houses to Tullivers. He had been very ill, and it was natural that Harold should be concerned first with his old friend's position so close to this shocking noise.

'I shall go and ring them,' said Harold firmly. Isobel heard him padding downstairs to the telephone.

There was a long wait, and then he returned.

'So much damn racket going on they can't hear the bell,' he fumed. 'I've a good mind to ring the police.'

'Wait a bit,' urged his wife. 'It will only make more of a to-do if the police come. It may stop soon.'

'I doubt it,' said Harold grimly, but he shut the window, and got back into bed.

He was not the only one to telephone Tullivers. Edward Young, outraged on his father-in-law's behalf, also failed to get through, and as he was just out of a hot bath, he did not feel inclined to traipse across to Tullivers to remonstrate in person.

Joan had been along to see her parents, and had found them quite cheerful and in bed. Philosophically, they had inserted the ear plugs which they always took with them when travelling, and they appeared less perturbed than their children.

Winnie Bailey had contented herself with viewing Jeremy's sleeping form and postponing complaints until morning. The cacophony ended about half past one. The lights went out at Tullivers. The residents at Thrush Green heaved sighs of relief, swore retribution at some more reasonable hour, and fell thankfully asleep.

Only Winnie Bailey's Jenny remained wakeful, and she was seriously considering the geographical advantages of Percy Hodge's farm house should she ever be invited to live there. There was now no doubt that Percy was seeking a second wife, and was being uncommonly attentive to her.

Jenny, brought up in an orphanage and later a drudge – though a grateful one – to the two old people who had taken her in, could not help feeling touched by Percy's devotion. On the other hand, did she really want to marry at all?

Life at Thrush Green with kind Winnie Bailey held all the happiness that she needed. Never had she enjoyed such luxury as her own small flat overlooking the green. Winnie's companionship was doubly precious because she had never known such warmth and generosity of spirit. And how good she had been to her during this last illness! And then she loved the house they shared. It was a joy to polish the lovely old furniture, to set the kitchen to rights, to shine the windows, the silver, the brass. The thought of leaving Winnie and the fine old home which they shared was insupportable.

And yet – poor Percy! He certainly missed his Gertie, and he was a fine fellow still. She would be cared for if she threw in her lot with his, and did he not perhaps need her more desperately than Winnie did? Jenny's warm heart was smitten when she recalled the buttons missing from his jacket, and the worn shirt collar that needed turning. What a problem!

St Andrew's church clock chimed four, and Jenny heaved a sigh. Best leave it all until later! She'd be fit for nothing if she didn't get a few hours' sleep, and tomorrow she had planned to turn out the larder.

She pulled up the bedclothes, punched her feather pillow into shape, and was asleep in five minutes.

Harold Shoosmith rang Tullivers at seven-thirty next morning to remonstrate with young Jack Thomas before he left for work. The young man was as profuse in his apologies as can be expected from someone at that hour, only partially dressed, and attempting to get his own breakfast. It wouldn't happen again. They would make sure that all the windows were shut, and the volume kept down, during future rehearsals.

Before Harold had time to enquire further, the telephone went dead. Other residents rang later in the day but did not get quite as civil a response as Harold had received.

Winnie Bailey decided to call in person during the evening when, she supposed, young Jack Thomas would be home and would have had a meal after his day's work. She found him sitting in the kitchen with Mary. As the motorcycle was not propped up near the front door, its usual resting-place, she imagined that the other couple were out.

The Thomases looked very tired and young, and Winnie wondered if she were being unkind in complaining. But the thought of further troubled nights, the disturbance of her charge Jeremy, and all the other neighbours nearby, hardened her heart.

They listened somewhat listlessly to her complaint. Even Jack's usual dazzling smile seemed dimmed, and he passed a hand over his hair as if bemused. As well he might be, thought Winnie tartly, after such a late night!

'The fact is,' he said, when Winnie had finished speaking, 'Bill and Lottie are going through a bad patch, and we offered them shelter while we're here. I used to run this band, and Lottie was our vocalist. Bill's the drummer – well, tympanist altogether really. Cymbals, triangle, the lot. Quite handy.'

'But can't he take it over? I mean, you seem to have a job of your own which must be quite demanding. I should have thought you needed your sleep as much as the rest of us.'

'Well, the job doesn't bring in much bread, you know.'

'Bread?'

'Dough. Money,' translated Mary. 'If we can get an engagement now and again, it would help all four of us.'

'I can quite see that,' said Winnie, 'and I am all in favour of earning extra money if you can. But not at the expense of your neighbours' well-being.'

'Well, we have to practise,' said Mary. 'No one's going to take us on unless we're competent.'

'We honestly had no idea we were making so much noise,' protested Jack. 'I promise you we'll take more care in future. I can't say we'll stop entirely. We need the money, and Bill and Lottie are even more hard up than we are. At least, I've got a steady wage coming in. They're skint.'

'They seem to have money for what they want,' commented Mary to her husband. She sounded very bitter, and Winnie suspected that she at least would be glad to see the back of her two fellow residents.

'Well, I'll say no more,' said Winnie, rising. 'But for pity's sake, spare Thrush Green any more nights like the last one. We're used to peace and quiet here after ten o'clock at night.'

The four young people at Tullivers were definitely in their neighbours' bad books. Apart from those who had accosted them openly with their complaints, there were plenty who stopped to tell each other how severely they had been disturbed, and how reprehensible such thoughtless conduct was.

'But there you are,' said Ella to Dotty as they shared a pot of coffee. 'Young things these days do exactly as they like. No respect for the older generation. No discipline, as we had.'

'Well, I certainly got enough,' admitted Dotty. 'As you know, Father was a trifle strict with his family.'

Ella privately considered this gentle censure as the understatement of the year. Tales of old Mr Harmer's punishments towards refractory pupils and his own children were enough to make even Ella blanch. The boys of his family had left home as soon as they could. Only Dotty had remained to look after her widower father in his old age, and a pretty thin time she had had, according to local gossip.

'One thing, they won't be here much longer,' said Dotty comfortably.

It was echoed, with considerable relief, by Miss Watson to her assistant.

'A *temporary* nuisance,' was her comment. 'I hear Mr Shoosmith and Mrs Bailey both complained the next morning, so I shall not bother to tell them how we feel about such behaviour. But if it happens again—' Here Dorothy stopped, with such a fierce headmistressy look, that even little Miss Fogerty trembled for anyone at Tullivers transgressing again.

Mr Jones at The Two Pheasants gave his opinion that that lot at Tullivers must have been dragged up in the back streets of some modern Sodom or Gomorrah to behave so badly, and he didn't know what the Hursts would find – or wouldn't find – when they returned. Which, he added, couldn't be too soon for him, and his audience at the bar agreed heartily.

Albert Piggott, nursing his half-pint of beer in the corner, gave a highly-coloured account of how he was awakened by the din, and a further discourse, with repellent details, of what it had done to his stomach in the middle of the night.

One listener, more squeamish than the rest, hastily changed the subject to the report of young Mr Venables' retirement, and this new topic engaged the attention of Mr Jones's clients until closing time.

'Never be the same without him,' asserted Percy Hodge. 'Had a lovely way with him in court. Look how he got old Dotty off the hook when she run down that Cooke boy!'

'*Miss Harmer*,' said the landlord reprovingly, 'never done it. That's why.'

'That's as maybe,' replied Percy, undeterred by Mr Jones's rebuke. 'The point is a young chap like Mr Venables is going to be missed in Lulling. He spoke up for me something wonderful when the cows got out and some fool fellow came off his motorbike among 'em. Luckily they wasn't hurt.'

'What about the fellow?' inquired a stranger from Nidden.

'Oh, he broke a thigh and something in his back, I believe,' said Percy vaguely. 'Nothing much. They took him off to hospital, so he was all right. But my poor cows was upset for days.'

The rector of Thrush Green had no hard feelings towards the young newcomers. Harold Shoosmith would have said, if asked, that Charles Henstock had no hard feelings against anyone, which made him the unique and saintly creature that he was.

As it happened, the affairs of the noisy night had not disturbed him, or Dimity, at all. They had both been deep in the sleep of the thoroughly exhausted, having had few good nights since their own tragedy.

So the rector's first pastoral visit to Tullivers was undertaken in happy mood. He felt rather ashamed, as he walked across the springy turf, that he had not called before, but so many pressing things in connection with the fire had engaged him, that he had found little time for his duties.

As he crossed the grass, he admired the rooks, swirling and dipping around the tall trees towards Nod. Perhaps they were 'winding up the water' as the old country folk said, and there would be rain in the night after this calm and sunny evening.

He purposely kept his eyes averted from the empty space where once his house had stood. He could not bear to look upon the gap. Would the church build him another house there? The ground belonged to it, of course. Or would that plot be sold, perhaps, and another home found for him?

It was worrying not to know what might happen. Harold and Isobel were kindness itself, but he and Dimity could not stay indefinitely. As it happened, they were going tomorrow to see dear old Mrs Jenner along the Nidden road. He had heard that she had a flat to let. It would be conveniently placed for church and parish, and he felt sure that it would be approved as temporary accommodation.

By now he was at Tullivers' front door, and even the unobservant rector could not help noticing that the late Admiral Trigg's massive brass knocker, in the shape of a dolphin, was tarnished as though it had been weeks since its last polishing.

Jack Thomas opened the door and looked a little startled when he saw the parson's collar.

'Oh, do come in,' he said, hastily remembering his manners. 'Mr Hendrick, isn't it?'

'Henstock. Charles Henstock,' answered the rector. 'And I must apologize for being so tardy in making your acquaintance, but you know we've had a little trouble lately.'

'We heard. Jolly tough luck. Did you lose much?'

He opened the door of the sitting room and ushered in his visitor. Charles could not help wondering what had happened to the chintz-covered armchairs and sofa which normally furnished the room. Now only three or four upright dining chairs stood against the wall, whilst a collection of wires, a microphone, and various instruments littered the centre of the carpet.

Charles perched on one of the chairs to which he was waved. Jack Thomas reversed another and sat facing him, with his arms folded along the back. Charles felt a flurry of panic, as though he were about to be cross-examined. He took a grip on himself.

'My wife and I wondered if we could be of any help while you are with us,' he began.

'As a matter of fact, Mrs Bailey has been very – er – *motherly*, and helped us quite a bit.'

'Oh, I'm sure of that! We are with the Shoosmiths at the moment. So handy for the church.'

There was a pause.

'Perhaps you are church goers?' he went on gently. There was a curious smell in the house. Some herbs, perhaps, used in cooking? He found it rather disquieting.

'Would you like to meet the others?' asked Jack abruptly. 'They're a bit tied up at the moment, but I could fetch them.'

'Dear me, no!' replied the rector. Tied up? What an odd expression! 'But perhaps you would tell them that I called and hope they would like to attend any of our church services. I took the liberty of bringing a list of the times.'

He put a slip of paper on a small table beside him. There were marks of wet glasses upon its once glossy surface, and Charles was perturbed to see that one corner of his list turned darkly damp.

'Thank you,' said Jack, turning upon the rector the smile which had so dazzled Winnie Bailey. 'I don't know about Bill and Lottie, but Mary and I used to go to church once. We were both christened, I know, and I was confirmed at school, the same week that I was vaccinated during a smallpox scare.'

Really, thought the rector, getting to his feet, he speaks as though he were doubly insured in the space of a few days! However, he found himself smiling kindly upon the young man. There certainly was something very fresh and attractive about him, and he was remarkably frank about being a lapsed church goer.

'Well, give my regards to your wife and friends,' he said, opening the front door, 'and we'll hope to see you all again before long.'

Jack walked with him to the gate, gazing about him and breathing deeply.

'One thing, we're enjoying Thrush Green,' he told the rector. 'It really is a marvellous place to live.'

'We think that too,' replied Charles simply, and allowed his eyes to stray to the ravaged plot which he had once called home. For the first time since the dreadful event, he found he could look at it with less pain. Was it a case of Time-the-great-healer? Or simply that he was getting accustomed to that sad gap in the skyline? Or was it that he felt that one day a house would rise again where his own had fallen?

Whatever the reason, the good rector was grateful for this small blessing of relief, and hurried back to the Shoosmiths with a lightened heart.

Much to the relief of Thrush Green's inhabitants, the cacophony from Tullivers was not repeated. True, rehearsals went on, but Jack Thomas had kept his word. Windows were closed, and the lights went out around midnight – quite late enough for the early-to-bed neighbours, but certainly an improvement on the first night's prolonged din until the small hours.

Occasionally, the musical equipment was packed into the van when Jack returned from his work at the estate office, and all four would drive off for the evening. Presumably, some engagements had been secured, and rumour was rife at The Two Pheasants about how much they would be paid.

'I'd pay to get *out* of the room if that Lottie girl got screeching,' commented one.

'Some likes that sort of racket,' said his neighbour. 'My two kids has it on all the time on the telly.'

'More fool you to let 'em.'

'They wouldn't get no more than twenty quid between 'em,' surmised another. 'Wouldn't go far between four, would it?'

'The landlord at The Star over Lulling Woods way gave 'em ten quid apiece, I heard, for an evening there.'

'Then he wants his head seen to,' said Mr Jones firmly, and switched the subject.

But there was a change of feeling towards the young people now that some improvement had been made in their behaviour. Bill and Lottie were seen but rarely, but Mary and Jack were about the green and in the shops at Lulling, and were much more sociable.

Winnie Bailey, who knew that the girl was pregnant, invited her to coffee one morning and renewed her offers of help. She had the feeling that Mary did most of the housework, and the shopping and cooking. She suspected too that the girl resented the other couple's presence. They certainly did not seem to pull their weight in the running of the household, and the girl appeared tired, as well she might be, as her pregnancy advanced.

Winnie asked how Jack's house-hunting plans were progressing, and Mary showed signs of enthusiasm for the first time.

'There's a small house near the office – the end one of a terrace, which I think we'll be able to have in a month's time. It will mean staying at a hotel for a few days after the Hursts come back here, but we shan't mind that.'

'And Bill and Lottie?'

'With any luck, they will have found somewhere in the next week or two. Not that they're searching very hard,' she added.

'Can they go back to their parents?'

'They *can*, but they don't want to. The first thing is to get a job. They're always hard up. Well, who isn't? I know I'm always staggered at the amount of money we seem to get through each week. I hope we'll be able to budget more satisfactorily when we get our own place. At least we shan't have Bill and Lottie scrounging for a loan.'

'Things will certainly be simpler,' agreed Winnie diplomatically, refilling her guest's cup. 'There's nothing so exciting as one's first home.'

She looked about the familiar sitting room, crowded with personal treasures of many years.

'This was my first home,' she told the girl, 'and my last, I hope.'

'If I'm a quarter as happy,' said Mary, 'I shall be quite content.'

10. A Golden May

Mrs Jenner, who had a sizeable old farmhouse a mile along the road to Nidden from Thrush Green, was a cousin of Percy Hodge's. Like Dotty Harmer, her contemporary, she had been the only daughter, and when her mother died she kept house, and occasionally did a little nursing for neighbours. She had trained at one of the London teaching hospitals and had worked in the capital until her mother fell ill. She was a large strong woman, eminently kind and practical, and well thought of in Lulling and Thrush Green.

On the death of her father she had refurbished the empty bedrooms, and had two or three paying guests who were in need of home nursing. The service she gave was outstanding, and many a local family blessed Mrs Jenner for the help she gave with elderly or invalid relatives.

But when Mrs Jenner's seventieth birthday had come and gone, she took stock of her situation. She now found it increasingly difficult to care for her patients as she wished. Carrying heavy trays upstairs, turning matresses as well as elderly bodies, and facing disturbed nights all took their toll, and though Mrs Jenner's heart was as willing as ever, her ageing limbs were beginning to protest. Reluctantly, she decided that she must give up her nursing.

The next step was to provide a small income for herself. The old farmhouse was her main asset, and after considerable planning she decided to turn the top floor into one good-sized flat to let, and to live on the ground floor.

Her last patient had left her in February, and the alterations to the house were virtually complete by the time the fire had ravaged

Thrush Green rectory. After she had heard that Charles and Dimity were settled temporarily at Harold's, she wrote to the rector and offered them the flat if it would be of any help to them. They welcomed the suggestion. No one could have a better landlady than Mrs Jenner, and the accommodation was conveniently placed for all the rector's parish duties.

The top floor flat was light and spacious, the furniture was of good solid country-made workmanship, but Mrs Jenner obligingly offered to move some elsewhere if the rector preferred. In truth, the farmhouse was infinitely more comfortable than the rectory had ever been. Large windows overlooked the sunny garden with fields beyond.

'Perce has those now,' said Mrs Jenner, naming Jenny's admirer. 'His father and mine farmed this place together, and it was split up when they died. I only need this garden, and I let my few acres to Percy who can do with them. He's a good help to me when it's needed. Keeps me in vegetables and milk, and can turn his hand to anything to do with wood or metal.'

'He's a very skilled fellow, I know,' agreed the rector.

'Great shame about Gertie. He misses her sorely,' went on their landlady, 'But there, you know all about that. Come and see the kitchen.'

As she led them from one room to the next, Dimity realized that she was going to be more comfortable in these quarters than she had been anywhere in her married life. The carpets and curtains were well-worn, but beautifully clean. The armchairs were deep and snug, the windows gleamed, the furniture was glossy with years of polishing. Above all, it was warm.

Whatever the future held for her, Dimity became more and more certain as she followed Mrs Jenner about the old thick-walled house, that her new home, whenever it materialized, was going to be as similar in light, warmth and comfort as it could possibly be to Mrs Jenner's house. It would be smaller, she supposed. Some of the new church houses were even bungalows, she believed. How wonderful to have a home which would be easy to keep warm and clean! She recalled, with an inward shudder, the bleak Victorian rectory – its wind-tunnel of a

passage, leading from the north-facing front door to the back one, its vast Gothic windows which rattled in the wind, its high ceilings, its wintry bedrooms and the ever-damp cellars. She knew that Charles grieved for its loss. She did too, for that matter, for it had been her first home as a bride. Nevertheless, she realized, as never before, that the place had been ugly, cold, impractical and hideously expensive to run.

She gazed about Mrs Jenner's neat kitchen. A small stove gave out a steady warmth. A kettle purred upon it. The saucepans winked from the walls, and a row of fine geraniums basked in the sunshine on the window sill.

'You won't want to make up your minds just yet, I feel sure,' said Mrs Jenner. 'But let me know when you decide.'

Dimity's eyes met those of Charles.

'I think we've decided already,' said the rector, with a smile.

'Then we'll have a cup of tea,' said their new landlady, lifting the kettle.

The next morning Dimity crossed the green to visit her old friend

Ella Bembridge and to tell her about their new temporary home. She found her engrossed in the morning post. Willie Marchant was wheeling his bicycle from one gate to another, and had acknowledged her presence with a casual wave as she passed.

'Anything exciting?' asked Dimity.

'Two bills, a catalogue about Shetland woollies and a very vulgar leaflet about some hideous pottery with an order form headed: PLEASE RUSH ME THE FOLLOWING. That's enough to put you off for a start, isn't it?'

Dimity agreed.

'Besides this awful pottery, they do jewellery based on Viking designs. Cashing in on those telly programmes, I suppose, though anyone less lovable than the Vikings it would be hard to find, I imagine.'

'Well, I suppose you could call them *brave*,' said Dimity tentatively.

'Don't you start,' growled Ella. 'The more I saw and heard about them, the greater grew my admiration for dear old King Alfred. *Great* he certainly was, coping with those dreadful chaps with names like throat-clearings.'

'I've got some good news,' said Dimity, feeling it was about time to leave the inflammable subject of the Vikings. She told her about Mrs Jenner's flat, and Ella grew equally enthusiastic.

'Well, you couldn't do better. I should settle there permanently if I were you.'

'That would be blissful, wouldn't it? But I daresay the church people have other plans for us.'

At that moment there was a knock at the door, and Winnie Bailey entered. After greetings, she unfolded a snowy linen napkin to display a minute piece of knitting.

'Do you, by any chance, have a spare number twelve needle, Ella dear? Mine has vanished. Jenny and I have turned everything upside down, and it's nowhere to be seen, and I want to give these bootees to Mary Thomas before they go.'

'Do babies wear bootees now?' asked Ella. 'I thought they were brought up in grow-bags.'

'I think the term is something like "growies",' said Winnie

vaguely, 'but I always imagined they had bootees on inside those things.'

'My little brother,' said Dimity, 'had a long flannel which was folded over his feet and secured with two enormous safety pins.'

'Well, these grow-bags are simply the modern equivalent,' explained Ella, 'and I'm sure I have another twelve needle somewhere, unless I used it to stake a drooping indoor hyacinth last winter.'

She set about rummaging in the drawer of a side table, scattering knitting needles, crochet hooks, carpet needles, bodkins, safety pins, stitch-holders and a mixed assortment of other metal tools for handicrafts.

While she was thus engaged, Dimity told Winnie about their new plans.

'Yes, I did know,' admitted Winnie. 'Percy Hodge told me last night when he came to see Jenny.'

'I might have guessed,' said Dimity, 'that everyone in Thrush Green knows the news now.'

'Well, I didn't know, did I?' said Ella comfortingly, advancing with a bristling handful of knitting needles.

'There you are, Winnie. All twelves, and ranging from my Aunt Milly's bone ones to pseudo tortoiseshell via steel and modern plastic. Take your pick.'

Winnie studied the needles.

'And how is Jenny? Is she likely to marry Percy, do you think?'

'I'll take the steel ones, if I may, Ella. And about Jenny – well, I really don't know. She still looks washed-out to me, I'd like her to have a few days away. To my mind, she's worried over Percy, too. I hardly like to dissuade her – she might think my motives were a trifle self-centred – and I don't feel like doing the opposite. She must make up her own mind. I'm strictly neutral. All I want is Jenny's well-being.'

'But she might find that with Percy,' cried Dimity earnestly thinking of her own late marriage to her beloved Charles. 'I mean it really seems so *cruel* to turn down the love of a good man like kind Percy. Especially when he misses Gertie so much.'

Her two companions gazed upon her with mingled affection, amusement and exasperation.

' "When in doubt, don't", is my motto,' said Ella forthrightly. 'And as for *love*, well, you know what the Provincial Lady maintained. She reckoned that a sound bank balance and good teeth far outweighed it in value.'

'I can hardly put that forward to Jenny,' said Winnie, rolling the needles with the bootees into a white bundle.

'Well, just tell her to look before she leaps,' advised Ella, accompanying Winnie to the door.

'I can only speak from personal experience,' said Dimity, 'but I have never for one moment had regrets about my marriage.'

'Naturally,' agreed Ella, 'but then Charles is in a class of his own.'

'You are particularly fortunate,' said Winnie.

'As though I didn't know!' exclaimed Dimity.

One golden May day succeeded another. In the growing warmth of early summer Thrush Green shook out its leaves and flowers, to the delight of its inhabitants. The school children spent every playtime out in the sunshine, much to the relief of Miss Watson and Miss Fogerty, and even Albert Piggott looked less morose, and had taken off two of his winter waistcoats and his disreputable muffler.

Farmers surveyed their promising hay fields, gardeners plied hoes and gardening forks and bustled about with packets of seeds, twine and knives sticking out of their pockets. Birds flashed to and fro, feeding young, or scrapping with others who approached too near their own particular territory. Activity was everywhere apparent.

Except, it seemed, at Tullivers.

There the garden grew more neglected. Harold Shoosmith, surveying it worriedly whenever he passed, wondered if he should offer to mow the grass and clip the hedges. It was Frank and Phyllida he was thinking about, not the present occupants whose laziness appalled him. As it happened, Jack Thomas emerged one evening with the Hursts' mower, and cut the lawns, and one

Sunday he snipped away the longest of the sprouting twigs in the hedge.

Obviously, Mary was in no condition to garden, and the other pair were seldom seen. Winnie began to wonder if they were still living there, and asked Mary one day over the dividing hedge between their gardens.

To her surprise, the girl's face flushed with anger. 'We've sent them packing,' she said shortly.

'I'm sorry. I shouldn't have asked. I didn't mean to upset you.'

'You haven't. Actually I'm so relieved, I can't tell you. They never fitted in, you know.'

'It looked rather that way.'

'Jack's too kind-hearted. They told him this sob story just before we came here, and he was sorry for them and offered them shelter until they found a job.'

'And have they?'

Mary gave a snort of disgust. 'They haven't exactly tried. They made a great thing of going down to Lulling to the Job Centre, but as far as I could see, they had no intention of taking anything offered them. I think they thought that the group would make a bomb. But of course it hasn't. Anyway, it was agreed that we should split any fee four ways, so that no one had very much.'

She paused for a moment.

'Especially if you're on pot,' she added.

'Pot? Drugs, do you mean?'

'Cannabis, and a bit of cocaine. I don't think they've got to the hard stuff yet, but I bet they will pretty soon. The stink of the stuff made me so ill. That's what finally decided Jack to send them packing.'

'So I should hope,' said Winnie.

'The final straw,' said Mary, 'was pinching the housekeeping money last week. I thought it had been vanishing for some time, a fiver here and there. You know how easy it is, especially when four people use the purse.'

'What was your system?'

'Oh, whoever went shopping for meat or eggs or groceries just took the purse. We all put in a fiver at the beginning, and then had a share out at the end of each week, and refurbished the funds again.'

'It sounds a good idea.'

'In theory, yes. In practice, particularly with half paying out for drugs, it was hopeless. My gold bangle's gone too. I may have lost it – the catch was loose – but I can't help feeling they pinched it. Jack refused to believe me – he's much more high-minded than I am. Anyway, I got some of that powder you can scatter in cash boxes and so on. It stains a thief's hands bright red. It certainly worked with Bill and Lottie last Thursday. We caught them literally red-handed. I've never seen Jack so furious. They were out within an hour.'

'Where have they gone?'

'I don't know. They can go back to their parents, but of course they don't want to. We had our last share out and they pushed off with about three pounds apiece. The motor bike's in good order. It's up to them now. Frankly, I hope I never clap eyes on them again. They've thoroughly spoiled our time here.'

'Put them out of your mind,' advised Winnie. 'It's over and done with, and now you must look ahead to the baby and take care of yourself and Jack.'

'You are quite right. We should be able to move into the new house next week, and we're both looking forward to making a fresh start.' She looked about her at the sunny garden, murmurous with bees among the wallflowers. 'We shall miss Thrush Green. It would have been perfect if only we had been alone.'

'You won't be far away,' said Winnie cheerfully, 'You'll be able to visit us, I hope, and see Thrush Green in a more favourable light.'

'See Eden without its serpent? I'll look forward to that.'

That same day, after the school children had raced home, Miss Watson and Miss Fogerty enjoyed a well-deserved rest in the school house garden. In common with the majority of Thrush Green residents, a modest tea was before them. A tray with two cups and saucers, milk jug, teapot and a plate bearing half a dozen delicious lemon curd tartlets made a brave sight.

The two friends were content to bask in the sun in silent companionship. An inquisitive blackbird made forays from the hedge, its bright eyes focused on the tea tray. Apart from its pattering claws upon the dead leaves, and the distant shouts of tardily departing children across the green, a blissful somnolence enwrapped them.

Agnes allowed her mind to drift from school matters to the more personal needs of her modest wardrobe. Should she buy another cotton frock, suitable for school, or should she get Miss Crookshank to make up the length of blue checked gingham she had prudently bought before material became so expensive?

The difficulty was that Miss Crookshank would probably need quite a month to get the frock made, pleading pressure of business, her mother's illness and other excuses, all probably quite genuine, Miss Fogerty told herself, but the result would be that the fine spell would probably be over by the time the garment was completed.

And, of course, she must get a new pattern. That princess-style, button-through one which had done so well for so many years, had its drawbacks. Far too often the bottom button had burst off when showing the children how to be a really energetic galloping horse in the playground. And, on occasions, she had discovered that the bodice gaped, which was immodest to say the least. Perhaps something with a yoke? No zip, of course, and certainly not at the back. Far too difficult to reach.

There was a lot to be said for buying a frock ready-made. She had seen some attractive ones in two of the Lulling shops, but the prices had been excessive, and it was really a shocking waste not to have the gingham made up. On the other hand, was the gingham perhaps too light in colour for school wear? One must remember how quickly clothes grew grubby in contact with such things as coloured chalks, modelling clay, charcoal sticks, paste and poster paints, not to mention innumerable infants' fingers clutching at one's raiment.

Agnes, juggling gently with this problem, was brought to earth by a squeak from her companion.

'Oh dear, I didn't mean to wake you,' began Dorothy.

'I wasn't asleep, dear, I assure you. Did something sting you?'

'No, no. I was about to get up to carry in the tray, and my leg gave a twinge. All over now. I think I must have been sitting awkwardly.'

'Should you see the doctor again?' asked Agnes, full of solicitude.

'No, I'm really quite fit. Well, as fit as I'm going to be, I suspect.'

'But surely,' protested Agnes, 'you will go on getting stronger? It isn't all that long ago—'

'It's well over a year,' said Dorothy. 'It may improve, of course, but I seem to have been at this stage for months now. It doesn't worry me, Agnes dear, because I just face the fact that I'm slower and can't walk as far as I did. On the whole, I can do all I want to do.'

'I sometimes think you do too much,' said Agnes loyally. 'You should let me help you more.'

Dorothy laughed. 'You spoil me as it is. Besides, you are quite a few years older than I am.'

Agnes nodded, and silence engulfed them again. A bold robin now came to reconnoitre, and the blackbird rushed at it, scolding furiously. The robin stood its ground.

'Agnes,' said Dorothy at last, 'have you ever thought of retiring?'

'*Retiring?*' cried Agnes. 'Why, do you think I should? I mean, am I working as you would wish? Do I do my duties satisfactorily—?'

Dorothy broke in upon this panic. 'Of course, you do *everything* quite beautifully, Agnes. I've yet to meet a better teacher, as you should know. No, I only passed the remark because retirement is rather in my mind at the moment.'

'You don't mean it!' gasped Agnes. 'Why, you are still in your fifties – and don't look it, I assure you! I thought you would want to stay at Thrush Green until you were sixty-five.'

Dorothy nodded absently, her eyes upon the robin. 'So did I. But since this fall, I've been thinking about things. Everything is much more of an effort. I'm beginning to wonder if I should go at sixty. I could give a year's notice when I get to fifty-nine next birthday. That should be ample time for a new head to be found.'

Agnes's mind, so recently swinging indolently from ready-made frocks to Miss Crookshank's versions, was now in a state of violent agitation. To think that dear Dorothy was even contemplating such a step! She had always looked upon her as so much younger and stronger than herself. After all, her own birthday would bring her to sixty-two, and she had quite resigned herself to the idea of staying until she was sixty-five. In any case, she hoped to put a little more in her Building Society account before she drew her pension. She had thought about returning to modest lodgings when the time came for Dorothy to give up the school house or even earlier. It was not a very exciting prospect, she knew, but she could hardly expect Dorothy to want her for the rest of her days, when the job they did together was over.

In her bewilderment, she scarcely took in all that Dorothy was saying.

'I should have thought about it long ago,' Dorothy was saying. 'Something really modest, a bungalow perhaps with a small garden and a view of the sea, of course. What do you think, Agnes?'

'I don't quite follow you, Dorothy,' said little Miss Fogerty unhappily. Everything was awhirl in her mind.

'If I decided to retire at sixty,' said her headmistress patiently, 'I should have to have a house. I was thinking aloud really – wondering about dear old Barton-on-Sea. What do you think?'

'You've always loved it there,' said Agnes carefully.

'But would you love it too?'

Agnes turned bemused eyes upon her. 'Would I be there too?' she quavered.

Miss Watson gave one of her famous snorts. '*Of course* you'd be there too! I hope you don't intend to desert me when we've both retired.'

'Oh, Dorothy!' began Agnes, appalled at the idea of treachery.

'Unless,' said Dorothy, suddenly and surprisingly unsure, 'you would rather not?'

'Rather not?' echoed Agnes. 'Just do let me get my breath, Dorothy dear, and I'll try to tell you how I feel.'

'I'll pour us both another cup while you're pondering,' said Miss Watson, lifting the teapot.

11. A Sea-Side Interlude

June arrived, and Tullivers stood empty again awaiting the return of Phil and Frank Hurst.

Jeremy grew more and more excited as the time drew nearer, and Winnie shared his joy. She admitted to herself that she was relieved at the departure of the young people next door, and she and Jeremy were glad to be putting things to rights after their slapdash housekeeping. It did not take long to get Tullivers looking ship-shape, although there were one or two things which would need more specialized attention than Winnie and Jenny could give.

A coffee table was badly stained, and someone appeared to have trodden tar or some equally viscous material into the sitting room carpet. The latter defied all their combined attempts to clean it. Obviously, the whole thing would need to go to professional cleaners.

Upstairs, there was a cracked hand basin and a peculiar stain down one wall in the back bedroom. But, at first sight, Tullivers gave its usual peaceful sunny welcome.

'Well, we've done all we can,' said Winnie, shutting the front door. I'll put some flowers inside on the day they arrive. How good it will be to see them back!'

They went next door, and Jenny filled the kettle for Winnie's tea tray. The children were already coming out of school, and Jeremy would be looking forward to a slice of her gingerbread.

'Leave that for a minute, Jenny,' said Winnie, 'and come and sit down.'

She led the way into the sitting room and she and Jenny sighed with pleasure at being at rest after all their activities next door.

'Now, Jenny,' began Winnie, 'I've something to put to you. Are you happy here?'

'Happy?' exclaimed Jenny. 'You know I am! Never been happier. It's like a dream come true.'

'Good,' said Winnie. 'And I'm equally happy, except for one thing.' She looked across at Jenny's bewildered expression. 'And that's your health, Jenny. You have never really picked up after that wretched illness, and I'm going to see that you have a little holiday.'

'But I don't *need* a little holiday!' wailed Jenny. 'I shouldn't know what to do! Honest, I wouldn't.'

'Well, I should like a little break myself as soon as Jeremy's back at Tullivers, and I have made inquiries at a very quiet hotel in Torquay where I propose we go together. I shall stay for the weekend and leave you there for another week. The sea air will do you a world of good.'

'But what—' began Jenny, when Jeremy burst in.

'I'm *starving*!' he cried.

'Hear that?' said Winnie rising. 'We'll talk about this later on, Jenny, but meanwhile we must get the tea ready. We can't have the Hursts coming back to a boy skeleton.'

And Jenny, her head awhirl with these holiday proposals, went to cut up the gingerbread.

On the same afternoon, at the Youngs' splendid house, Joan and Molly were busy taking down the long and heavy velvet curtains which had kept out the bleak winter draughts of Thrush Green, and were replacing them with light chintz ones for the summer.

'Do you know,' said Joan, 'that these windows are almost fifteen feet in height? I hope to goodness all these curtains last out our time. We should never be able to afford more.'

Molly, perched on a kitchen chair, was doing her best to reach the hooks at the top, and deciding that she must fetch the step ladder after all.

'How many metres would you need, I wonder?'

'Heaven alone knows, and I don't intend to try and work it out at my age. I'd have to tell the shop people in yards, and let them do the sums.'

At that moment, Molly gave a little cry, swayed on her precarious chair and was caught by her alarmed mistress. She helped the fainting girl to an armchair, and pressed her head down upon her knees. She was much agitated. Molly never ailed. Should she send for her brother-in-law, Dr John Lovell? But then he would probably be out on his rounds at this time.

She crouched on the floor gazing anxiously at her patient. To her relief, she saw the colour returning to Molly's cheeks, and the girl sat up.

'Lean back,' advised Joan, 'and I'll get you a drink.'

She hastened into the kitchen and collected a glass of water and some brandy. What could be the matter?

'Only the water,' whispered Molly, 'that other stuff makes me sick.'

Joan watched her as she sipped.

'Have you felt faint before?'

'Once or twice. Nothing much. Let's get on with the curtains.'

'Not on your life! They can wait. You're going upstairs to lie down. I shan't be able to look Ben in the eye if he finds you ill.'

'You know what I reckon it is?' said Molly.

'Tell me.'

'A baby on the way. To tell the truth, I thought it might be, and this seems to settle it.'

'Well, I'm glad to hear it, Molly dear, and you're going to see Dr Lovell first thing tomorrow. When do you think it's due?'

'If I've reckoned aright, it should be late in December.'

'A Christmas baby!' cried Joan, 'Now, isn't that good news? You were very naughty to clamber about on that chair. If only I'd known!'

'No harm done,' said Molly cheerfully, getting up. 'You know, I'd much rather carry on here than go upstairs.'

'You'll do as you're told for once,' said Joan firmly. 'Edward will give me a hand with these curtains when he comes home. What are husbands for, I'd like to know?'

*

The Hursts returned to an ecstatic welcome from Jeremy and a heartfelt one from all their old friends at Thrush Green. At first, they forbore to tell them of the shortcomings of Tullivers' temporary residents, but as Harold Shoosmith told Isobel: 'It is only a matter of time before all is revealed – and that much embellished, I have no doubt.' He was to be proved right within a week.

But before these unwelcome comments were made, Winnie and Jenny had packed their bags and taken the train to Torquay.

Jenny's agitation at first hearing of the plan had gradually changed to pleasurable anticipation. This was increased when she recalled that an old childhood friend, another inmate of the orphanage, had married a draper in the town. It was true that they only wrote to each other at Christmas time, exchanging handkerchiefs or bath salts, but they shared potent memories of their early home and had a strong affection for each other.

Winnie was delighted to hear of this link, and an invitation to Harry and Bessie to have tea with them at the hotel on the Sunday was warmly accepted.

The hotel itself gave Jenny confidence at once. She had secretly feared that everything would be over-poweringly grand. Certainly all in sight was harmonious and beautifully kept, a virtue which appealed to house-proud Jenny immediately. But besides this, the hotel staff were welcoming, the service unobtrusive and efficient, and the windows overlooked a well-kept garden with the sparkling sea beyond. Jenny's spirits rose as she unpacked in the bedroom next to Winnie's, stopping to gaze at the view on each trip to the wardrobe. Who would have thought she would ever be in such a lovely place? And so far from Thrush Green too?

To her surprise she felt relief rather than sadness at the thought of the distance between her present bedroom and the one at home. Somehow it was good to get away from the old familiar view, the chestnut avenue, the children running to school, Mr Jones watering the hanging baskets outside The Two Pheasants. Above all, she had to admit, it was a relief to get away from Percy Hodge. Perhaps now she could see things more clearly without his presence to upset her.

Ah well! Tomorrow she would see Bessie again, and her husband for the first time. It was good to be looking forward to new interests. She would forget Thrush Green for a while, and really make the most of this wonderful holiday.

The sunshine which enhanced Jenny's first view of Torquay bathed the entire country. At Thrush Green, early roses graced the window sills of Miss Fogerty's classroom. Mr Jones's geraniums burst into exuberant bloom, and the sound of the lawn mower was heard in the land.

The meadow leading to Lulling Woods was ablaze with buttercups. Daisies starred Thrush Green itself, and mothers watched their toddlers clutching bunches in their fat hands. The wooden seats were warm to sit upon, and young and old, eyes closed against the dazzling light, dreamt and dozed in perfect bliss.

Even Albert Piggott appeared less malevolent and, billhook in hand to show that he was mindful of his duties, sunned himself upon a flat tombstone by the churchyard wall.

Along the lane to Nod and Nidden, the cow parsley frothed and shed its lacy flowers in the breeze. Dotty Harmer admired its fragile beauty as she took Flossie for her afternoon walk. To tell the truth, the spaniel would have much preferred to spend the afternoon lying in the plum tree's shade in Dotty's garden but, obliging as ever, accompanied her beloved mistress with every appearance of pleasure. She was grateful to her owner, and had not forgotten how she had been rescued by her and given such a loving home. What if the melting tar did squeeze between her claws in this unpleasant way? It was a small price to pay for the pleasure of sharing a walk with Dotty and making her happy.

The elderflowers were beginning to open, turning their creamy faces to the sun, and Dotty turned her mind to making elderflower champagne if only she could remember where she put the recipe. Behind the kitchen clock? In the Coalport vegetable dish? In mother's secretaire? She would have a good look round when she returned home.

She came within sight of Thrush Green, shimmering in the

heat. Perhaps it would be a good idea to call at Ella's. The recipe had come from her in the first place.

She crossed the green, a scraggy shabby figure topped by a frayed coolie straw hat, the object of mirth to two young mothers lolling on one of the seats. Flossie panted obediently behind her.

Ella was in her garden, sitting in a deck chair. Across her lap was draped a small sack, and across that lay some strands of raffia in gaudy colours. A large needle threaded with a piece of scarlet raffia was in Ella's hand, but it was not being used. She was asleep, her mouth ajar, her head lodged sideways. Dotty surveyed her for a few moments, trying to decide if she should tiptoe away. However, the recipe was needed immediately if she wanted to pick really fresh elderflowers.

She coughed discreetly, and Ella awoke.

'Golly!' exclaimed Ella, reverting in her bemused state to the ejaculations of her childhood. 'You made me jump!'

'I'm sorry about that, but the front door was wide open, so I just came through.'

'And quite right too,' said Ella. 'Pull up that other chair and relax. What weather! That's why I opened the front door. You get a nice breeze right through the house that way, though I don't suppose the police would approve.'

'Was that young officer a good speaker? I couldn't come to the W.I. last Wednesday. One of the hens was indisposed, and I felt I should be at hand, you know.'

'Quite,' said Ella, envisaging Dotty crouched in the hen run holding a flaccid claw in her own skinny hand. 'How is she now?'

'Oh, quite recovered, thank you. I was sorry to miss the talk. About safety precautions, wasn't it? Not that I ever think of locking the house, though I suppose one should.'

'He seemed to think that *opening* the door to strangers was even worse.'

'But why? After all, one is obliged to open the door to see if they really are strangers.'

'Evidently, they are inclined to knock you on the head,' replied Ella, 'and then take anything of value before you come round.'

'How very unpleasant! I can't say I get many strangers, do you?'

'The odd tramp now and again. I always fill their billycans with hot water as requested, and give 'em a slice of bread and cheese.'

'I must admit that I do, too. My father was quite outspoken about tramps, and said some very *wounding* things to them, I thought. You know, about Satan finding mischief for idle hands to do, and able-bodied men always being able to find work if they really looked for it. They seldom called twice.'

'I must say, I try to protect myself from an inundation of tramps by warning them not to leave any of their cryptic signs on the gate post.'

'Do they do that?'

'So I'm told. You know – a circle means: "Here's a soft touch", or a cross means: "Look out! The old cat chucks water over you!" Something of the sort.'

'I must look out for those things. By the way, Ella, what are you making with that sack?'

Ella held up her handiwork. 'Peg bags. Always sell well at sales of work, and the raffia brightens them up, doesn't it?'

'Yes, indeed,' agreed Dotty doubtfully. 'But won't the colours run if the bag gets wet?'

'Why should it get wet?' protested Ella. 'You don't leave your peg bag out in the rain, do you?'

'Yes,' said Dotty.

Dotty would, thought Ella.

'But as it's a good stout bag made out of father's old Burberry years ago, it doesn't come to any harm, you see.'

Here Flossie, who had taken advantage of some shade under a lilac bush, yawned noisily and thumped her tail upon some defenceless forget-me-nots.

Dotty took the hint. 'Time we were off, Ella dear.'

'Won't you stay to tea?'

'No, thank you. Dulcie must be picketed elsewhere for the rest of the day. She's eating voraciously now she's pregnant, and I thought a short spell by the hazel bushes would enliven her diet. Goats really do appreciate variety. That's why I never get cross when I find that the dear thing has pulled something off the line for a snack. She's obviously short of some particular mineral or vitamin.'

Flossie struggled to her feet and lumbered over to her mistress.

'She feels the heat,' commented Ella, charitably ignoring the havoc caused by the spaniel's progress through the flower bed.

'Perfect weather,' she went on, 'to be on holiday. It will do Winnie and Jenny a power of good by the sea.'

Ella accompanied Dotty though the cool hall and out into the blaze of Thrush Green. She watched her old friend cross the grass and turn into the walled lane of golden Cotswold stone on her way to Lulling Woods and the most pampered goat in the locality. It was not until next morning that Dotty realized she had forgotten to ask for the recipe.

At Torquay, the Sunday tea party was a great success, and

Winnie departed for home on the Monday morning feeling relieved that Jenny had such good friends in the neighbourhood.

Bessie and Harry lived over the shop, not far from the harbour, and from their upstairs sitting room there was a view of the sea which delighted Jenny. She was invited to lunch on the Tuesday, and when Harry had returned to his duties below, the two old friends settled down to compare the course of their lives since leaving the orphanage.

They sat comfortably on a little balcony overlooking the steep street and the distant sea, their feet lodged in the decorative ironwork and their heads in the shade of the canopy above them.

Jenny sighed contentedly. 'Who'd have thought we should find ourselves so comfortable when we were at the orphanage?'

'We've both been lucky,' agreed Bessie. 'And Harry's the perfect husband. I wonder you didn't marry, Jenny. You were always a pretty girl.'

'Never had much chance,' replied Jenny. 'Ma and Pa took up all my time. Not that I grudged it, mark you. They was good to me, and I was glad to pay 'em back, but I didn't get out and about much.'

'But now they're gone,' persisted Bessie, 'don't you ever think of it?'

In the silence that followed, only the distant sea gulls cried. Jenny wondered if she should unburden herself to her old friend, and perhaps get her advice. On the other hand, her natural shyness made her reluctant. But the sun warmed her legs. The sea air was exhilarating. Thrush Green and its gossipers were far away, and for once Jenny threw aside her caution.

'Well, as a matter of fact, Bessie, there is someone at the moment,' she confessed, and the tale of Percy's attentions, her own embarrassment and uncertainty, Winnie Bailey's kindness and her needs, all came tumbling out.

Bessie, eyes closed against the brilliance of the afternoon, listened attentively. In common with the rest of mankind, Bessie loved a story, and here was a romantic drama of real life – its heroine lying close beside her and, better still, asking for her advice.

'So there it is,' finished Jenny, feeling mightily relieved after such an outpouring, 'and I hope I'll know what to do by the time I get back. It's my belief Mrs Bailey got me away to give me a chance to sort out my feelings rather than improve my health.'

'It's a bit difficult to know where one ends and the other begins,' said Bessie sagaciously. 'I had sty after sty on my eyelids when Harry was courting me, but as soon as I said "Yes" they vanished.'

'But what do you think? He's such a good chap and he does miss his Gertie terribly. She was a wonderful manager, and the best cook in Thrush Green some said. He's lost without her, and his clothes are getting something dreadful – buttons off, cuffs frayed – you know how men get their things.'

Bessie sat forward and propped her chin on her fist. She gazed out to sea as she spoke slowly.

'It's like this, Jenny. I don't doubt he's in need of a wife, and I don't doubt he'll find one pretty soon, if he's the nice fellow you say. But it's *you* I'm thinking of. Do *you* want to live with this Percy for the rest of your days? Do *you* want to give up the life you've just found simply because Percy's clothes need mending? You've always been unselfish. I can remember that from when we were little kids, and you've spent all your time till now looking after Ma and Pa. I don't say Percy wouldn't be grateful, and would treat you right. I'm sure he would, but is it what you want?'

'If you put it like that,' said Jenny, 'I suppose I should never have thought of Percy in that way, if he hadn't come – well, I suppose you could say – *courting*.'

'I'll tell you something else, Jenny, which always helped me when I was trying to decide about a man. I was no flibbertigibbet, mind you, but I did have quite a few lads in my time, before I met Harry, and I used to say to myself when they started to get serious: "Now, would it break my heart to see him with someone else?" And, d'you know, half the time I used to think it would be a relief if they *did* find someone! Then I knew my own feelings!'

Jenny laughed. 'What a sensible way of looking at it! I can't tell you how you've helped, Bessie, and I think I'll know my own mind before I go back to Thrush Green. It's just that I hate to think of Percy being hurt.'

'Nice men aren't hurt for long,' said Bessie robustly. 'They find someone else quite easily, believe me. Mark my words, if you turn down your Percy he'll be married within the year! I've seen it happen time and time again, and no hearts broken either.'

And then the subject of Percy was shelved, and for the next few hours the talk was of what happened to Mary Carter, and to Joan King, and to the two sisters who ran away and incurred the wrath of the Principal.

Later, Jenny walked back to the hotel through a rose and lavender sunset, and loitered in the garden before going to her room. The air was fragrant with night-scented stock, mignonette, and the aromatic spiciness of the cypress trees.

For the first time for months, Jenny felt at peace. That old saying about a trouble shared being a trouble halved was perfectly true, she reminded herself as she went thankfully up to bed.

12. BESSIE'S ADVICE

Winnie returned to her empty house and, much to her surprise, found that she quite enjoyed having it to herself.

Jenny's presence was always a comfort to her, particularly after dark, and she certainly missed the chatter of Jeremy after his few weeks' stay. But now that high summer was here, and the scents and sounds of Thrush Green floated through the open windows, Winnie felt no hint of loneliness and found a certain quiet pleasure in having no interruptions to her train of thought as she moved about the house she had lived in for so long.

Perhaps, after all, she would not miss Jenny so desperately if Percy's suit were successful. It was a surprising thought, and one which gave Winnie some pleasure. It must mean that she was over the worst of the shock of her dear Donald's death. Time, it seemed, as everyone had kept telling her, did heal wounds. She had not really believed it, but now she wondered. At least, this new-found confidence was welcome, and if Jenny were to leave her then she could bear it with greater fortitude than she had thought possible.

Her happiness continued through the week. Jenny was due to come home at tea time on the Saturday, and Winnie had instructed her to take a taxi from Lulling Station, despite Jenny's protests about the expense.

'I'm not having you walk over a mile, and uphill at that, struggling with a suitcase and all the rest of the luggage. And suppose it rains? No, you must do as I say, Jenny.'

And Jenny had agreed.

But on Friday afternoon Percy Hodge had appeared on the

doorstep with a bunch of Mrs Sinkin pinks as big as a cauliflower and had announced that he would be meeting the 4.10 train.

'But we've arranged for Jenny to come up by taxi,' explained Winnie, somewhat taken aback.

'I know that. But I'd particularly like to have a word with Jenny, and it's a pleasure to meet her off the train. No need for a taxi when I've got the car.'

Winnie could do no more than thank him, but the expression 'like to have a word with Jenny' sounded ominous. Was he going to propose marriage between Lulling Station and Thrush Green? And what would Jenny think when she found Percy waiting at the station? And suppose that Percy was a little late and Jenny had already taken the taxi? Oh dear, what a muddle!

By the time seven o'clock came Winnie was decidedly agitated, although she realized that Percy and Jenny's affairs were their own business. In the end, she decided to ring Jenny at Torquay, and to let her know that Percy was meeting the train, and to leave it at that. At least, the girl would be prepared.

As it happened, Jenny spent her last evening with Bessie and Harry, but Winnie left a message with the girl at the switchboard and could only hope that Jenny would get it when she returned. In a way, it was a relief not to have to speak directly to her. She might have wanted lengthy explanations.

Winnie went to bed, telling herself that she had had quite enough for one day, and the morrow must take care of itself.

The morrow, as it happened, brought Ella Bembridge to the door at ten o'clock in the morning.

Winnie had been in her garden picking roses and inspecting the raspberry canes. It looked as though there would be a fine crop this year, but rain would be needed to plump up the berries. The sky was cloudless, as it had been now for a week or more, and despite the needs of the raspberry canes, Winnie could not find it in her heart to pray for a change in the weather.

'Another glorious day!' she greeted Ella.

'Not for the Lovelock girls!' replied Ella.

As none of the three sisters would ever see seventy-five again

Winnie could not help feeling that *girls* was not the exact word for her three aged friends.

'Not ill?' exclaimed Winnie.

'Burgled!' said Ella, sitting down heavily on a delicate Sheraton chair which creaked a protest.

'No! When? How? What have they lost?'

'The answers are: Yes. Yesterday. By a person or persons unknown. And they're not sure yet what has gone, but it's nearly all old silver.'

'Poor old darlings! It will break their hearts. They loved their bits of silver.'

'Well, they were told often enough to keep it in a cupboard or a bank, but you know them! They said they enjoyed seeing it about them.'

'And why not? What's the fun of having lovely things if you don't enjoy them? My mother was left a diamond bracelet by her grandmother, and it was so wickedly valuable that it never saw the light of day but was in the bank's vault. My mother often grieved for it, I know.'

'Best place for it,' said Ella sturdily. 'You remember what that police officer told us about keeping valuables out of sight?'

'Of course I remember. And as a matter of fact, I've even locked the front door when I've been shopping in Lulling recently. What's more, I forgot where I'd hidden the key, and had to wait for Jenny to let me in. I'm sure people weren't so dishonest in our young days. It does make life very difficult for everyone.'

'Well, I thought I'd let you know in case you were seeing the girls some time soon.'

'I'll ring them to see if I can help,' said Winnie, 'but quite what to do is the question, isn't it? Their silver must have been worth a fortune. I suppose they were insured?'

'Lord knows!' replied Ella, heaving herself from the protesting chair. 'By the way, d'you want gooseberries? Bumper crop I've got, so come and help yourself. The Lovelock girls were picking theirs when the thief got in evidently.'

'What a bold fellow! And yes, please, I'd love some gooseberries to bottle. Nothing nicer than hot gooseberry tart on a bleak December day. Can I come one day next week when Jenny's back?'

'Any time you like,' said Ella, and stumped out into the morning blaze.

It was Miss Violet Lovelock who spoke to Winnie on the telephone, and although she sounded upset, her account of the burglary was remarkably clear and detailed.

'It's the *effrontery* of the crime that has so shaken us,' she cried, in her high quivering voice. 'We were only in the garden, you know, all busy picking our beautiful golden gooseberries for bottling. The wretched fellow must have pushed open the front door and seen us at it through the hall window. It gives a clear view of the garden, as you know.'

'But why should he open the door?'

'Well, dear, the milkman normally leaves our bottles in that rather fine cache-pot by the doorstep, but in this hot weather Bertha said it might be wiser for him to put it just inside the front door, and she left a note to that effect in the cache-pot. The thief must have seen it.'

'Very likely.'

'The milkman has been so unpunctual lately. We never know when he will appear. He's courting May Miller at the draper's, and his van stands outside for *hours*. I wonder he's not had up for loitering with intent.'

'You can't have a van charged with loitering, Violet dear.'

'Well, anyway,' went on Miss Lovelock, 'this wretched fellow lifted a carrier bag from the hall stand, went into the dining room and put *everything* – simply *everything* – from the sideboard into it. He also took everything from the hall table, too.'

'And no one saw him?'

'Well, dear, a man on the bus saw him, we gather. The thief must have stepped into a bus as soon as he emerged. Extremely fortunate for him when you consider the paucity of public transport these days. This man – who saw him, I mean – has given a description to the police. He noticed that the carrier bag *clanked*, but as it was a Debenham's bag – such a *respectable* firm – he simply supposed that he had been buying kitchenware of some description, saucepans and fish kettles and so on.'

'Do Debenham's sell kitchenware?'

'I'm not sure. Shops sell such odd things these days, though never what you want. Bertha is having such a job buying double satin baby ribbon to thread through her best nightgown. It seems to have vanished from the market.'

'What's the next move, Violet? Are the police being helpful?'

'Oh, very! Most sympathetic. The only thing is that we are having such difficulty in providing a correct list. I wake in the night and think: "Now, did I mention the pseudo-Lamerie posset cup which although made in Birmingham in 1905 was solid silver and quite charming?" The young officer who is dealing with us is patience itself, and always ready for a cup of Earl Grey tea. Luckily, he doesn't take sugar.'

There speaks a true Lovelock, thought Winnie, frugal even in adversity.

She put down the telephone after further expressions of sympathy, and went about her domestic duties.

The news about Molly's coming baby was soon general knowledge at Thrush Green. Everyone, with the exception of the baby's grandfather-to-be, Albert Piggott, was delighted.

'Lot of fuss about nothing,' growled Albert when congratulated by his fellow-drinkers at The Two Pheasants. 'If you ask me there's too many people in the world already, without adding to 'em.'

'You'll have to look after yourself a bit more, Albert me boy,' said one sagely. 'Can't expect Molly to do as she usually does for you, with another on the way.'

'D'you think I ain't thought of that meself?' snapped Albert, and gazed gloomily into his empty glass.

Little Miss Fogerty decided to put aside the cardigan she was knitting for next winter and to buy some baby wool at once for a jacket for the new child. She was somewhat agitated about the choice of colour for the finished garment.

'I like pink myself,' She told Miss Watson, as they cracked their boiled eggs, 'and I've no doubt Molly is hoping for a girl this time. But if it is another boy, pink looks so *effeminate*, doesn't it? Perhaps blue would be safer. Girls look just as pretty in blue, don't you think?'

Miss Watson agreed somewhat absent-mindedly, and Agnes was instantly alert.

'Tell me, Dorothy, is your leg paining you?' Her own problems were forgotten at once.

Miss Watson sighed. 'To tell you the truth Agnes, I had a most disturbed night with it.'

'Then we'll call in Dr Lovell immediately.'

'No, no. I saw him not long ago, you remember, and he told me then that it was nothing to worry about. It was only *referred pain*, he said.'

'So what!' remarked little Miss Fogerty, quite militant on her friend's behalf. 'If it's pain, it's pain, and hurts! What's the difference between *legitimate* pain and this *referred* variety?'

'I quite agree,' confessed Miss Watson, wincing as she moved her chair. 'All very unsatisfactory, but is one in a position to argue? I think we'll wait a day or two, and see how it goes on. I may have slept in an awkward position, and put my pelvic girdle out a little.'

'Maybe,' agreed Agnes. 'That's the worst of bones. They're all joined on and, I must admit, in the most careless fashion at times. But I warn you, Dorothy, I shall have no hesitation in summoning the doctor if I see you are suffering.'

Miss Watson smiled at her good friend. On the rare occasions when she was roused she looked, as she did now, like a ferocious mouse.

'I've no doubt I shall be as fit as a flea tomorrow,' she assured Agnes.

But even fleas, she reminded herself, as she rose painfully from the table, must have their off days.

Dimity and Charles Henstock, now happily installed at Mrs

Jenner's, met Dotty Harmer in the lane leading from Thrush Green to Nidden. They told her the news of Molly's expectations.

Dotty stood stock-still, looking bemused, while Flossie snuffled happily at Charles Henstock's legs, her plume of tail greatly agitated in her pleasure.

'Due in December? What a long time. Are you sure that's correct, Charles? I've forgotten the gestation period for humans. Goats, rabbits and cats I am perfectly sound on, but *babies* now . . .'

'I can assure you, Dotty, that December is correct,' said Dimity. 'Nine months, you know, is the time needed, and now it's June, so in six months' time the baby will arrive.'

'Yes, yes, I'm quite sure Molly would know. Such a competent little mother as she is. It's just that I had forgotten for the moment.'

'Come and have some tea in our new home,' suggested Charles. 'You've thought no more by the way, about adopting a child of your own?'

'I can't say I've had any encouragement,' retorted Dotty, 'from the adoption societies – or from you, for that matter, if you recall, Charles dear. I've decided to give up the plan. With much regret, I may say.'

Charles heaved a sigh of relief.

'And, yes please, I should love a cup of tea with you at Mrs Jenner's.'

They began to retrace their steps, Flossie bounding ahead.

'Of course,' said Dotty conversationally, as they entered Mrs Jenner's gate, 'elephants carry their young for two years. I think that is what was confusing me. Poor things!' she added pityingly.

Charles and Dimity, following Dotty's scarecrow figure up the path, exchanged glances of shared joy.

What would they do without Dotty?

As Jenny's train rushed eastward from Torquay through the June countryside, she looked back upon her holiday with great contentment. To have been by the sea would have been happiness enough. So seldom had she seen it that the wonder of its immensity and its changing moods, even viewed from the serenity of Mead-foot Beach, filled her with awe and excitement.

She remembered the thrill of paddling at the edge of the waves, watching them frilling round her ankles. She had not ventured to bathe, paddling was as much as she dared to do, but the sight of her feet, grotesquely distorted beneath the green water, filled her with joyous amusement.

The sea itself and the soft salty air had worked wonders for her spirits. Jenny began to realize how very run down she must have been, and she would always be grateful to Winnie Bailey for recognizing the state of affairs, and for dealing so briskly and generously with it.

Swaying gently to the rhythm of the train, Jenny watched the telegraph poles flicker past against the background of green woods and fields. She would never be able to repay Winnie's kindness. The holiday had been wonderful, and an added bonus had been the joy of meeting Bessie again. The warm contentment which now engulfed her was due as much to Bessie's friendship and advice as to the healing properties of Torquay's sea and air.

Yesterday evening Bessie had raised again the subject of Percy Hodge, guessing that Jenny must be feeling some tremors again at the thought of returning to Thrush Green and to facing her admirer once more.

She did not know, of course, that Percy was to meet Jenny's train. Winnie Bailey's guarded message still awaited Jenny's return to the hotel. But she thought it would do no harm to see if her old friend were more settled in her mind. She raised the matter delicately, and Jenny sighed.

'I remember what you told me about imagining someone else with your young man,' she said, 'and it worked, you know. If only some nice woman would take on Percy, I think I'd be truly relieved. He does *need* someone so.'

'I'm glad to hear you say that,' replied Bessie. 'But it needn't be you who supplies it. After all, Jenny, if his lost buttons and frayed collars worry you, then you could always offer to do some mending for him, as an old friend. You don't have to *marry* the fellow, now do you?'

And Jenny had laughed and agreed.

How sensible Bessie was! Of course, that was the right way to deal with Percy's ardours. Perhaps if she had had as many admirers as Bessie had in her young days, she would not have worried so much about dear old Percy's attentions. It was the sheer unexpectedness of being wanted by someone which had so agitated her. Bessie was probably quite right to say that Percy would find someone else within the year. She hoped he would. He was a good man and deserved some comfort and companionship.

As for her own feelings, well – it was nice to have been courted. She would always be grateful to Percy for singling her out. But what a relief it would be to be freed from the necessity and embarrassment of thanking him for flowers, eggs, soap, plants and all the other kind presents which he had brought to the door!

She closed her eyes against the Wiltshire meadows flashing past, and gave a sigh of contentment. Now she knew what to do. Now she could face Percy at the station. Probably he would say very little and just pick up her case, and talk about the weather. Then there would be no need to say anything much, except to tell him about Torquay. That should last beautifully until they reached Thrush Green. There really would not be much time to discuss feelings, thought Jenny with relief, and in any case, Percy was not a demonstrative man. And who knows, with any luck, his passion – such as it was – might have cooled in her absence, and meeting the train might simply be the gesture of an old friend.

As would be her offer to do his mending, thought Jenny, if the occasion arose. Well, at least she was in command of her own affairs now, and could cope with whatever Percy offered.

She dozed a little as the sunlight roamed around the carriage. The train's brakes squealed and the rhythm altered. Jenny awoke to see familiar fields running alongside.

She lifted down her case and stood by the window, swaying in the movement of the rattling carriage. In the distance she could see a little knot of people, and one figure standing alone. It was Percy.

He ran along by the side of the train and wrenched open the

oor. Jenny smiled and handed down the case as the train queaied to a halt.

Perfectly in command of her feelings, she began to step down, but before her foot had reached the platform, she was lifted bodily by Percy and enveloped in a great bear hug.

'How I've missed you, my girl!' cried Percy.

And Jenny's heart sank.

13. Jenny Decides

Winnie Bailey awaited Jenny's arrival eagerly, but with a certain amount of anxiety. Had she received her message about Percy? How would Percy greet her? Would she have come to any firm decisions about her future whilst at Torquay?

The train was due at Lulling Station soon after four o'clock. Winnie prepared a tea tray. Jenny would need some refreshment after her journey, and over it perhaps she would hear something of Jenny's plans, as well as an account of the holiday.

By a quarter to five Winnie was beginning to feel slightly worried. If Percy had driven Jenny straight through Lulling High Street and up the sharp hill to Thrush Green, they would have arrived by half past four at the latest. Of course, she told herself, the train might have been behind time, but the more disturbing possibility was that Percy had made a detour to find a quiet spot to make a proposal.

She surveyed the tea tray. There were two cups and saucers, some tomato sandwiches and home-made biscuits. It might be as well to put out another cup in case Percy was now a fiancé. Trying to control her agitation, Winnie went to find a third cup and to check the kettle. At that moment, she heard a car stop, and hurried to the window.

Jenny alighted, and Percy lifted out her case from the back seat. They held a short conversation, and Winnie thought that Jenny seemed rather put out. Percy's face expressed his habitual happy bemusement when in Jenny's company, and he seemed to want to carry the case to the door.

Jenny lifted it herself, said farewell to her suitor, and strode determinedly up the path. Percy waved, and got back into the driver's seat as Winnie hurried to open the front door.

'Won't Percy come in?' she asked.

'He's got to get back,' said Jenny shortly, watching the car pull away from the kerb.

'Well, my dear, it's lovely to have you home, and I'm just making some tea, so come and sit down.'

'I can do with a cup,' said Jenny thankfully. 'Percy can be a bit of a trial at times.'

And Winnie, pouring boiling water in the teapot, felt a pang of blessed relief.

Over the tea cups, Jenny gave an account of her surprising welcome at the station.

'I was fair taken aback, as you can imagine, and I told him pretty straight not to behave so silly. But, bless you, he don't seem to take much notice when he's set on something, and he drove round the back way – he *said* to dodge the traffic, but that was all my eye and Betty Martin – which is why I'm so late. He would stop in the old avenue, and there he went on about how he'd missed me, and now I was back we could think about getting married, until I could have hit him.'

'And what did *you* say, Jenny?'

'When I could get a word in edgeways, I said I was sorry but I wasn't planning to get married to anyone, and certainly not to him. But you might just as well talk to a brick wall as Percy Hodge. He didn't seem to take it in. In the end I got quite wild, and begged to be put down so as I could walk home to get a bit calmer. But he wouldn't have it.'

'A persistent fellow,' agreed Winnie, feeling more cheerful every minute. 'More tea, Jenny dear?'

Jenny passed her cup.

'It's thirsty work turning down chaps, I can tell you,' she said, 'especially when they're as pig-headed as Percy. Well, in the end he said he was off to Wales tomorrow morning to get some cattle, and he'd be away two or three days so I could get used to the idea of being engaged, and he'd call when he got back.'

'Oh dear, Jenny! Are you sure what you want to do?'

'Mrs Bailey,' said Jenny earnestly, 'I've thought of all this ever since I've left here, and I'm positive I don't want to marry Percy. What's more, I don't want to leave you.'

Winnie felt tears of relief pricking her eyes.

'Well, it's wonderful news for me, of course, and I'm glad you know your own mind. But I shouldn't like you to throw away your future happiness out of loyalty to me. Percy's a good fellow, and would make a kind husband, I'm sure, and he's obviously devoted to you. It's a good thing you have these few days to think things over.'

'I don't need a few days,' said Jenny robustly. 'I know now, and I feel all the better for coming to a decision. When Percy comes back I'll make it quite clear to him.'

'But do be *kind*!' pleaded Winnie. 'He'll be so disappointed.'

'Bessie says she wouldn't mind betting he's happily married within a year,' said Jenny shrewdly. 'But it won't be to me! I'll just go and rinse the tea things.' She jumped to her feet.

'You won't,' said Winnie. 'You've had enough to cope with in the past hour. Tea things can wait.'

There was no doubt about it. Jenny's holiday had set her up again, and she attacked her work with renewed vigour. Winnie rejoiced in her return to health and good spirits.

She said nothing more to Jenny about Percy, nor did she breathe a word to anyone else in Thrush Green, but somehow or other it seemed to be general knowledge, by the end of a week, that Percy Hodge had received his marching orders from Jenny.

Comment at The Two Pheasants was now completely contrary to earlier views expressed. Far from thinking that Jenny might have done very well for herself as Percy's second wife, the general opinion seemed to be that she had shown very good sense in repelling his advances.

Some went even further.

'Take my word for it,' said one worthy, 'she found something better down in Devon. You can tell by the look of her. Fair come to life since going to Torquay. There's a man at the bottom of it, I shouldn't wonder.'

'Can't blame her. After all, old Perce has been no more'n a thin string of misery since his Gertie went. Jenny's got herself to think of, and she's well enough off as she is in Dr Bailey's place.'

'Talk about a lot of women clacking,' cried the landlord. 'You chaps is worse than the lot! Putting two and two together and making half a dozen! Maybe Perce hasn't asked her yet.'

'He ain't been near the place since he called after he got back from Wales. Why, he was everlasting mincing along with ruddy great bunches of flowers and that before she went away. Now look at him! Ain't I right?' he appealed to his fellow drinkers.

There were confirmatory grunts of agreement. Albert Piggott had the last word.

'It's my belief they've both seen the light, mates. This marrying and giving in marriage, what is cracked up so, can be a terrible let-down. And I'll have another half-pint of bitter, please, seeing I'm a free man without a wife to nag me.'

It was soon after this that Harold and Isobel Shoosmith had a little party. Encouraged by the blissful spell of June weather, when the roses and pinks were at their most beguiling, and the sun still above the horizon at nine at night, they invited some two dozen old friends to have a drink with them.

The Henstocks and the Hursts arrived together. Frank Hurst had known Harold for many years and had been introduced to Phyllida by him when she was trying desperately to earn her living as a freelance writer and had first come to live at Thrush Green.

Agnes Fogerty was one of Isobel's oldest friends. They had met as girls at college, and it was a shared joy now to live next door to each other. Dorothy Watson, chic in navy-blue silk, accompanied her assistant. The Youngs, the Bassetts, Winnie Bailey, Ella Bembridge and Dotty Harmer were all at the party, as well as several Lulling friends, including Anthony Bull, Lulling's handsome vicar.

The evening was warm and windless, and the guests wandered about in the garden congratulating Harold and Isobel on their superbly mown lawns and weedless garden beds.

'All Harold's doing,' Isobel told them. 'I'm just the deadheader of roses and pansies – a very lowly assistant gardener.'

'Any news about your new home?' inquired Anthony Bull of Charles, as they stood together under a copper beech tree.

'I gather there is some debate about building a smaller place on the old site, or finding a ready-made establishment and selling the existing plot. I suppose that the land might command a good price, although I know very little about these things.'

'It is not very big,' observed Anthony. 'I wonder if it would fetch a good price. Doubtful, I should think. But tell me, are you comfortable at Mrs Jenner's?'

Charles's chubby face was lit with a smile. 'Incredibly comfortable! Dimity and I had no idea one could be so warm and happy. The windows face south, you know, and the light is wonderful. I never need to put on my desk light when I am writing. I can't get over the joy of it.'

'It's a house I've always admired,' said Anthony. 'Much the same age as our vicarage. Those eighteenth-century builders knew what they were doing, didn't they?'

'Without a doubt,' agreed Charles. 'Without a doubt. Although I grieve for our poor departed home, I'm just beginning to realize that it was badly designed, and dear Dimity must have put up with most uncomfortable surroundings without a word of complaint.'

'Ah! You married an angel, Charles, and I did too. We are fortunate fellows.'

Phyllida Hurst came up to them. 'Good news! The Thomases' baby arrived yesterday. A boy, and Jack sounded so pleased on the telephone. Wasn't it sweet of him to ring?'

'A charming young man, I thought,' said Charles. 'And of course he would let you know. After all, they were greatly obliged to you for letting them have Tullivers.'

Anthony Bull had walked away to have a word with Miss Watson and Miss Fogerty.

Phil spoke rapidly. 'I've only just discovered that the other young couple must have been a sore disappointment to you all.'

'Really?' replied Charles, his face puckered with bewilderment. 'I hardly saw them, I must confess.'

'They were on drugs, you know.'

'The sort you smoke?'

'I gather so.'

'That must have been the peculiar smell I noticed when I called. I thought it was something cooking – herbs, I imagined, of some sort.'

'Well, that's one way of looking at it!'

'How did you find out? Did Jack Thomas tell you?'

'No. Jeremy did.'

'*Jeremy!*' exclaimed the rector. 'But how on earth—?'

'One of the boys at school has an older sister who has been on the stuff. She knew that the Thomases' friends bought it, and told her brothers who told Jeremy evidently. I gather she's given it up now, thank God. Foolish girl to start, of course.'

'Well, you have surprised me,' said Charles. 'I can only hope that the other two will follow her example. And I am delighted to hear about the baby. Do congratulate the Thomases for us, if you are in touch.'

His eye alighted on the three Lovelock sisters who were admiring two small silver dishes containing nuts.

'Ah, do excuse me, Phyllida. I must have a word with the Lovelock girls. I haven't seen them since the burglary.'

He hastened away. Phil noted the predatory gleam in Miss Violet's eye as she put back the little dish on the table. Was she already replacing their lost collection, wondered Phil? She hastily quashed the unworthy thought, and went to talk to Joan Young.

Later that evening Dorothy Watson and Agnes Fogerty rested in their sitting room and discussed the excitement of the party.

'I thought that Joan Young looked very well in that bottle green frock. A very pretty neckline.'

Dorothy had a great eye for dress, as Agnes knew, and took enormous interest in the clothes of others. Agnes herself was content to be clean and respectable, but ever enthralled to hear her friend's comments on others' appearance.

'And did you notice,' continued Dorothy, 'that Ada Lovelock's evening bag was freshly adorned with some jet edging which looked to me remarkably like the stuff I sent to be sold at her recent coffee morning? I have never known such greed as those Lovelock sisters show when it comes to gewgaws.'

'You can't call all their lovely things *gewgaws*,' protested Agnes. 'And in any case, you can't be sure that the trimming was the material you sent.'

'Agnes dear, I am quite sure,' said Dorothy firmly. 'I am the first to admire your fair-mindedness, but you must not deceive yourself. That trimming was undoubtedly *appropriated*, one might say *purloined*, by the Lovelocks, well before the coffee morning.'

'That's as maybe,' agreed Agnes, 'but the poor souls have suffered terribly from the loss of all their beautiful things, and I do think that they might be forgiven for buying in that jet edging. They might easily be in a state of shock.'

'They've been in that particular state of shock ever since I've known them,' said Dorothy. 'However, they're much too old to change their ways now, so we won't waste time in censuring them. Agnes dear, after all that sherry I'm uncommonly thirsty. Do you think a glass of fresh orange juice would be a good idea for us?'

'Of course it would,' said Agnes, getting up at once. 'Keep your legs up, my dear, you have been standing quite long enough, while I get us both a drink.'

One day, thought Dorothy, watching her friend bustling towards the kitchen, I hope I shall be able to repay the kindness of that completely selfless soul. But will it ever be possible?

A few mornings later, Charles Henstock sat at his desk and gazed out at the sunlit garden. He was attempting to write next Sunday's sermon, always a difficult task, and not made any easier on this gorgeous June day by all the happy distractions outside the window.

A blue tit, with a mimosa yellow breast, clung to the coconut half which swung from a branch of the old plum tree. His antics were as delightful as they were graceful. A bullyboy of a blackbird bustled below, chasing all the other groundlings away from the crumbs which fell from the tit's energetic assault on the coconut.

Above, a tiny silver aeroplane ruled a fast-fading line across the blue sky, and over in Percy Hodge's field a red and white cow lay chewing the cud with the same vague bliss in its surroundings which now enveloped the good rector. And curled up in the chair beside him was their cat, which had settled down at Mrs Jenner's as happily as they had themselves.

Dimity had gone to Lulling to shop and Charles found his new abode very quiet. Dimity's parting words had been to the effect that he would have peace in which to compose his sermon. He certainly had that, he thought, putting down his pen and propping his head on his hand. How pretty the young leaves looked on the plum tree! How beautifully fashioned was the wing of the fluttering tit! How vivid the beak of the blackbird!

This was a very pleasant place to live, and he thanked God humbly for leading him to such a haven after the tragedy of the fire. Where, eventually, would his home be, he wondered yet again? It was surely time that he heard something from the Church. Anthony Bull, who always seemed to be so much better informed about things, had said that the new rearrangements of the parishes may have held up Charles's particular problem, but it was all rather unsettling. One would like to know one's future.

The good rector sighed, and picked up his pen again. He must make a start at least before Dimity returned. A great black rook now alighted on the grass and began to sidle timidly towards a crust thrown out by Mrs Jenner. The small birds took no notice of this formidable figure in their midst.

The rector decided suddenly to turn his observant idling to good account. His sermon should be about the joy of living in the present, and of looking at the wonders around. Did not Our Lord Himself tell his followers not to worry about the morrow, what they should eat, what they should put on? Now inspired, Charles began to settle down to his writing and to sharing his own happiness with his beloved parishioners.

While he was busy scribbling, Molly Curdle was being driven in the local taxi to the County Hospital for an ante-natal examination. Dr Lovell felt certain that all was well, but decided that a check on his own findings would be a sensible precaution at the splendid new maternity wing.

Joan Young would have taken her but had promised to go to a Women's Institute meeting in the neighbouring county. This involved lunching with the as-yet-unknown president, delivering her talk, judging the monthly competition – almost as hazardous and thankless a task as judging a baby show – and then driving back some twenty-five miles. Arthur Tranter was taking her place.

He was a cheerful man, some years older than Molly, but they had both attended Thrush Green School, and knew each other fairly well. She sat beside him in the taxi, and they chatted amicably of this and that. Molly was careful not to mention her condition and congratulated herself on her still trim figure. However, she need not have troubled to hide anything from the percipient Mr Tranter.

'Havin' the baby up the County then?' he remarked conversationally.

'Possibly,' said Molly.

'I'll take you up if you want me to,' he offered. 'I gets no end of young mums to take there from Lulling. Bit far though, I always think. Too far sometimes for some of 'em. I've brought three into this world in my time, so you don't need to worry.'

Molly remained silent.

'I always say they can name 'em after the old taxi. Maurice, say, or Austin – both good names. I had a Cadillac once, bought off of an American chap up the air base, but none of the mums would name their kids after that. Might be called Cad for short, see?'

He roared with laughter at his own joke, unaffected by Molly's disapproval. She was glad when they began to run through the suburbs of the county town. It was quite bad enough having to face a strange doctor without Arthur's coarse remarks.

'You'll want the ante-natal, love, won't you? I'll be waiting. I've got a flask of coffee and today's paper so don't worry if you're held up. You never can tell with hospitals, can you?'

'No, indeed,' agreed Molly tremulously. Now that they had actually stopped outside the door, fear gripped her, and distasteful as she found Arthur Tranter at least he was an old acquaintance and a link with all that was familiar at distant Thrush Green.

As if he guessed her thoughts, he leant out and patted her arm. 'Cheer up, duck. All be over in next to no time, and we'll step on it and get you home before you have time to turn round.'

She gave him a grateful smile, and went in to face the trial ahead.

14. AFTER THE STORM

The beautiful spell of June weather broke with a violent thunderstorm one torrid night. Lightning flickered eerily for several hours before the thunder asserted itself, and the rain began to rattle on the parched earth. Gutters gurgled, rivulets rippled down the hill to Lulling, and water butts, which had stood empty for weeks, filled rapidly.

So violent was the storm about three o'clock that Harold and Isobel decided that a cup of tea would be a very good thing, and Harold went down to make it. As he waited for the kettle to boil, he surveyed the wet world of Thrush Green through the window.

Other people were awake too, it seemed. There was a dim light at Tullivers, and Harold guessed correctly that it had been put on to allay young Jeremy's fears. There was another light at Ella Bembridge's. No doubt, thought Harold, she is brewing tea, as I am.

No lights showed otherwise. Presumably the Youngs, the Bassetts, Winnie Bailey, Jenny and all the other good folk of Thrush Green, were either deep in slumber or riding out the storm in the darkness of their bedrooms.

Harold thought, not for the first time, how fortunate he had been to settle at Thrush Green. Thousands of miles away when he was in business, he had first heard of this tiny English village, the birthplace of Nathaniel Patten, a zealous missionary, whose work Harold admired deeply. It was Harold who had been instrumental in raising funds to buy the fine statue of Thrush Green's most distinguished son. He could see it now, glinting as the lightning lit the view. It was good to think that such a good fellow was properly honoured, and Harold was proud of his part in the affair.

He had not bargained though for the generous welcome he had received from the inhabitants of his chosen village. That was a bonus. He had found several people, much of his own age and interests, in this little community who had a now become firm friends. He thought with affection and gratitude of the Henstocks, the Baileys, the Hursts, and many others who had made his path here so pleasant. He was lucky to have such good neighbours and Betty Bell to minister to his domestic comfort.

But luckiest of all, he told himself, as he attended to the boiling kettle, was the stroke of good fortune which had come unwittingly through little Agnes Fogerty next door. Her friendship with Isobel, her old college connection, had given him his wife, and a happiness he had never dared to hope for at his age. Balancing the tray with great care, Harold mounted the stairs, ignoring a crash of thunder which rattled all the window panes.

Isobel, as beautiful as ever, was sitting up in bed, serenely ignoring the violence which raged outside.

'A quarter past three,' she exclaimed, catching sight of the bedside clock. 'What a time to be drinking tea!'

'Anytime,' Harold told her, 'is time to be drinking tea.'

Some half-mile to the west, out of sight of Thrush Green, Dotty Harmer was awakened by the din and lay worrying about her animal charges.

Would Dulcie, the goat, be alarmed by the storm? She was of a nervous disposition, and goats were generally acknowledged to be sensitive to climatic conditions. The chickens and ducks were much more phlegmatic by nature, and were no doubt quite unperturbed in their roosts. As for the many cats, they always took events very philosophically, and dear old Flossie, apart from flinching at any particularly ferocious roll of thunder, seemed quite calm at the end of Dotty's bed.

No, it was dear Dulcie that was her chief worry. Possessed of enormous strength and sleeping in a somewhat battered shed, even by Dotty's standards, she might well crash her way out and do extensive damage to her garden.

There was no help for it, Dotty told herself, but to get up and investigate. The rain lashed against the cottage windows, the wind howled, and the lightning was alarming, but Dotty knew where her duty lay, and clambered out of bed.

She went as she was, barefoot and in her nightgown, down the stairs, followed by the faithful Flossie. In the kitchen she thrust her feet into wellingtons and dragged on her old mackintosh. As a token concession to the elements she also tied a scarf over her skimpy grey locks, took a torch, and set off to Dulcie's shed.

The onslaught of the rain quite took her breath away, but she battled down the path beneath the flailing branches of the old fruit trees, which scattered showers of water and leaves with every gust of wind.

She looked into the hens' house and, apart from some squawks from her disturbed charges, all seemed well. No sound came from the ducks' shelter, and Dotty decided to leave well alone. She struggled on, and was suddenly aware of what hard work it was. Her legs seemed leaden. Her heart raced. Water ran down her face from the already sodden scarf, but she pressed on.

By the light of the torch she saw that Dulcie was lying down. Her chain was slack and in good order, and she was licking a lump of rock salt with evident enjoyment.

'Dear thing,' said Dotty. 'Good Dulcie! Just ignore this dreadful noise, my dear. It will all be over by morning.'

Much relieved, she shut the door again. She trundled the glistening garden roller against it, for good measure, and decided that all would be safe until morning.

It was easier going back with the wind behind her, but Dotty was glad to get to the porch where Flossie, who had taken one look at the weather, had prudently waited for her mistress.

The kitchen was a haven, and Dotty was thankful to rest on the kitchen chair before taking off her wet clothes. Five cats looked at her from their various resting places, ranging from a stack of newspapers to a pile of Dotty's underclothes which were awaiting ironing. When she could breathe again more easily, Dotty struggled out of her coat and boots. The hem of her nightgown was drenched, but she could not be bothered to change it.

She wondered if it would be worthwhile making a hot drink. She felt uncommonly exhausted. Perhaps she needed a tonic? Perhaps she should see Dr Lovell? She had not felt her heart behaving in that odd jumpy way before.

She sat for a few more moments, savouring the warmth of the kitchen, the cats' presence, and pondering upon the possibility of visiting the doctor.

'Oh, drat doctors!' exclaimed Dotty at last, and wearily climbed the stairs.

Most of Thrush Green's inhabitants had been disturbed in the night, but the morning dawned still and grey. A light mist veiled the distance, and the warm earth, thoroughly drenched by the night's heavy rain, caused a humidity which reminded Harold of his days in the tropics.

Betty Bell, arriving like a whirlwind from Lulling Woods, gave a vivid account of the devastation caused in that usually coma-tose hamlet.

'And my neighbour's nappies – well her *baby's* nappies, of course, but you know what I mean – was wrenched off of her line and went all which-ways. Why, one of 'em blew into the pig sty! Think of that!'

Harold, who was trying to read his post in the study, made suitable noises. Despite the feet that his wife now ran their house, Betty still sought him out as soon as she arrived, to keep him up to date with local affairs. It could be rather trying.

'And they do say that one of them poplars up the rec was struck. Felled to the ground, Willie Marchant told me, and all frizzled round the edges. When you think – it might have been you or me!'

'I doubt if we should have been standing on the recreation ground at two in the morning,' commented Harold, slitting open an unpleasant looking envelope with OHMS on the corner.

'I was going to pop in to see if Miss Harmer was OK, but I was a bit behindhand after collecting some flowerpots and a bucket and that what had been blown into our hedge. Still, I'll look in on the way home.'

'That would be kind,' agreed Harold.

'Well, I'm glad nothing happened here,' said Betty. 'No tiles off, nor trees broken and that. I'd best get on. Anything particular you want done? Windows, say, or silver?'

'You'd better have a word with my wife,' said Harold.

'I'll do that,' replied Betty, and vanished.

Next door, Miss Fogerty found her charges unusually heavy-eyed. She had planned to teach them a charming little poem of Humbert Wolfe's, but gave up when she found them bemused from lack of sleep and a prey to sighs and yawns. Always a realist, she faced the fact that such a delightful poem deserved full attention, and at the moment something less intellectually demanding was called for.

'Give out the modelling clay, George dear,' she told young Curdle. 'You can choose which you want to make. Either a basket full of different sorts of fruit, or a tea tray with cups and saucers, and something nice to eat on a big plate.'

'And sugar lumps in a bowl?' asked Anne Cooke.

'Of course. And don't forget the teaspoons.'

There was a marked improvement in interest as the boards and glistening wet balls of clay were distributed. Miss Fogerty watched them attack their work, and smiled upon them. Baskets of fruit and tea trays were always good for twenty minutes at least, thought Agnes with satisfaction.

Albert Piggott, not many yards from Thrush Green School, felt as lazy and out-of-sorts as the children. To his disgust, the storm had blown leaves and twigs into the church porch, ripped one or two notices to shreds, and soaked the heavy mat which was bad enough to shift when it was dry, let alone sodden with rain. He set about his duties dourly, one eye on the door of The Two Pheasants.

His indigestion was even worse than usual this morning. Per-haps fried food was not good for him, but what could a chap cook when his lawful wedded wife had took off with the oil man? He could not fiddle about with pastry and vegetables and mixing gravy and all the other nonsenses his Nelly had mucked about with.

He plied his broom lethargically. Waste of time, all this clean-ing. Come tomorrow it would be as bad again.

There was a welcome rattle from the door of the public house. Jones was unlocking, and about time too! Maybe half a pint, and a slab of cold pork pie, would settle his stomach. Albert propped his broom against a Zenana Mission poster which had escaped the full fury of the storm, and set off with more vigour than had been apparent all the morning.

'Well, Albert, what a night, eh?' the landlord greeted him. 'I feel a bit washed out this morning, and that's the truth.'

He spoke for all Thrush Green.

*

A few mornings later, Ella Bembridge was surprised to see Dotty Harmer approaching, carrying the milk can which she usually brought about tea time with Ella's regular order of goat's milk.

Her old friend looked wispier and greyer than ever, she thought, as she ushered her into the sitting room. Flossie followed like Dotty's shadow.

'You're early today,' she said, taking the milk can from Dotty's bony hand. 'My word, you're jolly cold. Dotty! Are you all right?'

'Perfectly,' replied Dotty, looking about her vaguely. 'I've just milked Dulcie, so I thought I would come straight up with your milk while it was fresh.'

'And very nice to see you,' replied Ella. 'But you usually give me the afternoon milk.'

Dotty did not answer. Ella thought that she looked more than usually dishevelled and extremely tired.

'Let me get you a drink,' she urged. 'Coffee? Tea? Orange squash?'

'Could I have a small whisky? Father calls it a sundowner.'

'Of course you can have a small whisky, but it's not exactly sundown, you know. It's hardly ten o'clock.'

'Such light evenings,' agreed Dotty. 'I shall shut up the hens when I get back. Which reminds me, I can't stay very long. Father had one of his little tantrums this morning, and didn't want me to come out.'

She sat nodding to herself, oblivious of Ella's shocked silence. What on earth had hit poor Dotty? Her dreadful old father had been dead for twenty years! 'One of his little tantrums', as Dotty euphemistically described it, would have struck fear into the stoutest heart when he lived, but he was now resting with other Thrush Green worthies under Albert Piggott's sketchy care.

'Dotty,' began Ella, 'you are not well. It's only ten o'clock *in the morning*, and you know you haven't had a living parent for years! I'm giving you coffee. I'm not sure if whisky would be the right thing for you just now.'

'I certainly don't want *whisky*,' responded Dotty. 'If Father smelt strong liquor on my breath he would be most upset.'

She looked down at Flossie. 'What's this dog doing here?' she enquired. 'You didn't tell me you were getting one.'

By now, Ella was seriously alarmed. The poor soul's mind was wandering, and what on earth did you do with such a patient? John Lovell would be in his surgery now, but she could not leave her. She decided to get to the telephone in the hall where she would have a clear view of the front door if Dotty attempted to escape.

'I'm going to put on the kettle, Dotty, so lean back and have a rest. I must ring the butcher too, so don't worry if I'm a minute or two.'

'Pray take your time,' said Dotty graciously. 'It stays light until almost eleven o'clock, you know, so there's no hurry.'

She leant back obediently in the armchair, and closed her eyes.

Ella, much agitated, hurried to summon help.

John Lovell came himself before starting on his rounds. He was greeted by Ella with almost incoherent gratitude, and by Dotty with considerable hauteur.

When Ella had taken in the coffee she had found Dotty fast asleep, and snoring in an eminently genteel fashion. Ella, much relieved, hoped that she would stay in this state until the doctor called. She awoke as Ella went to the front door.

'I'd like to examine her on a bed, Ella,' he said. 'All right?'

'Of course,' she replied. 'Dotty dear, you don't mind if Dr Lovell has a look at you?'

'I mind very much,' cried Dotty, her papery old cheeks flushing pink, 'but as he has been called – *not* at my request, I hope he understands – I shall let him examine me, but I trust that you will be present.' She seemed to be more her old self since her nap.

Ella and John Lovell exchanged glances.

'Of course Ella can stay,' said the doctor. 'Let's go up.'

He was wonderfully gentle with their old friend, Ella noticed. She could not help noticing too, with considerable alarm, how pathetically frail Dotty was. Her legs and arms were like sticks.

Her rib bones could be clearly seen as well as the bones of her neck and shoulders.

Ella turned to look out of the window as the examination went on. Dotty bore all in silence, but sighed with relief when he said that she could get dressed again. They left her to do so and descended the stairs.

'What is it?' asked Ella.

'You can have it in one word. Malnutrition. She's in a pretty bad way, Ella, and I'm getting her into the Cottage Hospital right away. Can I use your phone?'

'Carry on. I'm shattered, but not surprised. She eats next to nothing, and works far too hard with that menagerie of hers.' She stopped suddenly, hand to mouth. 'We'll have to get someone to look after them. I'll take on the cats and the poultry, and dear old Flossie can stay here – but that damn goat is beyond me, I don't mind confessing.'

'Don't worry. We'll get something sorted out. But she must get some attention immediately.'

He went into the hall, and Ella slumped inelegantly on the sofa, feeling as if she had been sand-bagged. Flossie lumbered across the room and put her heavy head on Ella's knee. Ella fondled her long golden ears.

'Flossie, my girl,' she told her, 'we're in a fine old pickle this morning.'

Surprisingly enough, Dotty submitted to all the plans made for her with unaccustomed docility. John Lovell gave the two friends and Flossie a lift back to Lulling Woods and left them there to pack a bag for Dotty while he continued on his rounds.

Ella had expected a spate of instructions about food for the animals, and her own domestic arrangements, but Dotty scarcely said a word. She gave Ella directions about where to find clean nightgowns, a sponge bag, soap and so on in a weak voice, but seemed content to let her do the work. It was as if she had had quite enough of present problems and was already drifting into oblivion. Ella had never seen anyone in such a state of exhaustion, and was very much alarmed. It was a great relief when a car from the hospital arrived and she could get into it with the patient.

A cheerful nurse, whose face seemed vaguely familiar to Ella, took charge of Dotty, and said that Ella could see her at any time. This sounded ominous to Ella, who knew little about modern hospital methods. She had a confused idea that only those at the point of death were allowed visitors. Surely, one had to come between two and four, or six or seven, and then only with one other person at the bedside?

She kissed Dotty goodbye, and wandered out into Lulling High Street. Where on earth had she seen that nurse before?

It was odd to be at large in the town at almost twelve o'clock. She felt shaky, and the thought of the hill up to Thrush Green was a little daunting. She made her way to The Fuchsia Bush to get a cup of coffee, and to rest.

She had not been inside since the new arrangements had been made. It had been redecorated in a hideous shade of plum red which clashed appallingly with the old mauve curtains and made the interior unpleasantly gloomy. Two waitresses, who had been busy painting their nails, now broke off their conversation, and the taller one advanced reluctantly to Ella's table.

'Just a cup of coffee, please.'

'We don't do coffee after twelve.'

'It isn't twelve yet,' Ella pointed out.

'But it will be by the time I get the coffee,' replied the girl, huffing on her nails to dry the varnish.

Honest wrath began to give Ella back her usual strength. 'If I don't get coffee within three minutes,' she said flatly, 'I shall see the manager immediately.'

'Oh well!' replied the girl, flouncing off, and casting her eyes to heaven as she passed her friend.

The cheek, thought Ella, taking out her tobacco tin and beginning to roll a cigarette with shaking fingers! Bad enough closing this place at tea time and making it look like a third-rate brothel – whatever they looked like – without having chits of girls making a song and dance about fetching a cup of instant when requested.

In the old days there had been some very pleasant waitresses here, thought Ella, blowing out a cloud of acrid smoke.

Ah, that was it, of course! That nice nurse had worked here years ago. No wonder her face was familiar. Some relation of dear old Mrs Jenner's, if she remembered rightly.

The coffee arrived, with only a small amount slopped in the saucer. It was hot and refreshing, and by the time Ella had drunk half of it, she was feeling more herself.

She must buy some meat for Flossie on the way back, and go and collect her at Dotty's and see that the rest of the animals were safe until the evening. As for Dulcie, she must find someone to milk that wretched animal, but at the moment she could not think of anyone brave enough to tackle the brute.

She stubbed out her cigarette, left the exact money on the bill slip – no tip for that young woman today – and went out into the sunshine.

As much refreshed by her little skirmish as by the coffee, Ella set off briskly to tackle the hill, and all that lay before her at Thrush Green.

15. DOTTY FACES FACTS

While Dotty Harmer lay, unusually quiescent, in her bed in the women's ward of Lulling Cottage Hospital, and Ella puffed up the hill to Thrush Green trying to decide if it were better to collect Flossie immediately or after she had eaten an early lunch, her old friend Dimity Henstock was busy discussing household matters with Charles.

'We really must buy more bed linen, Charles. Everything in that line went, as you know, and the July sales will be starting quite soon. I could save quite a lot of money.'

'Well, my dear, you know best, of course, but the insurance people haven't paid out yet, and our bank account is as slender as ever, I fear.'

'I do know that. The thing is that we shall have so much to buy with it. Beds, for instance. I think it would be sensible to have two single beds in the spare room. We've only had the double one there which means larger sheets which are expensive to launder.

'But only *two* sheets,' pointed out Charles, 'instead of four.'

'Now I come to think of it,' said Dimity, 'Ella has some of my single sheets that I used when I lived there. I left them with her, but I don't think she has used them. Perhaps I could find out.'

'But we can't take Ella's sheets!' protested Charles.

'Strictly speaking, they are mine. Of course, if they are in use I shall leave them for Ella, but it would save me buying quite so many new ones. We shall need new blankets and covers too, of course.'

'Can you get all you want with fifty pounds?' asked Charles, his chubby face puckered with anxiety.

'No, Charles, I'm afraid I couldn't. But I shall spend fifty pounds to the very best advantage, believe me.'

'I know that.'

'If only the insurance people would pay up! Couldn't you write to them, or get Justin Venables to prod them?'

'I really don't like to do that.'

'Well, it's getting rather desperate, you know, Charles. I know we are very happy and comfortable here with Mrs Jenner's things, but we must look ahead to when we have a place of our own.'

The rector sighed. 'We have indeed been blessed. If only we could have a house as warm and light as this, Dimity.'

'And as old and beautiful,' agreed his wife. 'Well, whatever it is it will be lovely to settle in again, I'll call on Ella this afternoon, and find out about the sheets.'

'You won't rob her of them, will you?' pleaded Charles.

'Good heavens! I knew dear old Ella long before I met you, Charles, and you can rest assured that neither of us is going to fall out over a few rather shabby sheets!'

And with that the good rector had to be content.

Dimity set off to walk the half mile or so from Mrs Jenner's to Thrush Green. It was a calm day – 'soft weather' as the Irish call it – and there were very few people about.

Dimity enjoyed the peace of it all. She walked slowly, relishing the sounds of the countryside heard so clearly in the still air. A cow lowed in one of Percy Hodge's distant fields on her left. In the high branches of a walnut tree on her right she heard the excited squeaking of what she guessed were some long-tailed tits searching busily for insects, and she stopped by a farm gate to listen to the rare summer sound of a cricket in the grass.

It was all so very soothing, and Dimity's anxieties grew less pressing now that she was in the fresh air and able to enjoy the slower tempo of life about her. She wished that their plans were more definite. Surely they should know by now if a house were planned for the old site, although she was beginning to hope that somewhere else might be found for them. It would be good to make a fresh start. Not that she would ever want to go far from her friends at Thrush Green, but she felt that she could not face the effort needed to supervise the plans for a new abode, nor the delays which were bound to arise.

If only some pleasant place, like Mrs Jenner's, within a mile or so, say, from their old home could be found, how perfect it would be! Both she and Charles were now getting over the first numbing shock of their loss, and were beginning to long for a place of their own. Dimity knew Charles too well to expect him to take any positive action in asserting his needs. He would be content to wait humbly for what the Church provided, secure in his belief that all would be for the best. Dimity, a little less quiescent, was beginning to wonder if some pressure might not be a good thing.

She strolled on, and soon came in sight of Thrush Green. A sturdy figure, leading a spaniel, emerged from the lane which led to Lulling Woods, and Dimity recognized her old friend. She caught up with her as she crossed the grass towards the home they had once shared.

'I was just coming to see you,' she cried, bending down to pat Flossie. 'How's Dotty?'

And Ella told her the sorry tale.

'Well,' declared Dimity, with unusual firmness, 'it's a blessing in disguise, Ella. She's looked really ill for months now, and won't take any advice. I'm quite relieved to hear that she's being properly looked after for a change.'

'But that's only temporary, Dim, that's what worries me. I think, in a way, this trying to adopt a child was her muddle-headed way of having companionship and a bit of help with the work. Honestly, I'm pretty tough, but after clearing up the worst of that kitchen of hers, I was whacked. It wants a complete turnout from top to bottom, that house of Dotty's, but who is going to take on the responsibility?'

'Do you think the niece might come for a bit when Dotty comes out of hospital?'

'Connie? She might. But she's got a small-holding of her own, I believe. Mind you, they get on pretty well, and Connie's got a good head on her shoulders. I don't think she'd stand any of Dotty's bullying. By the way, did you come for anything special?'

Dimity explained about the bed linen.

'I shall be glad to know they're in use,' replied Ella. 'They've been stored on the top shelf of the airing cupboard ever since you got married. Do them good to see the light of day.'

'And you're sure you have enough? Charles is most anxious that we don't take anything away which might be useful.'

'My dear old Dim, I've all my own stuff, and when mother died I inherited hers, including some lovely heavy linen sheets with lace insertion. Perishing cold in the winter, but bliss on a hot summer's night, so have no fear on that score. And incidentally, I have a pair of her rugs up in the loft which I shall never use. Say if you want them when you move into the new place. Heard any more yet?'

Dimity told her how things stood, and how she was beginning to worry about the delay.

'It'll sort itself out,' said Ella, rising. 'Let's get those sheets down before we forget them. And do you want some black-currants? The bushes at the end of the garden are laden.'

'Yes, please. It's Charles's favourite fruit. Nothing so good as blackcurrant tart in the winter.'

'Unless it's dear old rhubarb,' said Ella. 'Can't think why people turn up their noses at rhubarb. Good for you all the way through, I reckon.'

They were upstairs retrieving Dimity's sheets when Ella looked at her watch. 'It's Dulcie I'm worried about. She's due to be milked before evening and I haven't found anyone to do it. I'm damned if I'm going to. Any ideas?'

Arms clutching sheets, Dimity turned her mind to Ella's problem. 'Percy Hodge might do it, I suppose, but he's pretty busy. Let's ring Charles. He might know of someone. He comes across all sorts of interesting bits of knowledge on his parish visiting.'

'And tell him to come down to tea,' said Ella, as her friend dialled. 'You'll need the car to get the sheets home, let alone the blackcurrants.'

Dimity relayed the message and then broached the subject of Dulcie.

'Albert Piggott once had goats,' said Charles immediately. 'I'm sure I could persuade him to take on a little task like that. He would be delighted to help Dotty, I'm sure.'

Dimity could not feel quite as positive about Albert's delight as her warm-hearted husband, but passed on the good news to Ella.

'God bless Charles!' cried Ella. 'If anyone can persuade Albert to take on extra work then he's the man to do it.'

Charles was as good as his word. He left the car outside Ella's house and walked by the church to Albert's cottage. He found his sexton standing at the sink, washing up some crockery in water so murky and afloat with unsavoury flotsam that Charles wondered if it would really be more sanitary to leave the china unwashed.

He explained the purpose of his visit while Albert prodded morosely at the congealed food in a pie dish. His expression brightened considerably when goats were mentioned.

'Now, they're animals with a bit of character,' said Albert. 'It was my dad, not me, sir, as kept goats. We had two nannies and a billy. We was brought up on goats' milk, all the lot of us. My old mum swore you could get the tubercular from cows' milk. Lor' bless you, I can milk old Dotty's – I mean Miss Harmer's – Dulcie, with one hand tied behind me.' He waved the dripping dish mop confidently.

'It's uncommonly good of you, Albert,' said the rector. 'I shall pay you myself while the arrangements last, of course. And I'm quite sure that Miss Harmer would want you to have any surplus milk. It would do your indigestion good, I'm sure.'

'I always enjoyed a mug of goat's milk,' said Albert. 'And my cat'd help out.'

'That's settled then,' said Charles, getting to his feet. He gazed thoughtfully at the bowl of filthy water in the sink.

'Is there any hot water in the kettle?' he asked.

'Plenty. Want a cup of tea?'

'No, thank you, Albert. I'm having tea with Miss Bembridge who will be so grateful to you for coping night and morning with Dulcie's bounty. No, I just thought that some fresh hot water might make your present task easier. I fear I interrupted your work.'

'They're clean enough by now, I reckon,' said Albert, casting a perfunctory glance at his handiwork. 'They'll soon be dirty again time I've used 'em. Housework's a thankless job at the best of times. Fit only for women, I always say.'

Charles, thankful that no woman was present to take up the cudgels, hastened out into the fresh air of Thrush Green.

The summer term proceeded with increasing activity, as Sports Day, Open Day, a Leavers' Service and end of term examinations all took place during the last few weeks. Dorothy and Agnes coped with their usual efficiency, but both confessed to being inordinately tired one summer evening.

'You have every excuse,' Agnes told her friend. 'After all, the responsibility of the school's running falls largely upon your shoulders, and you have to be ready at any time to meet parents and managers and people from the Office whenever any problem crops up. As well as coping with your poor leg,' she added.

'I greatly fear,' replied Miss Watson, 'that it's old age as well. So often I have told friends that they can't expect to get through as much work as they did when they were twenty years younger. Now I realize that I ought to take my own advice, but somehow, Agnes, one never thinks of oneself as old.'

There was a note of dejection in her voice which aroused Agnes's immediate sympathy.

'You do too much, you know. I hesitate to put myself forward, Dorothy, but I would willingly take on some of your less important duties if it would help.'

'I know you would. You are a great support and comfort, but I really think that the time has come to make a decision about retirement. I'm fifty-nine in a fortnight's time, and I intend to let the Office know unofficially, early next term, that I propose to go at the end of the next school year.'

'Whatever you decide to do will be right, I am sure,' said loyal little Miss Fogerty, 'but won't it be a terrible wrench?'

'It will be *whenever* I go,' said Dorothy. 'But I shall feel much happier if I can see the end in sight. Can you remember how much in advance one's official resignation has to go in?'

'Three months, I think.'

'Then I shall put mine in at the end of the spring term. Plenty of time for advertisements to go in. Thrush Green School should draw many applicants. It's a pleasant spot to live in, and an efficient school, although perhaps it's not my place to say so.'

'You are quite the right person to say so. And whoever takes on the job will have you to thank for a splendidly working and happy school.'

'Thank you, Agnes, but I don't forget my staff too. The one big problem now is where we shall live. Do you still favour Barton-on-Sea, or somewhere close by?'

'It sounds perfect.'

'Well, I propose that we both spend a few days there when we break up, and have a look at some of the properties the agents have sent. We can stay at that nice little guest house, and take our time over things. Agreed?'

'Yes, indeed, Dorothy. I shall look forward to it.'

Miss Watson gave a sigh. 'It will be a comfort to start moving towards retirement. And best of all, Agnes dear, to know that you feel you can be happy there with me. We must go into ways and means one evening when we feel more energetic, but I think my savings should be enough to find us somewhere modestly comfortable.'

'I hope you will use mine too,' said Agnes. 'Now, can I get you anything? Something to drink? Something to read? Your knitting?'

'What about a game of "Scrabble"? Always so soothing, I think.'

And little Miss Fogerty hastened to get out the board.

To the surprise of all Thrush Green, Albert Piggott approached his new duties with comparative zest.

He was observed setting off soon after eight in the morning towards Dotty's and again about six in the evening. Ella's milk was delivered as usual, on his return at night, and Betty Bell's left in the cool larder at Dotty's for her to collect on her way home from her many duties at Thrush Green.

Dulcie, always a generous nanny with her milk, seemed to take to Albert, and he carried home a plentiful supply for himself and his cat. Both appeared to flourish on it, and although Albert was teased by his colleagues at The Two Pheasants because he took to asking for half a pint of bitter instead of a pint, he put up with their joking with unusual good temper.

'It's a durn sight better dealing with animals than that church and graveyard,' he told them. 'That Dulcie's got more sense than any of you lot here. We gets on a treat. Goats is intelligent animals. And that's more'n you can say for men.'

'You'll be getting fat,' someone said, 'swigging down milk.'

'It's my belief it's doin' me good,' declared Albert. 'Wonderful soothing to the stummick. I reckon I'll buy some regular from Miss Harmer when she gets back. Saves me cooking too. Dr Lovell said himself as milk's a *whole food*, and he's nobody's fool.'

To Ella's delight, he also offered to feed the hens and ducks in the mornings to save her making two trips a day. Such a change of heart in such a curmudgeonly character made a fascinating topic for the inhabitants of Thrush Green, and all agreed that Charles Henstock had never done a better day's work than calling on Albert for help.

Meanwhile, Dotty remained in hospital. Her recovery was being very slow so that she had plenty of time to think things over.

She was a surprisingly good patient. When some of the nursing staff had discovered that Dotty was in the women's ward, there had been misgivings. Dotty's eccentricity was only exceeded by her obstinacy, as was well known in Lulling. The reputation of her fearsome father was still remembered, and in fact one of the doctors attached to the hospital was a former pupil of his, and could tell blood-curdling accounts of his late headmaster's disciplinary methods.

But, in truth, Dotty was a realist, and quite prepared to endure cheerfully what had to be. She saw now, as she rested against her pillows, that she had been foolish to think that she could cope with her energetic way of life without properly fuelling the machine which was her ageing body.

She accepted the nurses' ministrations with grace and gratitude. She believed the doctor, who remembered her father, when he told her gravely of the risks she ran by neglecting herself. He made it clear to her why she had been suffering from dizziness, why her back had a perpetual ache, why her legs throbbed and her heart palpitated so alarmingly. She would have to alter her way of life, he told her. If she intended to keep so many animals then she must have help. There really should be somebody living in the house with her. Had she thought of giving up altogether, and going to live in an old people's home? He could recommend several, very comfortable places, and with a warden to keep an eye on things.

To Dotty, the prospect appeared bleak in the extreme. Not that she had anything against homes for old people, and in fact her regular visits to local alms houses had always been enjoyable during her father's lifetime, when she was younger and took on such duties. And several of her friends lived in just such places as Dr Stokes mentioned, and seemed remarkably happy with their little coffee parties and handiwork, and visits to the hairdresser and chiropodist obligingly laid on by more mobile friends.

But Dotty knew quite well that such a way of life would never do for her.

For one thing, she would be *tidied up*. The haphazard clutter of objects, beneath her own thatched roof, which constituted home for Dotty, would have to be sorted out, given away or just put on the bonfire. She did not think that she could face such upheaval.

And then the thought of living without any animals was quite insupportable. To Dotty, her animal friends were far more dear than her human ones. Like Walt Whitman she could easily 'turn and live with the animals, so placid and self-contained'. They demanded so little and gave so much in return. She appreciated, with the poet, that:

> They do not sweat and whine about their condition,
> They do not lie awake in the dark and weep for their sins

and that they faced life with the same robustness as she herself faced it. The idea of living in a home, no matter how warm, clean and cared for she might be, but without even one animal for company, could not be borne.

She came in the end to a compromise. As the animals died, she would not replace them. She could not betray them by giving them away unless it were possible to place them in as perfect a setting as their present one. Perhaps young Jeremy Hurst might like two of the rabbits? Or Joan Young's Paul? They would be well cared for there, she knew.

The chickens and ducks were elderly, and Mr Jones from The Two Pheasants could dispatch them humanely when the time came, as he usually did. And she must resist the temptation to buy more pullets, or to put twelve lovely pearly eggs under a broody hen. How she would miss yellow chicks running around!

The cats had been spayed, luckily, so that there would be no more kittens, sad though the thought was. As for Dulcie and

Flossie they must stay on, and for a very long time too, Dotty hoped. She had been amazed to hear how willingly Albert Piggott had coped with the milking. With luck, he might be persuaded to continue, and of course, once Dulcie was dry, there must be no more mating.

Well, it was all very sad, thought Dotty, and gave a great sigh. A little fair-haired probationer nurse hurried to her side.

'All right, Miss Harmer?'

'Yes, thank you, nurse. I was only making a few plans for the future. Rather exhausting.'

'Like a cup of tea?' asked the girl, offering the panacea for all ills.

'Do you know,' said Dotty, sitting up and straightening her bed jacket, 'that would be most acceptable. Only a little milk and no sugar, please.'

She was feeling better already.

16. SUNDAY LUNCH AT THE MISSES LOVELOCK'S

One Sunday morning the Misses Lovelock fluttered along Lulling High Street to St John's church. This large and beautiful building stood in an open space south of the town, and its tall spire was a landmark for many miles around.

It was three times the size of St Andrew's at Thrush Green and was noted for its stained glass windows, dating from the sixteenth century. Throughout the summer, coach loads of tourists came to see the church and to take photographs, particularly of the fine east window above the altar.

In their younger days, the Misses Lovelock had taken their turn in manning the modest stall near the vestry where books and pamphlets, bookmarks and slides of the outstanding features of St John's were on sale. Invariably, after their visit, the tourists wandered across the green into the High Street and sought tea at The Fuchsia Bush.

It was this recollection which formed the theme of their conversation as they proceeded towards morning service.

'I really can't think that The Fuchsia Bush is any better off for closing at tea time. Why, only yesterday, Violet, I saw a coach stop, and the driver banging on the door. There were quite thirty people on board, and I'm sure they all looked the sort who would want sandwiches, scones and home-made cakes.'

'Some,' said Miss Violet, with a sniff, 'looked as though they would want fish and chips as well.'

'What I'm trying to say, dear,' pointed out Miss Ada, 'is that The Fuchsia Bush is turning away good money.'

'Well, they get it at night, I suppose, at dinner time.'

'I think not. I was talking to one of the staff at the fishmonger's

and she says they are never more than half full. People are finding it too expensive, she said, and prefer to eat at home.'

'And very sensible too,' put in Miss Bertha. 'I only hope that The Fuchsia Bush will see the folly of its ways, and remember that it is there to *serve* people. And people want *tea* from four o'clock onward. And if they desire to partake of fish and chips then, why shouldn't they find it provided?'

She gave a stern look at Miss Violet who pretended not to see, but rearranged a dove-grey glove.

'Winnie Bailey was wondering if a petition might be a good idea, with lots of signatures, you know, to persuade the management to open again at tea time.'

Bertha bridled. 'I shall certainly not append my signature. I do not intend to kow-tow for the sake of a cup of tea which I can brew for myself rather better next door.'

'I was thinking of the visitors, Bertha,' ventured Violet.

At that moment, the chiming of the church bells changed to one steady tolling of the tenor bell.

'We must step lively,' said Bertha, quickening her pace. 'It looks as though our hall clock must be running slow.'

During the sermon, Violet allowed her gaze to dwell on the glowing glass of the famous window. To be sure, she had never been able to see with absolute clarity just what the pictures showed. She knew that the incidents depicted were the draught of fishes, Jairus's daughter, and the miracle of water turning into wine. The illustrated pamphlet told her so. The colours were really magnificent, but there were so many pieces of glass in each picture, and all so intricately interposed, with those squiggly worms of lead everywhere, that she had often wondered if that really was a net full of fishes (Herring, perhaps? Surely not in the Sea of Galilee?) or simply the lower part of the fishermen's robes. Not perhaps the most *practical* garment for a fisherman, when one came to consider it.

Thus musing, she let her eyes pass from the mystery of the windows to the frank and handsome face of dear Anthony Bull as he stood declaiming in his beautiful voice.

What an actor he would have made, thought Violet! Such a presence, such manly beauty, such clarity of diction! And he really gave very sound sermons, nothing too highbrow and yet not patronizingly simple, as though his congregation was composed of non-intellectuals. This morning's subject, for instance, on the theme of good fellowship and the need to consider the feelings of others in everyday life, was being very well expressed.

She only hoped that Bertha, who could be rather unnecessarily tart at times, was listening attentively. How lucky they were in Lulling to have such a fine vicar! He really deserved a larger and more knowledgeable congregation than this quarter-filled church. A *better house*, thought Violet, was how it would be put in theatrical circles. Certainly, such a star performer, she decided, admiring a graceful gesture of his hands, deserved a truly discriminating audience, and no doubt he would have one some day.

Meanwhile, it was to be hoped that he would remain the vicar of Lulling for many a long day, delighting them all with his outstanding looks, his kindly manner and the genuine goodness of his way of life.

Sunday lunch at the Lovelocks' was always cold. Violet had set the table before going to church. Starched linen, heavy silver and

Waterford glass dressed the table with splendour. It was a pity that the meal set upon it was so sparse.

Six thin slices of corned beef were flanked on one side by a Coalport dish containing sliced cold potatoes, and on the other by equally gelid carrots. A beautiful little cut glass bowl contained beetroot in vinegar. Liquid refreshment to accompany this inspired course consisted of lemon barley water in a glass jug covered with a lace cloth beaded round the edge.

'A very good sermon this morning,' commented Bertha, chewing her corned beef carefully with her few remaining teeth.

'Such a pity there were not more to hear it,' agreed Violet. 'I was thinking so in church.'

'Well, we appreciate dear Anthony even if we are only a few,' said Ada. 'I think we can pride ourselves on being discriminating here in Lulling. We are very lucky to have him.'

Bertha cut a ring of beetroot carefully in half. 'But for how long, I wonder?' she said.

Her two elderly sisters gazed at her with curiosity. Had Bertha heard a rumour? And if so, from whom? And why had they not been told?

Bertha attempted to assume an air of nonchalance under their scrutiny. She was not very successful.

'Oh, it was just a chance remark of Mrs Bull's when I saw her at the draper's yesterday. She was buying some hat elastic.'

'Bertha, people don't buy *hat* elastic these days!' cried Violet.

'Well, no, but I imagine she needed it for her undergarments, and one wouldn't want to ask for *knicker* elastic in a public place.'

'*Knicker* or *hat*,' pronounced Ada, 'is beside the point. What did she say?'

'Oh, something about changes in the air, and Anthony much perturbed about decisions to be made.'

The two sisters looked disappointed.

'That could be anything from altering the site of the compost heap in the churchyard, to replacing those dreadfully shabby hassocks in the Lady Chapel,' said Ada.

'Or some little matter of church ritual,' added Violet, putting her knife and fork neatly across her empty plate.

'Maybe, maybe!' agreed Bertha airily. 'Well, time alone will tell.'

She rose and collected the plates. When she returned she was bearing a dish full of glossy black cherries.

'A present from dear Colonel Fisher yesterday evening,' she said, 'when you were both in the garden. I thought I would keep them as a surprise for dessert today.'

'Do you remember how we used to hang them over our ears?' said Violet, picking up a pair. 'We used to pretend the black ones were jet ear-rings and the red ones were ruby.'

The three old faces glowed at the memory, Anthony Bull's affairs forgotten in the excitement of this delicious surprise.

'I remember it as if it were yesterday,' declared Ada. 'You were always the pretty one, Violet, with your fair hair. The red cherries suited you best.'

'We were all pretty children,' said Bertha firmly, 'though no one would think so to see us now. Still, we are clean and healthy, and I suppose that is something at our age.'

They enjoyed their cherries, removing the stones politely from their mouths, behind delicately curved bony hands.

Later they stacked the china and silver in the kitchen to attend to later, and went into the sunshine to rest. The sun warmed their old bones and Bertha yawned.

Violet began to giggle.

'Do you know, Bertha dear, your tongue is as purple as a chow's!'

'Really? No doubt yours is too after eating black cherries.'

The three old ladies put out their tongues and surveyed each other's. Laughter shook their thin frames, and for a brief moment they reverted to the three little girls who had played in this same sunlit garden, wearing starched pinafores and cherry ear-rings, over seventy years earlier.

A week or two later, the problem of Dotty Harmer's convalescence arose. Ella Bembridge had offered to have her at her cottage, but Winnie Bailey, secretly fearing that Ella's home might not provide the peace which Dotty would need for a week or two, suggested to her old friend that the invalid might stay with her.

'The spare room is empty, as you know, Ella dear, and Jenny is longing to do a bit of spoiling. We are both in the rudest of health now, and it would be a real pleasure to have Dotty. You've done more than your share with Flossie and the other animals.'

Ella gave in with good grace. 'Well, to tell you the truth, I am rather behind with my weaving, and the garden's been neglected. Not that I mind much, first things first, you know, but if you're quite sure, I'm happy about it.'

It was arranged that Harold Shoosmith and Isobel would collect Dotty, and Flossie would be transferred to Winnie's to be reunited with her mistress. And so, one August afternoon, Harold and Isobel set off in the car, which had been polished for the occasion, to fetch their old friend.

She still looked remarkably frail and her steps were faltering as she made her way to the car on the arm of matron – a high honour not lightly bestowed. But Dotty's spirit was unquenched, and she chattered cheerfully all the way along Lulling High Street, up the hill, and past Ella's cottage, the gap left by the destroyed rectory, and the grass of Thrush Green.

Winnie welcomed her with a kiss and Flossie with ecstatic barking. Harold and Isobel promised to call the next morning, and then withdrew, leaving Winnie and Dotty alone in the sitting room.

Dotty's thin hands were caressing Flossie's long ears as she gazed happily about her. 'I can't tell you how good it is to be here. They were so *very* kind to me at the hospital, but I pray that I may never need to go there again.'

'Well, I hope you will stop with me for as long as you like,' said Winnie. 'You must get your strength back, you know.'

'My strength?' exclaimed Dotty in amazement. 'But I am quite strong now, Winnie. I shall thoroughly enjoy staying overnight here, but of course I must get back to the animals tomorrow morning.'

'We'll talk about that later,' said Winnie diplomatically, 'but now I am going to ask Jenny to make the tea.'

'How is she?' asked Jenny when Winnie appeared in the kitchen.

'The same old Miss Harmer,' Winnie told her, with a smile.

'Oh dear!' cried Jenny. 'That means we might have trouble!'

Dotty's niece, Connie Harmer, had kept in touch with her aunt's Thrush Green friends throughout Dotty's illness, and had driven some fifty miles from her home at Friarscombe to see the old lady in hospital.

She was a sturdy woman in her forties, with auburn hair now streaked with grey, and a square weatherbeaten face. She was as much attached to the animals as was her aunt, and perhaps this was why she had never married, finding the human race, and particularly the male of the species, very much inferior to her own charges.

The Henstocks, Ella Bembridge and Winnie Bailey were old friends of hers, and were glad to see her when she came to see Dotty in her hospital bed. She was frank with them all.

'It's like this. I'm quite willing to have dear old Aunt Dot to live with me, but will she come? If she's too groggy to cope alone at Lulling Woods, I'd certainly consider selling up and making my home with her, if that seems the right thing to do, but I don't relish the prospect, and that's the truth. In any case, I'd need a month or two to make arrangements for some of the animals, and selling the house would take time.'

'Let's see how things go,' said Winnie, at whose house this conversation took place. 'It's best that she convalesces here, near Dr Lovell, and we'll all keep in touch. But somehow, Connie, I can't see any of us persuading Dotty to leave that cottage of hers.'

'Nor me. Ah well, she's lucky to have such noble friends around her, and you know I'm willing to take on any permanent responsibility when the time comes. I've always been very fond of Aunt Dot, crazy though she is at times.'

'That goes for us all,' Winnie told her.

Luckily, Dotty was persuaded to continue to stay at Winnie's for at least another week, and appeared to have forgotten her resolve to rush back to the animals by the next morning.

It was one of the disconcerting things about the invalid at this time. She was vague about time. 'Let's say more than usually vague,' amended Charles Henstock, and although Dr Lovell was optimistic about the full recovery of his patient, even he admitted that Dotty would be better in the permanent company of someone like her reliable niece.

It was while Dotty was still recuperating that Lulling was agog to learn that the Misses Lovelock had been summoned to the local police station to view some pieces of silverware which had come into the hands of the police.

Full of hope, the three sisters tottered along one bright morning, stopping only by the Exchange to read some extraordinary messages, written in chalk, on the walls of that building. The words were not familiar to the three ladies, but the content of the slogans was. The writer presumably did not approve of the Prime Minister nor of the country's police force.

'But, Violet,' said Ada in bewilderment, 'does one spell that word like that?'

'Ada dear,' said Violet, with some hauteur, 'it is not a word that I find myself needing to spell.'

Bertha, as usual, took charge. 'We must draw the attention of the officer on duty to this defacement, when we call in. I'm sure he will deal quite competently with the matter, correct spelling or not. It is not the sort of matter for ladies to concern themselves with.'

'Should you end your sentence with a preposition, Bertha?' asked Violet innocently.

But she was ignored, and the three mounted the steps of the police station.

Sadly, there was only one of the Lovelocks' lost objects among the display set out on the trestle table in a back room with Police Constable Darwin on guard.

'Father's rose bowl!' cried Ada.

'What a miracle!' cried Violet.

'Given to him on his retirement!' cried Bertha. 'How wonderful of you to recover it.'

They walked slowly round and round the table, gloating over the beautiful objects before them.

'And where did you find all these lovely things, officer? So clever of you.'

'Well, miss,' said Police Constable Darwin, 'I'm not at liberty to say, but it wasn't us chaps at Lulling as came across this lot. But several people, besides you ladies, have lost stuff around here, so it's our turn to show it.'

'And have the other people found theirs here?'

'You was the first to be asked,' the constable told them.

'Well, that is most gratifying. Most kind. We feel quite honoured, I assure you. Now, are we allowed to take home Father's rose bowl?'

'I'm afraid not, miss. It'll have to be exhibited in court, see, when we've picked up the thieves. There's still a lot missing. If you notice, miss, all this is the big stuff, salvers and bowls and that.'

With commendable delicacy he ignored a seventeenth-century toilet set, with a pair of silver chamber pots to match, and directed the Misses Lovelock's attention to trays, teapots and other tableware, including the rose bowl, which stood at the farther end of the table.

'We reckon this is only about a quarter of what's missing. The smaller stuff's probably been passed on. Melted down already, I don't doubt.'

There were horrified gasps from the ladies, and Police Constable Darwin hastily tried to make amends for his gaffe.

'But let's hope not. After all, this lot's turned up. Keep your fingers crossed, ladies. Anyway, I'll mark this rose bowl down in the book as belonging to you. Want another look round to make sure?'

'No, thank you, officer. You have been most helpful. There was just one other little matter,' added Bertha, the natural spokesman of all three.

'Yes, miss?'

'Have you been on outside duty this morning? On your beat, I believe is the correct expression?'

'Well, no, miss. I was detailed by Sergeant Brown to stand by this lot this morning. Very valuable stuff here. But I'll pass on any message.'

Bertha wondered if this fresh-faced young man would really be experienced enough to deal with the unpleasant matter of the Corn Exchange's graffiti, but she decided swiftly that he had probably been adequately trained and was quite used to seeing – and perhaps even hearing – the phrases written on the wall.

'We just wanted to direct your attention, officer, to some quite dreadful messages written with some prominence on a public building near by.'

'Oh, them scribbles on the Corn Exchange,' replied the constable, with relief. He had begun to wonder just what else these old tabbies were going to disclose. 'Don't you worry about them. One of the Cooke boys, no doubt. Anyway, young Armstrong's been told off to clean it up, so everything's under control.'

'I'm delighted to hear it,' said Bertha graciously.

'In very bad taste to deface a building with such words,' added Ada in support.

'And not even correctly spelt,' said Violet, adding her mite.

'I think,' said Bertha ominously, 'it is time we returned home.'

17. HOUSING PLANS

The first two weeks of the summer holidays were spent by Miss Watson and Miss Fogerty recuperating from the rigours of the term. They also managed to fit in a number of personal arrangements which had been postponed during term time. Miss Watson had her hair permanently waved, one troublesome tooth extracted and two filled, and several shopping expeditions for new corsets and other underwear.

Miss Fogerty, whose hair was straight 'as a yard of pump water', as she said, dressed it in a neat bun, and washed it herself. She did, however, need to visit the dentist who luckily only found one filling which needed attention. Her modest shopping resulted in a new flowered overall for school use, a pair of light sandals, and a petticoat. She was sorely tempted to buy a navy blue jersey suit, reduced in the summer sales, but with the possibility of helping with the purchase of a shared home she decided it would be imprudent to spend too lavishly.

The friends had reserved rooms at their favourite Barton guest house on the front for two weeks from the middle of August, and both ladies looked forward to the break eagerly. The discussion of money affairs about the buying of a permanent home there did not take place until a day or two before their departure. Dorothy Watson had obviously given the matter much thought.

'Now, I know just how independent you are, Agnes dear, and I very much appreciate your offer to help in buying a place to share, but I've decided against it.'

'But, Dorothy—' protested Agnes, but was cut short. Miss Watson was at her most decisive, a schoolteacher at her firmest and fairest.

'It's like this. I should like to buy the house so that I can alter my will and leave it, with any other little things of value I might have, to be shared between my three nephews. I do not intend to leave anything to Ray and Kathleen apart from my mother's tea service which I know Ray would like. They have quite enough as it is, and I consider that they have forfeited any claim on my property after their dreadful behaviour. But I like the three boys, and I think they are making their way in the world quite splendidly despite their parents.'

'Yes, I do see that, Dorothy, but nevertheless—'

Miss Watson drove on relentlessly. 'Of course, I shan't see you left without a roof over your head, Agnes dear, should I go first. The house will be left so that you can stay there for as long as you wish, and when you have done with it, then the three boys shall have it.'

'Oh, Dorothy, you are too good! But I pray that I may go first.'

'First or second, Agnes, hear me out. I've given a great deal of thought to this matter. Now, if you *insist* on putting something towards this venture—'

'I do. I do indeed!'

'Then I suggest that you could contribute to the furnishings which we are bound to need. No carpet or curtain ever seems to fit a new home, and I'm sure we shall need various extras, and possibly redecoration, although I think we should share that expense.'

'I agree wholeheartedly with anything you suggest, Dorothy, but it really isn't enough from me. At least I can pay rent, surely?'

'I was coming to that. If you feel that you can pay the same amount as you do here, Agnes, it would be a very great help, believe me. Now, what do you think?'

'I think you are being uncommonly generous, as always, Dorothy.'

'Well, it seems the simplest and most straightforward way of arranging things. I thought I might go and put the matter to Justin Venables. He will deal with things if we do find somewhere, and I should like him to know what we have in mind. Will you come with me? I only hope he won't retire before we've finished with his services. One wonders if those youngsters in the firm have quite the same wisdom as dear Justin.'

'Of course I will come. And I don't think we need to have any doubts about the junior partners, Dorothy. I am sure that Justin has trained them quite beautifully.'

'Let's hope so,' said Dorothy. 'And now that that's over, I think I'll go and look out some of my clothes ready for packing.'

'And so will I,' replied little Miss Fogerty.

The two ladies retired to their bedrooms, one congratulating herself on a difficult matter successfully dealt with, and the other to think, yet again, about the boundless generosity of her friend.

The abrupt conclusion of Percy Hodge's courtship of Jenny had occasioned plenty of comment at the time, but as the weeks had gone by, other topics had taken its place until Percy's suit had almost been forgotten, if not by Jenny, at least by the majority of Thrush Green's inhabitants.

It was some surprise then to Harold Shoosmith when Betty Bell, crashing about his study with the vacuum cleaner, shouted the information that Percy was looking elsewhere for a wife.

To tell the truth, Harold had not heard clearly for the racket around him, and was on the point of fleeing to more peaceful pastures. Betty, seeing that she might be baulked of her prey, switched off the machine and began to wind up the cord.

'Percy! You know, Percy Hodge as was hanging up his hat to Jenny at Mrs Bailey's,' she explained.

'What about him?'

'I just told you. He's courting someone else now.'

'Well, good luck to him. No harm in angling elsewhere if he hasn't succeeded in landing his first fish.'

'I don't know as Jenny'd care to be called a fish,' said Betty, bending down to wind the cord carefully into figures of eight on the cleaner's handle.

Harold watched this manoeuvre with resignation. If he had asked Betty once to desist from this practice which cracked the cord's covering he had beseeched her twenty times. It made no

difference. At some point in her career, Betty had decided to wind cords in a figure of eight style, and stuck to it.

'Well, who is it, Betty? Come on now. You know you're dying to tell me. Someone we know?'

'You might, and you might not. Ever been up The Drovers' Arms?'

'Beyond Lulling Woods? No, I can't say I have. Does the lady live there?'

'Works there. Name of Doris. She cleans up, and helps behind the bar of a Saturday. She's from foreign parts, they say.'

'Really? What, Spain, France, or further afield?'

Betty looked shocked. 'Oh, not *that* foreign! I mean she speaks English and goes to our church. No, she's from Devon, I think, or maybe Cornwall. A long way off, I know, but speaks very civil really.'

'And you think Percy calls there? It may be that they keep the sort of beer he prefers.'

'Percy Hodge,' said Betty, setting her arms akimbo and speaking with emphasis, 'was always content to have his half-pint at The Two Pheasants. What call has he got to traipse all the way to The Drovers' Arms, unless he's courting? Besides, he's always carrying a great bunch of flowers, and he gives 'em to this Doris.'

'Ah!' agreed Harold. 'That certainly sounds as though he means business. I hope you all approve at Lulling Woods?'

'Well, he could do a lot worse. She's a hefty lump, and can turn her hand to helping on the farm, I'm sure. Clean too, and cooks quite nice. Not as good as Percy's Gertie, I don't suppose. She was famous for her pastry and sponges. But still, this Doris can do a plain roast, they tell me, and is a dab hand at jam making. She should do very nicely, we reckon.'

'I'm glad she's approved,' said Harold gravely, 'and I hope that Percy will soon be made happy.'

He nodded towards the cleaner. 'Finished in here?'

'I wondered if you'd like your windows done. They look pretty grimy from your tobacco smoke.'

'Better leave them,' said Harold, deciding to ignore the side swipe at his pipe. 'No doubt Mrs Shoosmith will tell you the most urgent jobs.'

'Come to think of it,' said Betty, trundling the cleaner towards the door, 'she's waiting for me to help turn the beds. It flew right out of my head with you chatting away to me.'

She vanished before Harold could think of a suitable retort.

That same afternoon, Ella Bembridge left her cottage to post a letter at the box on the wall at the corner of Thrush Green. It was warm and still, and she was just wondering if she would take a walk along the lane to Nidden to call on Dimity and Charles when she saw her old friend approaching along the avenue of chestnut trees. Dimity was on the same errand with a half a dozen letters in her hand.

'Coming back with me?' enquired Ella, after their greetings.

'I mustn't, Ella. I've a nice joint of bacon simmering away, so can't be long. Charles has gone sick visiting at Nidden.'

'Well, let's sit down for a minute or two here,' replied Ella, making her way to one of the public seats generously provided for exhausted wayfarers at Thrush Green. 'Heard any more about your housing plans?'

Dimity looked perturbed. 'Not really, but Charles had a letter this morning confirming these rumours about amalgamating the parishes.'

'First I've heard of it,' announced Ella. 'What's it all about?'

'Well, Anthony Bull's two parishes of Lulling and Lulling Woods are to be merged with Charles's Thrush Green and Nidden.'

'Good heavens! Anthony will have a massive parish to work won't he?'

'It looks like it.'

Ella suddenly became conscious of Dimity's agitation. 'And what happens to Charles?'

'Nobody knows. All the letter gave was the news that the four parishes would be merged.'

'Do you think this is the reason for not hearing about rebuilding the rectory?'

'It looks very much like it. I simply can't get Charles to do anything about it, although I've done my best to press him to make enquiries. We really ought to know where we stand. It is almost worrying. I'm so afraid he will now be moved. If it is too far from Lulling and Thrush Green, as it might well be, I shall be so lost without all our old friends.'

Dimity sounded tearful, and Ella patted her thin hand comfortingly.

'Cheer up, Dim! Worse troubles at sea! You'll probably hear in a day or two that building's beginning on the old spot over there, and you'll have a spanking new place to live in.'

'Somehow I don't think so. I'm afraid any spanking new place we have to live in will be miles away.'

She blew her nose forcefully, and jumped to her feet.

'Well, it's been a comfort to talk to you, Ella, as always, but I must get back to the bacon. You shall be the first to know if we hear anything definite.'

She hurried away across the green, and Ella returned more slowly and thoughtfully to her own house.

As it happened, it was Edward Young, the architect, who heard more about the empty site at Thrush Green. The rumour reached him by way of an acquaintance who was on one of the planning committees.

'About eighteenth hand,' Edward told Joan, 'so one takes it with a pinch of salt, but I think there's something brewing all right. Evidently, the Church is putting it on the market and the local council would like to buy it.'

'But what for?'

'Well, it's only a small area, but this chap seemed to think that a neat little one-storey unit of, say, four or six houses for old people might be put there. Actually, he said there were plenty of tottering old bods at Thrush Green that could do with them.'

'He's not far wrong,' commented Joan.

'Or perhaps a health clinic. I think that's a better idea myself. The one at Lulling's had its day, and it's a long way to walk there. Particularly if you are pregnant like our Molly.'

'It would certainly be useful,' said Joan. 'Which do you think it will be?'

'My dear good girl, don't ask me! You know what these rumours are. But I'm pretty sure he's right about the site being sold. And we'll keep a sharp eye on what gets put up on it, believe me. We've had our years of penance with that eyesore of a Victorian rectory. I hope our children will see something less horrific in its place one day.'

The day of Dorothy and Agnes's departure to Barton dawned bright and clear. The taxi had been ordered for ten o'clock to take them to Lulling Station, and the pair were up early.

Harold and Isobel called to collect the key and to get last-minute directions as they had offered to keep an eye on their next-door neighbours' property. They had been told about the proposed house-hunting and were full of good advice. Both Isobel and Harold had gone through this exhausting experience within the last few years, and did not envy the two ladies. But they heartily endorsed Miss Watson's desire to retire at the age of sixty, although they wondered if her successor would be quite so good a neighbour. Time would tell.

Meanwhile, they urged them to enjoy their break, promised to look after the premises, and waved them on their way.

'I shall miss Agnes dreadfully,' said Isobel, as they returned to their garden. 'She means a lot to me.'

'It only takes an hour or so to drive to Barton,' replied Harold. 'We'll make a point of visiting them as often as you like.'

Naturally, the Shoosmiths said nothing about Miss Watson's future plans, but nevertheless it was soon common knowledge in Thrush Green that she was going to retire and planned to live elsewhere.

'We shall miss them both,' Winnie Bailey said to Frank and Phil Hurst. 'Miss Watson's been a marvellous headmistress, and dear little Agnes is a real institution. It won't be easy to replace two such dedicated women.'

'Well,' said Frank, 'they're doing the right thing to get away while they still have their health and strength.'

'And sanity!' quipped Phil. 'At times Jeremy alone drives me mad. How they can cope with dozens of them round them all day beats me.'

'They finish at four,' said Frank. 'And look at the holidays they get!'

'They certainly do not finish at four,' said Winnie firmly. 'I've often seen the light on at the school and I know those two have been getting something prepared for next day. I wouldn't want their job for all the tea in China.'

Comment at The Two Pheasants was less complimentary.

'Time old Aggie packed it in,' said one. 'Why, she taught my mum as well as me! Must be nearly seventy.'

'But Miss Watson don't look that age! Mind you, she's no beauty but she've kept the colour of her hair and still hobbles about quite brisk with that bad leg of hers.'

'Living at Bournemouth, I hear.'

'I heard it was Barton.'

'Well, somewhere where all the old dears go. Bet that'll cost 'em something to find a house in those parts.'

And this gloomy prognosis gave them a pleasurable topic for the rest of the evening.

Meanwhile the two holiday-makers were finding that property was indeed expensive, especially of the type they had in mind. The house agents who attended to them all pointed out, with depressing unanimity, the fact that most retiring people wanted just such a place as they were seeking, small, easily-run, with a view and not too much garden.

'Of course, people come from all over England, and particularly from the north, to enjoy our milder climate,' said one exquisitely dressed young man. 'There are always plenty of clients – usually elderly – who are waiting for something suitable. It won't be easy to find you exactly what you want.'

This was the fifth estate agent's they had visited that day. Dorothy's feet hurt, and her temper was getting short.

'I imagine that these elderly clients of yours die fairly frequently,' she said tartly.

The young man looked startled. 'Well, of course, in the fullness of time they er – pass on.'

'In which case there must be vacancies cropping up,' pointed out Miss Watson. 'You know what we are seeking. Please keep us informed.'

She swept out before the young man could reply, followed by her equally exhausted friend.

'No more today, Agnes,' she said. 'Let's go back to the hotel for a cup of tea, and I will write a few postcards when we've had a rest. Isobel and Harold were absolutely right. House-hunting needs a great deal of stamina.'

After tea, the two sat on the verandah with their tired legs resting on footstools. Agnes was busy knitting a frock for Molly Curdle's expected baby and Dorothy busily filled in her postcards.

'I shall send one to Ray and Kathleen,' she said, sorting through half a dozen on her lap. 'So much easier than writing them a letter which, in any case, they don't deserve. Still, I should like them to know our plans. What about this one of the sunset? Or do you think they would like this clump of pine trees?'

Agnes, sucking the end of her knitting needle, gave both pictures her earnest attention. 'I think the sunset,' she decided.

Dorothy nodded, and set to work, as Agnes returned to counting her stitches. She wrote:

> *Very much enjoying a few days here. Good weather and comfortable hotel.*
> *Also looking for a house, as I am planning to retire next year. Agnes joins me in sending*
> > *Love,*
> > *Dorothy*

'There,' said she, thumping on a stamp, 'that should give them something to think about. I've two more to do, and then perhaps we might walk along to the pillar box if you are not too tired.'

'I should like to,' said Agnes, obliging as ever. 'I have only to finish my decreasing and I shall be ready.'

The two ladies bent again to their tasks, while overhead the gulls wheeled and cried and a refreshing breeze from the sea lifted their spirits.

18. HELP NEEDED

Dotty Harmer returned to her cottage after ten days with Winnie Bailey. To everyone's relief, Connie came to Lulling Woods once a week, staying overnight and seeing that the larder was stocked, the laundry done and that Dotty was taking her pills.

Albert Piggott, of his own volition, offered to continue to milk Dulcie. The two had become very fond of each other, and whether the free milk, enjoyed by Albert and his fast-fattening cat, had anything to do with the arrangement, no one could say, but everything worked out well for everybody.

Betty Bell called in each morning on her way to work, and often on her return, and Ella and the Henstocks called frequently.

It was not the ideal arrangement for it was quite apparent that Dotty needed a constant companion, but it was the best that the community could devise for someone as independent and head-strong as Dotty. They were aware that Connie was keeping a sharp eye on things, and knew that she would come to the rescue if need be.

Meanwhile, Dotty began to put into practice some of the good resolutions she had made in the hospital. Within a month of her return, the ducks had been dispatched and their remains rested in the deep freezer of the Lulling butcher. Jeremy was the doting owner of two rabbits: ('Of the same sex, *please*,' Phyllida had begged), and although Paul Young could not take on any more pets as he was now away at school during term time, he knew someone in Lulling who would give two more rabbits a kind home. Some of the more elderly chickens ended their lives humanely and became boiling fowls for Dotty's friends, and very soon the animal population at Dotty's home was halved.

She was philosophical about these changes, and also did her best to feed herself more adequately. She had promised Dr Lovell that she would sit down at midday to eat a meal.

'Even if it is only a boiled egg and some milky coffee,' he told her. 'You'll be back in hospital if you neglect yourself. And after the meal, you are to lie down on the bed for a full hour. Understand?'

The threat of hospital kept Dotty obedient to his demands, although she found it a terrible waste of time. But gone were the days, she realized, when she chewed an apple for lunch as she stood by the stove stirring the chickens' mash.

Lying down on her bed seemed even worse – positively sinful to be so slothful. However, she found that she frequently fell asleep during her enforced rest, and so grudgingly admitted that young Dr Lovell must be speaking the truth when he said that she would be bound to tire easily for some time.

Still, she told herself, with every day that passed she must be getting stronger, and with Albert to manage Dulcie, and kind friends rallying to her support, she told herself that everything would be back to normal in no time.

Albert Piggott's daughter, Molly Curdle, was particularly pleased to see the improvement in her father's health.

'You know,' she said to Ben one evening, 'it's not just the milk that's setting him up. It's having a job that he likes.'

'Well, it certainly seems to suit the old boy,' agreed Ben. 'And I've a feeling he'd be better off helping out with animals round here somewhere than trying to keep the church going.'

'It'd be ideal. I know he don't really pull his weight as sexton, and never has, to tell the truth. But these days some of the work's too heavy for the old chap. I wondered if we might have a word about it with Mr Henstock. What d'you think?'

Ben looked thoughtful. 'Best have a talk to your dad first in case he cuts up rough. Might think you're interfering. But if he don't mind, I'll speak to the rector. I reckon he might be pleased to get someone to take proper care of the church and graveyard. At the moment they're both a shocking sight. Coke crunching underfoot whenever you walk in church, and weeds up to your knees round the graves. It must vex the rector, and plenty'd complain, but you know Mr Henstock! Too good by half!'

'I'll speak to Dad this week,' promised Molly.

To her relief, Albert agreed with uncommon docility that the work was too much for him, and that he would welcome some help. He was not quite so keen to accede to Molly's suggestion that more work with animals might be found, if he liked the idea.

'Depends what sort of animals,' he said. 'I ain't going to Percy Hodge's, for instance, to muck out his cow shed. That'd be jumpin' from the frying pan into the fire. But I don't mind helping out with pets like Miss Harmer's.'

'Well, I'm sure Mr Henstock will have some ideas,' said Molly hastily. 'Ben might mention it when he sees him.'

Charles Henstock was as pleased as Molly at the turn of events. For a long time he had realized that his curmudgeonly sexton and caretaker was not doing the job satisfactorily. He had hesitated to call him to account for two reasons. First, was there anyone else willing to take on the work, and second, would Albert be hurt to be thought incapable of carrying on?

With Ben's disclosures it was plain that the second difficulty was overcome. If Albert were given the lighter duties, such as sweeping, dusting and cleaning the silver and brass-work, then the outside duties in the graveyard, and the heavy work of keeping the boiler filled with coke, could be offered to a younger and more energetic man.

'The snag is,' said Ben, voicing the rector's fears, 'there don't seem to be many suitable chaps available. Of course, Bobby Cooke has given our dad a hand now and again in the past – but them Cookes—' His voice trailed away.

The rector replied cheerfully. 'Well, I know that the Cookes as a family do tend to be a little *feckless*, but Bobby as the eldest child was always more *reliable*. Poor Mrs Cooke had so many children, and so fast, you know, that I think the later arrivals were somewhat neglected.'

No one, thought Ben, could have put the Cookes' case so kindly as the rector. On the whole, the tribe was dismissed as dirty, dishonest and a disgrace to Nidden and Thrush Green.

'And I happen to know,' went on the good rector, 'that poor Bobby Cooke was made redundant – if that is the correct expression – last week, from the corn merchant's. He may be glad to take on some of Albert's duties. I could certainly find out.'

'I'm sure you'll do what's right, sir,' said Ben. 'It would be a great weight off our shoulders if we could see the old man settled.'

'I shall do my best,' said Charles. 'And how is Molly keeping? When is the baby due?'

'Around Christmas,' Ben said.

'Ah! Then I shall look forward to a christening in the New Year. Another little Curdle to greet! We still remember your wonderful grandmother here, Ben.'

'I never forget her. Never for a day,' replied Ben soberly.

And Charles Henstock knew that this serious young fellow was speaking the truth.

After a remarkably dry summer, the latter part of August turned cold and wet. Luckily, the bulk of the corn crop was gathered in, and although strongly denied by the local farmers it had been a good year. Not, of course, that this made the farmers happy. A good harvest meant that prices would be low, and that ruin faced them. A poor harvest meant that they had little to sell and so, equally, ruin faced them. Farmers have always had hard lives.

'No good trying to please 'em,' declared Albert in The Two Pheasants. 'If the weather's right for the turnips, it's all wrong for the wheat. And if the sun shines for hay-making, it's too dry for the kale to grow. Farmers is kittle-cattle, to my way of thinking. Always on the moan.'

'He can talk,' observed one to his neighbour, but he said it behind his hand. 'Is that what Percy Hodge does?' he enquired more loudly. 'Moan, I mean?'

There was general laughter.

'Percy's too taken up with that Doris up The Drovers' Arms to worry over much about harvest this year. Come October I'll bet he's getting wed, with all the other young farming chaps.'

'But his Gertie's not cold in her grave,' cried one.

'She's been gone over a year,' said his drinking companion. 'I bet that house of Percy's could do with a spring clean by now.'

'His sister, Mrs Jenner, goes in now and again, they tell me. She'll see him right. Pity Jenny wouldn't take him on, but then why should she?'

'If you ask me,' said Albert, although nobody had, 'girls is too choosy by half these days. Comes of learning 'em the same as boys. They wants a good wage, see, and forgets they ought to be glad to look after a good husband for the love of it.'

There was a short silence after Albert's little speech. Most of them were thinking privately of Albert's wife Nelly. She certainly hadn't had a good husband, and one could hardly blame her for leaving Albert's abode to take up residence with that oil man chap who, though markedly unpopular with the males in Thrush Green, seemed to have had a way with the women.

And that, both sexes would agree, was a quality singularly lacking in Albert Piggott.

'Well,' said one at last, putting his tankard down, 'I'd best get back to work.'

He opened the door, and a squall of wind and rain blew in.

'Looks like summer's gone,' he commented, as he went out into the wet.

Rain streamed down the windows of the local school house as Miss Watson and Miss Fogerty unpacked after their holiday. They had returned much refreshed, although little progress had been made with their plans for buying a house. However, they had met several house agents who promised to keep them informed about suitable properties as they became available, and from what the two ladies had seen they were even more sure that Barton and its immediate neighbourhood would suit them both very well. Their efforts had not been wasted.

'How lucky we were to have such a fine spell,' remarked Agnes, gazing out at the driving rain veiling the houses on the farther side of Thrush Green. 'Somehow I don't mind a bit if we get rain now. It's quite restful, isn't it?'

'It is while we're still on holiday, Agnes dear. But quite a different kettle of fish if it continues into the beginning of term next week. You know how fractious infants get if they are cooped up indoors.'

'I do indeed,' said little Miss Fogerty, with feeling. 'By the way, I've sorted out the post, and your letters are on the dresser. Not much for me, I'm thankful to say, but a pretty card from Isobel's daughter on holiday in Ceylon. Always so thoughtful.'

'You mean Sri Lanka,' corrected Dorothy, turning her attention to the pile of letters.

'I shall always think of it as Ceylon,' said Agnes, with gentle dignity. 'Fancy asking one's friends if they would like China or Sri Lanka tea!'

It was an hour or so later, when the two ladies were enjoying a cup of the latter, that Dorothy opened the letter from her brother Ray.

'Well!' she exclaimed, putting down her cup with a crash. 'Of all the effrontery! Really, Agnes, Ray and Kathleen would try the patience of a saint! Do you know what Ray is asking?' She tapped the letter with her teaspoon. 'Listen to this: "If you are getting rid of any of your furniture when you move, would you please let us have first refusal of the following." And then, my dear, he gives a list of about *twenty* of my best pieces of furniture! What a cheek! What a nerve! I've a good mind to ring him – after six, of course – and tell him what I think of his grasping ways.'

Agnes, recognizing the flushed cheeks and heaving cardigan as danger signals, assumed her most soothing air.

'Don't upset yourself over such a thing. I should ignore the letter, and if he writes again, or telephones, you can answer him then.'

'I expect you are right,' conceded Miss Watson, stuffing the objectionable message into the envelope. 'And in any case, now that the telephone charges have gone up again, it would be a most expensive call.'

'Have another cup of tea,' said Miss Fogerty diplomatically, and refilled the cup.

Across the green, Phyllida Hurst was also drinking tea, with Winnie Bailey. She had called to deliver the parish magazine, and had been divested of her dripping mackintosh and persuaded to stop for a while.

'Have you heard this rumour about Albert getting some help with the church?' asked Phil.

'Dimity said it's pretty certain that Bobby Cooke is going to do the heavy stuff. Albert seems to be past digging graves and humping coke about.'

'Wasn't he always?'

Winnie laughed. 'Well, he hasn't exactly strained himself over any of his duties, all the time I've known him, but I think he really does need some help now. The Cooke boy is as strong as an ox.'

'And about as bright, I'm told.'

'At least he's honest,' responded Winnie, 'and you can't say that about the rest of the family.'

'And speaking of church matters, is there anything in this tale about Anthony Bull leaving St John's?'

'I've heard nothing except from Bertha Lovelock, and it's my belief she's got hold of the wrong end of the stick. Not that one would be surprised to hear of his advancement. He's much too decorative and ambitious to stay long here, I fear. He always reminds me of dear Owen Nares.'

'I never came across him,' confessed Phil.

Winnie sighed: 'It's at times like this that I realize how old I'm getting,' she said. 'But what's your news? Any more lecture tours?'

'Yes indeed. They want us to go again next year. I'm not sure if I shall accompany Frank, though. In any case, we don't intend to let the house again. That was rather a disaster, I feel.'

'No harm done,' Winnie assured her. 'And don't forget, I will caretake very willingly. And Jenny will help too. It's a great relief to me that she is still with me.'

'And likely to remain here, I imagine,' said Phil, getting up. 'I must be on my way, rain or no rain. We see Percy sometimes ploughing along with a nice bunch of roses for Jenny's successor. Does she mind, do you think?'

'Frankly, I believe she's relieved. It was an embarrassment to her to have the poor fellow calling here so often, and she's quite sincere, I'm sure, in saying that she's happier as she is.'

'It's all worked out well then,' replied Phil. 'Better to be single than unhappily married,' she added as she went into the porch.

Winnie watched her splash down the path.

'Poor Phil,' she thought. 'She knows all about an unhappy marriage. Thank goodness this second one has turned out so satisfactorily.'

The rain grew heavier as darkness fell, and by ten o'clock a strong wind added to the unpleasantness of the night. It tore the leaves from the horse chestnut trees on Thrush Green, and buffeted Nathaniel Patten as he stood on his plinth, gazing with sightless eyes upon his windswept birthplace. It howled round the grave-stones in St Andrew's churchyard and screamed down the alleyway by Albert Piggott's cottage.

The signboard at The Two Pheasants creaked as it swung, and very few inhabitants of Thrush Green dared to open a window more than a slit in the face of such violence.

Charles Henstock, lying awake at Nidden, listened to the tapping of the plum tree's branches against the window pane. The old house creaked now and again, and occasionally gave a shudder as the full force of the gale caught it, but it stood as sturdily four-square as it had done for centuries, and it was a comfort to be in such a solidly constructed building.

There was no doubt about it, Charles told himself, he had grown uncommonly fond of this ancient farmhouse and would miss its mellow beauty when they had to leave. Of course, a new house would have advantages, but there was something about an old loved house, where generations had lived, which gave one a comforting sense of continuity.

He realized now that his old rectory had never provided such a consolation to the spirit. It was not only the bleakness of its position and its poorly planned interior. This earlier house, where now he awaited sleep beside his slumbering wife, had an indefinable feeling of happiness. Perhaps builders in Georgian times enjoyed their work more than their Victorian successors? Perhaps the families who had lived here were contented with their lot, and their happiness had left its mark? Whatever the cause, Charles thanked God for giving him this pleasant place in which to recover from the shock of that disastrous fire.

He hoped for, but was too modest to pray for, as pleasant a home in the future, but was confident that by putting his fate in God's hands all would be for the best. He was sorry that Dimity worried about the delay. He knew that most men in his position would press for information about any proposed plans, and would make demands about their rights. Charles knew, as Dimity knew, that he was incapable of behaving in such a way. Before long, he would hear something. God would never desert him.

He remembered the story of the falling sparrow, turned his face into the pillow and, ignoring the storm raging outside, was comforted.

The next morning, the garden was littered with wet leaves and twigs. Willie Marchant splashed up Mrs Jenner's path, and put a letter through the box.

The rector opened it carefully at the breakfast table. It was a beautiful thick cream-coloured envelope and bore a crest on the back.

The letter was short, and Dimity, watching its effect on her husband, felt some alarm.

'My dear,' said Charles, 'the Bishop wants to see me next Thursday afternoon. He doesn't say much, but I expect it is to do with the rearrangement of the parishes.'

'What time?' asked Dimity.

'Two-thirty, he says.'

'Well, I'll come too and you can drop me in the market square. I've so much shopping to do it will keep me busy while you are gallivanting with the Bishop.'

'I don't suppose we'll be *gallivanting*,' said Charles, smiling, 'but I've no doubt you will be able to get in two hours' shopping quite comfortably.'

And so the matter was left.

19. CHARLES MEETS HIS BISHOP

The start of the new school year fell on the following Tuesday and, as the two friends feared, the wet weather still shrouded Thrush Green with veils of windswept rain.

Miss Fogerty's new arrivals were unusually tearful, and there were one or two trying mothers who wanted to stay with their offspring until they had cheered up. Little Miss Fogerty, who had been coping with the reception class for more years than she cared to remember, had great difficulty in shooing them away. She knew perfectly well that once their mothers had vanished, the howlers would desist from their lamenting and would resign themselves, after vigorous nose-blowing organized by Miss Fogerty, to threading beads, making plasticine crumpets, or having a ride on the rocking horse.

Within an hour, peace reigned in the infants' room and Miss Fogerty had pinned up the weather chart, found two clean Virol jars to receive the bunches of asters and marigolds brought by the children, and decided to appoint George Curdle as blackboard monitor.

Dear George, for whom Miss Fogerty had a very soft spot, was becoming rather boastful about the new sister he was hoping for at the end of term, and a little energetic board cleaning might channel his energies usefully, thought his teacher. Besides, he would have the inestimable privilege of going outside with the board rubber now and again to free it of excessive chalk dust by banging it briskly against the school wall. To be appointed board monitor was recognized as an honour. George Curdle, she felt sure, would perform his duties with proper zeal.

Meanwhile, Miss Watson's older children were busy writing

their names on the covers of their new exercise books, exhorted by their teacher to be neat and clear in their calligraphy.

While they were thus seriously engaged, Miss Watson surveyed the rain-drenched view through the window and wondered if she would write or telephone to the Office when informing them of her decision to retire. Of course, the formal resignation would be written, well in advance of the specified three months' notice required, but as her mind was now made up it would be helpful, no doubt, to the Office to know her plans well ahead.

She turned to look at the bent hands, the carefully guided pens and the odd tongue protruding with the effort involved. Her last class! After all these years, her very last class!

Well, they looked a nice little lot, and she would do her level best by them. But a warm glow suffused her when she thought that, this time next year, she would probably be looking through the window of some charming little place at Barton, and admiring the sea in the distance.

Thrush Green had been a happy place to work in, and had brought her the ineffable good fortune of meeting dear Agnes, but she would not be sorry to go. A complete change of scene would do them both good, and Thrush Green, after all, would still be waiting for them whenever they wished to pay a visit to their old friends.

'I can see some *beautiful* writing,' said Miss Watson, limping down the aisle towards her desk. 'I think we are going to do some good work in here this year.'

Molly Curdle, dusting her flat at the top of the Youngs' lovely house, wondered if the rain would stop in time for George and the other children to have their break in the playground.

He had run off on his own to school this morning, looking forward to seeing his friends and Miss Fogerty again. No doubt, he'd be blabbing to all and sundry about the new baby, thought Molly resignedly. Not that she worried unduly. Most people knew now, anyway, that a second child was coming. She only hoped that it would be as amenable and happy as George.

Strange to think that in five years' time another little Curdle would be running to Thrush Green School! Who would be there to teach them then? Not Miss Watson and Miss Fogerty from all she had heard. But of one thing she felt certain. She and Ben would still be at Thrush Green whatever occurred. In all his years of wandering with his grandmother's fair, this place was the nearest he had had as a settled home. Now old Mrs Curdle lay in the churchyard, and her grandson and great-grandson lived close by. Molly prayed that they might never have to move again.

She stooped, with some difficulty now that her pregnancy was advancing, and attended to the legs of the chairs. This afternoon, rain or no rain, she must go across to see her father and collect his washing, and hear his news. Sometimes she wished that Nelly, trollop though she was, would return to look after her husband, but there was small chance of that, thought Molly, and one could hardly expect it.

Well, things could be a lot worse. She had her health and strength, and Ben was happy in his work.

If this new baby was a boy, she was determined to call him Benjamin after his father. Ben had said it would be muddling to have two of the same name, but Molly was adamant.

'You can't have too much of a good thing,' she had told him. 'He'll be Ben – another Ben.'

'With any luck,' he had replied, 'it'll be a girl.'

Albert was newly returned from The Two Pheasants when his daughter called early that afternoon.

'Was just about to have a nap,' he grumbled. 'Come for the washin'?'

'That's right, Dad. How's the job? Seen young Cooke yet?'

Albert grunted. 'Ah! He's coming down one evenin' this week, so he says, to see what needs doing. Rector's coming too, and we're goin' to sort things out then.'

'What about wages? Will you have to share now with Bob Cooke?'

'Seems I'll be havin' a bit less, but that's only fair if I'm not doin' the work. Anyway, old Dotty's paying me well for the milking, and the rector wanted to know if I'd take on odd jobs like feeding people's hens and cats and that when they're on holiday. I've said I'll see to young Jeremy's rabbits when they go to Wales at Christmas – that sort of thing. Suit me fine, that will. Probably make as much like that as digging the dratted graves in this 'ere clay.'

Molly doubted it but kept her counsel. In any case, the old man's temper was better than it had been for many a long year which was all that really mattered.

'And Jones next door said he could always do with a hand with the empty beer crates at closing time, so I shall have plenty to do.'

'Will you get paid for that?' asked Molly suspiciously.

'Well, not in hard cash, like,' admitted Albert. 'More in kind.'

'I was afraid of that,' said Molly, picking up the bundle of washing.

After tea, the rain ceased. The clouds scudded from the west, leaving a strip of clear sky on the horizon. Lulling Woods stood out clearly, navy blue against the golden strip, and Jenny, looking from her window, guessed that tomorrow would bring a fine day. Perhaps she could take down the landing curtains? It would soon be the end of summer, she thought sadly, and time to put up the velvet curtains again to keep out the bitter winds of a Cotswold winter.

As she stood surveying the scene, a well-known figure trudged into sight from the lane to Nidden. In earlier times, Jenny's heart would have sunk, for without doubt the man would have turned left along the chestnut avenue to approach her house. Now, to her relief, she saw that Percy Hodge was plodding straight ahead, past The Two Pheasants, no doubt on his way to see his new love, Doris.

He was carrying a basket this evening. What delectable present was in it this time, Jenny wondered. A chicken, perhaps? A dozen pearly eggs? Some early plums? Whatever it was, Doris was more than welcome, thought Jenny cheerfully. She only hoped that Percy's second attempt at wooing would end successfully.

She remembered with amusement what Bessie had forecast.

'He'll soon find someone else,' she had said, 'if he's as nice a man as you say he is.'

Well, thank goodness he had found someone, decided Jenny. Whether he would be married again before the year was out, as her old friend had surmised, was in the lap of the gods, but at least she would be relieved to know that dear old Percy was settled.

She watched him turn down the lane by Albert Piggott's on his way to Lulling Woods and Doris. And with a sigh of relief, and no regrets at all, Jenny turned back to her happy solitude.

Jenny's weather forecast was correct. The rain had gone, leaving a sodden countryside and dripping trees and gutters, but above the sky was clear and blue and there was a freshness in the air that made one think of autumn.

'Bit parky coming along,' cried Betty Bell, bursting in upon Harold and Isobel Shoosmith still at the kitchen breakfast table. 'Are you late or am I?'

'We've been taking our time,' replied Isobel. 'Lots of letters this morning. But we've finished now, and we'll get out of your way.'

'No hurry,' said Betty. 'I called to see Miss Harmer as I came by. Actually, I popped in last night after I'd done the school. She don't look right to me.'

'Oh dear! Is she eating properly?'

'Seems to be. I mean, she'd got a bowl of cornflakes this morning with some brown sugar on it, and Dulcie's milk. Nourishing, I should think, if you can face goat's milk and brown sugar. Which I can't, and that's a fact.'

'Shall I go down there, Betty?'

'I don't think I would today. She'd think I'd been telling tales, see? Anyway, Miss Connie comes this afternoon, and stays there tonight, so she'll have company.'

Betty tugged off her coat and hung it on a peg on the back of the kitchen door.

'If you haven't got any particular plans for me,' she said, 'I thought I'd have a bash at the china ornaments in the drawing room. They look a bit grubby.'

As the china ornaments were Chinese porcelain, very old, beautiful and valuable, it was hardly surprising that Harold winced. 'Having a bash' was exactly how Betty attacked her work.

Isobel, with habitual aplomb, coped beautifully with this kind offer.

'I'd rather hoped to turn out the spare room today, Betty. I'll come up and help you turn the mattress and we'll make up the bed.'

'Right,' said Betty, rummaging in the cupboard for the carpet sweeper, handbrush, dustpan, polish, dusters and other equipment for the onslaught. 'See you pronto.'

She lugged the paraphernalia into the hall, and then returned.

'You know them two next door are going to leave next year?'

'Yes,' said Harold, folding his newspaper.

'And Albert Piggott's givin' up half his job?'

'Yes,' said Harold.

'And the Hursts are going to America again?'

Harold nodded.

'And they're not going to put up another house for poor Mr Henstock? Ain't it *mean*? There's going to be an ugly great clinic place there. Heard anything about that?'

'Not a word,' said Harold, rising from the breakfast table. 'And you don't want to believe all you hear, Betty.'

'Sorry I spoke!' said Betty, flouncing from the room.

Husband and wife exchanged rueful glances.

Charles Henstock polished his old car during the morning, ready to visit the Bishop promptly at two-thirty. The Bishop detested unpunctuality and was not above saying so. Charles respected the great man's principles, and was determined not to offend.

'Let me just see how you look, dear,' Dimity said, before they set off.

She scrutinized her husband from his pink and shiny bald head to his old but gleaming shoes.

'Very nice, Charles, but do remember to pull up your socks before you go in. The Bishop is always so beautifully turned out.

He's as immaculate as Anthony Bull, and that's saying something.'

'Anthony has a great advantage. He is a fine-looking fellow. Anything would look well on him. The last time I saw him he was tending his bonfire, and he still looked as though he had just emerged from a band box.'

Dimity privately thought that Anthony Bull's stipend allowed him to buy expensive suits made by his tailor, while dear Charles was obliged to purchase his off the peg. However, she did not voice this unworthy thought.

'Well, you look very well yourself,' she told Charles comfortingly, 'and now we must be off.'

The rain had freshened the countryside, and the shabby hedgerows of late summer were now sparkling with moisture. Already the ploughs were out, turning over the bright stubble into long wet chocolate furrows.

Dimity noted the yellowing leaves already showing on the beech and wild plum trees. Soon autumn would be upon them, and although she loved the mellowness, the rich colouring and the joys of bringing in the harvest fruit and vegetables, she felt a little shiver of apprehension about the cold weather to come.

The rectory had always been so bleak. Surely, wherever they went would be more comfortable than their last domain! Perhaps the Bishop would give Charles some firm idea of his plans for their new home. It was certainly most disconcerting to be kept in such suspense.

However, Charles knew her views well enough on this matter, and it was useless to try to make him assert himself. Charles was Charles – sweet, far too humble and a living saint. She would not have him changed one iota!

'If you drop me at the back of Debenham's,' she said, 'I can go through their bed-linen department, and you won't hold up the traffic by trying to stop at their main entrance.'

Charles did as he was told, promised to pick her up again at four o'clock, and set off, feeling a little nervous, to his appointment.

The Bishop lived in a fine red-brick house at the end of a long

drive bordered with lime trees. Charles parked his car in as
unobtrusive a spot as possible beside a flourishing prunus tree,
and tugged at the wrought-iron bell pull by the white front door.

A very spruce maid welcomed him and showed him into the
Bishop's drawing room.

'I'll tell the Bishop you are here,' said the girl. 'At the moment,
he is telephoning.'

She departed, leaving Charles to admire the silver cups on a
side table, and the oar hanging above the fireplace. The Bishop
was a great oarsman, Charles remembered, a true muscular
Christian. Perhaps that contributed to his good looks, thought
Charles, and bent to pull up his wrinkled socks as Dimity had
told him.

The solemnly ticking grandfather clock by the door said two
minutes to the half hour when Charles heard the Bishop approaching. He stood up as the door swung open.

'My dear fellow! I hope I haven't kept you waiting. You are
wonderfully punctual. Come into my study. We'll be unmolested
there.'

He strode through the hall, followed by the good rector who admired the clerical grey suit which clothed those broad shoulders and neat waist. He certainly was a handsome fellow.

But at least, thought Charles, I remembered to pull up my socks.

Connie Harmer arrived at much the same time as the Bishop invited Charles to take a seat in the study. She found her aunt resting obediently on her bed, kissed her affectionately and enquired after her progress.

Connie's expression was as calm and competent as ever, but inwardly she was much alarmed. Dotty looked old and haggard. Her lips and cheeks wore a purplish tinge. She was definitely vaguer in manner than at her last visit.

'I'm dying for a cup of coffee,' said Connie, pulling off her driving gloves. 'I'll bring you one too.'

Dotty nodded dreamily in agreement, and Connie went downstairs.

Her first job was to ring Dr Lovell. His receptionist promised to tell him the minute he returned from his rounds. Then she put on the kettle, and thought hard while it came to the boil.

Well, the time had come. She had made her plans, and friends had offered a good price for her house and land. Aunt Dot had always been good to her, and she could live very happily here in her cottage, bringing only a few of her most cherished animals to share the rest of their lives with Dotty's.

She carried the tray upstairs and put it down on the bedside table.

'There we are, Aunt Dot. And when you've finished it, we're going to have a little talk about the future.'

At four o'clock Dimity waited in the vestibule at the rear entrance of Debenham's, surrounded by parcels.

Charles arrived soon after and they piled everything into the back of the car in great haste as a van man drew up, practically touching Charles's back bumper with his own, and putting his head out of the window to address the rector.

From his accent he would appear to be a Glaswegian, thought Charles, and so – perhaps fortunately – his message was entirely incomprehensible to southern-English ears. His demeanour, however, was threatening and abusive, and Charles and Dimity were relieved to drive off.

'I was going to suggest that we had a cup of tea at Debenham's,' said Charles, 'but it wasn't a good place to park evidently. We'll stop at the Oak Tearooms instead. Anyway, they have quite the best toasted tea cake in the district.'

Dimity knew better than to question her husband while he was driving in traffic, and it was not until they were safely ensconced among the oak panelling and chintz curtaining of the renowned tearooms that she began.

'And how did you find the dear Bishop?'

'As upstanding as ever. He inquired most kindly after you. Ah! Here comes the girl!'

The girl was approximately the same age as the rector, must have weighed thirteen stone, and was dressed in a rather tight flowered coat overall.

'Could we have some of your delicious toasted tea cake? And a pot of China tea for two?'

The waitress wrote busily on a little pad.

'Any jam, honey or other preserve? We have our home-made apricot, mulberry and quince.'

'How lovely that sounds!' cried Dimity. 'Like a list of jams from Culpeper!'

'We only keep our own, madam,' said the girl with some hauteur.

'Then shall we try mulberry, dear?' asked Dimity. 'I don't think I've ever had it.'

The waitress added MJ to her pad and departed.

'And now tell me, what happened, Charles?'

The rector began to look quite shy. 'Did you know that Anthony Bull is leaving Lulling?'

'Really? Now you come to mention it, I believe Bertha Lovelock said something about it.'

The rector's look of shyness was replaced by one of startled exasperation. 'But how on earth could she know? It isn't general knowledge yet!'

'Well, you know how things get about in a small community,' said Dimity soothingly. 'Anyway, where's he going? Not retiring surely?'

'Far from it. He's been appointed to a splendid living in one of the Kensington parishes. Rather High Church, I gather, and a most beautiful building. Anthony will be just the man for it, the Bishop said. I'm so glad he has got preferment. I always felt that Lulling was only a stepping stone to greater things for Anthony.'

The waitress reappeared with the tray and set out the teapot, milk jug, hot water container and a large dish covered with a silver lid.

A small bowl containing a wine-coloured confection aroused Dimity's interest. 'And this is the mulberry jam? What a beautiful colour.'

'We make it on the premises,' replied the waitress, thawing in the face of Dimity's enthusiasm. 'We have a tree in the garden. It is reputed to be a hundred and fifty years old.'

'How wonderful!'

The waitress made off again, and Dimity applied herself to pouring out the tea.

'But what about us, darling? Did he mention anything about our new house?'

'He did indeed. I think two of those sugar lumps. They seem rather small.'

'They're called *fairy* lumps, I believe,' said Dimity. 'Well, go on.'

'I'm afraid there won't be a new house, my dear.'

Dimity dropped the sugar lumps in her dismay. 'Not a new house? Then where on earth are we to go?'

Her husband had now bent down to retrieve the tongs from beneath the table. When he reappeared his face was very pink.

'To an old one, Dimity. I have been offered the living of the four merged parishes, and we should live at Lulling Vicarage.'

Dimity gazed at him open-mouthed. 'Charles!' she croaked at last. 'I can't believe it! That lovely, lovely house!'

'Don't cry, Dimity! Please don't cry,' begged Charles. 'Aren't you pleased?'

Dimity unfolded a snowy handkerchief and wiped her eyes. 'Of course I'm pleased. I'm just completely overwhelmed, that's all. Oh, Charles dear, this is an honour you so richly deserve. Won't it be wonderful to have our own home at last?'

'I'm glad you are pleased. It means we shall still be among our friends, and I shall still be able to take services at St Andrew's.'

'And when do you take over?'

'Probably before Christmas. Anthony expects to be inducted in October or November.'

'And then we shall be able to move in,' said Dimity happily. She spread mulberry jam in reckless bounty upon a slice of tea cake. 'What a blessing I didn't fall for some curtaining remnants this afternoon. They would never have done for the vicarage windows.'

She looked with surprise at the jam dish. 'Oh dear, Charles! I seem to have taken all the mulberry preserve.'

'I think we might be able to afford some quince as well,' said Charles. 'By way of celebration, you know.'

And he raised a plump hand to summon the girl.

20. LOOKING AHEAD

After the long dry summer, autumn came early to Thrush Green. The great leaves of the chestnut avenue turned golden and soon the boys from the village school would be collecting conkers.

In the cottage gardens, Michaelmas daisies and golden rod flourished, and Mr Jones began to wonder if his hanging baskets would last out their time before the first frosts came.

Ploughing and sowing was done, and the fields lay brown and bare. Busy housewives bottled the last of the fruit, the blackberries, the bramley apple slices, and the quartered pears, and added them to the richness of the earlier summer fruits in their store cupboards.

Ella Bembridge added two more handwoven scarves to her Christmas collection, and decided that she must buy a replacement for the tweed suit she had had for ten years, not to mention a stout pair of brogues ready for the winter.

Miss Fogerty and Miss Watson decided to go to their favourite guest house at Barton for half term at the end of October. At least three houses sounded hopeful, judging from the estate agents' information. Naturally, one expected them to over-egg the pudding a little, as Dorothy pointed out to her more trusting friend, but even so, things looked promising. It would be lovely to clinch a deal, and thank heaven they had no house of their own to dispose of, added Dorothy. With any luck, they should have a place before the winter had passed.

The news of Charles's new appointment gave enormous pleasure to everyone.

'The ideal man!' said Harold. 'The Bishop's done the right thing.'

'And we shan't really lose you,' as Ella said to them both. 'I mean, you'll be nipping up to take early service just as usual, and Dimity can still get the crib ready for Christmas at St Andrew's.'

Connie Harmer arrived to take up residence with her aunt during November. The old lady appeared to be delighted at the arrangement, and her doctor and friends who had feared that she might suddenly dig in her heels and refuse to countenance any change in her way of life, breathed sighs of relief and welcomed Connie in their midst. Dotty herself was so absorbed in the half a dozen new animals of Connie's that her health seemed to be much improved, though, no doubt, as Betty Bell pointed out, Connie's cooking, which was first-class, had a hand in the old lady's improvement.

Doris, at The Drovers' Arms, displayed a pretty engagement ring, and Percy Hodge put up the banns at the end of November.

'And thank heaven for that!' said Jenny to Winnie. 'I must write and tell Bessie she was dead right!'

Albert Piggott continued to help at Dotty's and elsewhere when needed, and also found time to supervise Bobby Cooke's church duties. The young man received rather more kicks than ha'pence, but his upbringing had inured him to such discomforts and he seemed happy enough.

The most encouraging news for Thrush Green and Lulling came one afternoon at the beginning of December when a notice appeared on the door of The Fuchsia Bush in Lulling High Street.

THIS ESTABLISHMENT WILL BE OPEN FROM 9.30 A.M. UNTIL 6.00 P.M. IN FUTURE read the astonished passers-by.

'I hear they hope to get the Christmas shoppers in,' said Miss Bertha.

'And I heard that those evening meals never really caught on,' added Miss Violet.

'About time they realized that it is *tea* people want,' said Miss Ada, voicing the view of all.

*

It was during the last few frenzied days of Christmas shopping, when The Fuchsia Bush was certainly doing a roaring trade from four o'clock onwards, that Molly Curdle's baby was born.

'Just think,' said Winnie Bailey to Jenny, 'it weighed nine pounds!'

'Poor thing!' said Jenny. 'But at least it's a girl. I know Ben hoped it would be. I wonder what they'll call it? It was going to be another Ben, if it had been a boy.'

'I have a shrewd idea that it will be "Anne" after Ben's dear old grandma,' said Winnie, 'If she grows up as splendid as her namesake she won't hurt.'

One mild January afternoon, a small entourage walked out from the Youngs' gate.

Skipping ahead was young George Curdle, unnaturally clean and tidy, from his watered-down hair to his well-polished shoes.

Behind him walked his mother, holding the new baby well-wrapped in the beautiful old shawl which had first enveloped Ben himself. Beyond his parents came Joan and Edward Young and Mrs Bassett, Joan's mother. Her father had promised to come to the christening tea, but did not feel equal to standing at the ceremony.

The air was soft and mild. It had a hint of springtime in it, and some early snowdrops and aconites, near the churchyard gate, made an encouraging sight. Against the church wall, a shower of winter flowering jasmine spilled its yellow flowers.

As Ben passed his beloved grandmother's tombstone he patted it approvingly, noting the name and date anew.

'Pity she can't be here to see this one named for her,' he said to his wife.

'Maybe she knows anyway,' was her reply, as they passed into the church porch.